Praise for
The Secrets of a Fire King

"Stunning . . . [Edwards's] sinuous prose and endless empathy work their spell. . . . Radiant, original, and passionate, these are memorable stories."
—Andrea Barrett, author of *Ship Fever*

"*The Secrets of a Fire King* gives eloquence to their astonishing range of discoveries and leaves the reader entranced."
—Nina Sonenberg, *The New York Times Book Review*

"This collection introduces a writer whose name will soon be familiar to lovers of clean, direct, responsible prose and an interest in characters—many of them women—who are unique. These lives are often exotic; they are electric with risk, violence, and sorrow. And we will remember them."　　　—Frederick Busch

"Impeccable, a treasure . . . [Edwards] shows herself to be a fully realized writer. . . . Edwards's brilliance is evident in the way she constructs a story."
—Patricia Lear, *Chicago Tribune*

"Striking . . . powerful."
—Amanda Heller, *The Boston Globe*

"Ambitious and moving . . . Edwards writes quietly and intelligently. . . . Each story here is finely crafted and deeply felt."　　—Jane McCafferty, *Pittsburgh Post-Gazette*

"The stories . . . are infused with a quiet intensity that is bewitching and disturbing. Edwards's prose is concise, rich, and poetic."
—Stephanie Browner, *Lexington Herald Leader*

"*The Secrets of a Fire King* is a brilliant collection. Its range of deeply felt characters alone ought to inspire in a very broad audience the conviction that the short story form is now safely in the nurture of a very gifted and compassionate young master."   —James A. McPherson

"This collection is rich with subtle wisdom. Kim Edwards is a penetrating writer and in every story gives us the opportunity to glimpse—and comprehend—the elusive mysteries of love."   —Joanna Scott

"Kim Edwards has not only a gift for storytelling, but something far more rare—an interesting mind. I enjoyed her subtle characters, her unusual settings, and the risky and perilous situations that propel these skillful stories. *The Secrets of a Fire King* is a remarkable and rewarding first collection."   —Lynne Sharon Schwartz

"Kim Edwards is a marvel, an enchanter, a weaver of spells. . . . You'll be unsettled and disarmed, and when you catch your breath, you'll remember why you came to love stories in the first place."   —John Dufresne

"Beautifully focused . . . [Edwards's] tales read like the work of a wise traveler who returns home with uncommon souvenirs from other lands."   —*Publishers Weekly*

PENGUIN BOOKS

THE SECRETS OF A FIRE KING

KIM EDWARDS is the author of the #1 *New York Times* best-seller *The Memory Keeper's Daughter*. *The Secrets of a Fire King* was an alternate for the 1998 PEN/Hemingway Award, and Edwards has won both the Whiting Award and the Nelson Algren Award. A graduate of the Iowa Writer's Workshop, she is an assistant professor of English at the University of Kentucky.

The Secrets
of a Fire King

Stories by
KIM EDWARDS

PENGUIN BOOKS

PENGUIN BOOKS

Published by the Penguin Group
Penguin Group (USA) Inc., 375 Hudson Street, New York, New York 10014, U.S.A.
Penguin Group (Canada), 90 Eglinton Avenue East, Suite 700, Toronto, Ontario, Canada
M4P 2Y3 (a division of Pearson Penguin Canada Inc.)
Penguin Books Ltd, 80 Strand, London WC2R 0RL, England
Penguin Ireland, 25 St Stephen's Green, Dublin 2, Ireland (a division of Penguin Books Ltd)
Penguin Group (Australia), 250 Camberwell Road, Camberwell, Victoria 3124, Australia
(a division of Pearson Australia Group Pty Ltd)
Penguin Books India Pvt Ltd, 11 Community Centre, Panchsheel Park,
New Delhi – 110 017, India
Penguin Group (NZ), 67 Apollo Drive, Mairangi Bay, Auckland 1311, New Zealand
(a division of Pearson New Zealand Ltd)
Penguin Books (South Africa) (Pty) Ltd, 24 Sturdee Avenue, Rosebank, Johannesburg 2196,
South Africa

Penguin Books Ltd, Registered Offices:
80 Strand, London WC2R 0RL, England

First published in the United States of America by W. W. Norton & Company 1997
Published in Penguin Books 2007

1 3 5 7 9 10 8 6 4 2

Copyright © Kim Edwards, 1997
All rights reserved

These stories have appeared in the following publications: "The Way It Felt to Be Falling,"
The Threepenny Review; reprinted in *Pushcart Prize XIX*. "Gold," *Antaeus*; reprinted in *Best
American Short Stories of 1993*. "A Gleaming in the Darkness," *Story*. "The Story of My Life,"
Story. "Spring, Mountain, Sea," *American Short Fiction*. "Balance," *American Short Fiction*.
"The Great Chain of Being," *The Paris Review*. "Sky Juice," *Chicago Tribune*. "Thirst," *Mid-
American Review*. "In the Garden," *Ploughshares*. "Aristotle's Lantern," *Zoetrope*.

THE LIBRARY OF CONGRESS HAS CATALOGED THE HARDCOVER EDITION AS FOLLOWS:
Edwards, Kim, 1958–
The secrets of a fire king : stories / by Kim Edwards.
p. cm.
ISBN 978-0-393-04026-5 (hc.)
ISBN 978-0-14-311230-3 (pbk.)

1. Title.
PS3555.D942S43   1997
813'.54—dc20   96-28794

Printed in the United States of America

To Tom,
who built me a room of my own

These stories have appeared in the following publications:

"The Way It Felt to Be Falling," *The Threepenny Review*; reprinted in *Pushcart Prize XIX*. "Gold," *Antaeus*; reprinted in *Best American Short Stories of 1993*. "A Gleaming in the Darkness," *Story*. "The Story of My Life," *Story*. "Spring, Mountain, Sea," *American Short Fiction*. "Balance," *American Short Fiction*. "The Great Chain of Being," *The Paris Review*. "Sky Juice," *Chicago Tribune*. "Thirst," *Mid-American Review*. "In the Garden," *Ploughshares*. "Aristotle's Lantern," *Zoetrope*.

Contents

The Secrets
of a Fire King

The Great
Chain of Being

MY FATHER WAS A MAN WHO BELIEVED HISTORY REPEATED itself. Not in the large ways, of nations and of wars, but in the smaller ways of families. He was a religious man, and he believed that the patterns of the universe were fixed in place, infinite but static, revealed to the devout through the pure concentration of prayer. What is destiny, and what is in the power of a single individual? Ask my father and he would have answered that everything is destiny. That is the answer of our religion, the answer he was obliged to give. That was the answer he applied to us, his children.

He was small, but powerful, with a smooth bald head that made him seem both wise and ageless. In those days before our country's independence he had great influence, and he carried himself with a dignity that was almost regal. I understand now that the legacies he gave us were not more than the quick glint of memory, the sudden surfacing of a half-remembered dream. But at the time I believed, we all did, that they came to him through some kind of divine inspiration, tumbling from his lips without warning, like coins spilling suddenly from a shaft of sunlight.

"Jamaluddin," he would say, peering at my brother with a gaze both terrible and intent, "takes after his great-uncle Sayed in every trait." And we would remember our great-uncle, who stood straight and clear-eyed even as an old man, who had led the army against the communist rebellion before we were even born. From that day on we would call our brother Sayed, at first jokingly, later in all seriousness, until his real name was only a notation in my father's files. One brother took after a healer, another resembled an ancient trader. When my sisters were born my father claimed they were direct images of my twin aunts, the most beautiful women in my father's village. Years later, when he said this about them, you could see their faces glow, you could see the way they pulled themselves up taller, straightened their shoulders, tossed back their hair, and smiled the smiles of lovely women.

Of his thirteen children I was the seventh, the first girl, and the one who waited longest for this legacy of names. My father was an important man, some would say a great one, and we had been trained not to intrude upon his days. Nonetheless, I strayed into his vision now and then, hoping to inspire him. I sang beneath his window, thinking of Shala, the great poet in the family, who soothed whole villages with her songs. I brought him plates of biscuits I had made, cut with a childish hand, thinking of my grandmother, whose house I remembered as being always full of the sweet smells of coconut and spice. My father took these offerings, absently; he ran his knuckles across my shoulder blades when he passed me, singing, in the hall. But although it was my turn, he never looked down twice. I remained Eshlaini, I had no other name.

One day my mother found me weeping in the kitchen.

"Eshlaini," she said, stepping lightly across the tiles and holding me close. She was pregnant with her eleventh child then, and I told my sad story into the curve of her flesh: two brothers, younger than I, had been given names when I had not. My mother listened, stroking my hair, and when I finished she took my face between her two hands and gazed at me for a moment before she spoke.

"Eshlaini," she said. "Listen to it closely. Eshlaini. It's a name that I chose for you, a name I hope you will keep forever. There is a star in the night sky, a lovely star, and bright. I watched that star the night you were born, and when I fell asleep I dreamed about that star and woke up with your name, Eshlaini, on my lips. Thanks to God I have had many children, given many names, but soon yours will be the only one that remains. Now, my daughter, stop your tears. Take joy in your pretty name, Eshlaini."

From that day on I stopped wishing for another name, and soon enough I had another brother. My mother let me hold him, new as he was. I remember the redness of his skin, his shock of dark hair, the way he was a moving bundle of heat in my arms. In those days they followed the traditional ways, and my mother had massages every morning in a bed placed over a stove of slowly burning coals. The midwife rolled the warm rocks on my mother's belly. I sat in the corner, my arms a tense and careful cradle, listening to what they said.

"How does that feel?" the midwife asked, pressing the rock this way, then that, against my mother's flesh. I heard my mother catch her breath, I saw the edge of her white teeth biting on her lower lip.

"It hurts," my mother said. "Though the labor was fast, it hurts this time like it has no other."

The midwife frowned, and probed my mother's belly with her fingers.

"You should have no more," she said. "If you give life again, you will pay with your own life. That's what I fear, Shalizah. Eleven children! You should be satisfied." There was a moment of silence before she spoke again. "You should. And so should he."

"Eshlaini," my mother said, raising herself on her elbows. "Bring the baby over here."

I did as I was told, and rocked my brother back and forth as the midwife bound my mother up with cloth soaked in herbs and oils.

"What will you name this one?" she asked, tugging a strip of cloth so tightly that my mother winced.

"I don't know yet," she said, studying my little brother's face. "I have to get to know him a bit first. Zul, perhaps. That seems to suit him."

The midwife handed my mother a glass of greenish liquid, so pungent it made my nose wrinkle up.

"It's not right," she said, wiping her herb-stained hands on her apron, "to give a child one name for the first years, then change it to another. What they become is not his choice."

My mother sighed and drank the green drink, then made a face and held her hand out to me.

"I have them for the first five years or so," she said. "He never takes an interest until then." She smiled at me and pulled me close. "And Eshlaini's mine. I'll always have Eshlaini."

"It isn't right," the midwife repeated.

"It's not for us to question," my mother said serenely.

SHE DID NOT QUESTION, or if she did my father's words soothed away her fears. After all, many people say that he was the most eloquent speaker of his generation. I remember glimpsing him in his study, straight and dignified in his hard chair, surrounded by other men, the ceiling fan making its slow rotation above their heads. No matter how many others were in attendance, it was my father's voice I heard most often, as dark and melodious and as forceful as a monsoon rain. It was my father's hands I saw, raised to emphasize his words, it was my father who spoke of choices they must make, of setting a course to guide them through the coming years. He claimed through his daily prayers to believe in destiny, but he spoke like a man who felt the world turn and quiver on his command.

As my mother must have done, for despite the warning of the midwife she was pregnant again within a year. From the beginning it was difficult, and she was confined to bed. I used to go and sit next to her, let her comb my hair beneath the steady whir and click of the ceiling fan. Her fingers were strong, massaging my scalp, and the braids she made pulled at the skin around my temples. Even today, so many years later, I sometimes braid my hair to evoke those moments: heat raising a fine sweat on our foreheads, the tropical sun muted by wooden shutters pulled tightly closed, the vile, medicinal glass of herbal tea she sipped at through the day.

My mother's labor began when the fruit trees ripened, just after the hot season and before the monsoon, and at first we believed it was an omen of good luck, that she would avoid the fevers of the first and the chilling cold of the second, that she would bear the fruit of her body in a timely way, and live.

Her labor began early in the morning, and by noon that day I had a sister. She was placed in the room next to my mother's, the room I sometimes slept in, and I was put in charge of her. Tiny sister, even wrapped in blankets she was small, just four pounds at birth. I touched her miniature fingers, the lobe of her ear, the blue veins visible beneath the translucent skin of her forehead. Through the open door I saw my mother sleeping, her dark hair like a shadow between the dual paleness of the pillow and her face. The midwife was gone, and I stood in the doorway for a moment, listening to my mother's even breathing in the rising heat of the room.

For the next two hours the peace held. I watched my sister and kept the silence like a long extended prayer. And I was startled, but not surprised, sometime in the afternoon, when I heard the panting begin again, the soothing words of the midwife interspersed with the groans my mother made. Alarmed, I left my sister and ran into the other room. The sheets were stained red, and the midwife barely glanced up from her massaging of my mother.

"What is it?" I cried. "What's wrong?"

"There is another coming," said the midwife. "Your first sister has a twin. Now go quietly and watch her, and do not worry about your mother. You must trust her to me now, and to God."

This second labor was longer than the first. It seemed to me that way even with no clock to measure it. I fed my sister, changed her, felt the day's heat rise and culminate and finally recede. Later they told me that it took twelve hours, but to me those hours of muffled screams and groaning felt like days, like years. It was past midnight when the midwife brought the second sister to my room. She was smaller than the first, and more fragile.

"Eshlaini!" the midwife said. With the strain of birthing she had forgotten all about me. "Have you been here all this time?" I nodded. There was a bed in the room, but I sat stiff and alert on a single straight chair. I was exhausted, and very afraid—the night air seemed to crackle with spirits and emotions never visible in the day.

"Child," she said, putting her hand on my shoulder. "You must sleep."

"I want to see my mother," I said.

"She's sleeping now. The best thing you can do is sleep as well."

"She's dead," I said. "I know it."

The midwife looked surprised, then troubled. "No, she isn't dead. Oh, child," she said, and even though I was nine years old and tall for my age, even though she herself had worked past exhaustion, she picked me up and carried me to my mother's room. My mother's breathing was shallow, uneven, she looked as pale as the new babies she had borne. But when I touched her on the arm I felt her warmth, and some string held tight within me started to release.

"There," the midwife said, stroking my hair, pressing my head against her shoulder and leading me back to the other room, where the light breathing of my sisters filled the air. She pushed me down on the narrow bed and draped an old sarong across me.

"That's better, Eshlaini. That's it, now. Sleep."

I DID SLEEP, but not deeply and with many dreams. When I woke up the house, though very dark, was alive with movement and urgent, whispered voices. The door to my mother's room was slightly open. I could see my father sitting by the bed, my mother's hand in his. He was praying. I was only nine, too young to understand the words, but I remembered them from other deaths, I knew the portent of those sounds.

All that followed is no longer very clear. The words rained down around me, and suddenly I was standing up, illuminated with an idea of how to save my mother. I remember that the floor felt cool against my bare feet, that moonlight came in through the window and lit the crib where my two sisters slept. Their mouths moved, even in sleep, and their hands and feet jerked sometimes with the motions of the womb. In the sudden silence from my mother's room I reached for a thick pillow and placed it above the sleeping faces of my sisters. I was nine years old, with a literal mind, and I remembered the midwife's words. If these twins would cost my mother her life, then I reasoned I could save her if they died.

There is no way to know, now, what might have happened. I might have carried through, possessed as I was with the madness of loss, with the misguided logic of an egocentric child. But I was not an evil girl, or truly demented, and it's just as possible that I would have stopped. It's possible that, hovering above my sisters, I would have broken down, retrieved the pillow, and sobbed into the feathers. I can't know, now, which would have happened, and it no longer matters. For my father found me in that moment of intent. He appeared in the doorway quite suddenly, silhouetted by the terrible and empty light of my mother's room. He gave a roar so loud it froze the scene forever in our histories. It called my brothers forth; they tumbled into the room like birds spilled from a nest. They were witness to the blow my father gave me, the punch of a grown man inflated with wild fury against a death he was powerless to stop. And they were there to hear it when he gave me, finally, the name I would carry through my life.

"Take this one," he said, pushing me across to the oldest boy, the brother who was said to resemble the soldier. "Take her and lock her in her room. She has gone mad, like her grandmother before her. Rohila." He spat the name out like poison. "This evil girl, she is Rohila once again."

Rohila. It was a name we all knew, but rarely spoke. She was my father's mother, at one time young and lovely, known for both her beauty and her skill at sewing. Brides sought her out, and rich girls, and she sat night by night in the lamplight, her needle flashing like a minnow in the dark. Her own clothes were so elegant and graceful that she drew the eyes of every man. It is said that when she finally married, another girl was so distraught that she cast some black magic on Rohila. No one could have guessed this, for at first Rohila and her husband were very happy. It was only later that people remembered how she was plagued that year with headaches and strange dreams. Soon she was pregnant, but from the beginning there was something wrong. Rohila grew round without growing plump, and it is said that there was a nervousness about her, a kind of tightness that showed around her eyes.

Everyone knows about the fevers that can follow childbirth, the precautions that must be taken to prevent them. It was not Rohila's fault that the midwife was unskilled or forgetful, jealous or enchanted. It was not her fault that the herbs were not prepared, that the offering went unmade, so that after the birth of her first and only child my grandmother fell into a temporary madness. They found her standing on a bridge with the baby, my father, in her arms, ready to drop him into the creek. After that she was cast away by her husband in favor of another wife, the woman of sweet pastries, the woman I knew as Grandmother. Rohila was sent home, to live in isolation. She tended to her aging parents; when they died she went to help her brothers and their wives. I saw her once, a bent old woman who shuffled away from children, who gave us bad dreams. Aside from this I know nothing at all, though sometimes now I imagine that I understand her life.

For, in the way of our name legacies, her life became mine. I was only a child, but on the day my sisters were born and my mother died, my destiny was fixed. I became Rohila, the one who would not marry, the one who would remain at home to care for my brothers and, in his old age, my father. It was not spoken, but simply understood. Ask my family about the justice of it all, and they would have looked up surprised, they would have called it fate. They, named for the strong and sane and famous, could afford to believe in the preordained. If everything was destiny, then it was not their responsibility to intervene. And yet there was a truth I soon discovered that they never paused to think about. If I was to be an old maid, chained forever to that house, then this was also true: it was my father's will that made it so. It was his decree, his choice.

WHAT IS DESTINY, and what is in the power of the individual? By seventeen I was strong but petite, with long slender limbs, and wrists and ankles as delicate as bone. I learned quickly that the body is one destiny. No one who saw me would have guessed my fate within that house. The young men, watching me walking to and from my school, their eyes lingering on my skin like the warm light of sunset, none of them guessed. They followed me, slipped notes into my books that spoke of love and the future, of other lives. I should have been smart enough to see these for what they were, a lure connected to the hook of another predetermined life. I should have remembered my mother, turning her head away when the midwife warned her to make a choice she didn't have. But I was young and foolish, and those notes in my pockets were as light and persistent as hope. I smiled shyly at the young men, blushed becomingly, and soon they began appearing at my house, hoping to gain my father's permission to marry me.

On the night the first young man came, I stood at the upstairs window and watched him ring the bell. I had his note promising to win me, and I had a wild joy in my heart. I thought my father would reconsider. After all, no one wanted an unmarriageable daughter. My suitor had dressed very carefully, his hair had been combed with water until it looked polished. When he disappeared inside the house, I waited to be summoned.

Time passed slowly for me then. Still, not half an hour was gone when I heard the door slam, when I ran to the window to see that young man walking quickly to the road. The next day I looked for him, desperate to know what had happened, but although I saw him from a distance, across the classroom or the playing field, he never spoke to me again.

What had my father said, and why? I thought perhaps he'd found the young man unsuitable; he was, after all, a famous and important man, and particular about his in-laws. Which is why I was careful about the other notes I had, and finally chose one from another young man who was not in our school at all, but an officer in the army and stationed near our house. Wasn't my oldest brother also an officer in the army? My father must approve. After some time had passed, after a flurry of notes and shy glances, this man too approached my father's house. This time I left nothing to chance. I crouched beneath the window of my father's study, and listened.

"But I worry," my father said, tapping his pipe out in the ashtray. My young officer was seated across from him, hat in his hands, hope on his face. "I worry about this madness she has shown, and what might happen if there were children. You know, my daughter is not quite right. No doubt you've heard the stories—she nearly killed her two sisters when they were only infants. Even now I see her at the park sometimes, watching the children. Her eyes are quite unnatural then, the way they were that long-ago night. We keep a careful watch on her, you see."

"I had no idea," the young man said. There was trouble in his voice. I wanted to jump up, shout out loud, for what my father said about the park, about the children, was not true. Those children held no interest for me. Even the night my sisters were born seemed like a dream, like a story that had happened to another girl.

"If I were less honest," my father went on, "I'd let you go ahead and marry my daughter. But I can't condemn a young man like you to the uncertain life my daughter would offer. You need a strong woman, someone to support you. My daughter will spend her life in this house, as it has been willed. When I die, of course, this place will become hers. I've prayed on this, for guidance, and I'm sure that it is so."

The night was warm, yet as he spoke I was shivering on the porch, shaking so hard I had to tuck my hands within my armpits to keep my fingers from knocking on the wall. For I could understand the meaning of this night. My father was driving my suitors away, not for their sake, but for his own. He wanted to ensure himself a peaceful old age, someone here to care for him. I, Eshlaini, was to be the one. This was no divine destiny, but my father's will. The young man was standing up to leave, shaking my father's hand, expressing his thanks, and the sight impelled me to do what for years I had believed was an impossible thing. I stood up in that window and I spoke against my father.

"It is not true, what my father is telling you," I said.

Both men turned to me, shock on their faces. It was the young man I looked at first. I was so exhilarated at my own boldness, the blood pulsing in my heart, that I expected the same from him. I suppose I thought that he would take my hand and run with me out into the night, but instead he averted his eyes at once. I watched him for a moment, my blood pulse slowing with anger first, then with humiliation. He stared at the wall, a muscle twitching in his cheek. It was my father who finally spoke, in the gentle voice one uses on children and the mad.

"Rohila," he said. "This is not for you to decide. Go to your room at once." The young man turned away. He would not look at me, or speak.

"Rohila," my father repeated, but I interrupted him.

"I have been listening," I said. I knew that I probably looked half mad, my hair flying around my head, my face streaked with tears, my voice in a shrill pitch. "I heard you promise me the house. If you will not let me marry, Father, then at least do this: add my name to your will with this man as your witness. Ensure me that my future will be as you have decreed."

"It is not I who have decreed this," my father said. But he looked at me so strangely, as if it was the first time he had ever seen me clearly. Then he shrugged. "Nevertheless, it is a small thing. This is the least valuable of my properties, and it will only take a moment to add it to the will."

That night I sat up in my room for a long time, the paper in my hand. It was my true name they had used, my legal name, to will this house to me. Though the house was small, worth very little, and though I knew I would never have another suitor, a strange satisfaction mingled with my anger. I had this paper, after all, with my true name. I knew the small victory I had won.

WHAT HAPPENS to an anger, so fierce it burns the inner eyelids with a white light, when it goes too long unexpressed? I can tell you—it turns into a black nut, a bilious knot in the gut, a dark coiled seed. I could feel it every day, tending to my father's needs, the years of my own life passing one by one. At night I sat before the mirror, scanning the new wrinkles where none had been, clipping at the hairs that sprouted on my chin. I dreamed of leaving, but in those days there was no place a woman alone could go. I was tied to the house by the great chains of past and present circumstance. My anger leaked out in strange ways. Sometimes I broke things, secretly, that he would not notice missing for months—a small vase from my mother, the fountain pen from some famous general. I buried his medals in the backyard. At times it seemed that I was mad, as he claimed, but I had only to press my fingers against my stomach to reassure myself about the truth. That was where the anger had settled, tense as a muscle. I could feel it there, hard skinned, thick as a chestnut.

One day, after years had passed, I saw that my father was going to die. He was in his eighties, trim and to all appearances healthy, but that morning I noticed the tremor in his fingers as he ate his breakfast rice, and when he signed the letters I had typed his hand was shaking so badly that I could not read his name. He resisted doctors for the longest time, but when he finally went they confirmed what I had guessed long before: he had a year, or less, to live.

On that day the dark seed sprang open. I felt it releasing, the sap of it running through my veins. As each day passed and my father grew weaker, new shoots made their way through my arms and legs. I felt myself growing alive from within. When I held my father's elbow to assist him to the porch, when he took more and more frequently to his bed, I felt leaves unfurling, inner flowers blooming in my fingertips and cheeks. By the time he was bedridden it was nearly complete, a new self about to be born. I hummed as I cared for him, swabbing the loose flesh of his legs, arranging the sheets.

I began to speak to him too, though I had been a silent girl, curled quietly around my anger. Cancer had eaten through his voice box, and so he could not answer me when I told him what it was I planned to do with that house he had left me. His eyes followed me around the room as I opened windows, dusted the fan, poured water from a glass pitcher and held it to his lips. One day I told him I would burn it down, sending the blue flames high above the trees, curling the walls and furniture into nothing more than ash. Another time I told him I would rent it to people from different faiths, people who would cook pork in the kitchen, keep dogs to wander freely from room to room. A house of illicit women, I murmured, arranging his pillows, with lovers stepping in and out and sighs of passion floating from every room. I stood up, as if struck with an idea, and said I might even bring a lover here myself.

My father made a noise deep in his throat, and I look down. He was speaking without sound, his lips moving in exaggerated motions, easy to read.

"Rohila," he was saying. "No more. Don't."

"Rohila's dead," I told him briskly, pressing a damp cloth first against one cheek, then the other. "She's been dead for decades, you ought to know that."

There was a pause, then his hand against my sleeve again. I looked down. He struggled with the words, and I felt a bright tingling just beneath my skin.

"What was that?" I asked, though of course I had seen it. "Say it again?"

His lips trembled, his flesh shaped my name.

"I'm sorry," he said. "Eshlaini."

Roots shot to my toes, took permanent hold. It was only my name, yet to me it was like a flash of the sun, a trigger for the quick photosynthesis of joy.

FLESH IS THE ONLY DESTINY. In the end that's all I will concede to fate. My father lived his life as a powerful man, but even he could not die as he would have wished, quickly and with dignity. Instead he went with agonizing slowness, rotting from the inside out. It was not merciful, the way his body went before his mind did. Toward the end I discovered maggots living in the soft flesh around his few remaining teeth, and I had to watch his eyes, still knowing, while I plucked them out and swabbed his gums with antiseptic cream. Days later he burned with fever, his fingers like smoking sticks in my palm. He seemed to shrink before my eyes, his skin going tight and hard around his bones. He toughened, became nutlike. Though I bathed him with lightly scented water, though I pressed cool cloths against the pulsing heat of his forehead, I could not stop the transformation that was taking place. He shrank within himself, and his skin clung to the new shape. It was days and days before I understood. There he was, his skin gone rough and dark, his body coiled. I stared at him in recognition, then. He was the dark seed I had discarded.

As he lay dying, the family came. On planes, by car and train, from the distant foreign cities and the nearby villages, all came. They pressed my hands when they entered the house, they touched their fingers to their hearts and mouths in gestures of intimacy and love, but they did not see the transformation that had taken place, they did not look me in the eyes to notice.

What drew their attention was the will, and most especially the codicil that left the house to me.

Of course they knew about the promise, made twenty years ago to seal my fate. Twenty years ago, when mosquitoes clouded the dark rooms of that house, and the jungle rose up like a mystery behind it. No one wanted the house then, the least valuable of my father's properties, and so it was an easy promise. I, Eshlaini, would be made to give my life, and in return I would be guaranteed a house.

Twenty years ago. No one imagined then that the city would expand, pressing outward like a deep breath, to make this the most valuable land my father owned. This land, sold now, would make us all rich beyond belief. Before his death I heard them discussing this, in twos or threes. Carrying my father's bedpan, lifting him from the sheets to clean his sores, I heard the whispers coming from the bottom of the stairs, from around the corner. They could not take it from me, but they wanted it, and this was the most surprising thing of all: I could see on their faces, turned so kindly toward me, that they thought I would give it to them without a fight.

After my father died, there was a family meeting. The will was read out loud then, and discussed. Finally my eldest brother, named for the soldier, turned to me. He was short, like my father, with the same balding head.

"Rohila," he said. "This house is yours, as was once promised, though we can't imagine that you want it. It is so big, after all, hardly suitable for a woman alone. I would like to offer you a place in my own home, comfort and family for life. In return, of course, you would sign over the house to the general estate our father left."

He paused, and all the faces turned toward me. I felt the pressure of their eyes, and another pressure too. The idea of destiny is not an easy thing to shrug away. I knew it would be easier not to fight. I knew it would be easier to follow the path they had determined.

"You're right," I said. "I do not want this house."

I paused just long enough to see relief relax them. My eldest brother smiled. They began to turn to each other, putting me back in my shadowy place, but before they went too far I spoke again.

"I do not want the house. Nonetheless, I intend to keep it."

Words have power. I knew that from my father. Still, I watched with some surprise as what I had said rippled visibly through their faces. My eldest brother stepped forward and took my hands. Though it was said that he took after our great-uncle, in truth it is my father he resembles. I looked into his face, his expression so gentle, so concerned with my own good, and I saw the face of my father twenty years ago, when I was seventeen.

"Dear Rohila," he said. "You've had a shock. I'm sure you'll want to reconsider."

"Jamaluddin," I answered, slipping my hands from his, noting his surprise at the use of his dusty given name. "My father pledged this house to me. It was his dying wish. How can I, then, deny it?"

Jamaluddin shook his head. "We'd thought you'd live with one of us," he said. "We'll see to your future, no need to worry over that, Rohila."

"My name is Eshlaini," I told him.

It was only then that they noticed how I'd changed, the scent of new, insistent life rising from my skin, hair flowing out like a sea anemone. They stepped back from me when I passed them, their eyes followed me as I walked from the room. Later I heard them discussing their options, legal and otherwise, but in the end the will held. It was destiny, I told them, smiling. There was nothing they could do.

WHEN I SOLD that house I became a rich woman, but I live a simple life. I have a small apartment in the city, a few pieces of furniture, a brand-new car. And clothes—I threw out all my ragged sarongs, the little-girl and old-maid dresses I had accumulated over the years. In their place I bought the crisp tailored clothes I had admired in magazines, and as a tribute to my mother and my grandmother I wear bright scarves and jewelry, stones and precious metals that glisten in the dusk like tiny stars or a sewing needle flashing.

I think perhaps it was the bright colors, the glimmer of my jewels, that drew the little girl to me. She is from the orphanage around the corner from my apartment. I used to see her every day, kicking a takraw ball around the dusty, empty field or playing jump rope with a group of other girls. She is a serious child, friendly but self-contained. One day she waved to me, and after that I found myself looking for her when I passed, found myself disappointed if a day went by without her quick eyes, her bright triangle of a face, there to greet me. I began to think of her, to wonder what had put her there, what stories she was hearing about the choices fate had left her. I began to think of ways to help her—a scholarship, new clothes, a bicycle. And then one day I had another thought.

Why not a daughter of my own? Why not?

MY FATHER'S HOUSE is gone now. I watched them tear it down, the machine taking large bites out of the rooms I had scrubbed so many times, the rooms that had held so much unhappiness and death. It was a relief to me, finally, when nothing remained. I find it fascinating to watch the process they follow to make these new high-rises, the steel girders and poured concrete, the bamboo scaffolding alive with workers. These workers know it used to be my father's house that stood here, and sometimes they take me inside and show me what they're doing. I nod, impressed, listening to the echo of my footsteps in so many layers of empty space.

Tonight it's dusk, and the air is spilling over with sweetness from the flowers. I sit in the car, watching the workers move in the bright pools of light, thinking of the daughter who will come to live with me next week. I've prepared her room—new paint, a few toys—but I've kept it simple. She'll fill it up herself, soon enough, with things that are her own. I like to think of that, my house filling up with the unexpected. In the same way, it pleases me to think of the new lives that will soon occupy this space. Hundreds of people will live here, and they will have no connection whatsoever with my future or my past.

One by one the lights go out, the workers leave, and finally the last light flickers off and returns this building to the night. I start my car then, and pull out into traffic. It's a clear night, full of stars, and I wonder for a moment which one of them my mother looked at on the day I was born. No destiny in that, only a bright wish, a continuity of light to light. Look at me now, hands on a wheel, driving myself to a place where no one else has lived, where only the future lies waiting. I am that light. I have no other destiny. I am Eshlaini, and history ends with me.

Spring,
Mountain,
Sea

WHEN ROB ELDRED CAME HOME IN 1954 WITH HIS OVERseas bride, it was already winter. They drove north from the city, through the first fierce storm of the season, and the heavy snow seemed to fall invisibly through the roof of their new car, muffling their words and gestures until eventually they ceased to speak. Rob drove slowly and without stopping, fighting back a restless disappointment. The landscape he had dreamed of with such longing during his days in the navy had disappeared. In places the roads had been reduced by the storm to narrow lanes, and everywhere he looked the white fields faded into the pale horizon, the sea of white broken only occasionally by a bare tree, an isolated house, a stretch of metal fence. Even to Rob, who knew that the snow would give way to a spring of shimmering green fields and dark blue lakes, the place looked bleak and lonely. He stole glances at Jade Moon, who had pulled the collar of her red wool coat close around her neck, and whose dark eyes scanned the landscape as if seeking out a refuge.

That winter in upstate New York was especially harsh, and Rob Eldred would always remember it as the most difficult season of his life. Although Jade Moon had grown up in a village where snow drifted high over the thatched roofs and closed the roads for months at a time, during that first winter in her new country she could never get warm. Their house was small and set into a hill, protected from the worst of the wind, yet even so Rob was always turning up the central heat as far as it would go. He would come home from work, sawdust in his hair, still warm from the exertion of building, to find Jade Moon on the couch, huddled beneath several sweaters and a down quilt. Sometimes the telephone would be off the hook, emitting a low buzz into the room. He always replaced it discreetly, without comment, knowing her terror of the disembodied voices, the unfamiliar language unsoftened by a gesture, or a smile.

He was not a patient man, but during that long winter he was kind to her. Each evening he massaged her hands and made hot chocolate, which she drank like a child, greedily, holding the mug in both hands for warmth. He brought scented bath oils from the five-and-dime in town and drew the bathwater so hot that steam, smelling of roses or lilacs or lilies of the valley, swirled around her when she let her woolen robe slip off. He sat back on his heels, then, admiring her slender body, sculpted round by the baby that she carried.

"Like the hot springs," she murmured, stepping into the porcelain tub carefully, as if it were paved with hidden rocks. Once, before he knew her, he had seen her sliding into the hot water of such a spring, her skin as smooth and white as the snow drifted up behind her. Hidden behind a tree he had watched, her long legs easing through the steam, her hair like a sheet of black water to her waist.

Now, in a strange country, she closed her eyes at the familiar pleasure. Her eyelashes were thick, and her cheekbones were set high in a face that was delicately boned, the shape of an almond. He lifted her hair to wash her back, letting the soapy water drift over the tips of her breasts, which were darkening now against her pale skin in anticipation of the baby. Later, in bed, he held her close and spoke softly in her own language, describing the events of his day, comparing the people and the places to those of her own village, so impossibly far away. It was language that she craved, the steady wash of familiar syllables across her ears. And so Rob Eldred talked on, making up stories, singing bits of songs. Little by little he felt the tension drain from her, until at last she fell asleep in his arms, warmed by his voice, by the words.

The mornings of that winter dawned clear and cold, or softened with the gray light of another impending storm. It was always a shock to him, the way the warm dark nights gave way to the white light of morning, and he moved through the small rooms carefully, quietly, trying not to wake Jade Moon. Invariably, though, she appeared in the kitchen doorway as he was pulling on his boots. Her face was empty of expression as she watched him put his jacket on, but he knew the stillness was a mask against the long, silent day that awaited her. In all their happy dreaming in the high rocky seacoast she had come from, he had never anticipated her loneliness or understood that she would find it so difficult to learn his language. On those cold winter mornings he would not walk across the floor to kiss her because his boots were already on, and they followed the custom of her country, which allowed no shoes in the house. So he smiled at her across the space instead, and walked outside into the white light, into his own unexpected isolation.

Rob Eldred had enlisted in the navy as soon as he graduated from high school, fired with stories of the Second World War, dreaming of glorious and bloodless combat, the big guns exploding like fireworks over the dark water. He was disappointed when the navy discovered in him an aptitude for languages and sent him to school instead of to the front. When at last he was shipped out, it was not to do battle, but to sit at a desk on a radio ship, intercepting and translating messages. His war had to do with language, with the nuances of translation. He knew it was important work, though it did not always seem so. Eventually he was assigned to shore duty in the village where he met Jade Moon, and it was only then, hiking up the coast through the bombed and ruined villages, turning away from the beggars with their lost limbs and terrible scars, that he understood the extent of what he had been saved from.

The other carpenters knew his history, and it was something they could never quite forgive him. The transgression of his easy war was compounded by the fact that he had brought home an Asian wife. The last two wars were still felt acutely in the small town that had given half a dozen of its young men. Many of the carpenters Rob worked with were older men, and had long memories. Stanley Dobbs and Earl Kelly had lost a nephew each in Korea. Euart Simpson's only son had died during World War II, in a prison camp in the Philippines. One day Euart punctuated this fact by thrusting a photograph of his lost son at Rob. The picture showed a smiling boy in a man's uniform, his face the image of his father's before it grew so many lines of grief.

"I'm sorry," Rob said, handing the photo back. Euart sat down, the spite and challenge suddenly drained from his eyes.

"Sorry," Euart said, "doesn't settle with bringing home a Jap wife."

"She isn't Japanese," Rob said, struggling between anger and compassion.

"That don't make no difference," Euart said. He spat into the pile of sawdust around the planer. "She sure as hell isn't one of us."

THE BABY CAME in late April, just as the lilies of the valley opened on the shadowy side of the house. In the manner of those days Rob drove Jade Moon through the winding backroads to the hospital and sat through the piles of paperwork while his wife caught her breath and bit her lips against the groans. Then she was whisked away, and twelve hours later he was allowed in to see her, sitting up in bed with her hair tied back, holding their baby daughter. Jade Moon was ecstatic, and also very angry.

"I was asleep," she scolded, but he was relieved to see her spirit back, as if the drug that had kept her chilled and silent throughout the long winter had worked its way through her system and been expelled. "That whole time they made me sleep, and when I woke up it was finished. The baby was already born. I have no memory of it!" He recalled the practice of her own country, where women cloistered themselves with other women for a birth, and drank certain herbs, and let nature follow its course. Jade Moon went on, complaining softly but steadily, and Rob grew conscious of the curious glances from the two new mothers in the other beds. These grew longer and more amazed as Jade Moon slipped her gown open and let their new daughter begin to nurse.

"There is something wrong with them," she confided to Rob, tilting her head toward the two women. "Those poor ladies, they have babies but no milk. Every day the nurse brings them cow's milk, warm, in a glass bottle. Imagine!"

Rob turned to see the nearest woman, who was pale and thin with red hair twisted back in a bun. She was looking at him with a severe sort of pity over the dark bobbing head of her child. When their eyes met, she spoke.

"It's really none of my business," she said, "but someone should tell your wife about—about that." She nodded emphatically at the white slope of Jade Moon's breast, then at the bottle she held tilted to her baby. "This is a modern hospital. Civilized. We keep trying to explain it to her—we've even used sign language!—but she just smiles and looks embarrassed."

Rob, taken aback, did not know how to answer this. Jade Moon was being modest, he knew, and polite about her own full breasts when these women seemed bereft of milk. He turned to Jade Moon, who stroked his daughter's small head as she nursed, and then he forgot about the red-haired woman. He sat down on the bed, filled with joy and wonder.

"What were you discussing?" Jade Moon asked.

"You," he said, taking her hand. "Our beautiful baby."

Jade Moon glanced down and softened. "Yes," she said. "Isn't she a little cabbage?" Then she looked up at him, smiling, and said she wanted to name the baby Spring.

Rob was surprised. He knew that Spring was a common name for girls in her country, but he knew too that this child would grow up in America, and he tried to convince her to give the child another name. Lily, he suggested, thinking of the delicate white bells that fringed the house. Or why not Rose?

"No," she said, lifting the small bundle and cupping its head in her hand. "Flowers are too delicate, they don't last. I want my daughter to carry a name that can help her in life, give her strength. She was born in the spring, and spring is something that comes each year, renewing us."

"What about April, then?" he said. His daughter kicked and squirmed in her mother's arms, the restless water motions of the womb. Already she had her mother's eyes and hair, and already he feared for her, what she might suffer for her differences. "What about May, or even June?"

"No," she repeated, lifting the child easily to her shoulder, massaging its small back with her palm. "Spring."

At last he agreed, but during the two days that Jade Moon remained in the hospital, the name worried him. At work he stood in a newly framed house and handed out cigars to men who had barely spoken to him for months. He thought of the red-haired woman in the hospital and Jade Moon's lonely days in their house on the hill. When the time came to fill his baby's name in on the birth certificate, he found he could not honor Jade Moon's wish. He wrote down April Celeste, and signed. Jade Moon signed too, in Roman script, smiling as she finished the shaky letters. She could not read enough English to notice the change he had made.

"April," the nurse said, tickling the baby. "That's a pretty name."

Rob nodded and quickly moved his new family away from the talkative nurse, overcome with guilt. It was a moment he would always remember because, although it was a small thing, as tiny as a new shoot on the trunk of a tree, it was his first betrayal.

To Rob's GREAT surprise the birth of his first child made things easier for him at work. Many of the younger carpenters were new fathers themselves, and this shared experience became a narrow bridge across the flow of old animosities. He started eating lunch with them at the local bakery—thick homemade bread wrapped around tuna salad or slices of ham—and soon they invited him to join the local bowling league. For the first time since he returned from the war it seemed to him that the two halves of his life might be reconciled. He took up bowling, and then joined the Masonic lodge as well. Though it meant leaving Jade Moon home alone two nights a week, she was absorbed in the baby and seemed not to mind his absences as she had before. Also, church ladies had begun to visit her, bringing pies and casseroles, and they had seen with their own eyes that the Eldred home had the same sofa and coffee tables, the same crocheted doilies and blooming roses, that they would expect to find in their own homes. They left reassured, with promises to return. Miss Ellie Jackson, an aging spinster with a harsh voice and a no-nonsense manner, came back twice, the first time with a sheet cake and the second with an Early Reader borrowed from the primary school, determined to teach Jade Moon English once and for all. So Rob felt the pieces of his life were falling together in a complicated but understandable pattern. Their isolation, and the fact that the aspects of his life had seemed misaligned, had been a source of pain to him. Even though he had some reservations about finding Ellie Jackson in his house more days than not, he was glad that at least the bad time seemed to be coming to an end.

IN ANOTHER LIFE Ellie Jackson might have been a missionary, so great was her zeal, so pure was her determination. She was tall and lanky, with short gray hair and small but vivid blue eyes. She swept into their little house on the hill like a change in weather, and undertook Jade Moon's education with the same focused energy that she applied to spring cleaning or organizing church bazaars. She came by every afternoon from two till four, bringing with her cookbooks and measuring cups, and soon Rob came home not to rice and stir-fried vegetables or spicy fish, but to macaroni and cheese, hamburgers and hot dogs with beans, potato salad, and even roast lamb. Ellie was often still there when Rob arrived, gesturing at this utensil or that, making up for Jade Moon's lack of English by increasing her volume, notch by notch, until her loud voice sometimes woke the baby. This made Rob wince, because it was useless to shout, and because he himself was guilty of it. Jade Moon did not possess his facility with language, and he did not possess the patience of a language teacher. To his shame he had heard himself repeating words again and again, with increasing volume and exasperation, as if, through the sheer force of repetition, he could make her understand.

Thus, he was pleased to see that more English textbooks appeared, and to find, one day, that most things in the house had been labeled with their English names in Ellie's neat, blockish handwriting. The windows were open to the late spring breeze, and the paper labels fluttered softly. CUPBOARD, said one. STOVE, REFRIGERATOR, TABLE, CUP, SOFA, RADIO, SHELF. Jade Moon read them off proudly. Although Ellie was loud and aggressive, someone Jade Moon would have disdained in her own country, in America Miss Ellie was her only friend. It bothered Rob, sometimes, the way Ellie's advice became law in their house. *Use milk to remove ink stains,* Jade Moon would declare, scrubbing at the shirt pockets where his pens had leaked. *Vinegar and newspapers make the glass windows sparkle.* It worried him that Ellie treated Jade Moon in a somewhat patronizing manner, as if what they shared was not a friendship at all, but a great gift Ellie was bestowing on her diligent and fortunate student. That was why Ellie made him think of missionaries he had seen, but because Jade Moon seemed happy, and because her English was improving, he said nothing.

One day he came home from work to find Jade Moon pacing their small rooms with excitement. She had been invited to a mother-and-daughter dinner at the church. It was to be a potluck dinner, and Ellie had asked her to bring the dish they had learned that week: a tuna noodle casserole with a potato chip crust. Jade Moon had agreed to go, but she had a secret idea about what to fix. She would not tell him exactly what it was, but, laughing, said she wanted to drive into the city to find some fabric for a new dress, and then she wanted him to go to the lake and catch her a fresh rainbow trout.

On the evening of the dinner Jade Moon came into the living room wearing a fitted dress of dark rose. It had a narrow waist and a skirt that flared from the hips like an upended tulip. She carried the baby, whose frilly dress was the color of cream and decorated with lace and ribbons that matched her own. In the kitchen the mysterious dish was covered with tinfoil. Rob had spent most of the previous weekend floating on the still-cold lake, seeking the fish, and on their trip into the city Jade Moon had disappeared into several different grocery stores and one tiny Asian market, coming out with her arms full of packages and a private smile on her face. She had worked all week on the new dresses, copying hers from a magazine she had bought. Now she turned shyly in the room, waiting for his approval. Rob was moved to stillness by the sight of her white arms and dark hair against the deep red material. He thought he had never seen anyone so beautiful, and he told her so.

Before Ellie came, while Jade Moon was making a last-minute adjustment to her hem, Rob walked quietly into the kitchen and lifted the foil from the potluck dish. He saw at once that it was both splendid and completely wrong. Jade Moon had prepared a special fish. Turned on its side, the steamed trout was surrounded by vegetables cut into graceful shapes. Its one visible eye stared, and its tail was arched slightly, as if at any moment the fish might propel itself off the platter and into the green sea of the tablecloth. Rob stared back at the fish and wondered what he should do. Ellie was already knocking at the door. Perhaps, after all, the women would understand the importance of this gesture and be kind. So he nodded at Ellie, who was exclaiming over April's dress, and said nothing when Jade Moon carried the platter proudly out the door.

It was rare for Rob to be alone in the house, and he found himself restless, moving from one project to another, glancing constantly at his watch. He repaired a cupboard door, then put up new shelves in the bathroom. The familiar work calmed him, and he imagined the church ladies tasting the fish out of politeness, finding it good. He imagined them asking for the recipe, and Jade Moon giving it to them shyly, in slow but perfect English. The dinner lasted for over three hours, and the more time passed, the more convinced he became that things were going well.

At last, just as he was putting his tools away, he heard a car door slam. He met Jade Moon on the porch. Ellie's taillights were already disappearing over the hill. Jade Moon carried the platter balanced along one arm, and held the baby, who was sound asleep, in the other. She had stopped on the top step and turned to stare at the moon, which had risen as round and cold as a fish eye in the clear summer sky.

"Where's Ellie?" Rob asked, taking the baby. "Why didn't she help you?" Jade Moon did not answer, but turned in her red dress and walked into the house. By the time he had followed her to the kitchen, the fish, completely intact, was displayed for him in the center of the table. Jade Moon's face was expressionless, but nearly gray with embarrassment. He put the baby in the little reclining chair on the table. She was awake now, and wiggling happily, oblivious to her mother's disappointment, even when Jade Moon dropped her face into her hands and began to weep.

Little by little, he coaxed the story from her. He could imagine the women, of course, their small gasps, their looks of shock and then dismay as Jade Moon unveiled her fish. One woman had held her hand to her mouth and left the room. Even Ellie had been nonplussed. After a moment, the beautiful fish had been moved to the far end of the table. The rest of the evening had been equally humiliating. Whenever Jade Moon spoke in English, the others had laughed, or looked confused and walked away. Even when she repeated things twice, three times, they had not understood, and she had spent most of the evening listening to unintelligible chatter, while the women finished every dish and left her fish untouched.

"They are just ignorant," Rob said. He stood up and got a plate. The fish was soft, white, succulent, and he took a large portion. "Ignorant and foolish. If they had tasted it, they'd know what they were missing." He ate one mouthful, slowly, then another. "It is delicious."

When she did not answer him, he put his fork down and took her hand.

"Jade Moon," he said. "Remember the time I tried to compliment your mother's house, and instead I told her she had a lovely toilet?" He waited for her to smile at this old joke between them, but she did not. "Don't you remember? Everyone was shocked, and I was terribly embarrassed, but I didn't give up. You must make mistakes in order to learn."

Jade Moon's face was set. "English is an ugly language," she said, speaking to her hands. "It sounds like dogs barking. I don't want to know this language."

He looked at her profile, her narrow face and generous lips, and remembered how much she hated to do things unless she excelled at them. Once she had ripped out an entire piece of embroidery because of a tiny flaw she had discovered in the first stitch. He put his silverware down and spoke to her sternly.

"Jade Moon," he said. "You must learn. This is your country now. What if there is an emergency and you need to use the telephone? What if something happened to me?"

"I don't know," she said, glancing up, and he saw the worry move like clouds across her face. Then she composed herself and grew stubborn. "I will learn emergency phrases," she said. "But that is all."

He felt his patience ebb. If she would not learn, then she would be dependent on him all her life.

"You are nothing but a lazy woman," he said. "Lazy, lazy, lazy." He spoke the last word emphatically, aware of the great insult it would be to her, amazed, even as he spoke, at the depth of his own cruelty.

Her face changed and grew still, closed to him. On the table the baby kicked and cooed. Jade Moon picked her up, wiped her tears away with the back of her wrist, and turned away, leaving the ruined fish in the middle of the table.

That night Rob did not sleep well, and in the morning Jade Moon avoided him until he left for work. On his way out the door he paused, disturbed by both the silence and by some other, subtle change he couldn't name. Then it came to him. He looked around again, from cupboard to stove to table to chair.

All the small white cards had disappeared.

SPRING WAS TWO YEARS OLD when her brother was born, and by then the argument about language, about names, had become a tender, misshapen knot in the living flesh of their marriage.

When Jade Moon held the new baby on her shoulder and said she would call him Mountain, the air was tense with years of accumulated arguments. Jade Moon, stubborn, talked on. She herself had traveled too much in her life, as her name foretold. She wanted her son to stay in one place, as solid and steady as a rock cliff against the sea. She would give him the name to ensure him strength. She said all this defiantly. Rob sighed, eyeing their small son. When the nurse took him off to fill in the paperwork he tapped his pencil against the wooden desk, looking out the office window over the parking lot. He wrote down his father's name, Michael James.

Three weeks before their last child was born, just a year later, Jade Moon announced that if it was a girl, she would name the child Sea.

"Why Sea?" Rob asked, looking up from his newspaper. The two older children were asleep, and Jade Moon sat at the desk, slight even in this last month of her pregnancy, writing a letter to her parents. The translucent paper rustled softly beneath her pen. Though he spoke fluently, Rob had never read her language well, and the characters seemed both ominous and full of mystery. Was that how it felt to Jade Moon, he wondered, walking in the town or buying groceries? He tried sometimes to imagine how his language, divorced from meaning, might sound. Was it melodious, like French or Spanish? Was it the harsh singing of Chinese? Did it really resemble the sound of barking dogs? Sometimes he tried to listen to only the sounds of English, but for him sound was meaning, impossible to separate.

"Sea," she said, "for two reasons. First, because it is a sea that both separates and connects my family and myself. And second, because I am Jade Moon, and the moon controls the movement of the sea. I do not want my daughter to travel as far as I have in this life. Besides," she added, "it is a beautiful name, both in your language and in mine."

"When they go to school," he argued, "they'll need American names. Why not call her Maria? It's from Latin. It's an ordinary name, but it means sea."

"Maria," she spoke the words, blurring the *r* in a way that reminded him of a day, long ago, when he had tried to teach her the sound—*raspberry*, *rhubarb*—in the field behind the house. Now, as then, it sounded awkward in her mouth, and some of the old anger flared up within him. It was a difficult sound, true enough, but she had been in America now for nearly four years.

"That's right," he said. "Maria. Ma-*ree*-ah. That's her name."

"You call her Maria, then," she said, turning back to her letter. Her long hair was tied in elastic and made a black line down her back. "But I will call her Sea."

"Why are you so stubborn about this?" he asked, throwing down his newspaper. But she did not answer him. She kept her eyes fixed on the letter, her fingers shaping the complex, mysterious characters of a language he could not fully understand.

ONCE THE CHILDREN were born the years passed quickly, one following another in smooth succession, although Rob never lost the sense that he was leading a double life. Like the branches of a young tree, it seemed the parts of his life grew less and less connected with the passing of time. His days forked off into the community where he told jokes, swapped stories, argued, and worked in his own language. Pulling into his driveway in the evenings, he had to make a conscious effort to switch from one world, one language, to another. It was like stepping into the past, he sometimes thought, or walking with a single step from one country to another. He put his toolbox in the shed and stepped through the door with his pockets full of sawdust. There he found his family gathered around the table, folding animals out of paper, or singing songs while Jade Moon sliced narrow rings of spring onion, or working diligently at the complicated characters of her alphabet. The children were hers from birth until they went to school, and if their world was an isolated one, Jade Moon saw to it that it was full of learning, full of joy.

"They should learn to speak English," he said one night when the children were in bed. "Even if you won't, the children must."

She put down her embroidery and looked up at him.

"Let me tell you a story," she said. "When I was a young girl my parents had a friend who went to Hong Kong for business. While they were there they had a baby girl, and since they were rich, they hired a local girl to care for this baby during the days. Two years passed, then three, and though the baby was happy and healthy, still it did not speak. They grew worried, and even consulted a doctor. Then one day they were taking a walk, and they stopped in a shop for some food. The baby was babbling. They thought it was just baby talk until suddenly the store owner, an old Chinese woman who also spoke a little of their language, looked up smiling. 'How nice,' she said. 'Baby speaks Chinese!'"

Rob started to laugh, but saw at once that it was the wrong reaction.

"No," Jade Moon said. "How do you think that mother felt, missing her own baby's first words? How do you think she felt, not being able to speak with her own child? These are my children too," she said. "Not just yours and not just America's. I want to be able to tell them about my life."

THEY WERE HER CHILDREN until they went to school, but in the end Jade Moon lost each one to America. Rob grew to dread the early days of school, the way his children came home, one after another, at first in tears and later drawn into themselves, isolated and bewildered by the unfamiliar language. Yet it amazed Rob, too, how quickly they learned, with an aptitude that surpassed even his own. Within weeks they were chattering, imperfectly but fluently, to the other children. He tried to help by speaking English with them in the car, or while Jade Moon was outside hanging the wash or gardening. When they got older, he looked over their homework for mistakes. They were all bright, and their intelligence helped them overcome the thoughtless cruelty of other children. In the end they caught up and even surpassed their friends. April was editor of the newspaper in her senior year. Michael played the clarinet and drew intricate pictures that won awards. Maria ran for class treasurer, and won. They survived the hard years; they grew up. Like him, they had their secret lives outside the house, their lives of the telephone, of prom parties and clubs. He saw them roll their eyes behind Jade Moon's back when she refused to speak English, and he said nothing. He felt this complicity was the least he could offer, because he knew that sometimes still they were hurt. He could tell it from the tense, inward silences that enveloped them now and then. They didn't offer to share the sources of this pain, and for this he was, at first, grateful. He told himself that they took after him, that they preferred to work things out for themselves, in privacy and silence. It was only later when, one by one, the children left home for large cities and contained, controlled, anonymous lives, distant lives, that he wondered at the depth of pain they might have suffered, that he wished to go back, to touch the tense shoulder, to understand.

FIVE YEARS AFTER Maria graduated from college, Rob fell from a ladder at work and hurt his back. Lying on the ground, the wind knocked from his lungs, pain like nails in his spine, he understood that his construction days were over. Once he had finished physical therapy, the company gave him a desk job. He sat in the windowless office, pushing papers and answering the phone, and thought about the time, forty years before, when he had worked on the radio ship, his future spread out before him like the sea. Eventually they offered him early retirement, and he took it. He packed up his few remaining tools and removed himself from one-half of his life. As he parked his truck that final day, and carried his toolbox for the last time into the shed, he looked up to see Jade Moon standing in the kitchen window, preparing his dinner, humming. He paused for a moment in the driveway. The song was a light and haunting one, an old song from her own country. Jade Moon's voice wavered, and the August heat shimmered around the house. He felt an urgency then, a sudden panic, as if the house and his life within it were part of a mirage. It seemed that this time the attempt to leap from one life to another would plunge him from a terrible height. His fear was so sudden, and so great, that he actually turned to retrace his steps to town. Then a tug of pain in his back stopped him. After a few moments he grew calmer and was able to move forward, bridging the distance with a few steps, his feet on solid ground after all.

At first the days were difficult, long and restless, and he relieved himself by focusing on projects around the house, working late into the long summer nights. Then his back went out and he was forced to lie still in bed while Jade Moon moved quietly through the house. He observed her as she stepped from one room to another, surprised by her energy, her quiet grace, the traces of youth she had carried with her into middle age. There had been moments, even as a young man just married, when Rob would look at Jade Moon and see what she would be like old. She might be doing anything—reaching to a high shelf for a can, pouring water in a vase, stirring soup. For an instant he would see it—age in her narrow calves, bony as an old woman's, age in the careful grace of her gestures, age in the stiff curve of her fingers around a spoon. In an instant it was always gone, lost to the completion of her actions, to the resurfacing of her youthful self.

Now, alone again in the solitude of their home, he discovered an opposite phenomenon: beneath the surface of wrinkles and slow movements, Jade Moon had retained elements of her youth. Her hair stayed dark and her shoulders were still smooth and firm. Sometimes, as she stepped from the bath in a towel, her white shoulders broken by the black water of her hair, he was moved with a sense of collapsing time. She would laugh if he went to her then.

"But I'm such an old woman," she would say. "What do you still see in me?"

He would not answer, and she would laugh a young girl's laugh as the towel slipped away to the floor.

"We are so lucky," she said to him once. "We are able to live the happiest time of our lives over again."

Jade Moon remained slim and agile even as Rob, comfortable now in his retirement, grew a mild belly and felt stiffness settling in his joints. He expected that she would live longer than he would himself, and he took careful, secret precautions to make sure she would not lack for money. There was his life insurance policy, bought years before and now paying healthy premiums. There were blue-chip stocks and bonds locked away in a bank vault. Sometimes he got up early in the morning and drove the old truck into town. He had coffee and doughnuts in the bakery with the other retired men, easy conversations that were like surfacing from beneath the water, and then he went over to the bank to count his modest investments. He liked the rich scent of metal and leather in the safe-deposit room. He liked locking himself into a tiny booth and writing down the figures. Most of all, he liked the feeling he had when he returned the box and the key and left the bank. It was the same feeling as finishing a house and knowing that it was a solid house, that it would last. No matter what, Jade Moon would never go without. He drove along the country roads feeling sad at the thought of his own demise, but nonetheless deeply content with his arrangements.

He never considered what his life would be if she were the one to die first and thus, when the first signs came that this would be the case, he was able to ignore them. If Jade Moon was pale, well, she had always been fair skinned. When he saw her stop and touch her heart, as if with pain, he thought—well, she is getting old after all, and so am I.

At last the day came when Jade Moon fainted. She was working in the vegetable garden, but the day was overcast and she was only watering with a hose. He ran to her from where he was repairing the fence, and the expression on her face—something near the pain he had witnessed there during her three labors—compelled him to finally take her to a doctor. They drove to the same hospital, twenty miles away, where their children had been born. There was a new highway in place now, but Rob took the old road, reassured by the familiar curves and hills. Altogether, they made this trip three times over as many months, for tests. He expected something simple and curable: high blood pressure, a heart murmur, kidney stones. On their last visit the doctor escorted them into his office to tell them, quietly and gravely, that Jade Moon had cancer, advanced and inoperable. Rob was struck with such shock that he couldn't speak. Even after they left the hospital and were driving through the snowy white fields on the country road, he couldn't talk. He drove slowly, glancing now and then at Jade Moon from the corner of his eyes.

"So, I am dying," she said finally. "I thought I was sick, and now I know."

"You'll get better," he insisted, though the doctor had given them no hope. Then he turned fully toward her, surprised, for a moment, out of his fear. At the hospital he had been too stunned to translate, and yet Jade Moon had understood the terrible thing that had been said. On the far side of the truck she was looking out over the rolling white fields, and he saw a trace of a smile flicker at the edges of her mouth.

"Do you remember," she said, "the first winter you appeared in our village? It was snowing then, too, just like now, and we were all shocked at that fur hat you wore. So tall, it looked like something out of a Russian painting. That's what I thought. You were just as strange, and just as handsome, as a man from a painting. I really thought you were a Russian."

He tried to remember his first day in her village, but all he could bring up was a blur of staring faces darting here and there amid the snow.

"I remember some schoolgirls," he said. "I remember a whole group of girls watching me walk in. When I got close they all began laughing and ran away. They were wearing their high shoes and running in the snow."

"Not all of them ran," she said. "I was among them and I stayed and watched you. Do you know I decided right at that moment I would marry you? Even as you walked into town, I was planning to learn Russian so I could speak with you."

She laughed. Rob understood that she was telling him that she did not regret anything. She had made her choice that snowy day; she had wanted him and everything that had followed was justified by that moment. He felt a thickening in his chest and pulled off the road, into an area beneath a cluster of pine trees. He leaned over and put his arms around her. The old truck smelled of years of cigarettes and, very faintly, of kerosene. Jade Moon was small and frail beneath the bulky coats and scarves. Her cheek was dry against his. After a moment she pulled herself carefully away. She put her left hand on his cheek.

"Rob," she said, startling him with perfect, lilting English. "Please. I would like to go home."

THE DISEASE, which had made itself known so slowly, now progressed with an astonishing speed. For Rob, ignoring his bad back and chopping cord after cord of wood to release the wild energy that overtook him at the thought of her death, it was like learning a new word. For years the eye skipped over it, but once it became known, it seemed to appear everywhere. Jade Moon's symptoms were now so clear, so obvious, that he wondered at the time he had passed without seeing them. She lost weight, she tired easily. And then the medicine was less effective as the pain grew. Within two months she was spending her days in bed, watching TV and knitting. He had written the terrible news to the children right away, and they called home now at frequent intervals, encouraged each time by Jade Moon's bright, chatty tone. April was in California, working as an editor for a testing company. Michael was a lawyer in Seattle. Maria was married to a landscape architect and lived in Chicago. They said they would come when it got serious, and they did not believe him when he tried to tell them that it was serious already. They were all good at denying what they would rather not see; it was how they had survived, after all. It was only Rob who saw it, how she hung up the telephone and slumped back into her pillows, eyes closed against the lapping waves of exhaustion and pain.

"You must come," he said to them finally, one after another, and at last he convinced them. They would meet in Chicago, at Maria's house, and fly home together. Rob nodded at the phone, and told them each to hurry.

"I'm so worried," Jade Moon said on the morning the children were to arrive. He had told her they were coming and now her fingers moved in a fretful pattern across the sheets. The medication had made her drowsy and forgetful. "I'm worried, and I can't remember their names."

He smoothed her hair back from her head. "We have three children," he told her. She knew by now that he had given them other names, legal names, but today he spoke slowly and used the names of their childhood, the ones that she had chosen. "Spring. Mountain. Sea."

"Ah," she said, "yes." He was relieved to see how she relaxed then, as if each name had diffused through her like a drug.

"Spring," she repeated, and closed her eyes. "Mountain. Sea." Her breathing deepened, and he knew she was asleep.

He stood up and went to stand in the window. A few years earlier the city had widened the road and approved a stone quarry on the opposite hill. The traffic increased; machines had cut a great gash in the side, and now the huge boulders rested randomly on the hills, white and inert, like sleeping elephants. The noise, the tearing of the earth, had upset Jade Moon, and she had kept the curtains closed day and night against that sight.

Now he pushed them aside and, despite the thick heat in the house, the chill outside, he opened the window. The air, bright with sun and cold, rushed around his face. At the house of Jade Moon's parents he had stood just this way on a winter afternoon, leaving the suffocating warmth of the fire for the bitter, refreshing air of the unheated rooms. And it was in the spring, when the air was as fresh and crisp as well water, that he went walking with Jade Moon in the hills behind her parents' house. There was one spot they went to often, just beneath the crest of the mountain, where a shelf of rock thrust itself out over the sea. They used to sit there, the sun-warmed rock balanced by the chill of the air, Jade Moon picking the delicate wildflowers and looking, now and then, out across the expanse of sea to the places he would take her within a year. It was so long ago. They had left as planned, and in all the years of their marriage they had never been back.

Jade Moon stirred behind him; he wished the children would hurry. *Spring, Mountain, Sea*, he murmured, like an incantation, as if the words that had the power to soothe his wife could also hurry his children from their lives.

The image that came to him was incomplete, the way a frame merely suggests the finished house. He said their names again to help it form. *Spring, Mountain, Sea*. The four syllables were suddenly as powerful as a poem. How many times had he heard her speak them? Yet for him, until this moment, they had always evoked only the individual faces of his children and the weight of his double life. He had never thought of them this way, as Jade Moon must have, three small strokes of language that reconstructed their shared past. Spring, mountain, sea: he was sitting on a rocky cliff, gazing at an ocean as wide and full of promise as his future, and Jade Moon, young and lovely, was collecting flowers at his side.

She was sleeping now. Her hair, still dark, had slipped across her face. The stubborn beauty of her gesture clutched at him, and he thought of his many betrayals through the years. He shut the window. Crossing the room, he had again the fleeting impression of her youthfulness, but when he brushed the hair from her face he saw how tightly the skin was drawn now across her skull. He lay down next to her as he used to do on the nights before Spring was born, when she was so cold and he had talked her to sleep in his arms.

He did not know if she could hear him, or if she was past the power of words to soothe or build or comfort. Yet he spoke softly and steadily, both in his language and in hers, telling her what he had just now understood. When the children arrived that was how they found him, whispering their old, discarded names again and again—as if, by the sheer force of repetition, he could make her understand.

A Gleaming in
the Darkness

*Sometimes we returned in the evening after dinner for another sur-
vey of our domain. Our precious products, for which we had no
shelter, were arranged on tables and boards; from all sides we could
see their slightly luminous silhouettes, and these gleamings, which
seemed suspended in the darkness, stirred us with ever new emotion
and enchantment.*
                                                    —MARIE CURIE

I AM AN OLD WOMAN NOW, AND DYING, SO SURELY THE THINGS OF
this world should no longer have the power to compel me.
Yet in my final hours I am indeed distracted, and it is nothing from my own hard life that haunts me, but rather a woman I
barely knew, a person on the edge of all my living. It seems im-
proper, it is not right. If I am to be in this world a little longer,
then I should wish to dwell on my husband, Thierry, or the son
who looked just like him and fell beneath the German rifles, or
my only daughter, who disappeared so many years ago into the
countryside of France. I should wish to think of them, yet I do
not. Even my granddaughter cannot hold my attention, though
she comes to see me daily. For half an hour every morning she
visits, speaking brightly and fluffing up my pillows, rubbing the
cool balm into my hands, which are the color of a pig's liver, the
texture of bark, swollen now as thick as sausages. *Merci grand-
mère,* she whispers when she leaves. *Merci.*

She is good to me. She is grateful. I raised her after her mother

fled with the Resistance, and she has not forgotten. In her grati-
tude she has brought me to this hospital, the best in Europe, to
die in a room that is not my own. I watch her depart, delicate in
a dark blue dress that rustles lightly against her calves. She, of
course, does not remember Madame, who died when she was
still a little girl. She does not remember the years of hard work or
the blue jars glowing. It is only I who remember, but I do this
with such clarity that I sometimes imagine myself back in the
small glass building on the rue Lhomond, Madame in her black
cotton, Monsieur scribbling on the board, the scent of cooking
earth thick around us. As if my life had not yet happened. As if
time, after all, were of no lasting consequence.

It is strange, it is most disturbing, yet it is so. I run their images
through my mind like beads through my fingers, working something out. Madame was a small woman whose hands were often
cracked and bleeding from her work. She had a habit of running
her thumb across the tips of her fingers, again and again, lightly.
They were numb, she said once, absently, when I asked her. That
was all, a small thing. She would not remember it, and out of so
many things that have happened in my own life, why I dwell on
this is a great mystery. Still, I would like to call her here, to this
room with its walls of green tile, its single window masked by a thin
yellow curtain, a pale sea light washing through the air. I would
like to ask her what happened to her hands before she died.

LONG BEFORE she was famous in the world for her mind, Madame
was famous in the market for her shopping. That is how I first
knew of her, as the woman who stood baffled before the butcher,
uncertain how many people she could feed with a joint, as the
woman who bought fruit blindly, without pausing to test if it
was too young yet, or too ripe. The things any ordinary house-
wife knew she did not understand. In the market they said she
was unnatural, working side by side with men, leaving her small
daughter in the hands of others. At first, I must admit, I was no
different in my opinions. When the fruit sellers gossiped, I nodded in agreement. When she walked by on the street, in such
deep conversation with her husband that the world around them

might not have existed, I stared boldly, along with all the others. She did not go to church at all, a scandalous thing, and in the evenings, when I knelt on the hard pine boards of my little room and prayed, I wondered how she lived without that ritual, that comfort.

It was not until the day she came for the key that I began to see her differently. Up close she was more human, and more frail. We were similar in size and looks, she and I, two slight women with gray eyes and ash blond hair, and I felt an immediate affinity with her, despite the vast differences in our ages and our lives. I took her to the room full of windows, a rude and dusty space, abandoned for decades, which would become her first laboratory. Because it was a room the university did not require me to clean, I used to go there often, slipping unseen through the cloudy glass door, locking it behind me. Inside the air was still, moist and warm when the sun shone. I had cleared a little table of its dust and rubble so I could have a place to drink my morning coffee and to eat my lunch in peace. People said it had been a greenhouse once, and in that room of windows I could close my eyes and imagine the air around me growing thick with shiny leaves, spilling over with blooming flowers. I could pretend I was a rich girl, dressed in deep blue satin, wandering through the foliage like a bright pampered bird. When I told this to Thierry, who was then my most serious suitor, he laughed out loud, but two days later he brought me a little turquoise bird in a brass cage. For this I married him, for the extravagance of that little bird, for his deep laugh. I let him kiss me sometimes, in that deserted room, and I remember even now his lips, pressing mine like two pliant leaves, cool and alive. A shaft of sunlight fell across his arm, and all around us the air was full of dust, thick with the memory of growing things.

On the day they came to see this room, Madame and her thin, absentminded husband, I was newly in love, and thus sensitive to love in others, and so I noticed how he paused and took her arm, and the look she gave him in return—warm, full of an unspoken affection that softened the severity of her features. They said in all the shops that she was cold, like a machine, but that morning

I saw she had a tender heart. As they toured the room I watched with curiosity. They were not romantic, yet they suited one another exactly, just as a shell would fit perfectly within its fossil. In part it was the way they spoke, for they did not talk of ordinary things, the closeness of the air or the dampness of the floor beneath their feet, but rather of formulas and research. Each spoke, each listened, and as I stood quietly in the corner, watching their inspection, I thought that they spoke as two men might, as equals. She was intent, beautiful I thought, but wearing no adornment. She did not flirt or hesitate to contradict her husband. This was odd to me, for Thierry viewed his word as law, and I had learned not to oppose him even when I knew that I was right.

They took that room and soon moved in, though it was not possible to believe anyone could work there for an hour, much less for the decade they finally stayed, freezing when the winter came, plugging loose panes against whistling drafts, worrying about leaks or the roof caving in beneath the heavy snows. And in the summer it was worse, hot as an inferno with the sun flowing in and the great fires kept going for their experiments. Yet they would not vent the roof. Dust enough, they complained, came in already. No matter how carefully I cleaned, dust drifted into test tubes, coated instruments, tampered with their experiments like an evil force. Still, despite the bad conditions, they worked with such concentration that they forgot about meals and cold and heat, and everything in the world except the experiments before their eyes. I knew it was a rare thing, what they did, the way they did it. I have never seen the like of it, the twin heads bent over the glass and flames and measuring tools, the long silences broken by the bursts of talk, the shared excitement running like another flame, invisible, between them.

Now I myself have become an experiment, and people study my hands with the same intentness that Madame once turned, day after day, upon her jars. They examine me closely, but no one has any answers. Not the doctors, coming once each morning to make their tests; not the nurses, stepping through the doorway with their trays of bandages. I watch their smiles change, grow fixed, as they attend to me. *Your fingers look better,* they tell me, lying gently, and then, because they cannot say that soon I will re-cover, they talk about the war. *Soon the fighting will end for good. France is free again, Marie Bonvin, soon the whole world will be free and the soldiers will come home.* I murmur small words, smile my happiness. Of course I do. Who could disappoint the young nurses with their clear skin and hope-shining eyes? They save the news up, dwelling on the past, which for me, in their eyes, is a much greater place than my future. Pity glimmers on their faces, and compassion, yet their words are insulated with the smug knowl-edge of their youth. They do not believe that their unlined skin, their smooth and agile limbs, will ever fall into such a state of dis-repair as mine have done. They are sorry for my disabilities, my old age, my dying, and they pity me. They do not see I have no pity for myself. These young girls do not know it, and I cannot tell them, but I have discovered that past and present blur together, become one and the same, so that time means very little at the end.

I believe Madame understood this even in the heart of life. Absorbed in her experiments, she showed no awareness of the way the sun moved across the panes of glass and finally disappeared. She would look up suddenly, when it had become so dark she couldn't see, and she would blink then, surprised that the day, al-ready, had gone past. After many years, when I grew brave enough, I used to urge her to go home. It was always a great effort for me to speak to her, a foreigner and such a brilliant woman, famous al-ready for her mind. Still, we had the same name, Marie, a saint's name, and I had watched her long enough to know that with other people she was very gentle, though she pushed herself far beyond any human limit. Long after everyone else had gone home, when I myself had put away the brooms and rags and was setting off into the evening, she would still be bent over the single weak light. I worried for her, then. She was so pale, she rarely ate.

One time, long past the supper hour, she checked some bottles, wrote some numbers, then threw herself into a stiff wooden chair and rubbed her hands against her face. I was sweeping and for a long time I did not speak. But she was so still that at last I grew courageous.

"Madame," I said. "Madame, are you all right? Would you like me to fetch you a glass of tea?" She looked at me, startled, then shook her head. The dark circles ringed her eyes like clouds, and her eyes themselves were dull and weary, without the sparked focus of concentration that I had always seen in them before.

"No," she said slowly, sitting up straight and rubbing her hands. On the wooden table there was a beaker full of some dark liquid, and she picked this up, turning it before her, studying it. "I have made an error," she said. "Somewhere. That is all." She paused, and put the beaker down. "I will simply have to start again." She shook her head, then, and gave a small dry laugh. "A year's work," she said, "and it is gone, and there is nothing to do but to begin all over again."

I did not know what to say to her, of course. I knew her dedication, and it seemed that any words would sound petty against that pure intensity. Yet I felt a deep sympathy as well, for my second child had died as he was born, and so I thought I knew what it meant to lose in a moment what you had spent a year creating. And there was more, because following that loss my faith had disappeared, and it seemed to me that I alone among the shopkeepers had come to understand why she would not enter any church. I still attended—for Thierry, for my first son, I had to go—but prayer no longer brought me any solace. So on that dreary evening I took her hands in mine, her rough hands with their chapped fingers, and I pressed them.

"I'm sorry, Madame," I said, nodding to the brown jar. "It's a mystery to me, what you do. But you work so hard, I'm sure it will come out right."

She looked at me so oddly then. I pulled my hands away, suddenly embarrassed. "Excuse me," I said, looking down. "Excuse me please, Madame."

She looked at her right hand then. She held it flat and turned it in front of her, examining it as if it belonged to someone else entirely. She rubbed her thumb against her first finger, then all her fingertips, and then she turned her palm down and let her hand rest, very gently, upon my arm.

"Not at all, Marie," she said. "I thank you."

So you see how she was, her deep kindness. Her life was conse-
crated to her work, but it is not true that she lacked emotion. She
was a passionate woman, I can attest to it. She loved what she loved,
and if it was a strange thing for a woman to love her work, so be it.
Except for that love, what would be the difference between herself,
boiling up a kettle of her mysterious earth, and another woman
stirring the cauldron of her stew? Or even myself, for I worked as
hard as she did, scrubbing day after day at the dirty corners of that
university. I heard the men speak of her sometimes, with wonder
and derision. I cleaned their offices, their laboratories, so much
nicer than she had herself, and heard them gossip.

"She has a fine mind," they would acknowledge. "And she is
meticulous. But this business with the atoms—well, it is on the
wrong track completely."

Even after Madame and Monsieur were awarded a Nobel
Prize for the discovery of radium, I heard people say it was her
husband alone who deserved the credit—his labor, his intelligence,
that fueled the fascinating work. Years later, when the whole
world honored her discoveries, there were still those in France
who were grudging with their praise. All of Paris talked of her, of
radium, but she stayed in that small rude laboratory because they
would give her nothing else.

Yet for all the difficulties, there was joy as well. When the dirt
came, what joy then! Sacks and sacks of dirt, delivered to the
courtyard behind the glass laboratory.

"Pitchblende!" she exclaimed when I inquired, watching them
unload it. "At last, it is beginning!" She stood outside in her worn
black dress, her arms folded against the cold, a rapturous look on
her face. Before the unloading was finished, she was ripping open
a sack of earth and digging her hands in deeply. Over the next
many months she sifted and cooked this dirt in her big kettle, sep-
arating all the residue into smaller and smaller jars of various sorts
of mud. In that way she worked painstakingly through the entire
vast pile.

When I spoke of her at home, they could not believe such a
woman existed. Thierry disliked to hear of her, for he knew that

she and her husband did not go to church. So I told my stories when he was not at home, and my children came to believe that she and her husband were not exactly real, but people I had made up for their amusement.

"Tell us, Mama," they would beg, "about that magic lady who spends all day in her laboratory."

"Well," I would say, "today Madame made the things in the room blue—table, chair, door, floor—everything turned a lovely sort of bluish silver, like fog. Yet by afternoon the chairs and table and beakers and even the glass windowpanes had gone pure yellow, and best of all, in the middle of the day, around noon, everything was, just for a moment, an absolute shade of green." My children listened, fascinated, and I talked on. We were so poor, and I was happy that I could give them something lovely that would fall into their lives like shafts of light.

One day, however, when there was only bread for dinner, my son, then ten, complained loudly about Madame.

"If she is so magical," he demanded, "why doesn't she just turn the wooden chair and table into gold, and give some to us? Why isn't she the richest woman in the world, that's what I want to know!"

"Madame is as poor as we are," I explained. "She and her husband live in simple rooms as small as ours. She does not work for gold, but for knowledge." I paused, pouring heated milk into their cups. "I think," I said, "that if someone offered her a thousand francs, she would not spend one centime of it on herself, but would use it to buy another mountain of dirt, or a new laboratory, or something fine for science. She is trying to do something good for all the people of the world with her work."

"Well, then, she is crazy," my son said. In a dozen years he would be killed in the first great war, but on that morning he was only a small boy with his dreams. "Why, with a thousand francs I would buy a castle, and eat pastry and candy at every meal!"

It was not only my son who thought this, that Madame was a little crazy. All the shopkeepers still wondered at a woman who worked so hard for no money at all. They saw her daughter, cared for by the grandfather. They saw the family staying home on Sunday mornings, and they shook their heads, predicted disaster. When they spoke like this I felt myself growing angry, and I became famous among the fruit sellers for my defense of Madame. A genius, I would say. Leave her alone, she is doing things of which we cannot even dream.

I do not dream, I am awake, though the nurses think that I am sleeping. Like the famous scientists who did not notice a cleaning lady stooped low to sweep away their dust, these young nurses do not remember that a woman, even old, even dying, might have keen ears. They cluster sometimes at the foot of my bed, gossiping about their boyfriends, their liaisons, the new clothes they will make from bits of silk and lace they have been hoarding. They do not see that I was once like them, with blond hair that fell to my waist, washed once a week and dried in a the soft sweet light of the sun. Sometimes I want to rise up in this bed and tell them everything, the bicycle paths edged with flowers and the young men with their glances, and all of it yielding to the years of hard work, the children, the two fearful wars to end all wars, and finally to this bed, where I listen to their soft laughter. The world turns and turns and is always the same.

Yet one day, to my surprise, it changes. The chief nurse, who is older than the others and smart as well as pretty, comes in. Usually, she scatters the rest of them away. She knows about old ears. When she speaks in this room she speaks to me, telling me stories of her childhood in Breton, wrapping my hands in cotton so soft it feels like a breeze from the ocean she describes. Today she is serious, however, distracted, wrinkles spanning her wide forehead. Something has happened. She does not speak, but instead turns on a little radio. Immediately the nurses quiet down.

I listen too. The signal crackles, full of static, and the announcer describes the bomb that was dropped upon Japan. No ordinary bomb, but a weapon so strong it lit the world with light that blinds, with fire that burns everything but the shadows it creates. This atom bomb will end the war, they say, and that is good. Yet the nurses, for once, stay quiet. They leave, after a moment, even the smart one, silenced. They forget about my hands, which burn in their bandages, as if the flames have reached me even here, half a world away.

And in the silence I remember her jars, lined up on the rough boards, glowing softly in the dusk. There is terror now, yes, but truly the beginning was magnificent to behold.

I discovered the jars one day when my daughter had a fever. I nearly did not go to work at all, but late in the afternoon her fever broke, and I hurried out to do what I could. By the time I reached the glass building on the Rue Lhomond, it was dusk. The room was dark, and I realized that Madame and Monsieur had gone to take their dinner. I did not wish to stay there alone, so I decided that I would step inside, just briefly, to make sure that no one else was working. I knew they would not care if I came and cleaned tomorrow. I pushed the door open, and peered inside.

What can I say of what I saw? All the jars upon the table were glowing softly, as if each contained a small star that had fallen, as if shafts of moonlight had been gathered into each. The simple mud she had worked on for so long had become a thing of magic. I fell on my knees as if to pray, but I could not take my eyes from the light caught within those jars. It was so beautiful, so unearthly. I wanted to take one home, to keep it in the cupboard, to know I could open the door at any time and see that luminescence. I imagined the faces of my children, the wonder that would infuse them at the sight. That greedy thought was my first. I wanted this rare beauty for myself.

The dirt floor was very cold, and soon my knees ached with it. Slowly, I stood up. I went across the room, my skin growing pale blue as I drew closer. Gingerly, I reached out, holding a single jar in the loose vessel of my hands.

It was not terribly hot. That surprised me. I had expected the sort of heat you can feel coming from a flame. But this light was only slightly warm, so faint I thought I might be imagining it altogether. Some vibration seemed to come from the jar, though perhaps this was only my imagination. Perhaps it was my own excitement, making my hands tremble, making my fingertips tingle as if with new life. I held the jars and thought of a child, unborn, moving beneath my flesh. A ripple of life, the sense of a hidden thing, growing. I thought of all the plants that had once flowered in this room, grown and died and grown again, and it seemed that the essence of their green life was caught in the jar, like a spirit in a bottle. That is how it felt. I cannot explain it. I can only say that I went there, night after night, for many months, and held the jars in my hands, and every time I touched them I experienced the same wondrous surge. It seemed to me, too, that the light was healing. My stiff joints eased, my fingers felt alive.

One night I even brought my children there. I let them touch the jars, one by one. It is impossible to believe I did this secret thing. I meant no harm. But I tampered with knowledge that was not meant for me. And look at me now, paying the stiff price, my hands twisted like a thwarted bush.

One night Madame walked in and found me.

"Marie," she said sharply, "what are you doing there?"

"Oh Madame," I said, stepping quickly away, pressing my hands against the folds of my skirt. "Madame, it is so beautiful. What have you made, Madame? What is this light?"

She smiled then. Her jars were safe. And what mother can resist honest praise for her creation? "I call it radium," she said softly. "It is something very special. It will change the way we think about the world. It has the potential to do great good. Some day, Marie, no one will die of cancer because of what is in this jar." She came close, and took my hands as I once had taken hers, and she held them to the surface of the glass.

"You can feel it, can't you, Marie?" she asked, looking me in the eye. Her hands holding mine to the glass were very strong, the palms and fingertips as rough with callouses as mine.

I nodded.

"It is life," she said. "It is the very energy of life you feel."

"You took it from the dirt?" I asked, as she released my hands.

"Yes," she said. "I took it from the earth." She was looking at the jar, her face softened, her voice was low and dreamy. "Please," she said, "look all you want, Marie, but do not touch it again. It is very rare, this element."

I agreed, of course, but it was a promise I did not keep. Instead, every night, I put my hands against a jar, carefully, just for a moment, and felt the mystery. I remembered her great dreams. Madame believed that scientific progress would improve society. I heard her say this more than once, that the salvation of the world lay not in faith or social programs, but rather in the steady march of science. Later, during the first great war, she and her daughter traveled to the front with an X-ray machine, using the wondrous new tool to see inside the body, to examine shattered bones and ruptured organs, assisting surgeons with their grim task of mending broken bodies. Before he died in battle my son saw her once, and he remembered my old stories. He wrote to me of the way she worked, taking soldier after soldier to her tent, seeking to understand their wounds. *It is a fine thing,* he wrote to me, *what she does for us, the way she heals, but what I want to know is why doesn't she invent something really useful to rout the German bastards once and for all?*

FOR MANY YEARS, long after she had won her second Nobel Prize—this time alone, for isolating a gram of pure radium—and had become so busy that it was rare for me to even catch a glimpse of her, I kept the image of those jars, glowing a soft blue on the rough wooden tables, like a treasure in the back of my mind. My husband never knew that I had taken the children there, and in time they themselves forgot what they had seen. I asked my daughter once, when she was grown, what she remembered of that visit, and she looked at me blankly for a long moment.

"Oh yes," she said finally. "That funny woman. I remember that she worked in a glass house. I thought it must be so cold. It was cold, the day we went. I felt sorry for her. She was a little crazy, wasn't she?"

"What about the jars," I insisted. "Don't you remember?"

She paused over the carrots she was peeling. "Let me see," she said, frowning faint lines into her forehead. "Yes, I think so.

We walked a long way, and then you made us put our hands around the little jars of paint. They were blue, as I remember."

"Not paint," I sighed. "Something more extraordinary."

"Was it?" my daughter asked. She thought a moment, shrugged. "Well, extraordinary or not, it never did us any good."

She was like her father, that one, practical and to the point, but she was wrong about Madame and her jars. For they did me good, even the memory of them, which I held in my mind like a scrap of brilliant cloth hidden in a drawer, something rare and numinous to be fingered in a quiet moment. Late at night, drifting off to sleep, I took those memories out, the stuff of dreams. Or in church, when I should have listened to the priest, I remembered the way the jars had felt, alive against my flesh.

One mass we had a new priest, a visitor, and though I was not in the habit of listening anymore, his speaking was so forceful that he caught my attention. "Imagine the human soul," he said. "Look at each person present, and do not see a face before you, but a soul."

Curious, I tried to do this, but it was a concentration I could not hold. For weeks I had been feeling ill, dizzy when I stood, silverfish flying across my vision. This happened now, though I was sitting down. I stared hard at the graying hair of the man ahead of me, but he began to blur, until I could no longer distinguish him from the woman who sat beside him. I remember that I stood up, my hand gripping the cold smooth wood, my eyes scanning the faces in the crowded church, seeking some bright color, some odd feature on which to focus. But they too dissolved, became one. My own skin seemed to fade, and I grew so weightless that for an instant I seemed to merge with all that lived around me, as if, like minute particles of light, we were each nothing in isolation from the others.

I fainted then. They carried me out into the small garden behind the church. I woke up to the splash of water on my face, a cold slap back into the brilliant world. It was a sunny morning in early April and the crocuses were blooming in the priests' garden. Father Jean was kneeling over me, holding my hand. My husband was next to him, gazing at me with a puzzled wonder.

"What was it you meant?" he asked me when my eyes fluttered open.

"I'm sorry," I said. My skirts were up around my knees and I blushed to think of myself lying there, exposed, beneath the priest's eyes. I sat up too quickly, reaching to push my skirts down.

"Here," the priest said, tipping a glass of water for me to sip. "What happened, Madame Bonvin? Are you all right?"

"I'm fine, yes, I'm perfectly fine," I assured them, but they were still looking at me, puzzled, as if trying to decipher a mystery. "What is it?" I asked, turning to Thierry, who gazed at me gravely, with concern and a new, uneasy respect.

"Before you fainted," he said, "you spoke." He paused, and glanced at the priest, who nodded. "You shouted, Marie. You said, *Behold the light of this world.*"

I shook my head, embarrassed. "I don't remember," I said. When I tried to rise I could feel it still, the way the lines blurred between myself and every living thing, but I could not imagine telling this to my husband or the priest. "I'm sorry. I was listening to the sermon, and then I got dizzy, and the next thing I knew there was water splashing on my face. That's all. I'm very sorry."

While I was in bed recuperating from this spell, something dreadful happened. The weather changed for the worse, grew cold and so rainy that the days seemed like a chilly jungle, one long and foggy dusk. Madame was away, and one morning Monsieur, walking with his head down in the rain, was knocked over by a horse and killed, his skull crushed beneath a wagon wheel, his extraordinary mind splattered on the cobblestones. His death shocked the city. All France grieved, and within a month the Sorbonne offered Madame his post. To the surprise of many, she accepted, the first woman ever to teach at the Sorbonne. On her first day she wore her usual black dress, it was said, and she did not eulogize her predecessor, as was the custom. She simply started talking where he had left off, speaking in her clear, soft voice, running her thumb across her fingers. There was no grief manifest in her words or gestures, and in the offices, the hallways, later, they spoke of this. There were many who said it meant that she loved only science at the expense of human feeling.

It was not true. I can tell you that her grief was almost beyond enduring. I heard the story of how she faltered in the laboratory, overcome, when she tried to resume their shared work. And once, months later, I glimpsed her entering their old building full of windows, which was again abandoned. It was a summer evening, and she was alone. I went to the glass door and stood in the shadows and watched her. A shameful thing, but I could not help myself. She sat at the old wooden table where so many experiments had been done, and stared into the air. Her shoulders shook; her tears fell swiftly. She wept, I tell you, as deeply grieved as any woman I have seen. The blackboard had been left untouched, with his final thoughts, his last inspirations, noted in white on slate, and by then the soft city dust had grown thick upon it. Her lips moved in the dusky light as she gazed upon his writing. It gave me the chills to watch her, for although she had no use for religion and would not believe in spirits, I knew if she were speaking, it was to him.

I DID NOT see her again for many years. She was riding the rough wave of her fame by then, traveling across the country and the world, while I kept cleaning the same familiar rooms. My life went on, my children grew and later scattered in the war. My son was killed, my daughter fled with the Resistance. I grieved for them both, but I felt a deep pride in their lives, and thought sometimes that Madame would have approved of their spirit and their independence. I heard of her now and then during these many years, her speaking tour of America where she was given another gram of radium, and of course the news of her love affair with her colleague Monsieur Langevin, who was married and a father. All the fruit sellers were buzzing with this scandal. I stood among them with my lips pressed tight, but I remembered how they had laughed at her years before, for her coldness, for her shuttered heart. *All right,* I wanted to say. *So you see she is human, after all, what of it?* For myself, I remembered her grief and the way she had talked so easily with her husband, as if they were two sides of a single mind, and I hoped that she had found another happiness at last.

Then one day, after we were both grandmothers and I had become a widow too, I saw her walking toward me down a path. She was dying, though I did not know it at the time. From a distance she looked just the same. I saw her, and thought that her familiar paleness, her frailty, meant that she was still as strong as iron underneath. There were many people with her, standing in a circle around her on the lawn, and though I wanted very much to speak with her, I dared not approach. I stood beneath a tree instead, thinking of all the questions I would like to ask.

They moved together onto the path and came in my direction. I thought for a moment I would run away, pretending that I had not seen her, denying the opportunity to meet her one last time. But then, as she drew closer, I saw how her blond hair had faded white, how her skin was lusterless and stretched tight across her bones. She was ill. And so I stepped onto the path as they drew near. I spoke, loudly enough to be heard over the voices of the men.

"Madame," I said. "Madame, do you remember me from the glass building where you drew light from the earth?"

She stopped and looked straight at me, and when she recognized me—it took a moment, for by then her eyesight was not good—she smiled, and stepped through the ring of important men, and came to me.

"Yes," she said. "Marie. I remember you, of course."

She took my hands in hers. My fingers were not then as ugly as they are now. The color was still natural—there were only the lumps. These she felt, however, even though her own fingers were rough with scabs where her skin had broken open. She looked down and gazed at my misshapen flesh, my hands so much older than the rest of me. I did not know, then, anything of what would follow, but I remember that I thought of all the nights I had stood with my hands around her sacred jars, and I was overcome with guilt. I thought she must suspect my treason too, for a shadow fell across her features.

"You have worked too hard," she murmured. "Marie, look at your hands! Your life has been too hard."

She released me then, sadly, and turned back to the waiting men.

They walked with her across the snow, and one by one they disappeared into the building. It was the last I ever saw of her. Months later I heard that she had been taken to the country. It was said, at first, that she would recover from her illness, but time passed, and word came that she had died. It was her work, they said, that killed her finally, though even at the end she would not admit that her radium could cause such devastating harm. This news I heard in a hallway, one afternoon while I was sweeping, and I hurried to the broom closet where I put my face into my ruined hands and wept.

THE NURSES COME in with their bright chatter, snapping up the shades, preparing the soothing medicine for my hands. Despite the horror of the second bomb, dropped two days ago on a place called Nagasaki, they laugh now, and toss their hair. They have pushed the terrible flare, the dreadful knowledge, completely from their minds. They are full of the armistice, talking of brothers and lovers coming back from war. There will be a parade, I hear, down the main streets of this great city. These young girls talk about their dresses, their hair styles, the jewelry they will wear. Dreamily, they unwind the layers of cloth around my fingers. They do not understand that the world has stilled, for an instant, has paused in the persistent turning of the ages. The wind has stopped, and the leaves do not flutter, and there is no motion in the air. They say they will wear pink to the parade, or sky blue or a green as clear as emeralds. They will cluster at the train station, handkerchiefs fluttering from their fingertips, watching the men stream off until their husbands, their boyfriends, their beloved brothers are rushing into their arms.

They say they cannot wait.

They do not see that they are already waiting, as I have waited all these many years for them to bathe my tortured fingers, one by one, to lay their cool hands upon my forehead. Since the day I took the glowing vessels in my hands, I have been moving toward this moment. The present grows from the past, and contains it, and the cities that disappeared are connected to the mystery within those jars. These young women do not see that the world has paused, that even now they are tuned to its hesitation.

I do not tell them.

They leave me at last, their chatter, their bright laughter, drifting through the hall, falling into silence. In this empty room even the pipes have gone quiet, and the breeze has died within the curtains. I keep my eyes closed in the sudden stillness, remembering Madame running her thumb across her fingers again, and yet again. Three times our hands touched, in compassion, first, then in wonder, and finally in sorrow. What does it mean, I would ask her, that my flesh is so misshapen, that her fingers went numb by degrees? Why did she seek to tame this mystery, which in the hands of others turned a multitude to ashes? Her work exploded with the violence of a thousand suns, but I must tell her that it was not her fault, the way they twisted her creation, tampered with her dreams.

I will tell her.

They said she was inhuman, heartless, but it is not so. She is here now. Weeping, she awaits me. She is carrying balm for our hands.

Balance

THEY HAD COME ON THE EARLIEST POSSIBLE TRAIN, BUT NOW there was a mix-up. Their things had been sent astray and would not arrive until nearly noon. When they first heard this news, passed on to them by Marc, the juggler, everyone groaned and swore, rubbed the backs of their necks, and wandered in constrained circles around the station. The performance was scheduled for three o'clock so there was time enough, but it was their custom to set up early, fixing the trapeze frame on the brightest, sunniest corner they could find, choosing the shops where they'd change and store the props. These arrangements always drew a crowd in themselves. By the time of the performance word of the troupe would have spread, and the crowds would ripple from the main square and spill into the side streets.

That was their custom, because it left the day free. They went off alone or in groups of two or three, wandering around whatever place they were, seeing the sights and eating ice cream cones, watching the people around them with a certain detached curiosity that comes when you travel from place to place and never plan to stay. There was a certain superiority in it too. No matter how many stares they drew as oddly dressed strangers, they knew that soon they'd hold an audience of these same people breathless, spellbound. They knew that the waitress who tossed their food carelessly in front of them, that the shopkeepers who followed them suspiciously through narrow store aisles, would later realize their errors. Yes, they'd say to their friends, yes, they were right there. The man with the swords was sitting in that booth right there, I served him a root-beer float. And the woman? The lady trapeze artist? I sold her that hat she wore on the bicycle. That's right, it came from my shop, right here.

But now the baggage was late, and all these small pleasures were lost.

It was Françoise who pulled them together again. Standing on the platform she clapped her hands together and sang their names out, as if she were a mother, or a teacher with a group of schoolchildren. Marc, she called. Frank, Jack, Peter. Her voice was clear and loud, and other people paused to look at her too. They saw a small woman, her body lean and compact. It was a young body, wide at the shoulders, narrow at the hips, almost the body of a young boy. Only the face told otherwise. It was delicate, feminine, with deepening lines at the corners of the mouth and across the forehead. Her hair was very short, and she wore her makeup already: two bright pink circles on her cheeks, black lines making sad, exaggerated eyes.

"Now listen," she said, when the four were gathered around her. "There's nothing to be done about it, nothing at all. But it's certainly not the end of the world, either. The station people will see that the things are sent to the square, I've made arrangements for all that. So, we'll do what we want this morning, and meet at the square at noon to set up. How's that? All right then, there's no use mooning around."

She slung her bag over her shoulder and walked briskly to the stairs. Marc started to follow her but she smiled back at him.

"Errands, darling," she said, and he knew she wanted the morning alone.

He fell back and watched her, the quick sure gait down the stairs, the circle of space she seemed, always, to carry with her. She'd been a dancer when he met her, and she still walked as if every movement of every muscle had been choreographed: graceful, sure, deliberate.

Peter clapped him on the shoulder from behind.

"Want to have a drink, old man?" he asked.

Marc shook his head. Peter had just turned twenty-three. He could drink beer all morning and perform flawlessly in the afternoon. In fact, it seemed the more he drank the better he was at urn-balancing. With every drink he grew looser and more flexible, some tense veneer he ordinarily wore dissolved away.

"Come on," Peter insisted, pushing Marc on the shoulder. "Françoise won't mind."

"She'd mind if I dropped her," Marc said. "Go on," he added. "You know me. I'll drink with you later."

They had emerged from the station now, and were standing in a small park. There was a diagonal pathway, and at the end of it Marc could see the square where they'd perform. He'd never been to this town before, but nevertheless he was sure of the place. He watched Peter walk off, hurrying to catch up with Frank, who was walking slowly toward the square, hands deep in his pockets. Frank had been small and tense and wiry all his life, and now Marc was surprised to notice that he was getting fat. A loose roll moved around his waist with every step until he and Peter disappeared into the crowd.

Marc sat down on a bench and took out a cigarette. He leaned back, enjoying the sun, and wondered where Françoise had gone. She was unhappy, that much was clear, and she had been unhappy for several months. Yet whenever Marc tried to talk with her about it, she gave him a quick, evasive smile and changed the subject. And he couldn't guess, had never been able to guess, the precise sources of her sadness. The things he expected to distress her never did, and the things that did upset her she kept hidden deep away.

It had always been so. He remembered it in the first night he had spent with her, over twenty years ago, the night she'd told him that for years, growing up, she'd dreamed of becoming a ballerina.

"Why didn't you?" he wanted to know. That morning he'd seen her at the competitions, doing an acrobatic routine so precise and graceful that he knew before the announcement that she'd win. "Why ever didn't you?" he asked.

She lifted one leg slowly. They were lying on a mattress on the floor of his apartment, and next to her were French doors that opened onto a balcony. They were flooded white with the street light, and it was against this background that he watched her leg rise, slowly, perfectly controlled, until it was silhouetted against the glass. Her toe pointed straight to the ceiling. Her leg stayed perfectly still, delicate, yet strong and finely sculpted.

"I didn't have the legs for it," she said. She rotated her leg, examining it as if it belonged to someone else.

"I can't believe that," he said.

"Oh, they're the right shape," she said. "They're the *perfect* shape, in fact. But look at the length. No, I'm afraid they won't do. I'm long in the torso, short in the legs. That's bad, for ballerinas. You don't see ballerinas with short legs."

She'd pulled her knee in then, so that the silhouette of her leg looked briefly like a wing. Then she swung it down, and across his waist, until with one smooth movement she was straddled across him.

"I used to go to the auditions," she said. "I practiced harder than anyone, I danced all the time. And I was good. All the judges agreed. But once I turned fifteen or so, once my body changed, I was never chosen. They all made sure to tell me I could dance, though. They let me know it wasn't lack of talent. Even when I knew it was hopeless, I kept dancing. I used to go to the studio alone. I was fifteen, and I danced by myself every Saturday afternoon."

He could imagine her, lithe and nimble, spinning through a room where sunlight fell in patches on the floor, where even the soft rustling of her shoes had a faint echo. He felt terribly saddened by her story. He had liked her from the moment they'd met on the bus. Now, from somewhere in the sadness his affection grew deeper.

"I'm sorry," he said to her. She looked down at him.

"No," she said. "Don't be. I'm not, anymore."

He reached up and stroked his fingers across her forehead, where she was frowning.

"What are you thinking about then," he said.

Her mood changed, and she smiled.

"You'll laugh," she said.

"Good. Tell me."

"All right." She clasped her hands behind her head and arched back, so that her breasts lifted and rose. He dropped his hands and ran them along the bony fan of her ribcage. "I was wondering," she said, her eyes half closed. "I wonder if it's possible for two people to make love while standing on their heads. You see," she added when he burst out in laughter. "What did I say?"

"It would require immense balance," he said, forcing the laughter from his voice, seeing suddenly that it was important to her, however ludicrous it sounded.

"It would," she agreed. "That's what I mean. And immense concentration. Because you'd have to maintain control, even as you lost control. You'd have to achieve an extraordinary frame of mind."

He picked her up, which was easy because she was so lean and light, and because, though thin, he was a gymnast and very strong. He put her down on the practice mat in the front hallway. She went into a headstand almost immediately, her white body lifting into the air. He did the same, so that they faced each other, only inches apart. He nearly laughed at her inverted face, altered by gravity, the cheeks and forehead plumper than usual, and pink with exertion. Then he felt the rough sole of her foot as it ran down his calf, the back of his thigh. He looked up and saw her narrow body tapering into the far point of her toes. Then her legs opened in a graceful V, they lowered very slowly and caught him lightly by the waist.

"I don't know if this is going to work," he said, feeling himself lurch closer to her, caught in the delicate embrace of her thighs. They looked at each other, eye to eye, and it seemed to him that he had never seen another person so clearly. Something about their inverted pose removed all distractions. Françoise had small eyes,

with an intensity and quickness that sometimes made him think
of a bird. Yet from such a distance her eyes were all he saw; they
changed, grew larger, and the darkness of her pupils seemed to
draw him closer, then closer still, the most intimate knowledge of
her he had ever had.

"It will," she said. "I'm sure."

But it didn't. They started laughing, simultaneously it seemed
to Marc, though later Françoise insisted he was the one to begin.
Either way, once they started they couldn't stop, and they had
ended up falling, gracefully of course, because they knew how to
fall. They didn't try again for several weeks. Then the posture felt
more familiar and they didn't laugh, but it was still difficult, the
most difficult thing Marc had ever attempted. That time it was
Françoise who moved too quickly and lost her balance.

"Still," she said later. "I'm sure now it's not impossible. It's just
something that will take some work, that's all. Some time." She
spoke as if they had all the time together in the world, and Marc
drew her close.

"Maybe you should move in here," he said. He tried to make it
sound very casual, for he had observed her independence and
didn't want her to be frightened away. From any angle, he knew
he was already in love with her. "It would give us more opportuni-
ties." He ran his hand up the back of her thigh. "To practice."

The sun had grown stronger, and Marc stretched his arms
against the back of the bench, closed his eyes, imagined that small
rays of light pierced like healing needles to his bones. He was very
tired. They had been doing this act for fourteen years now, and he
was tired. Several times he had mentioned to Françoise that they
should quit, but her answer was always the same: She tightened
the line of her lips, and worked more quickly at whatever was in
her hands.

"We're not old," she said once. She was sewing sequins onto her
costume, and the needle began to jab in and out with tremendous
speed. Then she threw the garment down and plunged forward
into a somersault that ended in a handstand. Her narrow legs
pointed to the ceiling, and her short skirt fell around her chin.

"See these legs," she said, making small scissor kicks in the air.

"These legs are not ready to retire." She let herself slowly onto the floor. "Besides," she said, not meaning to be cruel. "It was for you we started this."

Well, it was true, that part. Sometime in their middle twenties it had become clear to them both that they would never be famous gymnasts. This was a painful discovery because fame was something they had both expected from their earliest years on the floor. They were both very good, just not quite good enough. Younger and younger people were coming, with firm and supple bodies that bent in impossible ways. They were winning the prizes. Soon Françoise was offered a position as assistant instructor and Marc, realizing that his gymnastic days were at an end, packed the things from his locker and became an apprentice plumber.

He was a good plumber. He didn't mind the work, and at first it required all of his attention to learn the intricacies of joining pipes, the tricky dynamics of water. Soon, though, it became routine, and he became restless. He took up juggling, and sometimes he amused the older men by juggling his wrenches, tossing them in high arcs and amazing patterns. "That's it," they'd say, spellbound, "that's it, Marc." Later, he'd hear them telling the others about it. After work, drinking beer in one smoky tavern or another, they'd hand him things: boiled eggs, spoons, balls from the pool table. He remembered those days as happy ones, some calm equilibrium between the expectations of his youth and the quieter life to come. In his mind it existed as a perpetual summer, though surely it was longer than a summer's length. He walked home every night through the golden dying light of the solstice, the feel of round, weighty objects in his fingers, and found Françoise, freshly showered and dressed in something loose, pouring wine into clear glasses.

It ended soon enough. He scarred a marble floor when a wrench slipped through his fingers, and a week later he'd taken out a chandelier with a piece of pipe that flew unexpectedly high. He'd had to pay for that one, and he'd nearly been fired. That was the end of his on-the-job performances. He was back to solid plumbing, though his fingers itched now with the urge to toss small objects in the air. At home he juggled everything: eggs and bananas, matching bars of soap, the teacups Françoise's parents gave them when they finally married. The great restlessness that had entered him grew into an obsession. He exercised rigorously, morning and night, horrified by the slow softening of his flesh. He arrived home before Françoise and waited, some wild position trembling in his mind. *Come,* he'd say, as soon as her key was in the lock. He took her hand and led her to the practice mats, without giving her a chance to rest or shower or even put down her purse. *Come, let's try this.* He became obsessed with the thought of making love in a headstand. When Françoise, exhausted from a day of teaching, slipped or fell, he lost his temper. He knew it was irrational, but he felt as though everything depended on it, suddenly, that if they could not achieve this thing together then everything else would be lost.

"We have to do something about this," Françoise said, finally. They were lying on the practice mats, and Marc was turned away from her, his arms hugged close to his body. In his state of mind those days, he thought she meant they should be divorced.

"Marc," she said, touching his shoulder with her callous and chalk-smoothed palm. "Marc, you have to get your life back. This is what I think." She had stood up, pulling on a black silk robe with a dragon embroidered on the back.

And so it had begun, their troupe. Over the years the other members had changed, grown younger or older, more or less skilled. Drunkards had been fired, a woman who was flawless in practice but who shattered things in front of an audience was also fired. But always, at the center of it all, were he and Françoise. They went to nearby towns and villages, they performed for the children of the wealthy. Françoise kept her job as an instructor, and he was a plumber all week long. But on the weekends they were transformed, masters of a balancing act they had sustained for fourteen years.

Now it was Françoise who needed to continue. Eight months ago she had been retired as an instructor, promoted into the management of the school. The day she received this news she had stood before her three-sided mirror for a long time, flexing muscle after muscle and glancing back and forth, from flesh to glass. Then she had turned away sharply, closing the mirrored wings across the flat center piece. She had bought six new suits and had never mentioned her promotion again. Three days later she had found Peter tossing urns in the park, and had invited him to join the troupe.

Peter's youthful presence had forced Marc to look around. He noticed that the sword dancer was slower than others had been and that Frank, the magician, was growing fat. He wondered how much longer they could continue. Yet Françoise showed no signs of stopping. Marc imagined them years from now, he juggling bifocals, false teeth, pill bottles, all the evidence of his age, while Françoise twirled on the trapeze, her hair a blaze of white against the vivid sky.

The rattling of carts woke him from his pleasant drowsing in the sun, and he looked up. Their lockers were being wheeled across the park. He saw the trunks come first, containing equipment and costumes. Then came the trapeze, dismantled into long poles and bars and ropes. It took four men to carry it, balanced on their shoulders. Finally three men followed carrying the large boxes marked FRAGILE. These were Peter's porcelain urns, packed in layers of bubble plastic. The man before had used ordinary urns, the cheapest he could find, but Peter poked around in antique shops and flea markets, looking for pieces that would make the audience gasp as they floated through the air. Between shows he was very careful of them, treating them delicately, hovering anxiously around as they were unpacked.

Marc stood up from his bench, stretched, and followed the men at a distance across the diagonal of the park. As he had anticipated, they stopped at the edge of the square, at the junction of the two bricked streets, and began to unpack and measure, pausing now and then to point at the sky. In a while the trapeze would go up and Marc would climb up to test it, to check the sway and balance. But now he was hungry. He went into a cafe on the corner and ordered a cheese sandwich and tomato soup, taking some kind of reassurance from the ordinary food.

When he came out, Françoise and the others were already there. They were all dressed in sweatsuits and tennis shoes, but already Françoise stood at a slight distance from the others, a distance that marked her as the star. And it was true—though they had started the troupe together, it was because of Françoise that it continued. The man who could balance Oriental urns on the nape of his neck or the bridge of his nose, the man whose dancing partner was a bright flashing sword hugged close to his body, the man who could stand on half a dozen eggs without crushing them—all these came together because of Françoise. Every crowd knew this before she ever appeared. The trapeze hung above all the other acts, swaying in the slight breeze that came through the city streets. Even when Peter threw the delicate urn, its pattern of blue and white spinning to a blur as it rose and fell again, all eyes lingered on the empty trapeze. This was why they came, this was what they waited for. And Françoise was very good. She didn't disappoint them.

Now she was tugging the stabilizing rope of the trapeze into place, glancing up occasionally to gauge the angle. Marc did the same on the other side, and after a moment she climbed the rope ladder and lifted her weight onto the bar. Swinging, she turned her head and frowned slightly, as if listening to some barely audible vibration. Then she called down to him and had him pull his supporting rope six inches tighter.

When she was on the ground again he went over and put his hand on her shoulder.

"Are you all right today, darling?" he asked, thinking, even as he spoke, that it was a mistake to say this. She had repaired her makeup, and she turned her face toward him. There was a knack she had of making herself go expressionless. He'd seen it countless times when she climbed up to the bar, a smile on her lips but the eyes, if you looked closely, unreadable. She was like that now. Gazing at the straight, emphasized eyebrows, the mouth touched with orange, the eyes clear and edged with black, he had the impression he was looking at a mime. Hers was a face capable of assuming any expression, but for the moment it revealed nothing, nothing at all.

"Of course I'm all right," she said. The small smile. "Shouldn't you be getting ready?" She looked at her watch. "We'll start in just a quarter of an hour."

THERE WAS ALWAYS an instant when Marc, wearing green tights and a green felt hat, perched on a unicycle with balls and eggs tucked all through his clothes, felt he could not go through with it. He had felt this way even in the beginning when he still enjoyed the actual performance, the wonder in the faces of the children, the amusement in the expressions of adults. Lately he had not felt any joy, though. He was tired. It seemed the moment on the sidelines became longer and longer. And then he was out there, jerking through the square on one wheel, filling the sky with a blur of spinning objects, his hands flashing as though they were unconnected with himself. Once he finished he placed the eggs carefully in a basket, then went around the crowd with his hat held out. The city paid them, of course, but this revenue covered lunch and dinner, and drinks when they were done.

Peter had added a new trick to his routine, something he had been practicing all week with plastic buckets. He flung the urn high into the air and then leaped from his perch on a milk crate, spun himself in an aerial somersault, and caught the urn just before it brushed the ground. Marc was impressed. He glanced over at Françoise. She was standing next to her trapeze, her arms folded gracefully, her long fingers white against her black sweatshirt. She watched Peter intently as he bowed and bowed again.

The other acts were less successful. Jack dropped his sword on the cobblestones twice, and Frank failed to make one of his coins disappear. Finally it was time for the trapeze. The initial crowd had grown and was spilling over into the side streets, pushing close to the metal base of the trapeze. Marc urged people to step back, glancing now and then at Françoise, who was scaling the rope ladder to the swing. She grabbed the trapeze and secured it with one bent knee. Then she was on the bar, testing it, pumping like a small child on a swing set, except that her flight took her high, near the tops of the buildings, and far out over the cobblestones. He had seen her do this a thousand times, more, but it still gave him a clutch of fear when she rose against the sky like that, a clear dark line, resting with such a delicate grace upon the bar. He had never seen her fall from the trapeze, not even in practice.

"If I ever slipped," she'd told him once, "I could never do it again. I have to believe that it's impossible for me to fall. Otherwise I couldn't go out there without a net, over all those sidewalks."

Now Françoise, agile, lowered herself until she was resting across the bar on her hip bones. Slowly, slowly, she stretched her arms out, until she was balanced across the bar in a graceful arc, her narrow arms extended. She looked like a bird etched against the blue sky. Marc rubbed his palms against his thighs and listened to the murmurs of the crowd. Looking around, he saw all eyes fixed on Françoise. For an instant he was amused by the people around him, their parted lips, their bodies relaxed and vulnerable as they gazed up at his wife. Soon, Françoise would begin to lean forward. Slowly, so very slowly, she would lean into a fall, while the crowd below grew tense, stiffening their bodies and clenching their fists, or pressing their hands against their cheeks. He had seen it so many times, Françoise gazing out to the sky as if nothing was wrong, slipping, slipping, until she plunged straight down. The crowds always gasped at this point, and Marc hated them then. This was why they came, really, not for the miracle of balance, but for the possibility that she might fall, flattening onto the street before their eyes. But she did not. Her feet were clever hooks that caught her at the last moment. She hung, upside down, while the people around her sighed, from relief and disappointment, and clapped.

He had seen it a thousand times, so often that it was the tension from the crowd which signaled to him that she had begun her slow dive. He looked up then. But something was different. Françoise was not gazing straight out over the heads of the crowd. Instead, she was looking straight at Marc, something she had never done, not once in all the times he had seen this. He looked back. Her exaggerated eyes were steady on his, even as she moved in imperceptible degrees down and down. His breath quickened. He felt the hard tiles of the plaza beneath his thin-soled shoes. If she were to fall—but she never fell, not Françoise. Still, she was staring at him, her gaze no longer expressionless. The intensity of her look reminded him of all the times they had tried to make love upside down.

Once they had done it, only once. Hands clasped behind his head, he had stayed as still as possible while Françoise twined herself around him like a vine. He had felt himself letting go, he had felt himself falling, and he had opened his eyes to find her staring at him. They were so close that he could see only her eyes, and he had stared into them, steadied himself even as his body moved, judging the moments of her pleasure in the minute contractions of her pupils, the flutter of her eyelashes.

Now their eyes connected in just that way, despite the space of air between them, and her intentions were revealed. Marc knew before it even began that her toes would stay straight and pointed. That, unchecked, her dive would be straight down, straight toward the hard shiny tiles. Or to him, if he could catch her. He stepped forward, never taking his eyes from her. She was falling, slowly, so very very slowly, and he watched her coming toward him by minute degrees.

The moment came; the balance shifted, she was plummeting to him like something shot from the sky. He stepped forward, bracing himself for the weight of her familiar body. Dimly, he heard the gasps and shrieks of the crowd, but his eyes never left Françoise, her agile body shaped like a Chinese character against the blue parchment sky, her eyes dark with concentration, fear, and, he had time to think, a certain pleasure in what they were attempting to attain. It was her eyes he focused on, lifting his arms to her, hoping that the years of the past could balance them both against this moment.

The Way It Felt
to Be Falling

THE SUMMER I TURNED NINETEEN I USED TO LIE IN THE backyard and watch the planes fly overhead, leaving their clean plumes of jet stream in a pattern against the sky. It was July, yet the grass had a brown fringe and leaves were already falling, borne on the wind like discarded paper wings. The only thing that flourished that summer was the recession; businesses, lured by lower tax rates, moved south in a steady progression. My father had left too, but in a more subtle and insidious way—after his consulting firm failed, he had simply retreated into some silent and inaccessible world. Now, when I went with my mother to the hospital, we found him sitting quietly in a chair by the window. His hands were limp against the armrests and his hair was long, a rough dark fringe across his ears. He was never glad to see us, or sorry. He just looked calmly around the room, at my mother's strained smile and my eyes, which skittered nervously away, and he did not give a single word of greeting or acknowledgment or farewell.

My mother had a job as a secretary and decorated cakes on the side. In the pressing heat she juggled bowls between the refrigerator and the counter, struggling to keep the frosting at the right consistency so she could make the delicate roses, chrysanthemums, and daisies that balanced against fields of sugary white. The worst ones were the wedding cakes, intricate and bulky. That summer, brides and their mothers called us on a regular basis, their voices laced with panic. My mother spoke to them as she worked, trailing the extension cord along the tiled floor, her voice soothing and efficient.

Usually my mother is a calm person, levelheaded in the face of stress, but one day the bottom layer of a finished cake collapsed and she wept, her face cradled in her hands as she sat at the kitchen table. I hadn't seen her cry since the day my father left, and I watched her from the kitchen door, a basket of laundry in my arms, uneasiness rising around me like slow, numbing light. After a few minutes she dried her eyes and salvaged the cake, removing the broken layer and dispensing with the plastic fountain that spouted champagne, and which was supposed to rest in a precarious arrangement between two cake layers held apart by plastic pillars.

"There." She stepped back to survey her work. The cake was smaller but still beautiful, delicate and precise.

"It looks better without that tacky fountain, anyway," she said. "Now let's get it out of here before something else goes wrong."

I helped her box it up and carry it to the car, where it rested on the floor, surrounded by bags of ice. My mother backed out of the driveway slowly, then paused and called to me.

"Katie," she said. "Try to get the dishes done before you go to work, okay? And please, don't spend all night with those dubious friends of yours. I'm too tired to worry."

"I won't," I said, waving. "I'm working late anyway."

By "dubious friends" my mother meant Stephen, who was, in fact, my only friend that summer. He had spirals of long red hair and a habit of shoplifting expensive gadgets: tools, jewelry, photographic equipment. My mother thought he was an unhealthy influence, which was generous; the rest of the town just thought he was crazy. He was the older brother of my best friend, Emmy, who had fled, with her boyfriend and 350 tie-dyed T-shirts, to follow the Grateful Dead on tour. Come with us, she had urged, but I was working in a convenience store, saving my money for school, and it didn't seem like a good time to leave my mother. So I stayed in town and Emmy sent me postcards I memorized—a clean line of desert, a sky aching blue over the ocean, an airy water-fall in the inter-mountain West. I was fiercely envious, caught in that small town while the planes traced their daily paths to places I was losing hope of ever seeing. I lay in the backyard and watched them. The large jets moved in slow silver glints across the sky, while the smaller planes droned lower. Sometimes, on the clearest days, I caught a glimpse of skydivers. They started out as small black specks, plummeting, then blossomed against the horizon in a streak of silk and color. I stood up to watch as they grew steadily larger, then passed the tree line and disappeared.

When my mother was gone, I went back inside. The air was cool and shadowy, heavy with the sweet scent of flowers and frost-ing. I piled the broken cake on a plate and did the dishes, quickly, feeling the silence gather. That summer I couldn't stay alone in the house. I'd find myself standing in front of mirrors with my heart pounding, searching my eyes for a glimmer of madness, or touch-ing the high arc of my cheekbone as if I didn't know my own face. I thought I knew about madness, the way it felt—the slow sus-pended turning as you gave yourself up to it. The doctors said my father was suffering from a stress-related condition. They said he would get better. But I had watched him in his slow retreat, dis-tanced by his own expanding silence. On the day he stopped speaking altogether I had brought him a glass of water, stepping across the afternoon light that flickered on the wooden floors.

"Hey Dad," I had said, softly. His eyes were closed. His face and hands were soft and white and pale. When he opened his eyes they were clear brown, as blank and smooth as the glass in my hand.

"Dad?" I said. "Are you okay?"

He did not speak, then or later, not even when the ambulance came and took him away. He did not sigh or protest. He had slid away from us with apparent ease. I had watched him go, and this was what I knew: madness was a graceless descent, the abyss beneath a careless step. *Take care* I said each time we left my father, stepping from his cool quiet room into the bright heat outside. And I listened to my own words; I took care, too. That summer, I was afraid of falling.

STEPHEN WASN'T COMFORTABLE at my house and he lived at the edge of town, so we met every day at Mickey's Tavern, where it was cool and dark and filled with the chattering life of other people. I always stopped in on my way to or from work, but Stephen sometimes spent whole afternoons and evenings there, playing games of pool and making bets with the other people who formed the fringe of the town. Some of them called themselves artists and lived together in an abandoned farmhouse. They were young, most of them, but already disenfranchised, known to be odd or mildly crazy or even faintly dangerous. Stephen, who fell into the last two categories because he had smashed out an ex-lover's window one night, and had tried, twice, to kill himself, kept a certain distance from the others. Still, he was always at Mickey's, leaning over the pool table, a dark silhouette against the back window, only his hair illuminated in a fringe of red.

Before Emmy left, I had not liked Stephen. At twenty-seven he still lived at home, in a fixed-over apartment on the third floor of his parents' house. He slept all morning and spent his nights pacing his small rooms, listening to Beethoven or playing chess with a computer he'd bought. I had seen the dark scars that bisected both his wrists, and they frightened me. He collected a welfare check every month, took Valium every few hours, and lived in a state of precarious calm. Sometimes he was mean, teasing Emmy to the edge of tears. But he could be charming too, with an ease and grace the boys my own age didn't have. When he was feeling good he made things special, leaning over to whisper something, his fingers a lingering touch on my arm, on my knee. I knew it had to do with the danger, too, the reason he was so attractive at those times.

"Kate understands me," he said once. Emmy, the only person who was not afraid of him, laughed out loud and asked why I'd have any better insight into his warped mind than the rest of the world.

"Can't you tell?" he said. I wouldn't look at him so he put his fingers lightly on my arm. He was completely calm, but he must have felt me trembling. It was a week after my father had been taken to the hospital, and it seemed that Stephen knew some truth about me, something invisible that only he could sense.

"What do you mean?" I demanded. But he just laughed and left the porch, telling me to figure it out for myself.

"What did he mean?" I asked. "What did he mean by that?"

"He's in a crazy mode," Emmy said. She was methodically polishing her fingernails, and she tossed her long bright hair over her shoulder. "The best thing to do is pretend he doesn't exist."

But Emmy left and then there was only Stephen, charming, terrifying Stephen, who started to call me every day. He asked me to come over, to go for a ride, to fly kites with him behind a deserted barn he'd found. Finally I gave in, telling myself I was doing him a favor by keeping him company. But it was more than that. I knew that Stephen understood the suspended world between sanity and madness, that he lived his life inside it.

One night, past midnight, when we were sitting in the quiet darkness of his porch, he told me about cutting his wrists, the even pulse of warm running water, the sting of the razor dulled with Valium and whiskey.

"Am I shocking you?" he had asked after a while.

"No. Emmy told me about it." I paused, unsure how much to reveal. "She thinks you did it to get attention."

He laughed. "Well it worked," he said, "didn't it?"

I traced my finger around the pattern in the upholstery.

"Maybe," I said. "But now everyone thinks you're crazy."

He shrugged, and stretched, pushing his large thick hands up toward the ceiling. "So what?" he said. "If people think you're crazy, they leave you alone, that's all."

I thought of all the times I had stood in front of the mirror, of the times I woke at night, my heart a frantic movement, no escape.

"Don't you ever worry that it's true?"

Stephen reached over to the table and held up his blue plastic bottle of Valium. It was a strong prescription. I knew, because I had tried it. I liked the way the blue pills slid down my throat, dissolving anxiety. I liked the way the edges of things grew undefined, so I was able to rise from my own body, calmly and with perfect grace.

Stephen shook a pill into his hand. His skin was pale and damp, his expression intent.

"No," he said. "I don't worry. Ever."

STILL, ON THE DAY the cake collapsed, I could tell he *was* worried. When I got to the pool room he was squinting down one cue at a time, discarding each one as he discovered warps and flaws.

"Hey, Kate," he said, choosing one at last. "Care for a game?"

We ordered beer and plugged our quarters into the machine, waiting for the weighty, rolling thunk of balls. Stephen ran his hand through his red beard. He had green eyes and a long, finely shaped nose. I thought he was extremely handsome.

"How goes the tournament?" I asked. He'd been in the play-offs for days, and each time I came in the stakes were higher.

Stephen broke, and dropped two low balls. He stepped back and surveyed the table. "You'll love this," he said. "Loser goes skydiving."

"You know," I said, remembering the plummeting shapes, the silky streaks against the sky, "I've always wanted to do that."

"Well," Stephen said, "keep the loser company, then."

He missed his next shot and we stopped talking. I was good, steady, with some competitions behind me. The bar was filling up around us, and soon a row of quarters lined the wooden rim of the pool table. After a while Ted Johnson, one of the artists in the farmhouse, came in and leaned against the wall. Stephen tensed, and his next shot went wild.

"Too bad," Ted said, stepping forward. "Looks like you're on a regular losing streak."

"You could go fuck yourself," Stephen said, but his voice was even, as though he'd just offered Ted a beer.

"Thanks," Ted said. "But actually, I'd just as soon ask Kate a question, while she's here. I'd like to know what you think about honor, Kate. Specifically, I want to know if you think an honorable person must always keep a promise?"

I shot again. The cue ball hovered on the edge of a pocket, then steadied itself. There was a tension, a subtext that I couldn't read. I sent my last ball in and took aim at the eight. It went in smoothly, and I stepped back. There was a moment of silence, and we listened to it roll away into the hidden depths of the table.

"What's your point, Ted?" I asked, without turning to look at him.

"Stephen is going skydiving," he said. "That's my point."

"Stephen, you lost?" I felt, oddly enough, betrayed.

"It was a technicality," Stephen said, frowning. "I'm the better player." He took a long swallow of beer.

"What bullshit," Ted answered, shaking his head. "You're absolutely graceless in defeat."

Stephen was quiet for a long time. Then he put his hand to his mouth, very casually, but I knew he was slipping one of his tiny blue Valiums. He tugged his hands through his thick hair and smiled.

"It's no big deal, skydiving. I called today and made the arrangements."

"All the same," Ted answered, "I can't wait to see it."

Stephen shook his head. "No," he said. "I'll go alone."

Ted was surprised. "Forget it, champ. You've got to have a witness."

"Then Kate will go," Stephen said. "She'll witness. She'll even jump, unless she's afraid."

I didn't know what to say. He already knew I wasn't working the next day. And it was something to think about, too, after a summer of sky gazing, to finally be inside a plane.

"I've never even flown before," I told them.

"That's no problem," Ted answered. "That part is a piece of cake."

I finished off the beer and picked up my purse from where it was lying on a bar stool.

"Where are you going?" Stephen asked.

"Believe it or not, some of us work for a living," I said.

He smiled at me, a wide, charming grin, and walked across the room. He took both my hands in his. "Don't be mad, Kate," he said. "I really want you to jump with me."

"Well," I said, getting flustered. He didn't work, but his hands were calloused from playing so much pool. He had a classic face, a face you might see on a pale statue in a museum, with hair growing out of his scalp like flames and eyes that seemed to look out on some other, more compelling, world. Recklessness settled over me like a spell, and suddenly I couldn't imagine saying no.

"Good," he said, releasing my hands, winking quickly before he turned back to the bar. "That's great. I'll pick you up tomorrow, then. At eight."

When I got home that night my mother was in the kitchen. Sometimes the house was dark and quiet, with only her even breathing, her murmured response when I said I was home. But usually she was awake, working, the radio tuned to an easy-listening station, a book discarded on the sofa. She said that the concentration, the exactness required to form the fragile arcs of frosting, helped her relax.

"You're late," she said. She was stuffing frosting into one of the cloth pastry bags. "Were you at Stephen's?"

I shook my head. "I stayed late at work. Someone went home sick." I started licking one of the spoons. My mother never ate the frosting. She saw too much of it, she said; she hated even the thick sweet smell of it.

"What is it that you do over there?" she asked, perplexed.

"At work?"

My mother looked up. "You know what I mean," she said.

I pushed off my tennis shoes. "I don't know. We hang out. Talk about books and music and art and stuff."

"But he doesn't work, Kate. You come home and you have to get up in a few hours. Stephen, on the other hand, can sleep all day."

"I know. I don't want to talk about it."

My mother sighed. "He's not stable. Neither are his friends. I don't like you being involved with them."

"Well, I'm not unstable," I said. I spoke too loudly, to counter the fear that seemed to plummet through my flesh whenever I had that thought. "I am not crazy."

"No," said my mother. She had a tray full of sugary roses in front of her, in a bright spectrum of color. I watched her fingers, thin and strong and graceful, as she shaped the swirls of frosting into vibrant, perfect roses.

"Whatever happened to simple white?" she asked, pausing to stretch her fingers. This bride's colors were green and lavender, and my mother had dyed the frosting to match swatches from the dresses. Her own wedding pictures were in black and white, but I knew it had been simple, small and elegant, the bridesmaids wearing the palest shade of peach.

"I saw your father today," she said while I was rummaging in the refrigerator.

"How is he?" I asked.

"The same. Better. I don't know." She slid the tray of finished roses into the freezer. "Maybe a little better, today. The doctors seem quite hopeful."

"That's good," I said.

"I thought we could go see him tomorrow."

"Not tomorrow," I said. "Stephen and I have plans already."

"Katie, he'd like to see you."

"Oh really?" I said sarcastically. "Did he tell you that?"

My mother looked up from the sink. Her hands were wet, a pale shade of purple that shimmered in the harsh overhead light. I couldn't meet her eyes.

"I'm sorry," I said. "I'll go see him next week, okay?"

I started down the hall to my room.

"Kate," she called to me. I paused and turned around.

"Sometimes," she said, "you have no common sense at all."

SECRETLY I HOPED for rain, but the next day was clear and blue. Stephen was even early for a change, the top of his convertible down when he glided up in front of the house. We drove through the clean white scent of clover and the first shimmers of heat. Along the way we stopped to gather dandelions, soft as moss, and waxy black-eyed Susans. Ted had given me his camera, with instructions to document the event, and I spent half the film on the countryside, on Stephen wearing flowers in his beard.

The hangar was a small concrete building sitting flatly amid acres of corn. The first thing we saw when we entered was a pile of stretchers stacked neatly against the wall. It was hardly reassuring, and neither was the hand-lettered sign that warned CASH ONLY. Stephen and I wandered in the dim open room, looking at the pictures of skydivers in various formations, until two other women showed up, followed by a tall gruff man who collected forty dollars from each of us, and sent us out to the field.

The man, who had gray hair and a compact body, turned out to be Howard, our instructor. He lined us up beneath the hot sun and made us practice. For the first jump we would all be on a static line, but we had to practice as if we were going to pull our own ripcords. It was a matter of timing, Howard said, and he taught us a chant to measure our actions. Arch 1000, Look 1000, Reach 1000, Pull 1000, Arch 1000, Check 1000. We practiced endlessly, until sweat lifted from our skin and Howard, in his white clothes, seemed to shimmer. It was important, he said, that we start counting the minute we jumped. Otherwise, we'd lose track of time. Some people panicked and pulled their reserve chute even as the first one opened, tangling them both and falling to their deaths. Others were motionless in their fear and fell like stones, their reserves untouched. So we chanted, moving our arms and heads in rhythm, arching our backs until they ached. Finally, Howard decided we were ready and took us into the hangar to learn emergency maneuvers.

We practiced these from a rigging suspended from the ceiling. With luck, Howard said, everything should work automatically. But in case anything went wrong, we had to know how to get rid of the first parachute and open our reserve. We took turns in the rigging, yanking the release straps and falling a few feet before the canvas harness caught us. When I tried it, the straps cut painfully into my thighs.

"In the air," Howard said, "it won't feel this bad." I got down, my palms sweaty and shaky, and Stephen climbed into the harness.

"Streamer!" Howard shouted, describing a parachute that opened but didn't inflate. Stephen's motions were fluid—he flipped open the metal buckles, slipped his thumbs through the protruding rings, and fell the few feet through the air.

Howard nodded vigorously. "Yes," he said. "Perfect. You do exactly the same for a Mae West—a parachute with a cord that's caught, bisecting it through the middle."

The other two women had jumped before but their training had expired, and it took them a few tries to relearn the movements. After we had each gone through the procedure three times without hesitation, Howard let us break for lunch. Stephen and I bought Cokes and sat in the shade of the building, looking at the row of planes shining in the sun.

"Have you noticed?" he asked. "Howard doesn't sweat."

I laughed. It was true, Howard's white clothes were as crisp now as when we had started.

"You know what else, Kate?" Stephen went on, breaking a sandwich and giving half to me. "I've never flown either."

"You're kidding?" I said. He was gazing out over the fields.

"No, I'm not." His hands were clasped calmly around his knees. "Do you think we'll make it?"

"Yes," I said, but even then I couldn't imagine myself taking that step into open space. "Of course," I added, "we don't have to do this."

"You don't," said Stephen, throwing his head back to drain his soda. He brushed crumbs out of his beard. "For me it's my personal integrity at stake, remember?"

"But you don't have to worry," I said. "You're so good at this. You did all the procedures perfectly, and you weren't even nervous."

"Hell," Stephen said. He shook his head. "What's to be nervous? The free fall is my natural state of mind." He tapped the shirt pocket where his Valium was hidden.

"Want one?" he asked. "For the flight?"

I shook my head. "No," I said. "Thanks."

He shrugged. "Up to you."

He pulled the bottle out of his pocket and flipped it open. There was only one pill left.

"Damn," he said. He took the cotton out and shook it again, then threw the empty bottle angrily into the field.

We finished eating in silence. I had made up my mind not to go through with it, but when Howard called us back to practice landing maneuvers, I stood up, brushing off the straw that clung to my legs. There seemed to be nothing else to do.

I was going to jump first, so I was crouched closest to the opening in the side of the plane. There was no door, just a wide gaping hole. All I could see was brittle grass, blurring then growing fluid as we sped across the field and rose into the sky. The force of the ascent pushed me against the hot metal wall of the plane, and I gripped a ring in the floor to keep my balance. I closed my eyes, took deep breaths, and tried not to envision myself suspended on a piece of metal in the midst of all that air. The jumpmaster tugged at my arm. The plane had leveled and he motioned to the doorway.

I crept forward and got into position. My legs hung out the opening and the wind pulled at my feet. The jumpmaster was tugging at my parachute and attaching the static line to the floor of the plane. I turned to watch, but the helmet blocked my view. I felt Stephen's light touch on my arm. Then the plane turned, straightened itself. The jumpmaster's hand pressed into my back.

"Go!" he said.

I couldn't move. The ground was tiny, an aerial map, rich in detail, and the wind tugged at my feet. What were the commands? *Arch,* I whispered. *Arch arch arch.* That was all I could remember. I stood up, gripping the side of the opening, my feet balanced on the metal bar beneath the doorway, resisting the steady rush of wind. The jumpmaster shouted again. I felt the pressure of his fingers. And then I was gone. I left the plane behind me and fell into the air.

I didn't shout. The commands flew from my mind, as distant as the faint drone of the receding plane. I knew I must be falling, but the earth stayed the same abstract distance away. I was suspended, caught in a slow turn as the air rushed around me. Three seconds yet? I couldn't tell. My parachute didn't open but the earth came no closer, and I kept my eyes wide open, too terrified to scream.

I felt the tug. It seemed too light after the heavy falls in the hanger, but when I looked up the parachute was unfolding above me, its army green mellowing beneath the sun. Far off I heard the plane as it banked again. Then it faded and the silence grew full, became complete. I leaned back in the straps and looked around. Four lakes curled around the horizon, jagged deep blue fingers. All summer I had felt myself slipping in the quick rush of the world, but here, in clear and steady descent, nothing seemed to move. It was knowledge to marvel at, and I tugged at the steering toggles, turning slowly in a circle. Cornfields unfolded, marked off by trees and fences. And still the silence; the only sound was the whisper of my parachute. I pulled the toggle again and saw someone on the ground, a tiny figure, trying to tell me something. All I could do was laugh, drifting, my voice clear and sharp in all that air. Gradually, the horizon settled into a tree line a quarter of a mile away, and I was falling, I realized, falling fast. I tensed, then remembered and forced myself to relax, to fix my gaze on that row of trees. My left foot hit the ground and turned and then, it seemed a long time later, my right foot touched. Inch by inch I rolled onto the ground. The corn all around me tunneled my vision, and the parachute dragged me slightly, then deflated. I lay there, smiling, gazing at the blue patch of sky.

After a long time I heard my name in the distance.

"Kate?" It was Stephen. "Kate, are you okay?"

"I'm over here." I sat up and took off my helmet.

"Where?" he said. "Don't be an idiot. I can't see anything in all this corn."

We found each other by calling and moving awkwardly through the coarse, rustling leaves. Stephen hugged me when he saw me.

"Wasn't it wonderful?" I said. "Wasn't it amazing?"

"Yeah," he said, helping me untangle the parachute and wad it up. "It was unbelievable."

"How did you get down before me?" I asked.

"Some of us landed on target," he said as we walked back to the hangar. "Others picked a cornfield." I laughed, giddy with the solidity of earth beneath my feet.

Stephen waited in the car while I went for my things. I hesitated in the cool, dim hangar, letting my eyes adjust. When I could see, I slipped off the jumpsuit and black boots, brushed off my clothes. Howard came out of the office.

"How did I do?" I asked.

"Not bad. You kind of flapped around out there, but not bad, for a first time. You earned this, anyway," he said, handing me a certificate with my name, and his, and the ink still drying.

"Which is more than your friend did," he added. He shook his head at my look of surprise. "I can't figure it out either. Best in the class, and he didn't even make it to the door."

I didn't say anything to Stephen when I got into the car. I didn't know what to say, and by then, anyway, my ankle was swelling, turning an odd, tarnished shade of green. We went to the hospital. They took me into a consulting room and I waited a long time for the X-ray results, which showed no breaks, and for the doctor, who lectured me on my foolishness as he bandaged my sprained ankle. When I came out, precarious on new crutches, Stephen was joking around with one of the nurses.

It wasn't until halfway home, when he was talking nonstop about this being the greatest high he'd ever had, that I finally spoke.

"Look," I said. "I know you didn't jump. Howard told me."

Stephen got quiet and tapped his fingers against the steering wheel. "I wanted to," he said. His nervous fingers worried me, and I didn't answer.

"I don't know what happened, Kate. I stood right in that doorway, and the only thing I could imagine was my chute in a streamer." His hands gripped the wheel tightly. "Crazy, huh?" he said. "I saw you falling, Kate. You disappeared so fast."

"Falling?" I repeated. It was the word he kept using, and it was the wrong one. I remembered the pull of the steering toggle, the slow turn in the air. I shook my head. "That's the funny thing," I told him. "There was no sense of descent. It was more like floating. You know, I was scared too, fiercely scared." I touched the place above the bandage where my ankle was swelling. "But I made it," I added softly, still full of wonder.

We drove through the rolling fields that smelled of dust and ripening leaves. After a minute, Stephen spoke. "Just don't tell anyone, okay, Kate? Right? It's important."

"I'm not going to lie," I said, even though I could imagine his friends, who would be unmerciful when they found out. I closed my eyes. The adrenaline had worn off, my ankle ached, and all I wanted to do was sleep.

I knew the road, so when I felt the car swing left, I looked up. Stephen had turned off on a country lane and he was stepping hard on the gas, sending bands of dust up behind us.

"Stephen," I said. "What the hell are you doing?"

He looked at me, and that's when I got scared. A different fear than in the plane, because now I had no choice about what was going to happen. Stephen's eyes, green, were wild and glittering.

"Look," I said, less certainly. "Stephen. Let's just go home, okay?"

He held the wheel with one hand and yanked the camera out of my lap. We swerved around on the road as he pulled out the film. He unrolled it, a narrow brown banner in the wind, and threw it into a field. Then he pressed the accelerator again.

"Isn't it a shame," he said, "that you ruined all the film, Kate?"

The land blurred; then he slammed the brakes and pulled to the side of the deserted road. Dusk was settling into the cornfields like fine gray mist. The air was cooling on my skin, but the leather of the seat was warm and damp beneath my palms.

Stephen's breathing was loud against the rising sound of crickets. He looked at me, eyes glittering, and smiled his crazy smile. He reached over and rested his hand on my shoulder, close to my neck.

"I could do anything I wanted to you," he said. His thumb traced a line on my throat. His touch was almost gentle, but I could feel the tension in his flesh. I thought of running, then remembered the crutches and nearly laughed out loud from nerves and panic at the comic strip image I had, me hobbling across the uneven fields, Stephen in hot pursuit.

"What's so funny?" Stephen asked. His hand slid down and seized my shoulder, hard enough to fix bruises there, delicate, shaped like a fan.

"Nothing," I said, biting my lip. "I just want to go home."

"I could take you home," he said. "If you didn't tell."

"Just drive," I said. "I won't tell."

He stared at me. "You promise?"

"Yes," I said. "I promise."

He was quiet for a long time. Bit by bit his fingers relaxed against my skin. His breathing slowed, and some of his wild energy seemed to diffuse into the steadily descending night. Watching him I thought of my father, all his stubborn silence, all the uneasiness and pain. It made me angry suddenly, a sharp illumination that ended a summer's panic. The sound of crickets grew, and the trees stood black against the last dark shade of blue. Finally Stephen started the car.

When we reached my house he turned and touched me lightly on the shoulder. His fingers rested gently where the bruises were already surfacing, and he traced his finger around them. His voice was soft and calm.

"Look," he said. There was a gentle tone in his voice, and I knew it was as close to an apology as he would ever come. "I have a bad temper, Kate. You shouldn't provoke me, you know." And then, more quietly, even apprehensively, he asked if I'd come over that night.

I pulled my crutches out of the back seat, feeling oddly sad. I was too angry to ever forgive him, and I was his only real friend.

"You can go to hell," I said. "And if you ever bother me again, I'll tell the entire town that you didn't jump out of that plane."

He leaned across the seat and gazed at me for a second. I didn't know what he would do, but it was my parents' driveway and I knew I was safe.

"Kate," he said then, breaking into the charming smile I knew so well. "You think I'm crazy, don't you?"

"No," I said. "I think you're afraid, just like everybody else."

I was quiet with the door, but my mother sat up right away from where she was dozing on the couch. Her long hair, which reached the middle of her back, was streaked with gray and silver.

I had a story ready to tell her, about falling down a hill, but in the end it seemed easier to offer her the truth. I left out the part about Stephen. She followed me as I hobbled into the kitchen to get a glass of water.

I didn't expect her to be so angry. She stood by the counter, drumming her fingers against the Formica.

"I don't believe this," she said. "All I've got to contend with, and you throw yourself out of a plane." She gestured at the crutches. "How do you expect to work this week? How do you expect to pay for this?"

"Give me a break," I said, shaking my head. Stephen was home by now. I didn't think he would bother me, but I couldn't be sure.

"Working is the least of my problems," I said. "Compared to other things, the money aspect is a piece of cake."

And at that my eyes, and hers, fell on the counter, where the remains of yesterday's fiasco were still piled high, the thick dark chocolate edged with creamy frosting. My mother gazed at it for a minute. She picked up a hunk and held it out to me.

"Piece of cake?" she repeated, deadpan.

My mouth quivered. I started laughing, then she did. We were both hysterical with laughter, clutching our sides in pain. And then my mother was shaking me. She was still laughing, unable to speak, but there were tears running down her face too, and when she hugged me to her I got quiet.

"Kate," she said. "My God, Katie, you could have been killed."

I held her and patted awkwardly at her back.

"I'm sorry," I said. "Mom, it's okay. Next week, I'll be as good as new."

She stepped back, one hand on my shoulder, and brushed at her damp eyes with the other hand.

"I don't know what's with me," she said. She sat down in one of the chairs and leaned her forehead against her hand. "It's too much, I guess. All of this, and with your father. I just, I don't know what to do about it all."

"You're doing fine," I said, thinking about all her hours spent on wedding cakes, building confections as fragile and unsubstantial as the dreams that demanded them. My father sat, still and silent in his white room, and I was angry with him for asking so much from us. I wanted to tell my mother this, to explain how the anger had seared away the panic, to share the calmness that, even now, was growing up within me. Whatever had plunged my father into silence, and Stephen into violence, wouldn't find me. I had a bandaged ankle, but the rest of me was whole and strong.

My mother pulled her long hair away from her face, then let it fall.

"I'm going to take a bath," she said. "You're okay, then?"

"Yes," I said. "I'm fine."

I went to my room. The white curtains lifted, luminous in the darkness, and I heard the distant sound of running water from the bathroom. I took off all my clothes, very slowly, and let them lie where they fell on the floor. The stars outside were bright, the sky clear. The curtains unfolded, brushing against my skin in a swell of night air, and what I remembered, standing there in the dark, was the way it felt to be falling.

The Invitation

Joyce Gentry's day began badly, early in the morning, when she discovered that the slender branches of her mango trees were crawling with ants. Not the tiny black ones, but the large coppery ants that seemed to have adhesive on their feet, clinging obstinately to her cloth gloves and stinging her wrists before she could brush them off. She cried out, more from the knowledge that her trees were endangered than from the sting of their bites. Jamal came at once. He was a little man, short and hard and thin, with a narrow mustache and deft hands, a habitual expression of worried concern on his face.

Fortunately, he knew exactly what to do. A kettle of water poured down each nest, some concoction of herbs slathered on each dissolving anthill, and a stiff spray of the hose to clear the branches. Joyce watched with fascination as the ants tried to escape, spilling frenetically out of adjacent tunnels, carrying their eggs. What resilient creatures they were! Still, she felt no pity for them. They had destroyed half a dozen trees already, and it was just luck that she'd caught them before they'd chewed their way into the bark and killed these young trees as well. Jamal worked quickly in the rising heat of the morning, ringing each trunk with pesticide and raking up the ruined anthills, and she brought him a glass of iced tea from the kitchen when he finished.

"You are so good," Joyce said as he wiped the sweat from his forehead with a bright bandanna. Jamal looked down, as if embarrassed, and she went on, extravagantly, "I would be simply lost without you."

Jamal kept his eyes lowered, but Joyce could tell he was pleased. She rarely had the chance to say what she felt to him; Sid was such a stickler about that. He managed a factory and disapproved of speaking with employees regarding anything but routine matters. If he heard Joyce pay a compliment, or even make an observation on the weather, he became so terribly annoyed. "I deal with people like this every day," he'd tell her, pouring himself another shot of scotch, "and once you cross that line with them, you're lost. Out goes your authority, right out the window, and you can forget about getting any sort of work out of them after that."

Sid was especially stern in regard to Jamal, for Joyce had not hired him in the ordinary way, through want ads and interviews. Instead, she had found him quite by accident on a day when she had gotten lost in a poorer section of the city, her big dark car moving slowly through the narrow lanes, children flocking at the edges of the road to watch her pass. The area was all dirt and squalor, the houses rickety, built of wood scraps and corrugated tin, the drainage ditches oozing green, stinking of rat and refuse. Yet in the midst of this depressing scene, Joyce had come upon a garden so enchanting that she had stopped her car at once. Hibiscus and bougainvillea flamed behind a wooden railing, and hundreds of flowers bloomed in window boxes, in tin cans, in neatly tended beds. Jamal had been standing in the middle of this garden on a little stool, watering several dozen pots of hanging orchids, patiently, with a cup.

Joyce had gotten out of her car, her heels sinking in the soft earth, the air making her skin go damp and oily. She had sized

Jamal up, his silence, his deft, long-fingered hands, the beauty of his garden, and offered him a job on the spot. It was a daring, reckless thing to do—that's what everyone told her later—and she'd never even asked for references. Yet Jamal had transformed her garden, and now she was the envy of her neighbors. Privately, Joyce liked to think that she had a knack for these things, that she could see in people qualities that others often missed. Sid, for instance, was often blind to the good in other people, and he would never quite trust Jamal, no matter how many times Joyce said, "It was the flowers, the way he tended to his flowers. No one with such a garden could be a demon, darling."

Jamal drained the tea quickly, sucking the juice from the wedge of lemon Joyce had placed on the rim of the glass.

"I'd like to stake these trees today," Joyce said, gesturing to the row of slender mangoes. "The rains are coming soon, and I don't want them to get toppled over."

"But Madame," Jamal said, looking past the trees to some point on the horizon. "That is not a good idea, I think."

"Why not?" Joyce asked. "What makes you think it's not?"

Jamal shrugged. "It will not help your trees," he said. "Putting stakes in the ground today."

Joyce waited for him to go on, but Jamal was as uncomfortable in English as she was in Malay, and he did not explain. The sun glared brightly off the concrete patio and for a long moment Joyce stood, considering. It was true that Jamal's advice, though often odd, almost always turned out to be correct: he had advised slashing the older mango trees to force them to bear fruit, and this had happened just as he predicted. Yet Joyce was thinking too of Sid, who just last week had come home exasperated because a surveyor had refused to go near the site of the new factory. It was, the man claimed, a spiritual place, full of ghosts. "A hunk of rock," Sid fumed, "in the middle of the jungle, and he wouldn't go near it. And he was an educated man!"

Perhaps it was because Sid was away that Joyce heard his voice so strongly. He'd warned her against these new trees in the first place. She could imagine him coming back and finding the work undone. He'd say it was laziness, pure and simple, Jamal's ingenious way of getting out of work.

"What is it?" Joyce insisted. "Is it the weather? Is that why you don't want to stake the trees today?"

She gazed at Jamal, waiting for him to answer, but he only lifted his shoulders lightly in a shrug.

"Well," she said crisply, thinking of Sid. "I think it's an excellent idea, nonetheless. I want it done by nightfall."

The garden dealt with, Joyce hurried off to run her morning errands. To the post office, first of all, where she waited in an annoyingly slow line, and to the market, where she bought a silver pin, a birthday present for her niece. Finally she ate a light lunch at the club, the ocean breeze flowing through her hair.

When she got back home the postman was just leaving on his little motor scooter, and Joyce paused in the cool hall, going through the mail eagerly, quickly, looking for the gilded envelope that would be the invitation to the sultan's birthday party. Last year at this time it had already arrived. Today, however, there was nothing but an electric bill and a fashion magazine six months out of date. Joyce tossed them down, feeling a little flurry of irritation. The sultan's birthday was only three weeks away, and she would need to have a dress made, perhaps take a trip to Singapore for shoes. She would need time to prepare, for the invitation was quite special, not one to take lightly, not at all. The sultan and his family were a visible presence in town, with a police escort and flashing sirens every time they went out, but only the most fortunate of the expatriate community ever set foot inside the palace. Last year Joyce had done a little favor for the sultan's wife—smuggled in some pansy seeds for her indoor garden—and that had resulted in her invitation. This year she had sent a whole box of such seeds, elaborately wrapped, and now she waited.

Joyce glanced at her watch and sighed. The new wife was due to arrive in less than an hour. Years ago, these initiation teas had been less frequent and more exciting, but even though the expatriate community had grown to nearly fifty people, Joyce refused to give up the practice of inviting them for tea. Joyce herself had been the first wife out, nearly thirty years ago, and she would never forget how much she'd longed for company, for someone older and wiser to give her some advice.

It made her smile a little now to remember how eagerly she'd come here, studying the atlas where the long bent finger of Malaysia dipped into the South China Sea. She'd imagined an adventurous life, rich with silks and spices and exotic people. The reality had been quite a shock. In those days the rubber factory was nothing but a glorified quonset hut, with hardly a village between here and Singapore, six hours south by car and ferry. Sid had been terribly busy trying to make a go of his new business, and they had not been able to have children, as they had hoped to do. Those languorous days, dissolving into years, had been so lonely that Joyce had often thought she would go mad. It was only after a decade, when the factory expanded, that the others started coming. All the wives, arriving with their leather suitcases, wiping their foreheads and squinting, bewildered, into the harsh midday light. From the beginning they had looked to her for help, and Joyce, grateful for the company, glad for an end to the long, still afternoons, had done what she could.

Now she hurried upstairs and flung open her closet doors, flicking the hangers back and forth, inhaling the faint scent of perfume. On an impulse she pulled out the gold silk gown on its padded hanger. It was a cool rush, shimmering in her hands like light. In deference to local custom the cut was very modest, with a high neckline and sleeves to the wrists, but this was subverted by the way the fabric clung to the body at every movement. Joyce had worn it to the sultan's last birthday party, causing the room to go absolutely silent at her entrance. She had paused to take it all in, the huge brass vases stuffed with orchids, the full orchestra, the marble floors, and the sultan himself in a white linen suit, surrounded by women dressed in bright shades of silk, like an arrangement of exotic flowers. Even now it gave Joyce a thrill to remember, all eyes turned in her direction, the tapping of her heels echoing in the sudden hush as she walked the length of the room.

She sighed, reluctantly putting the gown away. She could not wear it again this year, though she doubted she would find another dress that was its equal. She dressed quickly in a simple linen sheath and went downstairs to make the tea.

The new arrival was called Marcella Frank, and on the telephone she had sounded shy to the point of being demure. This, however, turned out not to be the case. Joyce glimpsed her through the window, arriving on an old-fashioned bicycle, her back straight, her dark hair and white dress vibrant against the shimmering air. Joyce went to the patio, where Marcella was slipping off her shoes and talking to Jamal. They were speaking Malay, and Joyce, who understood only a few words, was amazed. Jamal had spoken only rarely in the four years he had worked for her, but now he seemed quickened, charged, his voice flashing. Joyce had never seen him so; she stopped and took the scene in.

Marcella turned and smiled. "Hello," she said, stepping inside, her bare feet slapping lightly on the marble floor. She seemed very young to Joyce, fresh despite the heat and her recent bicycle ride. "I was just admiring your beautiful yard."

Joyce glanced at her garden, frowned slightly. The word "yard" was one Americanism she had never gotten used to; it conjured up an industrial wasteland in her mind.

"The garden," she said. "Yes, Jamal does wonders."

"Your fruit trees especially," Marcella added. Beyond the patio, heat shimmered against the foliage like a translucent veil. "They're really wonderful." She turned and spoke again in Malay, some rapid observation that caused Jamal to laugh, bringing his two hands together in a gesture of pure pleasure that Joyce had never seen.

"Jamal is staking the young mangoes," Joyce said. "We're worried about the monsoons knocking them down." She smiled at Jamal, but he had turned his attention back to the garden and did not answer. She watched him bend over a bush of flaming hibiscus, his hands moving deftly, silently, amid the leaves. "Please, sit down," she added, stepping back and gesturing to the living room, where ceiling fans stirred the air and their drinks were waiting. "Make yourself at home."

Marcella ran one hand through her dark hair and sank into

the nearest armchair. "Iced tea!" she exclaimed, reaching to pour herself a glass. "Do you mind? I'm absolutely parched."

Joyce smiled and nodded, gesturing to the table, then watched as Marcella took a long, thirst-quenching drink. She was reminded of her own young self, the bright energy she'd had, the way that the years, the endless heat, had transformed it into a sort of entropy. "I'm so glad you could come by, Marcella," she began, sitting down and pouring a glass of tea for herself. "You must feel free to ask me any questions, let me know whatever I can do to help. I've lived here for nearly thirty years, you see, and I know the country rather well. So I feel it's my duty, as well as my privilege, to offer what little assistance I can."

Joyce paused. The rest of her speech—well practiced after all these years—was ready to slip from her tongue, but Marcella Frank was making only the barest pretense of interest. Her dark eyes glanced around the room, taking in Joyce's things—the full set of china, the matching furniture and curtains—as if she found them faintly amusing.

"Thirty years," Marcella repeated, turning her attention back to Joyce. "You must have seen so many changes. Sometimes I look around and wonder what it was like here, say, fifty years ago, or a hundred. All jungle, I imagine. Lovely, unspoiled jungle."

"Yes, it must have been a completely different world," Joyce said. "My husband always says he was born in the wrong century. He's always saying to me, 'Fifty years earlier, old girl, and we'd still have had an empire.'"

Marcella's face sobered; all traces of amusement fell away, and her expression became very distant. She sipped her tea and stared out at the garden where Jamal was burying stakes in a ring around each mango tree. "I imagine Encik Jamal has a different opinion regarding that," she said at last.

Now it was Joyce's turn to be silenced. She felt a blush of anger rise on her face. This girl—this Marcella Frank, just off the plane—was judging her! As if a bit of nostalgia for the lost, romantic past made Joyce herself a staunch imperialist. She glanced out the window at Jamal, remembering the rapid exchange he'd had with Marcella Frank, and her own futile attempts to learn the local language. She had tried, at first, but she had no facility, and when her early attempts, practiced so conscientiously before a mirror, had elicited only soft giggles or confusion, she had given up. It was hard enough to communicate even in her own language. Between herself and this young American, for instance, there was a chasm, a gap, into which fell all the connotations of her sentences. It was as if her words were stripped of all their nuances and reached her guest in a bare and unadorned state, susceptible, then, to all the unknown meanings the girl herself attached to words. Still, Joyce took a deep breath. After all, she had been here so long, and it was her responsibility to reach out, no matter what. She asked Marcella what her husband did.

Marcella had been gazing out the window, too, but now she roused herself and turned back, pushing one hand through her dark curls. There was a fine line of sweat beading on her forehead. Even with the fan on high, the afternoon was very hot. "He's an ecologist," she said. "Soil conservation. We were in Indonesia for two years, and now he's working as a consultant for the new dam here. I'm a teacher," she added. "English. Though they've only hired me part-time."

"Well, that's something new," Joyce said, interested, for all the other women that she knew were wives of executives at the factory. "I once considered teaching. It doesn't pay much, though, as I recall."

Marcella put her tea down. "No, it doesn't," she agreed. "But I've met so many people. And last week, for the first time, another teacher invited me to her family home. She grew up in a village about half a day's drive from here. We sat on reed mats on the floor and ate with our hands, the way they do here, you know. There was tea, and these wonderful cakes made from coconut milk, cool and very smooth, like white jelly." Marcella smiled then, and stopped herself. "Of course," she added, "you'd know all about that." She laughed. "I'm sorry. After thirty years, this must seem very ordinary to you."

Joyce smiled, sipping her tea, but she was surprised, thinking of Jamal's rickety wooden house, or the modest bungalows of the lower managers at the factory. Places where, even in the depths of her great loneliness, she had never thought to go.

"You've certainly seen a lot," Joyce said. She paused, struggling against an uneasiness—an unfamiliar envy, even, that Marcella Frank's exuberant immersion into the local life had inspired. "Of course," she went on, "it takes quite a lot of time to *really* be accepted here. Why, it wasn't until just last year that I knew I finally had been. I received an invitation to the palace then, for the sultan's birthday. I'd often seen him, of course, and we'd met once or twice at the minister's house, but to be invited to his birthday celebration—well, it was really such an honor." She laughed lightly. "I was in a dilemma for weeks about what I ought to wear."

"And what did you decide?" Marcella asked. She had looked up, truly interested at last. Joyce allowed herself a moment of satisfaction before she answered, remembering the silence that had welled up around her when she entered the palace, her silk dress glowing like a shaft of golden light.

"I found a lovely piece of cloth in Singapore. Gold silk. And there's a rather wonderful tailor here in town. I had some illustrations of course, from magazines, to show him the sort of thing I wanted, and he created it from there."

"Gold, did you say?" Marcella asked.

"Yes," Joyce said. She smiled, thinking of the dress, like a patch of opaque sunlight. "It was a lovely shade," she added.

"Gold?" Marcella insisted. "And that was all right?"

"It was *lovely,*" Joyce said sharply, frowning now.

"No, no," Marcella said. She was leaning forward, quite intent. "That isn't what I mean. I'm sure it was beautiful. What I meant was, no one said anything about the *color?*"

"My dear girl, why should they?" Joyce asked. "There were women there in every color you can imagine."

"But gold," Marcella said slowly. "I was told that gold is the sultan's color. That no one else is allowed to wear it in his presence."

"Oh, that," Joyce said. She laughed and waved her hand in the air, but at the same time she felt a sudden horror ripple like a blush along her skin. She remembered the hush that had filled the room when she walked in, a stillness so complete that she'd heard only her own breathing, only the tap of her heels against the marble. It was true—the faces around her had seemed to freeze, mid-sentence, as she walked the length of the hall. She had taken it for a hush of admiration, but what if this girl, this Marcella Frank, was right? It was simply too horrible to consider. Joyce, after an instant of pure dismay, shook the thought away. The sultan, after all, had received her very graciously.

"Surely," she said, her voice a little strained even to her own ears, "surely they wouldn't expect a foreigner to follow these same customs. Why of course not," she went on, drawing assurance from her own argument. "Of course they wouldn't. I've been here almost thirty years and if they did, I most certainly would have heard about it."

"I could be mistaken," Marcella, seeing her distress, said hastily. "I'm sure I must be. It was the other teachers who mentioned it to me. They didn't want me to commit any social errors."

"Oh, I wouldn't worry about that," Joyce said, relieved. The locals had a thousand superstitions—about spirits and thieves, dangerous times of day. Even Jamal refused to do any work at dusk, because he claimed it was the hour when spirits roamed most freely. Joyce didn't suppose she should give any more credence to the rumor about gold dresses than she gave to the other nonsense. "Everyone always comes here with the same idea. They've read too many novels from the Raj. It was literally years before I received my invitation. In fact, you mustn't be disappointed if you never get one. You wouldn't be the first."

As she spoke, a monkey slid over the fence into the garden, stole a mango, and stood on top of the cistern, waving angrily at Joyce. She jumped up and scooped a smooth stone from a bowl by the patio doors. Her aim was true; she hit the monkey in the arm. He screamed and leaped up onto the fence, but not before he took one large bite from the unripe mango and threw it back into the garden.

Jamal came to investigate, and Joyce grew calmer as he collected the ruined fruit and threw it into the wasteland beyond the fence. Still, when she returned to her seat she was shaking, and she smoothed her skirt against her knees several times to regain her composure. "They're in my garden all the time," she explained to Marcella, who looked quite astonished. "I truly hate the creatures."

"Really?" Marcella said, finishing her tea. "I think they're kind of charming. The sultan's youngest daughter keeps one for a pet. It's just a baby monkey, so I guess it's harmless. She carries it around like a little doll."

"That seems completely irresponsible," Joyce said, wondering, as she spoke, how Marcella had come to know this. "Even small monkeys can be quite dangerous."

Marcella pushed her dark curls back, looking thoughtful. "She's never alone with it. They lock it up at night, and of course she always has a servant with her during the day."

Joyce glanced out the window. Jamal was working on the last tree, sunlight beating the back of his neck a dark bronze. "The local teachers are certainly full of stories, aren't they?" she said.

Marcella was silent for a long moment. "I've been tutoring the sultan's children, actually," she said at last. "The headmistress at the school asked if I'd be interested."

Joyce turned to stare at her young guest.

"You hold special classes at the school?" she asked.

"No, at the palace," Marcella told her evenly, meeting her gaze. "I go three times a week."

"My dear girl," Joyce said. Marcella Frank was obviously a lackey, a kind of servant to the royal family, but she was also the only other foreigner Joyce knew who'd ever been inside. "Come, my dear, you must tell me all of it, now that you've begun."

Marcella gave a modest shrug. "There's nothing to tell, really. I teach them English in the afternoon and sometimes, after class, the sultan's wife invites me in for tea. She's already fluent, but she likes to learn American slang. It's very casual. She tosses all these plump cushions on the floor, and then we sit and talk. She must be bored, don't you think, just hanging around in the palace all day, nothing to do but play the piano or float around in the pool? After tea her sisters come by, and they do each other's hair." Marcella touched her own thick curls self-consciously, and laughed. "Last week they wove jasmine through mine, and piled it up on my head. I thought I'd never get the pins out!"

Joyce, who had listened avidly, yet with disbelief, imagined white jasmine setting off the dark infusion of Marcella's wild hair, perfume rubbing from the petals into the skin at the hollow of her throat. Joyce's own hair was cut off in a stylish cap, and now her hand wandered to the nape of her neck, stroked the blunt hairline. She did not speak, puzzled by the intensity of feeling that passed through her at the thought of Marcella Frank with jasmine in her hair.

"I thought," Marcella went on, "that I might wear it that way for the sultan's birthday, as well. What do you think, Mrs. Gentry? Would that be too ostentatious?"

Joyce's hand dropped to her collarbone. She felt the sharp line where the linen neckline met her flesh.

"You're going to the sultan's party?" she asked.

Marcella nodded. "The invitation arrived two days ago. I think," she added, "that it was edged in real gold."

"Yes," Joyce said slowly. "Yes, they use real gold."

She heard her voice speaking, but the words were almost obscured by the sound of high heels tapping against marble, which echoed in her head. She kept a tight smile on her face as she stood and went once again to the patio doors. Jamal, finished with the mango trees, was tending to the shelves of orchids in the shade of the house.

"I'm feeling somewhat faint, I'm afraid," Joyce said, being very careful of her voice. "It must be the heat."

Marcella, concerned, rose at once. "Can I get you anything?" she asked.

Joyce shook her head. She placed one hand on the cool stone wall. "I'll be fine," she said, the echo still ringing in her mind. She wanted to tell the girl to go, but she was aware that this would be too rude. "Let me get Jamal to see you out," she said. "I'm afraid I'm suddenly in desperate need of a rest. He can give you a tour of the garden before you go."

"Are you sure I can't get you something?" Marcella asked. "Are you sure you're all right?"

"I'll be fine," Joyce said. She waved sharply to Jamal, called his name.

"He's a nice man, isn't he?" Marcella said after an awkward pause, reaching for her bag. "His daughter's in my class. He's so gentle with her. And so proud of her, too. You'll really be all right?" she finished. "It was nice to meet you, then. Thank you for the tea."

Marcella stepped onto the patio, and Jamal looked up, pleasure breaking across his face. Together they strolled from tree to bush, chattering away in a language Joyce did not understand. She watched them, feeling stunned and full of shame, as if she had been in a terrible accident and had awakened to find strangers staring at her naked, damaged body. She thought of the mailman, of Jamal, both of whom had witnessed her eager vigil for the invitation.

"Jamal," she called, more sternly than she'd meant to. "Don't forget to show the maze you are constructing."

Jamal turned toward the house and nodded, and for an instant his eyes met hers. She watched the laughter in them disappear, saw the flicker of pure contempt—of hatred almost—that surfaced in the brief seconds before he lowered his gaze. He turned away so quickly that she did not have time to react, but then her heart began to beat with a rapid intensity. How could he feel that way toward her, after all she had done? When she thought of that ruined house he lived in, all that chaos and filth from which she'd taken him. And she'd have done more, too, much more, if only she'd known he had a daughter. She watched Jamal and Marcella carry on an animated exchange, a twisted feeling moving through her. Yet if Jamal truly hated her, then why would he have built her such a lovely garden? Surely there was more than craft behind the well-tended bushes, the array of flowers?

Joyce roused herself and began to gather up the tea things. The kitchen was spacious, lined with windows that overlooked the garden. Hibiscus bloomed, violent red and a blush of peach, all along the border. The veranda was lined with bougainvillea, and everything was neatly trimmed. It ought to have given Joyce some relief to see it, the color and the order, but today it only made her feel a deep unease. For a moment she stared at the bright flowers without really seeing them. Then a movement caught her eye.

From each stake in the ground to each new mango tree, bridging the air over the circles of poison Jamal had put down just that morning, there was a dark, quivering line. Joyce blinked, and when the illusion didn't go away, she opened the screen to look more closely. Lines of ants were walking through the air. But it was not air, she realized, it was the fishing line Jamal had used to stake the trees, so transparent that she would not have seen it except for the ants. They were the large red ants, so dense and steady they seemed more substantial than the fishing wire itself. Joyce held herself still, as if a single motion would shatter something fragile. She hardly breathed, watching the steady progress of the ants. They were working very hard, each one excavating, then carrying away, the very heart of her trees.

Aristotle's Lantern

PHIL GAVE THE SIGNAL, HIS ARM A SWIFT BLUR IN THE HEAT-shimmering air. Pragna, her head tilted to catch the sun, dark glasses hiding her expression, lowered her book to her belly; at seven months pregnant, she couldn't dive.

"Go!" Phil called as his arm fell, and in the next instant Jonathan was over the edge, disappearing into that sea, so blue, so green, the water a liquid gem closing over him. Then Gunnar, lean and tan, plunged into the sea and disappeared. I sat on the edge of the boat, adjusting my mask. "Go, go!" Phil called, and I pushed off, sliding after Gunnar into that other world.

It was so quiet. Falling, I noticed this first. Light fell in shafts and then diffused, the water turning dimmer and more opaque and suddenly cooler. A school of tiny silver fish scattered before us like sparks. Below, Jonathan's limbs were luminous against the ocean floor. I felt the water shift as Phil dove in, and turned to see him silhouetted against the clear, wavering ceiling of the ocean, a wide stream of bubbles in his wake.

It was the fifth dive of the week. For me, the last. Tomorrow I would leave these islands, this resort built so unobtrusively amid the white beaches and jungled mountains. Jonathan's research on current-wave dynamics often took him to remote places. He always went, eagerly—it was the bane of his existence that he taught oceanography in Minnesota, a thousand miles from any ocean. He had discovered this resort while wandering around the archipelagos of the South China Sea on a grant. One morning I'd answered the phone in Minneapolis, heard static sweeping through the line like snow. Then Jonathan's voice came, fading, clear, echoing itself.

"Anna? Can you hear me?"

"Kind of," I said, sitting up.

It was eleven o'clock in the morning and I'd been sleeping, a Minnesota winter sleep, the kind of sleep you sink into for a few weeks after a patient throws up on you and ten minutes later a doctor tells you off for a mistake that was his own, after you go downstairs and hear the receptionist arguing with a woman who's maybe forty-five, maybe fifty, a woman who is clearly in great pain, and the receptionist is telling her that she can't see a doctor if she can't pay, but there's an emergency room in a hospital across town that still takes the uninsured. *I'm too sick to drive,* the woman says, and she looks it. Pale, she's leaning on the counter for support, like she might fall. She is well dressed, in a dark-red skirt and matching sweater, though her hair isn't combed. Her hands are shaking, and she's having a hard time catching her breath. *Please,* she says, and the receptionist looks grim and troubled; it's not her fault that there's nothing she can do, and you stand there in the doorway and hear yourself saying, *Look, don't worry, I'll drive you there.* Anna? the receptionist says, and the doctor, who moments ago was screaming that you were a bloody fucking idiot, totally inept because you didn't notice the medication error he'd written on the chart, comes in and says, Anna? I need you upstairs right now. And everything slows down as you cross the room instead and take the woman's elbow. She is puzzled but in too much pain to protest. There is a moment when your eyes connect, you see the fear in hers and you know it could be you standing there, your throat closing up, fear and pain making you light-headed, and that's when you decide. You take her across the narrow swell of the Mississippi River to St. Paul and get her admitted to that hospital and then you don't return to your job as a physician's assistant. You go back home and fall asleep, waking at strange hours to eat cold cereal or watch TV, wondering what the next thing in your life will be.

Jonathan, a world away, didn't know any of that, of course.

"How are you, Anna?" he asked. "You sound tired."

"It's a long story," I said, walking to the window. My breath clouded the frozen glass. Beyond, the suburban world was flat and white. Cars crawled along I-35W like bright-shelled bugs. Even here, in this clean midwestern city, traffic had multiplied; in the summertime, ozone alerts forced the very old and very young to stay inside. I'd treated them, the elderly gasping for breath, their heads arcing back to meet the plastic mask; the infants, limp and wheezing in my arms. That morning the cars were stalled, heat shimmering from their hoods into the snowy sky. I imagined the hospital, its regulated air and gleaming white walls and swarms of business managers in their cubicles, calculating and adjusting and maximizing the potential of every human resource. "What's new with you?" I asked.

"Look, cash in your vacation time, all right? Anna, I can't explain any of it long distance, but please. Say you'll come."

I didn't answer right away. We'd been together for five years and had reached some sort of intersection: whether an ending or a turning we could not yet tell. But I heard something different, imperative and inexplicable, in Jonathan's voice.

"Anna?" My name traveled through dark space, echoed from satellites. *Anna, na, na,* like a song. "Are you still there? I'm having trouble hearing you."

"I'm here," I said, and there was a pause as my words traveled back over the curve of the globe, over oceans.

"Just come," he said. "I've sent you a ticket."

"I'll think about it," I promised. But I already had—long beaches, deep seas, sun all over my skin. The minute I hung up, I started packing.

Jonathan met me in Singapore and then we traveled for two days more, by incrementally smaller planes and boats, until we reached this remote chain of islands. They emerged slowly from the horizon as we approached: the white lines of beach, the tree-dense hills. The low buildings were teak and thatch in the style of old sultans' palaces, their tile roofs the same dark red as the earth. Chalets, barely visible, were situated only yards from the sea. The resort was elegant, yet also an ecologist's dream: the toilets were self-composting in bathrooms of Italian glass tile, and the electricity came from windmills on the hillside and solar panels on the roofs. The airy rooms had high ceilings; windows and doors opened onto shady verandas. We slept to the sound of waves and waded each morning into water as clear as air.

That sea: limpid around our ankles in the shallows, dense blue now as we dove. Gunnar, my diving partner, kicked his way down to a giant clam nestled in between two boulders. Gunnar was elusive, I'd noticed, prone to floating off in his own direction. *Freedom first,* he'd said one night over beers, after a dive, and Pragna had looked up, her eyes narrowing. Her dark hair was swept back in a clasp and long silver earrings brushed against her neck. She spoke intensely, her eyes flashing. *Yes, but what frees a community must necessarily restrict the individual,* she said. Gunnar waved his hand, dismissive. *We will raise this child to be absolutely free,* he insisted, and Pragna flushed, clearly angered by this old argument between them.

Now, in the ocean winds, Jonathan and Phil drifted lower, examining anchor damage at the base of the reef, setting up the instruments that would measure tidal shifts and currents. I had done dozens of dives with Jonathan, in the weedy bottoms of the Minnesota lakes, to wrecks off the Florida coast, and in sinkholes in the Virgin Islands. I was struck, each time, by how happy he seemed in this world, isolated and self-contained, while I was always longing to erase the distance—to hear his voice, feel his touch. I ran my hand across the bottlebrush coral. The fronds, waving red and yellow and purple like exotic flowers, pulled inside and disappeared, leaving only a stony, pitted brain. A manta ray flashed, scattering a school of butterfly fish, silver and striped

with dark gold, each moving like the pulse of a wing. Chains of
clear eggs drifted near my face. The rush of air, and some faint,
distant clicking, as if the coral were speaking, or the stones. I hung
suspended for a moment in that blue silence, watching the others,
isolated and yet bound to them, the water around us a living thing,
embracing and sustaining.

I touched Gunnar's shoulder and gestured beyond the coral to
the field of sea urchins, their black spines waving like dark wheat
in the currents. He smiled and waved me off.

I swam low over the field, spines just inches from my skin. All
week I had been fascinated by these sea urchins. Each was the size
of a baseball and had a dozen spots, blue and orange set in white,
like bulbous eyes. Clustered on the ocean floor, they seemed to
watch me with an infinite and wary gaze. I was searching for a
skeleton. The inner shell of a sea urchin is a hollow globe, scored
in five curved sections that taper at the ends into a small hole at
the top and bottom. Echinodermata: Echinoidea, whose shell is
known as Aristotle's lantern. In the hushed lobby of the resort
there was a sculpture, delicate, made of bronze: an Asian goddess
with fifteen graceful hands, the shell of a sea urchin, white and
cream and rust, balanced on each open palm. The dark spines of
living sea urchins were quite poisonous—I'd seen a fellow tourist
with an ankle like a grapefruit, downing Valium and gin to kill
the pain. But this was my last day, and it seemed worth the risk: I
wanted a souvenir.

A glimpse of white. Mud bloomed from the ocean floor as I
cupped the shell, a fragile sphere, in my hand.

When I turned back, Jonathan and Phil had moved off into
the gloamy distance, but Gunnar was still drifting by the bank of
brain coral. A rush of guilt—I'd let him slip completely from my
mind. And something was not right: Gunnar's regulator trailed
free. Air rushed in my ears; even from this distance I saw Gunnar's pink lips, a wildness in his eyes. He waved, and then drew his
finger swiftly, definitively, across his throat, the diver's universal
signal of distress.

I swam to him, and he grabbed my arm with such force that
the shell slipped from my hand, tumbling slowly back to the spiny

field. The arrow on his oxygen gauge was in the red. His grip hurt. He was all desire, all desperate need, and yet I hesitated for an instant, taking one last, deep breath before I passed my regulator to him.

Water moved against my naked lips; the taste of salt, the taste of panic. It seeped into me, became a slow welling, as Gunnar breathed and breathed, as my own lungs grew taut. Jonathan and Phil were still dozens of yards away and did not notice what was happening. My lungs began to burn. I touched Gunnar's arm. He did not respond. I grabbed him harder. He opened his eyes, calmer now, and put one hand on my shoulder. He passed me the regulator, warm in my mouth from his lips.

Together, then, with many pauses, we kicked our way toward the surface. A deep breath, a passing of the regulator, acts as intimate and essential and full of question as a kiss. I breathed, and then Gunnar did. It was a kind of dance, urgent and calm, full of fluid grace. One creature, with one purpose: the surface of the water far above, that invisible border where the water opened to the sky. It seemed to take forever, but at last we broke through, flinging our heads back, releasing each other. I drank in the air.

"Anna!" Gunnar shouted, gasping. He ripped off his mask, sunlight in his dark blond hair. "Anna, you saved my life, you did."

THAT NIGHT, in the darkness of our chalet, my bags already packed, I lay next to Jonathan. We had eaten grilled fish with the rest of the group and had drunk a lot of beer in celebration and farewell, watching the sunset flare the world pink and gold. The manager had walked down the beach setting coconuts on fire, leaving them to blaze like skulls against the sand. Now it was late, the fires had died, and we were alone with the moonlight and the waves, but even though I was leaving in the morning with nothing settled, what Jonathan was talking about was the dive.

"I was right behind you," he said. "I know it must have been terrifying, but it was also beautiful to watch, Anna. You were splendid."

I shifted, turning to lie on my side. What went unspoken between us had always seemed like its own sea, full of mysterious shifts and currents. Jonathan's dark hair brushed my arm. He placed one hand lightly on my hip. I wondered when he was coming home to Minneapolis. When or if.

"I didn't want to be splendid," I told him. "It was awful to be without air. I was afraid every time that he wouldn't give it back."

Jonathan looked at me, his expression so intent, so focused, a sort of intimacy he didn't often allow. "Still, you did it," he said. "You didn't miss a beat."

I remembered the shell then, its slow, tumbling fall through the dark blue water. And I thought of Pragna, how she had stood up in the boat when we broke through the surface, leaning to help Gunnar in, her arms slender and muscled, his hands running down the swell of her belly, his cheek sliding down to rest there. An intimate moment, so passionate, so spontaneous; I'd paused in the water, watching, glad to be alive, yet struck with yearning.

"I'm a little bit in love with those two," Jonathan observed, as if he'd read my mind. We often had the same thoughts at the same time, a fact that had comforted me when Jonathan was gone or distant, distracted by his work. That night, though, for reasons I couldn't name, his comment made me restless and annoyed. I went to the dressing table and sat down.

"In love?" I asked, turning on a lamp and reaching for a comb. "What are you telling me? Are you in love with Pragna?"

"No." Jonathan sounded surprised. "With what they have between them."

He came and stood behind me then. He took the comb from my hand. We studied ourselves in the mirror, blond and dark, blue eyes and brown, the perfect twinning of opposites. *What they have,* I thought. *And what we don't.*

"You're not coming back," I said, meeting his gaze in the glass.

He shook his head, slowly. Then he surprised me again. He leaned down and kissed my neck, just at the point where my hair brushed the skin.

"You don't have to go tomorrow," he said, kneeling beside me, resting his chin on my shoulder. "You don't have to go at all."

"Not go?" I echoed, puzzled.

"Anna," he said. "There's something I want you to see."

"A secret?" I asked. The ceiling fan clicked. Jonathan put the comb down. Gently, he massaged the base of my neck, my shoulders.

"Yes," he said, his hands moving up then, through my hair. "A secret, yes."

AT DAWN, rather than leaving, Jonathan took me out in a small boat, pulling away from the resort into the pale white mergence of the sea and sky. The sun rose, becoming oppressive as we traveled through the chain of islands. At last Jonathan pulled the boat up to a narrow dock. Here the beach, crushed white coral, was sharp against our feet. A few yards into the trees we came to a single bright yellow car of a funicular railway.

I looked at Jonathan, who simply smiled. "You'll see," he said, fastening the door behind us. "Just wait and see."

The car lurched and we climbed high up the face of the cliff, the rock raw and rough behind us, the beach below sliding beneath the clear smooth water. I don't know what I expected to be shown—a fabulous view, a virgin jungle. But when the car came to a stop I stepped out into a clearing, lush with tropical foliage, coconuts and palms and swaying mango trees. A group of children played with a rattan ball on the grass at the far end, where a wide gate, like those outside Japanese temples, opened onto a village street. We walked on a path of finely crushed shells that caught the light and gleamed. Hundreds of people of every race, every age, were carrying baskets or babies, ringing the bells of their bicycles, hoisting packs with rice or bread on their backs, holding hands, pausing to talk beneath the shady casuarina trees. We passed one simple building after another, made of teak or covered with clapboard painted in pastel blue, yellow, peach, or mint green. Hibiscus and bougainvillea flamed by the doorways and the white fences. These buildings housed restaurants, coffee shops, stalls for fruit and vegetables. People sat at tables, drinking tea, cats weaving around their ankles. We passed a community center and a sign for the health clinic. After that the path narrowed and the buildings became small chalets, scattered amid the trees and overlooking the ocean.

Jonathan was known; people kept stopping him to talk. *Don't go,* he'd said, and I'd imagined some kind of nomadic life, just us, someplace where we might become slightly different, better people. I kept glancing at him, his long tanned arms and the familiar line of his jaw, trying to understand who he was. Just beyond the community center we turned down another path. Tropical flowers brushed my arms. There was a fragrance, dense and heavy as the heat.

"Here," Jonathan said as we came to a teak building. He held the door open for me, and I stepped into an astonishing room.

It was circular, half of it set into the cliff, half cantilevered out over the ocean and framed by high, curving walls of glass, filled with light. Filled, I saw as I drew closer, with a view of the sea. The room was vast, a full three stories high. People lounged on sofas, read newspapers, chatted by a fountain in the center. Gunnar was there, and Pragna too, sitting at a small table, empty cups before them. They smiled and waved. Jonathan and I crossed the room and sat on a sofa by the glass wall. A hundred feet below the waves slammed in, seething into a white spray flung skyward.

Nets of light, reflected in random and chaotic patterns from the waves, played over people as, one by one, they came to join us.

"Where are we?" I asked Jonathan.

I spoke softly, yet my voice filled the room. Everyone laughed. Pragna sat on the sofa opposite.

"This is the atrium, Anna. We'll explain."

She began to talk then, and others broke in, telling me the story. Ten years ago this chain of twelve islands had been purchased by a consortium of investors. They planned a development of high-rise hotels, the jungled hills denuded and flattened for airstrips, a restaurant built over the fragile coral reefs we had explored all week. I knew just what this meant and how bad it could be: Jonathan and I had spent a week on the southern coast of Thailand, where the beaches were littered with tourists and trash, where raw sewage poured into the sea and chunks of dead coral, loosened by anchors, washed up on shore. The villagers, fishermen for untold generations, had taken jobs waiting tables, their black shoes slipping against the sand. Nights were neon; young girls, lured from poor villages, flickered on the corners until dawn, and when the sun rose it was reddened by the haze, pollution from logging fires raging in Borneo. It was more hell than paradise, but it was profitable in the short term. The developers here had envisioned the same thing. The plans had been drawn: bulldozers had been lined up on the mainland like orange and yellow insects, set to invade.

Then Yukiko Santiago intervened.

Yukiko Santiago. I had never heard of her, but the people in that room spoke of her with something close to reverence. She was the daughter of a Japanese samurai family, whose grandfather had supported the imperial army and committed seppuku, whose father had rebuilt the family fortunes in the wake of the Second World War. Yukiko, as a child, had witnessed both the horrific machine of the state and the devastation of war. Half of her mother's family had died in Hiroshima. She had grown up to marry a wealthy Peruvian businessman, and when he was killed in a plane crash she had taken his considerable wealth, coupled with her own inheritance, and set about doing philanthropy. Reclusive, generous, she had a simple philosophy: she had seen the worst that human beings might do, and she wanted now to see the best. She had flown in to buy these islands, offering the investors cash settlements greater than the returns they would have seen for twenty years. Then she had turned the development plans inside out: the high-end ecotourist resort where we had stayed would preserve the coral reefs and island jungles, all the while funding her real interest, a global coalition of research stations known collectively as the Sea Earth Institute—SEArth.

"All right," I interrupted. "But there's a village out there. A town. Schools and a community center. Restaurants."

"Yes. We are a community." The woman who spoke was thin and strong, a sarong skirt tied at her waist. Her name was Khemma. A Cambodian, like many here she had been a refugee, a survivor of war or other atrocities. She was now the community librarian. "In the beginning this place was simply for research. The growth happened very gradually, very organically, as researchers brought their families. There has never been any plan imposed. But once it was clear what was happening, Yukiko Santiago appointed a board to assess and guide the evolution of the community. To provide what came to be needed. To see, in essence, where this other, new experiment would lead."

"Yes," Gunnar said. He was leaning forward with his elbows on his knees, his hands clasped. I remembered his fingers on my shoulder. "It is Aristotle's idea of entelechy, applied not to biology but to our human community. Entelechy—it is the science of the possible, of unlocking what is otherwise merely potential. As we see it, Anna, the ideal is like a vessel with which a community may select those possibilities suitable to its own nature—those which promise to further human development. We do not impose here. We discover."

I turned to Jonathan. That sensation I'd had on the path, that this man I'd known was suddenly strange to me, returned. I watched the way he spoke, his fingertips tapping on his bare knee. I couldn't believe we'd ever stood side by side at a counter, dicing vegetables, or that these same hands had reached for me last night.

"How long have you been here?" I asked, remembering the long Minnesota nights, his infrequent e-mails from what he said were Internet cafés.

He nodded, acknowledging his lies. "Ever since I left. Remember that trip, that conference, a year or so ago? I met Pragna there. Phil and Khemma, too. They invited me to visit. I'm sorry that I didn't tell you, Anna. I couldn't. But from the beginning I wanted you to come. And after yesterday," he added, "you're more than welcomed."

Everyone smiled. Understanding flashed through me, sudden and harsh.

"It was a *test*?" I said, too shocked to be angry right away. "That emergency was engineered?"

"My air was gone," Gunnar told me. "But the event was planned, yes."

I remembered my guilt at forgetting him. My fear and panic when I saw his air was gone, what it had cost me to trust him. And all the time they had known, they had been watching me.

When Jonathan touched my arm, I pulled away. I couldn't speak, but my feelings must have been working on my face.

"Is Yukiko on the line yet?" Khemma asked Phil, softly. "Can you get her? Because she will explain it best," she added, turning to me. "Of course you are angry, Anna. We would not expect otherwise. We have all been through this, and we have all been angry too." She flashed a slow smile. "You might even say that getting past the anger is the most real test."

And then Yukiko was there, flashing up on a screen against the rock-faced interior wall, a diminutive woman in a pale blue dress, her dark hair falling loose and streaked with gray.

"Hello, Anna," she said, and I was startled to be addressed so warmly and directly. She smiled, and her smile was kind. "You were tested, yes. Perhaps that was not very fair. But since you are in love with a scientist, I hope you will understand. This is not simply a community here, and it is not only about the coral reefs. We are engaged in a greater research, which involves charting currents and wave systems. We wish, ultimately, to harness the latent power of these forces. To find an alternative form of energy. It's important work, and many here are political refugees, whose lives could be endangered if their whereabouts were known. So we must be careful. We recognize our interconnectedness, and our own fragility. Not everyone suits. And not for everyone would this be a good place."

A skeletal light played over the array of faces, and the room filled with the muted crash of waves.

"You can talk normally," Pragna said. "She'll hear you."

I was still stunned, but at Pragna's voice, anger shattered through me. She had reached for Gunnar as if he were returning from the dead.

"Everyone in that boat lied to me," I said, and then I turned to Jonathan. "Including you. Especially you."

"Jonathan was your very strong supporter, Anna," Yukiko said. "He went through a similar experience on his arrival. He did not wish you to go through it also. Yet we had no choice."

"Anna," Gunnar said. "We were taking a risk, also. We did not want to lose Jonathan."

I closed my eyes for a moment, trying to take it all in, what had happened, what was happening.

"Take some time, Anna," Yukiko said, and I opened my eyes to see her smiling at me, one hand lifting, as if she might reach through the air and touch me. And I wanted that suddenly, to be a part of this, to please them, and yet—and yet—so much had happened so quickly. "Take your time," she repeated, and then her image disappeared.

"Here," Jonathan said after a few minutes of silence. "In case you think I wasn't paying any attention."

He handed me the shell I'd lost, or one just like it. Aristotle's lantern, round, slightly flattened, the surface rough, pierced with tiny holes.

When he spoke again Jonathan's voice had an urgency I recognized. This, I knew, was a moment he'd been imagining for weeks.

"Anna, the word 'test' comes from the Latin *testa,* meaning shell. In the Middle Ages, a test also was a kind of vessel, in which experiments were done. You just heard Gunnar say that the ideal is a kind of vessel, too. He's right. In some sense, every day here is an experiment. Every day, a test."

I turned the shell, so delicate, nearly weightless. I understood that he was offering me, in his oblique way, in the only language he could use, another way of seeing what had happened. And in that moment I saw how the curve of the glass wall swelling over the sea mirrored exactly the shape of the shell in my hand. I held it up on my palm, looking from shell to wall and back again.

"Yes," Gunnar said. "Good eye, Anna."

"But not good enough," I answered.

He looked up, sharply, at the bitter edge in my voice. Then he cleared his throat and went on.

"As you know, Aristotle classified the animals. He named this shell. You can see how the shape is like a lantern, how the light could flow out of the pattern of tiny holes. These urchins are indigenous, and beautiful, and so we took their name for our community. But Aristotle is important to us for another reason. He was the first to challenge Plato's ideal state. Plato's utopia was many good things, but it was also static. Plato did not allow for growth or change or self-transformation, and in some sense this flaw—of fixation—led very naturally to the dystopias we have all seen, and which many of us have experienced and have fled."

"Is that another test for admission?" I asked, glancing around the room. "Surviving oppression?"

Gunnar, unamused, shook his head.

"It is not. But people with such histories tend to understand our purpose. You see, while Aristotle's view, too, was flawed, for him the community was alive. He believed it could grow and change, like every living organism. For Aristotle, politics was the science of the possible. That is what we believe. And this belief sustains us."

I cupped the shell and remembered Gunnar's eyes, his finger making that frantic slash across his throat, the bubbles flowering from his lips.

"I risked my life," I said, still angry.

"Yes," Pragna said. "You risked your life for a man you hardly knew. Precisely."

That night, as Jonathan slept, I lay awake and listened to the pounding of the surf. If I stayed, as they had asked me to, I would become the community health-care specialist. There was a doctor who came three times a month whom I would assist, and in her absence I would oversee the clinic. And once a week I'd go to the mainland, to a community there, and work training nurses and midwives, treating patients, giving vaccines.

I dressed and walked to the park, where I sat on a bench above the vast ocean. The stars were vivid, near, and the darkness was filled with sounds I didn't recognize: birds and insects and the rustling of unseen animals. I'd never felt so unsettled, so unsure of what to do, the world unmoored, swimming. I wondered how my life would be if I stayed, what I'd gain and what I'd sacrifice forever.

Footsteps, then, on the crushed shells. Gunnar passed through a small pool of light from the community center. I remembered his voice, his passion, as he talked about this place. I remembered, too, the feeling I'd had on the dive, when we all swam, isolated from each other yet so intimately connected. I was flattered to have been chosen, it was true. And I wanted to explore the possibilities with Jonathan. But as Gunnar disappeared again into the darkness, as I made up my mind to stay, it was yearning, finally, that compelled me. A yearning to know what Gunnar knew, to understand this place at its unmoving center. A yearning, too, for that brief moment of connection, as elusive and beautiful as the changing color of the sea.

THE NEXT DAY I went to work. The village was small—only 867 people—and relatively young, so I was surprised to find the waiting room full, even at that early hour. On my first day I treated three kinds of skin rash and diagnosed two cases of giardia, several minor respiratory infections, a broken finger, one case of pinkeye, one urinary-tract infection, and a pregnancy. I did three well-baby checks and tested the eyesight and hearing of one of the retired scientists. The pharmacy was well stocked, and I was to prescribe within my own comfort levels. I'd never had such autonomy, such a feeling of accomplishment. And I liked the doctor, a no-nonsense Vietnamese woman who had trained in Poland, who invited me over for sushi and asked difficult questions about English grammar, and who could find a vein in any arm with a single try and no break in conversation.

There were, right from the beginning, crises: a septic infection, an ectopic pregnancy, an alarming lump in one woman's leg. A botanist in his mid-fifties came back from a jungle hike and dropped dead from a heart attack. There was nothing anyone could do.

The dives, too, involved risks. Much of the research happened underwater, and there was always the danger of a tank failure or an accident. One evening, just as I was about to close the clinic, Phil came in. He had been diving deep that afternoon, at a hundred fifty feet, working with a team to set up motion sensors, and as he worked he'd felt himself growing detached and dreamy. A slender white shark passed by; instead of fear he'd felt a surge of joy and reached to touch it. Phil was an experienced diver and knew what was happening: a kind of nitrogen poisoning that distorted reason. He knew he should rise to the surface—getting out of the deep would restore the balance in his blood—but he didn't. He swam on. After some time he floated over the shattered remains of a boat, where he thought he saw a human skeleton. He wasn't sure if it was real or a hallucination.

I was listening, making notes on his chart. When I looked up he was handing me a human bone, a femur. It was both smooth and porous, bleached deeply white.

"Boat people," he said, "that's what I figured, people fleeing Vietnam in the eighties who hit bad weather and drowned. It's not uncommon to find them. But the light was odd, you know, and I was narked. I knew I was narked, I told myself I ought to go up, but instead I kept floating by the boat. Little by little it seemed to me that there were people in it again. Alive, I mean, but underwater. I talked to them," he added, and then stared at me, defiant.

I put the femur on the counter. I'd heard these stories a lot over the years.

"It's lucky you had enough will to come back."

Phil nodded. "Gunnar saw me drifting off. He had to pull me by the arm, hard, because coming up was the last thing I wanted to do. I'm telling you," he said, laughing at himself even as he spoke. "I felt New Age or something, as if I'd become one with the universe. Sentient and yet diffused. That sounds crazy, I know."

"The rapture of the deep," I said, thinking not of Gunnar but of Pragna reaching to pull him into the boat. "There's a reason divers call it that."

We talked some more—he wanted, mostly, it seemed, to tell his story. I gave him some Valium to see him through the next few hours. After Phil left I studied the femur, wondering about the life that had surrounded it, the dreams that had propelled it. Wondering what should be done with it now. In the end I took it to the deck off the atrium, where I leaned far out over the water and returned it to the sea.

IN THIS WAY the days passed with the fluidity and continuity of waves. I was very happy. Even as I rose in the middle of the night to a knock on the door, even as I helped the ill or injured, I felt a sense of peace, of purpose. Once a week I traveled to the mainland village's makeshift clinic, where I taught the young nurses how to dress wounds, give shots, and disinfect equipment. Then I came back to swim at sunset in a sea as calm as glass. In Minnesota, Jonathan and I always had a hard time coming back together at the end of each day. Often, we'd sat together in the evenings, hardly speaking, each absorbed in our separate lives. Here, what we did connected us, and when we were together we talked as never before. In the distance windsurfers moved in slow lines, like the ever-shifting points of a triangle made from light.

I found myself thinking of Plato and his theory of ideal forms: a triangle drawn on paper, no matter how precisely, is only a crude representation of a triangle's essence. Plato believed in a framework of perfection hidden behind the visible; I believed we had discovered that framework here. Jonathan and I were determined to see what would evolve between us. There were details we would need to attend to—our house, our things—but we rarely spoke of them.

AT THE END of the hot season, near the advent of the monsoons, many people left the islands, either to escape the tedious weeks of rain or because they feared that rough seas and skies would make travel impossible. Pragna, now at the end of her eighth month, would go to Singapore and wait in an apartment near the hospital. Gunnar would join her near the due date. At the boat Gunnar put his hand on the curve of her stomach and I saw it again: something invisible but real passing between them, the glimpse of another country, a place they inhabited alone. I felt pierced with loss. Jonathan was standing next to me, and I reached to take his hand.

A week later, the rains began. I woke to what I thought was thunder, rain so loud that Jonathan, lying next to me, had to shout to be heard. Laughing, we went outside and stood in the deluge, the water hitting the earth and bouncing high again, already filling the dry gutters and sliding in sheets from the roofs. By noon the island was transformed, water standing in shallow places and dripping from leaves, the flagstones of the paths small islands in the mud.

Over the next days, mysteriously, the clinic filled up with crickets. When I came in the dusky light of early morning they were singing, and when I opened the door they jumped beneath the tables and onto counters, their narrow legs humming. I swept them out with a broom, great leaping piles of them. All day I leaned close to hear my patients, their breath against my ear. When the rains eased, momentarily, or for a few hours, we all relaxed, as if silence were a kind of space that had opened up around us. Our sheets and clothes grew damp. Mildew erupted overnight on Jonathan's huaraches. One morning, I found toads nestled in my shoes.

The rains were excessive, the worst they'd ever been. In meetings at the atrium, the sky and sea were indistinguishable. Just a few hundred miles away in Indonesia whole towns flooded, and a wedding party was washed away when a temple collapsed beneath a tidal wave. In the Philippines, an entire season of rice was destroyed. We left these meetings sobered, but sustained by Yukiko's vision, imagining these powers transformed into energy, into light, by the ways we might change the world.

Three weeks into the monsoons, the resort, emptied of its tourists for the season, began to flood. This was not supposed to happen. The work Jonathan had done on current dynamics and surface-wave prediction was supposed to have averted any major disaster on those beaches. We listened, helpless and disbelieving, to the reports the manager sent up. Jonathan couldn't sleep. At night I'd wake to the scent of kerosene and find him at the table, poring over his charts and graphs beneath a flickering lamp.

On the first calm day all of us boated over to view the damage. In places the beach had been totally resculpted. Two chalets had been swept away, the ceiling fans and Italian tile and comfortable deck chairs all carried out to sea. The main building had escaped damage, but its grounds had been flooded, and the receding water had left behind lakes of mud and debris.

We walked amid the beauty and the ruins, picking up trash,

skirting new lakes. Generators ran everywhere, fueling the electric pumps and vacuums. Jonathan was silent, his face as shattered as the landscape.

When we reached the sunken garden behind the main building, Phil, his beard three days old and stubbled with red, stepped down off the stone fence and waded between the ornamental bushes. Fish were swimming in the grass, a strange and joyous sight that cheered us all. Laughing, Phil reached down and caught one in his bare hands, holding it up, a flash of white against the gray rain dripping from the sky, the leaves, our clothes. We were still laughing when we heard the soft crack, the rush of falling branches in the air. I stepped into the water, looking in the wrong direction, thinking the rushing sounds were coming from the beach. Then someone, shouting, pushed me so hard I staggered. My foot slipped in a low ditch and I felt my ankle turn. So slow, it all was, I struggled to keep my balance and yet, even as I fell, I saw the branch floating down, taking wires with it. I saw Phil see what was about to happen, the line writhing like a snake and then dropping into that lawn where water was not meant to be, where fish swam. Electricity traveled through the new lake like lightning, traveled through Phil, who dazzled us all for a terrible instant, sparks flying from his hair, his fingertips, like the flash of silver fish in the air. Phil, who was dead before he could even gasp or scream.

Khemma started toward him—he had fallen facedown by the bougainvillea—but Jonathan grabbed her arm. The line was still alive in all that water.

"Someone shut off the damned generator," he shouted, his voice hoarse. And when no one moved, he went to do it himself, walking backward, his eyes caught on Phil. Already fish were beginning to rise up and float on the surface of the water. I stood up slowly, enveloped by the scent of burning flesh, singed hair. The generator ceased, and we all waded at once toward Phil, poor Phil. We pulled him out of the water, and I leaned close to do CPR, though his skin was blistered beneath his new beard, and I knew it was hopeless. Still, I held his face in my hands and pressed my lips against his, remembering his conversation with the dead at the bottom of the sea. They let me work for a while, and then there were hands on my shoulders, my arms, lifting me up.

"Anna, that's enough, Anna. Anna, look, you have to stop, you're bleeding."

It was only then that I noticed my leg, the gash on my shin from where I had fallen, streaming blood.

Jonathan tore his shirt into strips, and we wrapped my leg. His face was taut, a muscle jumping in his cheek. His eyes kept running over the ruined beach, Phil's body. I tried to touch him, but he shrugged me off. When the rest of us left the island he refused to come, determined to see where he'd gone wrong. Besides, he said grimly, someone had to stay with the body. When the hydroplane reached the other island, Khemma helped me all the way back to the clinic. At the doorway I paused, remembering the day not long ago when Phil had come to me, excited and disoriented, full of visions.

"What will they do with him?" I wondered.

"I don't know," Khemma said. Her smooth olive skin was pale, and she was shivering, her arms folded tightly across her chest. "Find his family, probably, send him home."

"I was about to step into that water. Someone pushed me."

"Yes," she said. "That was Gunnar." She helped me onto the examining table and brought me a light blanket. "I need to step out for a minute. Will you be all right? I have to call Yukiko right away."

"Go," I said. Alone in the clinic, surrounded by the hum of crickets, I held my leg out straight and unwrapped the layers of Jonathan's shirt. When I got to the wound, a neat dark slash against my shin, blood welled up at once. But not before I had glimpsed it, the flash of white bone beneath the flesh. Bone that had never felt the air.

I pressed the cloth back down, applied pressure. For a long time I just sat. When Gunnar appeared in the doorway, I was weeping.

"Let me see," he said gently, pulling the cloth away. "It's deep," he acknowledged.

I nodded, wiping at my eyes with the back of my hand.

"It's cut to the bone. But it's clean, fortunately. If you could get me the medical kit in the cupboard. And hold my leg while I do this, please."

Gunnar nodded and came back with the equipment. I filled a syringe with novocaine and took a long, deep breath before I injected the drug all around the gash. The numbness spread quickly, and after I'd cleaned the cut the blood subsided to an ooze. Still, when I put the first stitch in, catching my own flesh with the needle and then pulling the suture through, I felt a wave of nausea and was forced to stop. Gunnar reached up and pressed one palm against my forehead.

"You don't have to be so brave," he said. "Lie down, Anna. All right?"

"But I have to have stitches."

"I can sew," he replied. "My grandmother believed it was an essential skill for all human beings, male or female."

"Well, that's great," I said. "I don't suppose you practiced on human beings?"

Gunnar, wisely, ignored me. "My grandmother is still living," he said. I felt his fingers, and the pressure of the stitches going in. "She will be a hundred years old next year."

He told me stories of his country as he worked, the long tongues of glaciers reaching down valleys, the fertile rivers and charming cities. The interior of the island so rugged that American astronauts had used it to practice moon landings. Swimming pools filled by geothermal springs, where the snow melted in the rising steam as people swam. Every few months he went back to teach, and to collect data from the Icelandic seas.

"All right," he said, putting one hand on my shoulder. "Sit up."

The stitches were ugly, rough and uneven, but they were tight and secure. I dressed the wound and stood, testing my weight on my foot.

"Oh," I said, looking up at the pain, tears in my eyes. I was thinking of Jonathan, the lines in his face, but what I said was "Poor Phil."

Gunnar nodded, studying me.

"Can you walk, Anna?"

"Yes. Yes, I think so."

He studied me a moment longer, deciding.

"Good," he said. "Follow me."

We walked down an unfamiliar path and arrived at a black sand beach. The sea was rough, but the setting sun had broken from the clouds and everything was vibrant in the sudden light. There was a shallow cave in the cliff, stairs opening into a passage lit like the aisle of an airplane. Gunnar saw me limping and put his arm around my waist, helping me down the steps.

We emerged into a room underwater. It was built like a greenhouse, with walls of glass. But in the same shape, I saw right away, as the swelling walls of the atrium. We were in the deep water before the drop-off, so that the dome—*a pleasure dome,* I thought, remembering some long-ago poem—stood as if on the edge of a cliff, fields of coral, the spiny dark sea urchins all around us, and then on the far side of the drop-off, a sudden darkness, the edge of an abyss. Light fell in nets through the water and shimmered across the floor, across my skin, wavered on Gunnar's face as he turned to me. His eyes were the same blue as the water.

I went to the glass and pressed my hands against it, my face. My breath gathered and disappeared. A school of parrot fish swam by, an inch, no more, away.

"We are about thirty feet below the surface," Gunnar said. "The site was very carefully chosen. No coral was destroyed."

"It's so beautiful," I whispered. I felt as if I might cry, I wanted so to feel those fish brush against my hand.

Even as we spoke the light had begun to fade, the sun setting far above.

"It is a research station," Gunnar said, gesturing toward the drop-off. "We take AUVs out of an antechamber to this room and travel half a mile down to the site. I am talking about a series of hydrothermal vents on the floor of the deep ocean. Near them, we have discovered biological communities—novel, strange communities found nowhere else. And from these communities we are learning extraordinary things about the evolution of life. Unusual symbiosis we had never imagined possible. As a scientist, you must always ask yourself the same question, again and again: Why this form and not another? Why this path and not any other?"

In this short time the water around us had grown dark, and fish had begun to emerge, giving off their own pale light. Flashlight fish, shimmering blue-green, and bioluminescent plankton glittering in their wake. Gunnar was no more than a shadow beside me, but his voice, too, was lit with excitement.

"It is not fixed, is what I am saying, Anna. The evolution of life. In these communities we are not studying fossils or shells or the dead artifacts of creation. We are watching life evolve, before our very eyes. You see these fish, giving off their own light? This phenomenon happens very rarely in the world. In freshwater, not at all. In fireflies, yes, and in some worms, but on earth, almost never. Yet in the deep ocean ninety percent of all animals are luminescent. The chemical process has evolved independently in a dozen different paths. In that same way, these new communities are seeking a different form from anything that now exists. Discovering their potential is the center of our mission here."

"And the coral reefs?" I asked. "Jonathan's work on currents, on waves?"

"Also important," Gunnar said. "But not the center. Anna, do you understand? We are what we are, you and I. Our evolution has followed a particular path to bring us to this moment and no other. But imagine if another path had been taken, long ago. Imagine if a new evolution naturally occurred, so that an organism such as plankton, say, suddenly contained the chemical properties of fuel. Or of a perfect protein. Not something engineered by humans. Something natural, driven by evolutionary necessity. Imagine if these resources were plentiful and cheap, what this would mean."

On the surface far above, plankton glittered like a sweeping of stars. I felt a surge of excitement, power, the thrill of possibility.

"You would change the world," I said, softly. I thought of the streams of cars back home, exhaust hiding the sun, starving children, struck by drought. "You would save it."

"Yes," Gunnar said. "I would. I will. Perhaps it will take decades, but we will do this thing. Without Yukiko, of course, this would not be possible. Pragna knows, a few others here. But I would ask you not to speak of this."

"Another test?"

"No," Gunnar said. Medusa jellyfish hovered nearby, their light a translucent green. "This is me, trusting you to see what I am seeing. Sometimes I come here simply for the beauty. To remind myself of what is at the center. Of the mystery."

"You're a scientist," I said, trying to imagine this same passion in Jonathan's voice when he talked about boundary-layer data. "I didn't think scientists believed in mystery."

Gunnar laughed. "If there were no mystery, Anna, there would be no science."

I loved his voice, the way he spoke my name, as if there were waves running through it. We were quiet as we left, walking back through the passage and up the dark stairs. I had been given a gift, I knew this, a gift meant to ease my sorrow. And it had. I never spoke of that place to anyone, and yet I could not stop thinking of it. A rush of the surf and I might close my eyes, imagining the strange light of this other world, hidden beneath the surface of the usual. And sometimes, leaving Jonathan in his restless sleep, I returned to that silent room. I pressed my hands against the glass, plankton scattered high above like stars, fish moving past in their slow orbits, like planets, like strange moons.

PEOPLE BELIEVED it was the shock of watching Phil's death that had unsettled me, but I knew the source of my restlessness was more complex. Even as the rains abated and our things dried out and people began to return to the islands, I remained alive with secrets, changed by what I'd seen, and the act of not running into Gunnar became as deliberate as running into him would have been. Jonathan was distracted by his failures, and his small habits got on my nerves. The rituals of my life and work, once so satisfying, seemed increasingly empty. More than once I stopped in the center of the clinic, halfway across the room to fetch something I could not remember. More than once I went to the cliff edge and stood gazing out at the water, that high wind in my hair, and the abyss of air just a step away.

"This happens to everyone," Jonathan said one morning, handing me a cup of coffee, but I knew it had not happened to him, not in this way, not for these reasons. "Why don't you take a vacation, Anna? It's a bad time for me right now, anyway."

And so I traveled by boat to the mainland, where I boarded a prop plane and then one jet and then another, all the way back to Minneapolis. I had been gone five months, and I felt like a ghost, returning to a home I'd never inhabit again.

In the city, too, I felt this. Litter swirled, and sirens screamed through the streets. The papers were full of things I'd forgotten: murders and racial tension, car accidents and congestion. NPR did a story on a food shortage developing in Nigeria and the effects of drilling for oil in the frozen arctic sea, and I found myself sitting on the edge of my chair, gripping my coffee cup so hard my knuckles turned white. In this world, I was helpless. I fell asleep at all hours of the day, and dreamed of the waves, rushing one against the other on the shore. I dreamed of falling through the water, or of standing beneath it, my hand held flat against the blueness of that glass.

I had planned to stay for several weeks, but when Jonathan e-mailed that Yukiko Santiago was planning to visit the islands, I changed my mind. It took just two days to clean out our lives in Minneapolis. I didn't ask Jonathan about any of it—I just wanted it done. A few old pieces of furniture from his family I put into storage, but almost everything else I gave away. When the plane lifted off, I felt, for the first time in my life, completely free.

When I got back, patients were lined up in the waiting room. I was so busy, and so glad to be back, that for several weeks I hardly thought of Gunnar. I glimpsed him now and then, standing on the boat or walking along the beach. Sometimes he waved across the distance, and I waved back. Pragna had returned from Singapore with the baby, and I saw them too, sitting on the veranda of their chalet or strolling in the park at dawn or dusk. It was a girl, named Analia. After no one, they said, a name they'd invented, a name without the weight of history. I held her once, so small and warm, when Pragna came in for a well-baby check, and sometimes I saw her in the nursery, when Pragna stopped in after work to use the treadmill or the pool. Pragna seemed rest-less to me, as changed as I felt. One night, walking home late, I saw Gunnar pacing their porch with Analia in his arms. In the distance, behind the sound of the waves, I heard Pragna, faintly weeping.

The days slid by, one into another. The paths hummed with gardeners, painters, carpenters. Jonathan spent long days, and sometimes nights as well, on the other island, overseeing the in-stallation of new drainage and wave-forecasting systems. He took the damage, and Phil's death, personally, and worried that he might have made equally catastrophic errors in his greater re-search. Late at night, when he slipped into bed, I'd touch his shoulder and he wouldn't respond. *Jonathan,* I'd say, *are you all right?* And he'd sigh and say he was tired, too tired to talk. Often, when I woke in the morning, he was already gone.

Yukiko Santiago arrived on a brilliantly clear day. Diminutive, almost frail, with her hair swept into a severe bun, she wore a blue suit, black high heels, and glasses too large for her face. She walked among us in the park, Gunnar at her side, pausing to greet old friends. When she reached me she held my hand for a moment and said she was glad I had stayed. I was so pleased I could hardly speak. For several days I glimpsed her traveling along paths in a golf cart. I imagined her in secret meetings, or standing in that underwater room.

I did not expect to talk with her again, but on her final day she came to the mainland to observe my clinic. I was nervous during the hydroplane ride, the wind in our hair and salt spray staining her glasses. But in the clinic she was warm, pragmatic, easy to ap-proach. She prepared the plaster for a cast and held the boy's arm as I applied it. She noted vitals, took throat cultures, and talked through an interpreter to the nursing students. At the end of the day, we sat on the edge of the dock with our legs dangling. Below, the waves moved over the white sand.

"*Ganbatte*, Anna," Yukiko said. I felt myself flush with pleasure. "Very well done, indeed." She looked at me directly, taking me in. "Anna," she said, "tell me honestly: is there anything you need?"

I thought she meant the clinic and started to tell her about which supplies were running low, but she interrupted me with a wave of one hand.

"Not that," she said. "You. Are you happy here?"

"Yes," I said. "I am." But to my own surprise I started talking about Jonathan and his worries, the way he couldn't sleep at night, the growing gulf between us.

Yukiko nodded, staring out over the clear water to where the hydroplane was now visible, a dot on the horizon.

"His error cost a great deal of money," she acknowledged. "Still, I am not so concerned with the loss itself, which may open up a new path, a better path. That is always the advantage of failure. But Jonathan's reaction does concern me. He has not made much progress on the new plans. He's become too afraid to be bold."

"He loves this place," I said, dismayed, for I understood her implication, and the irony. Jonathan had brought me here; now he might have to leave.

The wind swept at Yukiko's hair. She took off her glasses and polished them on the hem of her shirt. "I know," she said. "It would be a loss if he left. But the community will survive. It is only Gunnar, finally, we could not spare. His vision is essential to us all."

I nodded, feeling helpless as I remembered his voice in the underwater room, the sound of Pragna weeping.

When I got back to the chalet Jonathan was sitting at the table, peeling a mango. We'd hardly touched in weeks, but now I put my hand on his shoulder.

"I spoke with Yukiko," I told him.

Jonathan put the knife on his plate and stood up. He walked over to the window, and when he spoke his voice was bitter. "Great," he said. "That's just terrific."

And suddenly, out of worry and frustration and a sense of impending loss, a fierce anger rose up in me. I remembered Jonathan sitting beside me in the atrium on that first day, watching me apprehend all that had been hidden. I remembered him putting the delicate shell into my hand saying, *This, too, is a test.* How disoriented I'd felt, as if the world were no longer a steady place, but something that swam and glittered and changed in every instant.

"I know how you feel," I said, trying to stay calm.

"You can't possibly," he snapped, and something in me broke loose.

"You're right," I said, preparing to be cruel and taking pleasure in it, too. "I'll never know what you're going through. After all, I passed the test."

I slammed the door and walked to the atrium, where a group was already drinking on the balcony. Gunnar was there, on his second beer, and I found myself watching him, remembering our time below the water, what Yukiko had said. There was a bright sheen of red on the water, phosphorescent algae that traced the waves. Someone suggested a night dive. I was a little drunk already, and I ran to collect the waterproof flashlights and our gear, then joined the others on the beach, where Pragna and Gunnar were arguing. Pragna was holding Analia, her voice rising above the waves.

"Gunnar," she said. "This is madness."

"It's perfectly safe," he insisted, and I remembered the play of skeletal light on his skin as we stood together in the silent dome, his fingers on my leg as he made his clumsy sutures. The others had already gone as he stepped into the waves, and when Pragna called to him again he did not stop. After a moment I followed him, swimming to the beam of light he held. The waves crashed hard against the rocks and the currents pulled at us. I touched his arm.

"It's Anna," I said.

"Anna."

"Gunnar!" Pragna's voice came to us, broken by the waves, edged with anguish. "Gunnar! Please, Gunnar. You are frightening me. Come back this instant! Gunnar! Do you hear me?"

"Ah, she is ruining it all," he said, and there was anguish in his voice, too. "She wants to leave. She wants us all to leave."

"No," I said, trying to imagine staying here without him. "No, don't, Gunnar. You can't."

Our hands brushed one another in the water and he reached for me. I couldn't seem to help myself. I ran my hand along Gunnar's leg. He did not speak, but faced me as he had on that other day, that last and first day, when we passed the regulator back and forth and each one, each time, saved the other's life.

We swam, breaking a path through the phosphorescence, past the rocks to the black sand beach, where we shed our gear, our suits. Sand gave way beneath our feet and then our bodies were on that sand, half in the sea and half on land, and with every movement the water eased from beneath my back and his. Faint light from the plankton trailed across his skin and mine, glowing where we touched each other—the line of his jaw, the curve of my shoulder, our lips. For a long time after we lay there, touching length to length, fading slowly back to darkness. I knew, of course, that the future might evolve in a thousand different ways, but in those moments I believed Gunnar would stay. I believed he would stay with me.

When he sat up, without speaking I knew what it meant. *Freedom first,* he'd said one night, long ago. His lips were on mine again; his hands touched my face, leaving coolness in their wake this time. *Anna,* he said. *You are so beautiful. And I—I am so sorry.* Then I heard the splashing, glimpsed the momentary break in the phosphorescence—he was gone.

I stayed where I was for a long time. I'd lost the flashlight. Also, my suit. Even my hands were invisible in that darkness. I felt my way to the edge of the path and began to climb, slowly, gradually, through dense foliage, feeling the air change, faintly, as the path rose. When I reached the ridge, the atrium was visible, swelling from the edge of the cliff and glowing softly.

I stopped, suddenly afraid. Loss gaped like an abyss. For I understood that I would leave this place, and that my leaving had been seeded long ago, when I handed Gunnar my regulator, when the live wire had fallen, twisting, to the lawn where fish swam, when Pragna had called out, her voice laced with anguish.

When Gunnar, yes, had turned to me.

I gazed out into the darkness of sea and sky, thinking of that hidden room, the secret locus of all yearning. A faint wind moved through my hair. I thought of Phil, conversing with the dead, and then of Gunnar, swimming. I imagined the fields of sea urchins unfolding beneath him, their perfect, hidden bones curved to hold the light, their thorns repelling, interweaving. So beautiful they were, so strange. Echinodermata: Echinoidea, with a thousand eyes, all blind.

The Secrets
of a Fire King

"JASPER," SHE WHISPERED, HER SHADOW MOONCAST AGAINST THE tent wall. Night smell of damp canvas and a dark wind off the river. My mouth watered, I imagined her lips as they rounded out my name. She whispered "Jasper!" And I told her, "I am coming." I said, "Wait," struggling into my clothes. "I am coming." I crawled right over Ogleby the snake man, who was snoring with his mouth wide open, his big feet blocking the door flap. She moved beside me, beyond the canvas wall, yet with me, just inches away. Then her shadow drew up suddenly and fell into the greater darkness. By the time I got outside, she was gone.

I stood there, searching, tents and wagons an eerie white in the moonlight. We were camped in the fairgrounds by the river. I listened past Ogleby's great snores and the nearby rustle of the animals and the tin pans of the mess wagon tapping in the breeze. I listened hard, to the susurration of the water rising up, to the air moving lightly through the trees. It was quiet but for the wind and thus, when the preacher spoke, his voice breaking the silence like a whip, I jumped a mile.

He said, "You are treading near fire, Jasper. You had better beware."

My fists clenched at his words, for I knew my young and willing girl was gone, my hours of sweet talk wasted. *"The righteous need no candle,"* he went on, mocking my night blindness, *"neither light of the sun."*

"Leave me alone," I demanded, turning toward his voice. "Do you hear?"

"Oh, I hear you," he said, his voice so soft I had to strain to listen. "But the great question is, do you hear? Jasper? Do you hear what the spirit sayeth?"

He shifted, stepping from the shadows. Moonlight streamed down his pale skin, caught on his ring, heavy gold, stones inset like a fireburst, which he waved before the sinners in each new town like a tiny piece of heaven, hard and shiny, of value beyond reckoning, nearly impossible to attain. The next day I might even see my sweet-talk girl hovering beside him, bedazzled and saved and lost to me forever. I stood poised, waiting. I would not stagger after him like a fool, but like a fool I was furious enough to fire the argument that had been smoldering between us all these years.

"You saved me once already," I reminded him. "And once was too much for any lifetime."

"Blasphemer," he said, his voice a whisper now, floating to me amid the tree sounds, the water murmurings. "You will burn in a lake of fire."

I knew he was gone. But of course, so was she. I walked to the edge of the river, leaving the cluster of tents behind me, willing her to appear, firm and supple, draped with light. The wind rustled in the leaves, tapped the hanging pans, but he had scared her good, and despite my longing she did not come again.

THEY CALLED HIM FATHER the next morning when they gathered at the river. *Father, will you save me?* He stood among them, his white robes catching the wind, bits of paper and refuse from the campground skittering through the long grass and settling in the

flowing water. I stood a safe distance away—on higher ground, in a
copse of trees—as he called the chosen forth, one by one, and had
them kneel together at the river's edge. An elderly woman in her
threadbare best, a bearded man whose wrists hung out below his
coat sleeves. A slender girl, with eyes as blue and pale as the sky at
the horizon, who was pulled from the crowd by her thick-waisted
mother. Four souls, only, yet the preacher acted as if he'd gathered
fifty, mayors and businessmen among them. He waded in, his robes
catching the current, the elderly woman's hand in his. There was
shock on her face as the cold water climbed her clothes, and she had
hardly taken her hat off when he dunked her under. She came up
gasping, dazed, her white hair pulled loose, stringy down her back.

The bearded man was next—he rose up with a whoop and
holler—and then the mother, all shades of gray, grasping both of
the preacher's hands and stepping gingerly, rock to rock. The
girl was last. The river eddied around her bluish skirts, climbed
darkly to her waist, spread like a stain up the bodice of her dress.
She was slender, but strong and supple as a sapling, and she held
her hands high, open palmed, refusing help as she waded in waist
deep. She was reluctant, that was clear, and when the preacher
reached for her she jerked away from him so hard she slipped.
Slowly then, like a leaf falling, she disappeared beneath the water. Right away the preacher dove. His hands flashed and he
came up gasping twice, the river streaming from his hair, his
robes. The world hung suspended, silent, as the minutes passed,
and the crowd rose to its feet, stirring and straining like some
great animal, certain that the girl was lost. But when the preacher
rose up a final time he had a skirt snagged in his fingers. The girl
was unconscious, maybe dead, her white arms limp against his
back as they rose out of the water.

The crowd gathered close as the preacher began thumping
on her back. Her face was pale and streaked with dirt, her thick
hair wet and tangled. I watched from the hillside, feeling the
blows on my own flesh. He'd pulled me from a different river,
years before, under other circumstances, but then, like now, he'd
pounded on my back until I'd coughed up enough muddy water
to fill a cistern.

"Praise God," he said that day, sitting back on his heels. "Young man, you are a miracle incarnate, the answer to a prayer."

I opened my eyes, taking in the sudden brilliance of the sky, and laughed.

"A lot you know," I told him. I pushed myself up and wrapped my arms around my knees, for it was late spring and cold. I was just fourteen, run away from the mission home two weeks before. I'd had my fill of preachers there, and I hadn't eaten in ten days. Nothing in my situation was funny, not my hunger, not my past, not the preacher sitting by my feet, making calculations, yet I kept on laughing, digging my fingers into my legs. After a while the preacher seemed to figure something out, for he gave up on praying and pulled two hard biscuits from his pack. I stopped laughing and sat up straight, my mouth already watering with desire.

"Hungry?" he asked.

I nodded, but he merely turned the biscuits over in his hand.

"You've got to earn it first," he said.

I hardly heard him as he talked, telling me about the farm down the road, with five fat chickens and only the farmwife home. He'd go to the front door and work to save the wife, while I went round back and brought a chicken to salvation. I'd get the biscuits for myself, and we'd split the chicken, fifty-fifty.

"Well," he said. "You willing?"

I'd never stolen anything before, but I didn't hesitate, and a few hours later the preacher watched me suck the meat off every bone, firelight gleaming on his bald head. He was like no preacher I had known before, and he took me on, offered me instruction in his craft. For almost three months I studied with him, learning plenty. How to get an old woman to sign over all her worldly goods. How to speak in tongues, raising people to a fever pitch, and how to slip their wallets from their pockets as they shouted praises. How to get the young girls so heated with the word that they would step into his tent without a second thought.

Yet though I slept in his tent and sat through his services and knelt dutifully beside him every night, I was a sullen disciple, an unwilling miracle, my attention wandering all the while. Of all the acts in that traveling show—the snake man, the acrobats, the sword swallower, the luminous dancers—the Fire King was the one who held me fast. In his flames I saw the beauty, the power mingled with the danger. He could pour molten lead into his mouth, then spit out solid metal nuggets. He ate burning coals with a fork, as if they were a pile of new potatoes. I had hung around to see if he was scarred in secret places, and I had pestered him so much, and so insistently, that when I showed up at his door one night with everything I owned, he simply waved a weary arm and took me on as an apprentice. He was a skilled old man, but he was a drunkard too, and although he never missed a show, there came a day when he inhaled accidently while chewing on a wad of burning cotton, and seared his lungs, and died.

I had his secrets by then, his red silk robes, and on the day we buried him I took his place. I was awkward at first, suffering my share of burns and failures, but from the beginning I was a natural with the rural crowds. I knew their lives so well, the dust rising off their endless fields, the flat somber light that filled their homes and churches. I knew what they came seeking, and I spoke to them. I was the Fire King, and they were mesmerized by the colors I gave off, by the way I moved and flickered. I swallowed fire, I became fire, and they could not stay away.

Very soon I was drawing crowds even larger than the preacher's. Tangible flames were more compelling than any promise of salvation. The preacher had never forgiven my abrupt departure, which he saw as a betrayal, and gradually a war grew up between us, his miracles escalating in response to my success.

Like this drowned girl, for instance. It would be too much to say that the preacher had deliberately made her fall. Yet surely he had seen her reticence, her desire to keep her distance. And just as surely he had reached out, causing her to start, to slip beneath the water. She was pale, one cheek on the muddy grass, her arms outflung, the preacher still pounding on her back. If he saved her he would pack his shows all week, get the county in a fever, and the girl would be so grateful she'd give him anything he wanted.

And, not much to my surprise, he did. The girl coughed

once, then several times, and a sigh went up from the crowd around her. The preacher waved them back, then helped the girl sit up. She looked a little stunned as he placed his hands firmly on her head, proclaimed her saved. I heard the murmur this aroused, and despite myself I was filled with a sharp admiration for the preacher's cunning. He looked up then, catching my eye across the distance, and smiled. I smiled right back, accepting his implicit challenge. For he might woo the crowds his way with water, but I would lure them back again with fire.

AFTER EVERY SHOW the young boys lingered, too poor to buy anything, too curious to leave. They pulled close together when they saw me coming, shy and skittish, looking anywhere that I was not, and that afternoon only one boy was brave enough to step forward as I passed. His pants were too short on him and his feet were bare, his young arms muscular with work. Everything was ordinary except his eyes, which were blue, like the color of the sky where it seeps toward the horizon and grows pale.

"Mister," he said straightaway. "Mister, we would like to know how you did that trick. We would like to look into your mouth and see if you are burnt."

"Is that so?" I said. There was something in his innocence, his persistence, that made me think of the life I'd had before my parents died, before I was sent to the mission home, before I ran away.

"They believe you are burnt," he went on, and now the other boys were braver, they were looking at me, too.

"And you?" I asked.

"I think it was magic," he said, and I was struck all the harder by his innocence, by the way he hungered for the mystery and was not afraid to say so. He looked me in the eye and I felt uneasy, for his face was so familiar, like one I had known well in a dream.

"Well," I said. "Watch then. Watch closely, and you will see." I reached into a pocket and procured a single coal.

"Smell," I insisted, waving it around. "It has been soaked in kerosene." And indeed the odor cut sharply through this group of boys, making them wrinkle up their noses. "Observe," I added, lighting a match and setting the coal on fire.

They gasped, for the coal burned brightly on my bare hand, yet my flesh was clean, untouched by fire. I watched with satisfaction at the looks of fear and wonder on their faces. Not even the preacher on his best days could fill them with a mystery like this. Subdued, they stepped away. Awestruck, they drifted off. All except the bold one.

"I told them," he said, fierce and triumphant. "I knew it was magic." He looked up at me and added, "I bet them also that I would get a job from you."

His request was a familiar one, and I braced myself to send him home, but before I could speak a voice called "Eli!" and the boy glanced back at a slender girl standing at the edge of the tent. Behind her the river glimmered through the trees. I remembered how she'd looked the day before, the way the current had caught and held her, the fabric of her dress clinging to her long legs as the preacher pulled her from the water.

"Eli," she repeated, low and clear. "You're late."

"Who is that?" I asked, still staring.

"Only Jubilee," he answered. "My sister. Will you hire me?"

She waited, looking straight at me just as her brother had, except that her gaze, while forthright and faintly curious, was edged not with wonder, but rather with contempt. Already the preacher had dazzled her to a state of righteous blindness. I had a sudden, desperate urge, a deep desire that was mixed with anger, to light another coal and press it in between her palm and mine, to sear her flesh while mine stayed cool, to burn through her resistance with my own.

"Mister," Eli said. "Will you hire me?"

I did not answer right away, considering. "Come inside," I said at last, gesturing to the row of smaller tents that functioned as our dressing rooms. "Bring your sister, too."

Behind me I heard their voices, arguing softly. Then Eli followed me inside. He paused in the dim light, blinking, captivated by his own image looking back at him from a full-length mirror set in a gilded, freestanding frame. Jubilee did not enter, but lingered in the doorway, arms folded. The air was hot, rich with the scent of warm canvas, and in the far distance I could hear the crescendo of organ music that closed each show.

"Come in," I invited, but she looked up coolly, then turned her eyes away. "Or stay out there," I added, shrugging. "It's all the same to me."

Eli was still staring at his image in the mirror.

"So you want to work for me," I began, speaking loudly enough for Jubilee to hear. "Young man, just what is it you can do? Can you swallow swords? Can you walk on coals? What talents would you bring along?"

Eli turned reluctantly away from his reflection, shifting his weight, jarring the mirror, sending motes of light across the canvas. "I don't have any talents," he said. "But I work hard. I learn fast."

"A quick study, are you then?" I said. I heard a rustling just outside. "But every young man believes himself to be so. Tell me, what makes you sure it's true of you?"

From the corner of my eye I saw her stepping through the door flap, drawn in by the mirror, by the wandering motes of light.

"What's that?" she asked, watching herself inside the glass.

"That? Why, it's a mirror," I told her.

She shook her head. "It can't be," she whispered. "Mirrors are small things. You hold them in one hand."

I was standing just behind her now, my red cape a glowing backdrop to her cool gray dress, to the whiteness of her skin. She wore no perfume, and it was the first time I had been up close to smell her pure and salty smell. I reached out slowly and guided her hand to adjust the frame, the narrow bones of her wrist like supple hinges beneath my fingers. I felt the heat of her along my arm. She tilted her head, examining the smooth curve of her jaw, the blond wave of hair, her shell-like ear. She stared and stared into the looking glass, and in that moment I knew she was like any other girl. Each one held a secret wish, and once I understood it, they were mine.

"You are beautiful," I told her softly, my breath against her ear.

But I'd gone too far, too fast, and she stepped away.

"I saw you baptized," I told her then, thinking of her legs beneath the cloth.

"So you saw me saved," she answered, primly.

"I've seen that many times," I said. "It never means too much."

We stared at one another. The air was hot and still, and full of her. The preacher had told her that she was chosen above others, chosen to be saved, and now I watched her struggle with the idea that I might not think her special after all. It gave me power over her, a hold the preacher could not match, but to my own astonishment I gave that power back.

"I will find you a looking glass," I said.

"I do not want a looking glass," she countered, flushing, yet glancing at the mirror with an expression full of longing. "Eli," she went on, stepping through the tent flap even as she spoke. "Eli, let's go now."

I had forgotten Eli until that moment. He was kneeling by my trunk, studying the cup I used to drink the boiling oil. It had a false bottom, a partition down the middle, so that oil poured in on one side would not come out the other. Eli was perplexed, but in the next instant I saw him understand, his face illuminated with a pleasure of discovery that just as quickly gave way to disappointment.

"I thought it was magic," he said, his voice soft. But he was a quick study after all, for he pushed aside his feelings and spoke up. "Now you'll have to hire me," he said, "so I won't tell."

I might have laughed then, and sent him on his way. As cruel as it might have seemed to him, it would have been a kindness. But I did not think of Eli, his dreams and hopes. Instead, I thought of Jubilee, her clean sweet smell, her presence in my tent. I thought of the way she'd looked the day before, when the preacher pulled her from the water.

"All right," I said, pausing long enough to let him think he'd won. "A week of work. But only if you tell me where to find Jubilee tomorrow."

He wavered, weighing everything, his desires and mine, his sister's honor. I waited, remembering the first chicken I had stolen, how it pecked my hands until they bled. My weakness had been hunger, whereas for Eli it was the darker mystery of fire. This was enough, however. In the end, he told me.

I EAT FIRE and am not scarred, but Jubilee had seared through my indifference, had settled in my flesh like ash. Everywhere I went, I smelled that sweet saltiness of hers. Every time the wind stirred, I felt the heat of her arm pressing mine.

I went to town and got a real looking glass, the biggest I could find. It was the size of me, six feet high exactly, thick, with beveled edges. "Vanity!" the preacher snorted when I carted it down the dirt path to my tent, and others in the show snickered too.

The next day, early, I loaded the mirror into a cart I had borrowed and drove to the place Eli had described. It was a path through a copse of trees, and Jubilee would travel here on her way to meet the preacher. I set the mirror up, reflecting leaves and bark and flickering light, and then I settled myself into the bushes, where I waited, still as a watchful fox, for Jubilee to come.

Half an hour later I heard her footsteps, and then she emerged, walking so quickly, so intently, that for a moment I feared that she would walk right past. However, some swift movement or flash of light caught her eye, and she stopped, staring at her image for a long moment before she turned and searched the bushes.

"Hello?" she called, and then again, more loudly.

I did not answer. Nothing but the distant sound of water, the rustling of leaves, filled her listening. She turned back to her reflection, placing both hands lightly to her cheeks. Then her hands fell, her fingers tracing lightly down her neck, lingering on her throat. I thought of the soft skin there and did not speak. And when those same fingers passed along the row of buttons, one by one, when they slid the sleeves off, revealing the narrow straps of her camisole, her bare and silky shoulders, I held my breath and watched her. She put her hands lightly on her hips and turned her head, studying her reflection. Slipping, she was slipping from the preacher now, even as she stood motionless beneath these trees.

"Jubilee," I whispered, standing up.

She heard me and turned in my direction, but she did not

leave. Her lips parted in surprise and her hands flew to her shoulders, but she stood still, paralyzed by surprise and fear, and also something stronger, which she could not name. I recognized it though, and I was motion to her stillness, catching her by the waist, slipping my fingers beneath the soft cotton of the camisole, pulling her with me into the swift, persistent, current of desire. She let me kiss her once, her lips soft, her expression when I pulled away as surprised and curious—as utterly newborn—as I'd ever seen anybody look. Her hands had fallen to her sides at first, but now she raised them to my shoulders, stood up on her toes with her eyes wide open, and kissed me back.

What I thought of with her lips on mine was fire, the way flames hold the power to both horrify and compel. Any conflagration draws a crowd. People gather, captivated by the beauty of the flames, by their sheer destructive power. So it was with Jubilee. I could feel both her reticence and her yearning. In my triumph then I kissed her hard, knowing that danger, like a shadow, only makes the flames seem brighter.

But I had not counted on Eli. She saw him first and grew stiff in my embrace, pulled away, was gone an instant later. Facing the mirror I saw him too, the anger and envy on his face reflected in the glass. He threw a stone then, shattering his image, raining broken glass onto the earth, and ran.

You must fight fire with fire, and only fire. This is something I understood quite well, but with my thoughts on Jubilee I missed the signs, the small initial flares of trouble. The preacher's sudden cordialness when I returned, his unusually large crowd, the conspicuous absence of Eli—I noted these events, yet paid them scant attention.

That very afternoon, however, my audience had shrunk, and the people who did attend the show soon broke up my act with boos and hisses. Some of the men had procured a healing elixir from the miracle cure demonstration, and now they stumbled through the meager crowd, shouting insults, demanding to look inside my drinking cup. I soon gathered that the preacher had denounced me during the morning revival, giving a detailed de-

scription of my drinking cup. I glanced desperately backstage for
Eli, who could have snuck me the real tin cup in a box of cotton
batting, but even as I searched I understood he'd been the one to
give away my secret.

"Gentlemen," I called out several times, until the jeering subsided somewhat. "Gentlemen, you are disturbing the good men
and women who have paid to see this show. Now, I am a man of
honor, and I assure you that of course you may—no, you *will*—
see this cup." I placed it on the table in front of me with a clang.
"You have my promise. Here it sits, and you will examine it once
the show has finished. In the meantime you may watch it with
your own eyes, as I perform the greatest feat of this or any show.
Ladies and gentlemen! Today you will see a rare sight, a feat so
dangerous that I do not do it every show, or even every fourth
show or every tenth show. In fact, ladies and gentlemen, I do this
feat only once every three years.

"Today, I will do it for you.

"Today, I will become a human volcano, before your very eyes."

This hushed them, for a moment anyway. I pulled out the cotton batting and piled it on the table, careful that some of it obscured the tin cup from view. Then I started stuffing cotton in my
mouth. The crowd laughed, and as I stuffed in more, then more,
they became uproarious. Finally, when my mouth was full to
bursting, I took a coal in my bare hand and lit it. Smoke strung my
eyes and made the rows of faces melt and waver. The coal flared
brightly, then turned to an ember, all while I held it steadily on the
palm of my hand. I waved my free arm to show I was ready. Then
I took a deep breath, put that live coal to the bale of cotton in my
mouth, and exhaled a stream of fire.

This is a wonderful trick, a splendid effect. It is dangerous,
too, the trick that killed my mentor. Fire flows forth like a hori-
zontal column, a fallen pillar, and a single inward breath proves
fatal. I kept it going as long as I could, the flames dancing a full
foot in front of my face. As I had hoped, they were so awestruck
by this display that when I stepped offstage between my first and
second bows, they did not think to question my brief moment
from their sight. They left, examining the real tin cup, nodding

soberly, apologizing for their earlier suspicions. I stood aloof, relief flooding through me like the cool, clean air.

THE AFTERNOON was pretty, one of those blue midwestern days when the sky is so clear and so large that it nearly hurts to look at it. You feel your own insignificance, is what I mean. We had a few more hours before the final show, and I was mixing up a batch of Storaxine, the salve I used to keep from getting burned. I'd rub it all over my mouth and hands before a show, gargle some vinegar to set it, and I was ready, impervious to fire.

The formula was secret, naturally, but I did sell Storaxine on a limited basis for treating scalds and burns. After becoming a human volcano my sales were up, my supply just about depleted. While I waited for the water to boil I carved up Ivory soap and tossed it in. Now and then I paused to skim some fallen leaves off the top of my preparation, which was starting to foam, the water going opaque as the soap dissolved. I tossed in sugar, cup by cup, aware all the time that there was someone standing in the foliage on the far side of the creek. I waited some, and finally I said, "Eli, you left me in the lurch yesterday, deserted a friend when he truly needed your help. Now what do you have to say for yourself about it?"

The bushes rustled, and after a minute he came out, walking carefully along the river's edge, placing his bare feet just so on the rocks. I caught his eyes, their fading blue, and thought of Jubilee.

"Well?" I said once he stood beside me.

"I thought they were going to run you out of town."

"Well, they might have, Eli, except that I was so quick thinking." I poured the liquid storax into the pot and stirred.

Eli squatted down on a stump nearby. He picked up a sharp stick and started drawing patterns in the soft earth. He wouldn't look at me.

"Do you love her, then?" he asked at last.

The question took me by surprise. Love. What could I say to this boy? That most of the time love boiled down to another word for loss, or for getting what you wanted? I wanted Jubilee to meet me in my dressing room, to shed her camisoles like leaves. I wanted to touch that tender skin of hers, watch her eyes go from innocence to knowing. I'd have done it, too, in the trees beside the mirror, if Eli hadn't followed me, then gone running to the preacher. I thought of the angry crowd the day before, of my own fear, rising like a burn in the back of my throat.

"Eli," I said. "You still interested in being an assistant of mine?"

"You mean it?" he asked, looking up at me at last.

"Well, if you're good enough," I said. "Then yes. We'll start with Brimstone on the Palm," I went on. "When you get good at that, you can graduate up to Brimstone on the Tongue. That's the real crowd pleaser. Here's how it's done, Eli. You watch close."

I took three small round pieces of sulfur, looking an angry yellow against the white saucer, doused them with kerosene, and set them on fire. Then I tipped them into my right palm, which was slathered with Storaxine already. I held those burning bits of rock for nearly a minute, and all the time Eli watched me, wonder and apprehension mingled on his face.

"Okay," I said, slipping the coals back into the saucer. "Your turn."

He looked scared, but nonetheless he poured the burning brimstones into his hand. *Good,* I thought, seeing the pain hit his face, *learn a lesson.* I expected him to drop the coals right away, but though his hand shook and sweat ran down his cheeks, he cupped his fingers and held on to those bits of burning rock as if they were the most precious thing he owned.

"Drop them!" I said. "Eli! It's a mistake!"

But he did not. I finally had to grab his wrist and jar the brimstones out, thrusting his hand into the cold water of the river. His palm was raw and red, blisters already rising on his skin. I applied Storaxine and bound his burns with clean cloths from my bag, studying his hands as I worked. For all their callouses, their nicks and scratches, Eli's hands were smaller than my own, not yet finished with their growing.

"I tried," he said after a while, his voice still tight with pain. "I wasn't good enough."

"Eli," I said. "You did just fine. The fault was mine. I tricked you."

He got quiet then, and I felt myself grow smaller, reduced from the Fire King to the mean mortal that I was. I saw that even angry, even disillusioned, Eli had believed in me till now.

"Why?" he asked.

"To teach you a lesson," I said.

Now his eyes were a deep blue, steady on mine, like the edge of a flame. "Tell me how you did it, then."

"I do not owe you anything," I said. But his hand seemed small beneath the bandage, and his fingernails were dirty. A boy's hand, this was. I thought of Jubilee, her stillness, her sudden kiss, and wondered what she'd be doing now, just how she'd feel, if Eli hadn't chased her off. I thought of her soft skin, the way her hands had rested on my shoulders, and remorse twisted through my heart like a dark curl of smoke. I started talking. I lined up the ingredients for Storaxine and explained the process. I demonstrated Brimstone on the Palm, and Brimstone on the Tongue. I gave away the cherished secrets of a Fire King.

"You'll travel with me now," I said, surprised at the relief I felt, unburdened of my secrets. "You'll work for me, as long as you like."

But Eli didn't thank me, or even speak. He just stood up and walked away, leaving me standing in the silence, in a shaft of light, the vat of Storaxine steaming at my back.

It's EASY TO SAY, in retrospect, that I should have known. That Eli with his envy and desires was not a force to trust. But though I was shaken by the incident, though I lingered over the bottling of my Storaxine until just before the final show, I did not foresee the consequences. The night was much as usual, clear and windy, alive with lights and music, the bright chatter of hawkers, the murmurs of the crowd. Phillipa, luminous in her butterfly costume, was coming from her dressing room just as I drew near. When I stepped aside to let her pass, she raised her painted eyebrows high.

"Somebody," she said, "thinks you really *are* the Fire King." Then she reached into her bodice and handed me a folded note.

Wait for me, it said. *Tonight. I am coming to your show. And after. I am coming. Jubilee.*

The handwriting was loopy, childish. I went into my dressing room and sat down, imagining her spelling the words out carefully, tearing away the strips of paper that held her small mistakes. I imagined her getting dressed, the clean petticoats and camisoles and undergarments, soft cotton brushing every surface of her skin. I had ruined such girls before and never cared. I had filled them full of fire and left them longing, I'd been gone before light flared on the horizon, and I had not looked back, not once. No reason, none at all, why Jubilee was different. A country girl with pretty eyes, who would fall all the harder because she thought she had been saved. I could take her anywhere and she would have me. In my dressing room, in the copse of trees, waist high in the river. That preacher was nothing to her now. But instead of feeling satisfied, I heard young Eli asking, *Do you love her?* And I thought of her sweet smell, the softness of her skin, and wondered.

Outside, the opening theme song rose above the voices of the hawkers and the crowds, and I knew that Ogleby was in the center of the tent, the audience agape as the python and the boa constrictor wound themselves around him. My own act would not start for another hour, and on an impulse I made my way inside the tent, slipping beneath the canvas near the back. I climbed high into the bleachers and stood on the uppermost seat, scanning the crowd for a glimpse of Jubilee.

I found her easily. She was sitting directly across the ring, on the second bleacher from the top, wearing the blue dress she'd been saved in and a matching hat, her feet resting on a small valise. Everything she owned was in that case, I knew. It made my heart constrict, thinking of her skin, so soft, so hidden, thinking of Eli's burns, the way his eyes had changed when he learned that I had tricked him. Like the rest of the crowd, Jubilee was staring down at Ogleby, but unlike them, she wasn't really watching. Her expression was serious, her thoughts turned inward, preoccupied with the magnitude of what she was about to do. I reached into my pocket, fingering her note.

Ogleby finished, took his bows, and I sat down. Next would be Phillipa and the other butterflies, the sequence of the acts so familiar that I paid no attention. My thoughts were on Jubilee, the scent of warm canvas reminding me of her sweet smell, of her wrists beneath my fingers as I helped her with the mirror.

Yet something was amiss. The music that began was not for the butterflies, after all, but for me. For the Fire King. I felt a surge of confusion, because these notes meant one thing and one thing only: that I should be standing ready in my cape, heart thrilling, curtain rising, about to make my entrance. I felt a nightmare panic as a flaming hoop, *my* hoop, descended from the ceiling.

The curtain lifted then, slowly it seemed, and a new Fire King bounded over the sawdust and leaped through the flaming hoop, my silk robes nearly catching fire, billowing and pooling at his ankles as he landed. He bowed, and the crowd laughed, thinking he was a parody. I knew better; I saw the determination on his face. His hand was still bandaged, making him clumsy, but nonetheless Eli managed to light the coals, to pick up a fork and put the burning embers in his mouth. His hands were trembling and some of the coals slipped off into the ring. Sawdust flared, and Eli interrupted his act to stomp out the little flames. The audience laughed again. Except for Jubilee, who was leaning forward with a frown of concentration.

Normally, people do not laugh at a Fire King. They gasp, they hold their breath, they sigh in relief, but they do not laugh. Thus, as I pushed my way downward, each roar of those around me let me know things were progressing badly, even when I could not see him. I was furious at Eli, at his audacity, his mockery, but more than that, I was afraid. I had seen the bottles of kerosene lined up carelessly beneath the table. I knew better than anyone how quickly sawdust could ignite, how fast a tent like this could disappear in flames.

The crowd around me laughed again. People jostled, standing on their toes. And then softly at first, but then more forcefully, I felt a pressure, as if everyone around me had taken a deep breath at once. I was standing on the ground now and could not see the ring for the press of people, but I felt the panic rising, felt the pressure as people turned to flee. The music was still playing. I pushed hard and broke through into the center ring. The sawdust on the floor had all caught fire, was shimmering in the heat like a field of grass. Eli was standing on the far side of the flames, trying to stamp them down with his feet, my silk cape discarded, already curling at the edges, the smell of burning silk pungent in the air.

Fire gone wild is like a seeking hand, grasping at the air in search of something dry. These flames moved quickly, pulling themselves up the canvas walls, crackling and hissing, catching on the dry kindling of the bleachers. Waves of heat rose off the flames, shimmering, and the thick black edges of the smoke drifted high, dissipating into hazy gray. I searched for Jubilee, but I could not see her. Within a few moments there was fire on every side, and the light grew eerie, flickering and bright, the air so hot my lungs went dry with every little panting breath I took. People swirled around me in the smoke, faces surfaced, disappeared, and the tent was filled with a determined silence as people pushed and struggled for an exit. I watched the flames climb high, leap and flare, turning green-edged as they consumed the canvas, bluer as they fed on wood.

Jubilee. Here to meet me. I wondered if the flames frightened or compelled her now, if she'd have the courage to push past them to safety, or if they'd hold her still and mesmerized, as I had done. I pushed against a surge of the crowd to try to find her, but I got knocked off my feet, trampled and kicked until I was pushed into a narrow stream of fire. My palms hit the flames and pain shot up my arms. I smelled the sickening scent of burning flesh. Remembering my mentor's words, I curled myself into a ball and rolled. In this way I escaped the flames, reaching the sawdust on the perimeter, which had already burned to ash. I thought of Eli as I started crawling, my hands burning on the still-hot earth, and like him I kept going despite the pain. Behind me, through veils of fire, I saw the surging shadows of the crowd, but I did not stop, not until I felt the air change suddenly, not until the grass grew damp and cold beneath my hands, not until I was a dozen yards from danger.

The tent burned for nearly two more hours, eating through the edges first, then flaring up, fluttering like a burning scarf, before it settled to the ground. A great crowd had gathered to watch this happen, and after a while I stood and joined them, my own hands throbbing as I watched them staring at the flames. There was a beauty to this fire, to all fire, a strange pleasure to be taken in danger and destruction. I was a Fire King and this pleasure was the source of all my power, but on that night I lost forever my taste for conflagration.

Seventy-nine people perished, and Jubilee's name was listed among the dead. Eli had escaped, I heard, though no one could find him. All that night, as my hands blistered and swelled, awash in waves of heat, I thought of her, of Eli, and the life that I had lost. Ended now, and as the preacher had foretold: in fire.

THE FLAMES ARE IRRESISTIBLE to those who see them, and if I found my destiny in conflagration, then it was, finally, Eli's fate to succumb to the preacher's missionary fever. The disaster he called forth must have shaped him absolutely, for many years later he came to the town where I was living, traveling with his own revival tent and an entourage of devotees. His face jumped out at me from a poster hung up on the pole outside my shop. I was by then a blacksmith, a trade where skill with fire is useful and delicate sensation in the hands is not essential. I feel things, certainly, their dull outlines, their density and weight. But I could not tell a feather from a razor on my palm, and even after all these years the slightest heat—a shaft of sun, the swell of living flesh—will radiate a deep aching in my hands.

The people of this town conjecture. I dropped hints, early on, and now they attribute my reticence, my strange scars, to my having fallen from a train on which I was a fireman. No doubt many of them believe that I was, and am, a drunk. No matter. They leave me alone. My life is simple, on the surface good, but for these last many years I have lived it around the image of Jubilee, sitting high up in the bleachers, her feet balanced on her old valise.

I went to the revival, though I had not set foot at a religious service since I traveled with the preacher. I heard the whispers, felt the looks of surprise as I walked into that tent, the smell of hot canvas and too many sweating bodies raising the memories of my dead life. Two women got onstage and swore they had been crippled once, and healed by Father Eli. A ringer in the audience began to speak in tongues. I saw the crowd swaying, saw how deeply they wanted to believe. By the time Eli came onstage he had them hooked and thrashing, desperate to rise up and let the air of their ordinary lives burn them clean.

He was older, of course, heavier, and he had grown some too. His voice had changed as well, thickened and roughened, as if the smoke he must have inhaled that night had seared his vocal chords. But he talked better than the preacher ever had, better than I had myself, filling the revival tent with a fervent cadence. He'd grown rich with the things of this world; his clothes were elegant, beautifully cut. I kept one hand securely on my wallet, but the other wandered to my chest, where the heat of my own flesh radiated an aching in my smooth palm. I thought of Jubilee, her skin warm beneath this same hand as we stood together by the mirror. Eli stood up on the stage, his face so like hers, his eyes so like the blue of a fading sky, that my throat went dry with memory, with desire.

Eli talked on. He got the crowd around me in a fervor. When he spoke of paradise, I held my peace. When he got going on sin and then redemption, it got a little harder. But when he started quoting Revelations, I stood up. I'd heard it all so many times, the beast, the burning lakes of fire. I heard his voice, and the voice of the preacher before him, and I could contain myself no longer.

"Eli," I called out, stepping into the aisle. "Eli, speak louder now, for surely you know everything there is to know about the brimstone and the fire."

He stopped then and looked straight at me. His hands were raised in benediction and I saw the scars I had given him. Slowly, his arms fell. A silence had descended on the audience. I felt the pressure of their eyes. And I waited, just as they did, to see what Eli would do next.

To my surprise, he merely smiled. And as he did so his eyes left mine and moved to the edge of the stage, where a little group of his followers—the gospel singers, the healed—stood gathered. She was in the midst of them, still unaware of the commotion I had caused, laughing up at a tall, bearded man who, just moments earlier, had claimed his sight had been restored. The child on her hip was patting her face, and she reached without looking to catch the little hand, press it with a kiss.

When the wave of silence finally reached her, she looked first to Eli, puzzled, and then, at last, to me.

"Jubilee," I said, but my throat constricted and it came out in a whisper.

She stared at me. I waited for some sign of recognition. There were murmurs in the crowd by now, but I did not shift my gaze, nor did Eli speak. All these years, the memory of Jubilee had lingered in the flesh of my hands, emblematic, finally, of everything I had squandered once, then lost. *Do you love her?* Eli had asked, and I had burned his hands for my reply.

When she finally moved she did so swiftly, handing her child to the bearded man. She was gone before I could even think to follow. They closed ranks as she went, filling the space she had vacated, and then the crowd shifted and blocked my way as Eli resumed speaking. I knew that no matter how long or hard I searched, I could never reach her now. Still, I went after her. I left the tent and ran until pain stitched my side and I could run no longer, until I fell into the tall grass at the side of the road. Jubilee. I lay panting, breathing dust and the bitter scent of wormwood, and my two hands burned deeply with the lack of her. *As it was,* I thought, staring at the sky, vast and blue and infinitely empty. *As it is. As it ever shall be.*

Thirst

THE BEACH IS AS WHITE AND SMOOTH AS THE CURVE OF A moon. I sit with an empty glass cradled in my hands, watching the waves slide their thin tongues along the shore. Late afternoon light escapes beneath low clouds, shooting through the surface of the water, making the waves glow for an instant before they lick the land and then grow dark, seething through the pale, gritty sand and disappearing.

My three daughters play just at that point of convergence, squatting where the sea and land meet, digging. When the waves recede, they write their names in the wet sand with sharp sticks, then stand and run, chasing each other, laughing, silhouettes against the sun. They grow serious again quite suddenly and concentrate once more on the tower they've been building. It's an intricate and fragile edifice rising out of the sand, taller than the youngest. My daughters, all slender limbs and bright cheeks and flashing hair, decorate their creation with flowers and shells.

They shape fanciful turrets and bridges. They are far away, but I hear their laughter, their voices calling softly, each to each.

When the boy comes, they are too absorbed to notice him at first, and when he beckons to my oldest, whose schoolmate he is, she looks up, startled. I imagine that she flushes, seeing him there, for she is at that age when even the most commonplace boys take on a sense of mystery. And this boy is not ordinary. He is wild and he has strange and fanciful perceptions. He lives nearby, and they have played together from the time they were very small. He has always been there, as constant as the sea and sun and sand, but now that he has taken on these new qualities he seems suddenly elusive to her. I have watched her watching him, reacting as she does this very minute, holding herself aloof, brushing sand from her palms and tossing her hair, which catches the light like new wheat, green and gold. He has some discovery he wants her to see; he calls her to come with him. Her sisters protest and she looks at them, wanting to stay, wanting as much to leave.

"I'll be right back," she promises. "I'll just be gone a moment."

She runs off, then, leaving them behind, and follows the boy to where a jellyfish is beached, thick and translucent. For a moment she is in two places at once, glancing back at her sisters and the magnificent tower, then turning her attention to the boy with his discovery. But when she leans over to study the jellyfish more closely, when she tilts her head and pokes at it, gingerly, with the edge of a shell, a wave from the turning tide lifts from the others a hundred yards out and begins to travel, gaining size and speed. It hits the shore with force, and it spreads far beyond the lovely castle, undermining its foundation. My smaller daughters cry out as the foam rushes around bridges, fills their moats, floods the first story. The eldest turns back in time to see the castle crumbling, and then it's her own cry on the air, above the waves. She's running back, but already their edifice—all imagination, sun, and air—has crumpled into dust.

Disappointment crests in her face. They all sigh and kick at the ruins. After a few minutes, my oldest glances down the beach to the boy by the jellyfish, but he, too, has disappeared.

My glass is empty. So is the pitcher, and the maid is nowhere in sight. But who can blame her? No one would expect a woman to drink so much so quickly. Even to me this thirst seems excessive and somehow shameful, a secret I should keep. For I have been drinking water all week, all month, all night, and all day, and still this thirst of mine seems only to grow. I wake in the night with my lips cracked and parched, my tongue rough and dry on the roof of my mouth.

The pitcher, blown glass, swings heavy in my hand. At the door I pause. My two younger daughters are rebuilding the castle, but the oldest stands alone at the edge of the sea, her arms folded, studying the waves that rush across her feet. All I can see on her face is yearning. Still, given my own condition, I must wonder if this is what is really happening, or only how it appears to me from my own particular vantage point of thirst.

My husband sees things differently, I know. He is arriving even now, a hand waving in the sun-washed air and a voice cascading, and then his feet in their dark leather shoes, polished to a shine, descending the staircase to the beach. A purposeful man, my husband, an important one. Ask him what he sees below and he would give a calm and straightforward answer: three girls, sand gleaming whitely against their tan and healthy skin, playing happily on the beach. And the boy would be just another playmate, a cheerful friend, the jellyfish a scientific study, the sandcastle built precisely so it might be destroyed, the loss inherent in its construction essential to the delight in its creation.

Yes, my husband is pragmatic, a man practiced at calm assessment, at managing disasters, at cutting losses. He's a prince, my husband, born to take the larger view, to seek the greatest good. When we came here, he anticipated how much I would miss the life that I had left, and he did what he could to assuage longings I had not yet even begun to feel. Two walls of every room he fitted with aquariums, floor to ceiling, and these he filled with the wavering plants I had loved so as a girl, the sea fronds and spiky urchins on a sandy floor, great turtles swimming high, revealing the soft pale undersides of their bellies. He did this at some sacrifice, for he loves the sunshine, and as a consequence of his great kindness we live in a watery light, the colors both subdued and made more intense by the darkness of the house. I was grateful to him; I am. For as the years passed and I grew more lonely, these tanks became my solace. I added fish, one by one, to cheer myself up. I collected them, such an array of dazzling shapes and colors, their scales so vivid, their puzzled and skittish yellow eyes.

On my way back to the veranda, I pause before the two glass walls, watching the flicker of tails, the sidelong, uncertain glances of these fish. Yes, pleasure—water in a pitcher and glass, smooth and heavy in my hands, and everything connected in a chain. This pitcher, once sand itself, was fired and so transformed. These fish, too, have had their lives completely altered. They are puzzled and wary, and they suspect me even now. One sudden movement and they will dart away, seeking refuge in the shadows. But I move slowly, and when I leave it's a shaft of sunlight that startles them and makes them scatter, bumping the glass walls in their haste to get away.

On the raw beach, my husband has taken off his shoes and socks and rolled his trousers to the knees in order to help with the castle. He squats before it, his handsome toes digging into the cool, wet sand. He approves of this, the purposeful building, the earth clinging to our daughters' hands. He sits back on his heels, considering, and makes suggestions for a larger, deeper moat, a drawbridge.

They set to work. Even the oldest has joined in, pushing her long, wet hair behind one ear. I pour one glass of water and then another, watching my husband, so intent and hardworking, so earnest and industrious, wielding authority and dispensing his ideas with a steady, judicious hand.

Perhaps the only time he abandoned himself completely was on the day he first saw me. I was standing on the beach, water still streaming from my hair, a dark and startling green. My legs were as white as bone against that whiter sand, my feet great weights I had hauled a few inches, then dropped. I remember feeling giddy at the pressure of sand between my toes, at the way the wind rushed up the skirt I'd fashioned, touching my thighs, the soft new skin between.

I remember that I stood still, watching. This man had been, for weeks, my great desire. And finally, to satisfy this yearning I had transformed myself, leaving everything behind to follow him. Although he had never seen me before, he knew me, for I had sung to him from where I floated on the surface of the water or clung like seaweed to the crevices of rocks. I had seen him turn, startled, searching for the source of my song, as delicate as the wind in his ears, as haunting as light caught inside a jewel. Fire in a stone, a voice in the sea. The songs of sirens burn within, a happiness so great it feels like pain, and when those songs stop, their absence is vast and even more painful, as if you have inhaled a starless sky. His handsome face grew lean with longing. And so I, still hardly more than a child, decided. I did not, in those days, understand the concept of exile. I was young enough to believe it was possible to discard one's past. Possible to leave a world, yet keep it alive in the heart. I never imagined longing for what I'd always had, and so when I looked up from my feet, so new and astonishing and pale, to find him watching me, stunned and somewhat repulsed by my rippling green hair, by my walk like a fish thrown on land, I opened my mouth and I sang to him once more.

Now the tide is coming in and the waves pound harder. A new castle rises out of the earth. My oldest pauses, curling her feet into the wet sand, glancing down the beach to the place where the boy stood earlier and beckoned.

She is learning now what it took me years to understand: that there is always a cost, that the past can be transformed but not discarded. I thought it could, for many years. If my last life was gone, well, there were other distractions, the continuing miracle of legs, and with those legs the miracles between them. In those days I could walk across the room to where my husband stood, absorbed, perhaps, by some state business. I could whisper the sea in his ears and dazzle him with the memory of light flashing on the surface of the water. One touch of my hand and he would look up at me, his hazel eyes going a deeper green with desire. I had not dreamed, never had I imagined, that by giving up the sea I would discover this, that legs were akin to wings, meant to flutter and to open and to carry me back to what I'd loved and left. When I woke up later and felt the surf pounding through the house, trembling through my flesh, I lived in both places, and I was happy.

What changed? I cannot say exactly. Perhaps it began with the birth of my daughters. In a rush of salt and blood each one pushed into the world. I held them in my arms, as slippery as fish, and watched them breathe. And it was in those first moments, seeing how easily they lived in this place, how much they were a part of it, that I realized my own world was something they would never know, my own language a tongue they would not speak. Just days after their births, alone at dusk on the beach, I put my infants into the water to see if they would know what to do. And one by one they did; they swam as they had within me, a reflex as sure as breathing. But one by one they forgot. Each day I would try, and one day they would know and the next day they would not. And then they would learn to walk and run, and they would play a game with the waves, a game whose purpose was to avoid the touch of water.

And so it came to happen that at night I would leave my husband dreaming and lean against the railing of the balcony, lean as far as my body would allow without falling. Or on those bleak days when we fought or when he traveled, I would wander as far as the edge of the water; I would wade in and let the waves lick my ankles, the backs of my knees, the soft skin of my thighs, until my skirts grew damp and I knew that in another step I would never stop. In those moments I would close my eyes and breathe deeply of the salt air. I would imagine my husband, and when his image rose up in anger or in the everyday blankness that must sometimes overcome all humans, no matter how fine or good they are, then I would think quickly and urgently of my daughters, my three small girls with their waves of hair, dark and light, splashing against their necks, with their small, perfect ears in the shapes of shells. My girls who had been born to walk on land.

I thought then that I could never leave them.

Yet desire creates itself from nothing, out of air. Seeking, we cast a light and the shadows rise up around us, flickering, elusive, and yet with cores as round and powerful as iron bars. What we long for defines us, finally. We are caged by our own desires. Until, yearning, we cast our lamps into the black and invisible sand, we open our arms, embracing *loss*, and *never*, and we give ourselves over to that night.

Or so, anyway, it is with me. My husband plants a flag in the tallest turret, my daughters laugh and smile, and on some unseen, distant border, the unthinkable merges with the irrevocable.

I step back into the cool, watery light of the house, where fish swim in the walls and where the air is blue, so subdued. I go to the buffet where the crystal is stored and take the glasses out, their sides and edges as thin as paper. One night last week, as I drank glass after glass of water and yet craved more, I grew terrified of my own dark longings, and I began to weep. A tear fell on my tongue, and for an instant my great thirst was quenched. Then I knew. I went to the ocean. Like someone about to die from thirst, I pressed my lips to the surface of the water and I drank. I drank so deeply and for so long that I came up coughing, salt rushing through me like a wind.

I forced myself to stop, of course. A woman cannot live on salt. But all week I have been dreaming of this decanter with its delicate etchings, which I filled with seawater, just to know that it was near. And now I cannot stop myself, nor do I want do. I fill all of the eight glasses, and I drink from each one, slowly, with great care and deliberation. I imagine salt sifting into my flesh, crystallizing every cell. I imagine my blood growing thick, and then ceasing, until I am a pillar of salt, a woman frozen in the flesh. I imagine how a touch would shatter me then, and I think of my heart, so complex and multichambered, grown as bleached and hollow as shell.

I drink, and from that moment on I move fluidly through the days, water hidden everywhere. In the cool jars on the buffet, old bottles tucked inside my drawers. I wake in the morning and stumble into the bathroom, turn on both faucets. Screened by the shower of rushing water, I drink from a discarded bottle that holds the sea. I slip back into bed before my husband wakes, and when he turns to kiss me, he licks my lips and murmurs that I taste like the ocean. His tongue is muscular, moving like a fish in my mouth, caressing all those dark curves, that wavery cave of flesh with its high, arched roof and stones of coral teeth. I sigh a song across my tongue and rise over him like a wave. And for a time, a little time, my thirst is gone, and his.

He is a very busy man, and he does not notice when, little by little, I begin to change. You look pale, he says one night. Are you wearing too much makeup? My fingers, touched to my lips, come away streaked white. Salt. I lick my fingertips slowly, one by one. In the bathroom, I squint, studying myself, these fluid waves of hair, the dark green eyes, all familiar and yet strange to me. And then there are footsteps on the stairs and my three daughters burst through the door, clamoring, their tiny fingers moving like anemones, touching me and plucking at my clothes while they chatter. They have brought me gifts: shells, smooth coral, the bony spines of crabs, the exotic zebra swirls. Their soft hands brush against my flesh, which is so brittle I fear it will crumble at their touch.

Listen, Mama, they say, and hold the shells to my ears. *Listen to the sea.*

Days pass in this way. Salt begins to drift from my skin. When I walk white crystals scatter, floating to the lawn, burning the grass beneath my feet. Trails appear on the ground, so that anyone looking could follow my path, where I run and where I linger, the wilted flowers I have touched.

It is fearful, what is happening. Yesterday I bit into a piece of bread and two back teeth shattered into dust, the bitter joy of salt.

Yet I do not stop drinking. I cannot.

One night my husband, arriving late, touches my shoulder as he climbs into our bed. By then it hurts to breathe and so I hold my breath. Anything could happen: My lungs might shatter into dust. I might dissolve beneath the kiss he places on my cheek. But nothing changes. I listen to his soft breathing as he drifts into sleep. Then I go downstairs and stand before the glowing walls of fish. In the beginning I encompassed him like a wave, I whispered my songs into his ears, I was the sea incarnate. In the beginning he could not bear to be without the salt of me, the steady pulse of me. I pulled tight around him and I spread out flat to let him rest, and my breasts rose like waves against his skin, and fell away, and rose. In those days this was enough, and our other longings we kept hidden.

But gradually, his eyes drifted to another, so lush and round that she might have been sculpted from the earth. My hair, so green and full of light, was suddenly too familiar. The taste of me grew stale. What he wanted I could not give him: a flesh that wouldn't yield, an embrace full of friction and resistance. He craved women with bare feet the color of earth, so firmly planted in the ground that the wind moved through their hair as if through leaves. Women with hands like soft branches, women who stood rooted in one place waiting for him to arrive, to stroke the delicate, white bark of their calves and branching thighs, so supple. Again, and yet again, he went to them, yearning for the earth.

I followed him, quiet as rain, as barely visible as mist. And after a time, when I could bear it no longer, I rose right over the ground around these women and embraced them with the sea.

It stunned them, the transformation that ensued. You can see that they are puzzled still, their yellow eyes glinting to all sides of the aquarium, as if they might understand a mystery that eludes them. Their tails flicker, they turn. I touch my fingers to the cool glass and imagine the feel of scales brushing lightly against my skin, the inward rush of seawater. They are beyond his reach, of no interest to him now, but I take no satisfaction from this. I watch them breathe, their rainbow scales moving slowly with each shift of gills, each pulse of water, and I envy them.

I take a small, silver flask back to bed. When I raise it to my lips, it catches the light, little gleams in that darkness. Later, when the pain begins, it is on this light, these shards and sparks, that I focus. The pain is as intense as that of childbirth, but not localized. It is everywhere and always. It comes in waves and pounds at me, and I clench my fists against it. It lasts all night, pain that pins me motionless in the bed, pain that turns me into molecules of stone.

Sometime, just before dawn, it ceases as quickly as it began.

I sleep and wake to narrow shafts of sunlight on the floor, a bed full of salt. When I raise my hands, carefully, lest they break off and shatter, I see that my fingers are as rosy and pink as the insides of shells. My husband wakes and touches the crusts of salt in the bed. He looks at me, trying to assess this latest mystery. "Are you all right?" he asks, caressing my arm. "Did you sleep well?" he asks, running his hand through my hair.

"I am all right," I say, rising to see if this is so. "I am very well."

When I stand my legs are strong and firm and supple and they carry me across the room. My thirst is utterly gone. In the mirror even my hair seems newly alive. Idly, I begin to comb it. The pain was so intense that it seems I should have been transformed in some visible way, but there is nothing. Just the slant of sun in the window, and my husband whistling in the bathroom, and water running. I consider this. What is pain? Something like passing slowly through glass. Excruciating, yet in memory transparent, a clear veil between before and after, yet in itself without substance. I think of my daughters, sleeping, and I raise my arms to twist my hair in place.

It is then that I notice. The soft flaps of skin, like tiny wings beneath my arms, tensile flesh that rises and falls and rises again with every breath. I run my fingers from my waist up over the bony ridges of my ribs, until I feel the beveled edge beneath the wing of flesh. I take a deep breath and it flutters. I hook my finger over the edge, feel the rush of air. And I know.

The comb clatters on the tiles. I leave my husband splashing in the bathroom, humming his way into the day. It is early. The stairs beneath my feet are still cool. I pass the open doors of my daughters' rooms, where they lie sleeping quietly, peacefully, their hands outflung, dirt beneath their fingernails. Through the dim foyer, past the yellow-eyed fish swimming in the wall. The floor is cool against my feet, and then the sand, hot. Waves circle my ankles. Water to my knees, my thighs, licking its way between my sturdy, human legs. And I keep walking. Water lapping between my breasts, a tongue on my neck, running up my earlobes. I fling my hair back to float like seaweed, gold and green. Waves in my mouth, my nose, filling my lungs. And why not, I think, for when my daughters grew within me they had gills, first, before anything else but heart and spine. This capacity was within us once, and so it is only a matter of remembering.

I dive so deeply. By the time I surface the sun is high, flashing whitely off the beach where my family has gathered. I see them in the distance, sand sprinkled across the warm feet and long legs of my daughters, their hair moving like young wheat in the breeze. I see my husband, too, his face dark with sorrow and cleft like a rock. He gazes helplessly in my direction, but the green of my hair, the whiteness of my skin, make me seem like just another wave from where he stands. I am not concerned for him. He will grieve, but he is a man of purpose. In a few days he will take action, and everything belonging to me will go. Staggering from the house with metal tubs, he will release those fish into the shallows, and he will stand astonished, amazed and also horrified, as they twist against the wet sand, flipping this way and that in an agony of wanting, and then turn to look at him with their startled eyes, their human eyes, their bright limbs flashing in the light. They will stand, naked and trembling, but his own eyes will drift past them to the sea.

My three daughters search now as they will search forever, shading their eyes against the sun. Their yearning will travel far across the water, and it will swell like a dark sky in my throat. At night they will stir from dreams, restless and yet soothed, believing that they have heard my voice rising from the sea. I linger here, drinking in the sight of them, but I will not return. Waves rush against the shore, one moment, and sand shifts beneath their force, another, and I am the fire in the emerald, the light behind the clouds, I am this song.

Sky Juice

LET ME TELL YOU, THEN, HOW IT BEGAN: MY ONLY BROTHER attracted the wrath of the heavens and stumbled into a fatal encounter with a cow.

The first time I told this story the man who was listening to me broke out in laughter. He did not see the great grief I carried with me, ugly and clumsy, a clay pot heavy with water, a perpetual weight. And so he laughed, blue eyes disappearing in his mirth. His teeth, as white and straight as small bones, were brilliant in his face. I stopped speaking. Even in that place I was shocked. But they had trained me well, and the smile never left my lips.

"A cow," he said, still laughing. "Unbelievable."

"No," I told him, pulling my hand away. "This story is the truth. You must not laugh at the memory of my brother."

He finished his beer and waved for another one. Then he recaptured my hand. "Whatever you say, honey." He was a cheerful man, round and good-natured, and he squeezed my fingers to prove his sincerity. Nonetheless, from across the room, watchful eyes glanced against my skin like the feet of a fly. I pulled my chair closer, smiled at the man. I knew the rules. But I could not stop my tongue.

"My brother," I began, and the memories were such that I did not heed the reluctance on the round man's face. I told him about my brother as a boy, the thick hair that fell flat against his smooth brown skin, his long fingers tugging at my arm until I followed him. Whenever it rained we went outside, chasing the chickens until they fled to the dry earth beneath the house. My mother came to the windows, warning us of fever, but he stayed outside and I stayed with him. One monsoon, many years ago, we tore off all our clothes and ran naked through the falling water, trying to catch the rain in our mouths. Sky juice, my brother called it. The sky was full of water fruit, a lush fruit that spilled juice, soaked through the clouds and fell to us. We were dripping with sky juice, sky juice slid cool on our tongues, ran rivers on our arms and legs. My mother called more urgently, warm in her dry dress, warning us, but we were never sick.

And there was more: When my brother fell into the swollen river, fell into deep water that carried him downstream, past two villages and through the long pipe that led to the sea, he did not drown. He swirled through the froth, bumped against bloated frogs and the carcasses of birds, skinned his hands on chunks of speeding wood, but he did not drown, and this filled us all with awe because he had never learned to swim.

Remembering this miracle, celebrated by a hundred candles burning in my village, I forgot where I was. I spoke dreamily, and told the stranger that I sometimes thought my brother was a saint.

The man put down his beer undrunk and looked at me. I blushed, because in that place we seemed what we were not. My dress was pale silk with a high mandarin collar, the blue cloth cut away from my shoulders to reveal my petal skin. My hair could reach my knees in those days. It had never been cut. I spent hours with it every morning, dressing it elaborately with tinsel jewels and falling sprays of flowers—the wedding style. I resembled a bride, but of course I was not a bride. The room was filled with smoke and the scent of champagne, and upstairs there were other rooms, small or large, simple or opulent, depending on the wallets of the men. The other girls joked about it, and ran a contest to see who would be the first to have been taken to every room. I laughed with them, in those days, and placed bets on a girl named Nangka who was both beautiful and very bold, and who was always chosen. We were like factory workers, or dreamy rich girls, seeking to relieve the long tedium of our days. We were like many things, but of course we were only one thing. This is what the man next to me had known all along.

"A saint," he said. "Imagine that."

He leaned so close to me I could feel his breath. His hand stroked my neck and fastened on the chain there, which he pulled up so slowly I felt every tiny link brush my skin. And then the small cross appeared, pure gold, hanging from the knobby ends of his fingers. His eyes were bright and mocking now, and I was suddenly afraid.

"Are you a religious man?" I asked.

"Oh yes," he answered.

"You are?" I tried to stroke his wrist but he shrugged me away. I felt the fly feet dancing on my neck again.

"Yes," he said. "And I'll bet you pray too, don't you? On your knees all the time, I bet. What do you pray for, sugar?"

I thought of many lies, all dangerous. And I thought of my mother, pinching my arm and telling me my tongue would cause me great trouble someday. So I looked him in the eyes and told him the simple truth.

"I pray to leave this place," I said. "I pray to be forgiven for these sins."

His hand twisted on the chain. I thought he meant to break it. Instead, he let it go, abruptly. The man we all feared was standing beside me, rubbing the place on my neck where I had felt his insect gaze, the small insistent feet of his power and lust.

"This one," he said to the man. "She is being good to you, yes?" His fingers pressed my neck so that I had to bend my head, as if in supplication, as if in prayer. The sounds of the bar, voices, falling glass, drew closer. Through them I heard the man speak, I felt the brutal edges of his smile.

"This one?" he said. "Why, she's a regular little saint."

THERE ARE SAINTS, I have seen them, hanging bright and tormented on the high walls of the district church. They have smooth stone skin, slender fingers cupped and held to the sky, tears of glass on cheeks as cold as mountain earth. We went each year to watch them emerge, carried in the ancient way on canopied platforms. They swayed, floating above the torch-lit city streets. The men who carried them were hidden beneath, under folds of velvet cloth, so that the saints, trembling against a smoky sky, turned and seemed to move unaided. The sisters scuttled like black birds and held us back. Do not touch, they whispered. Pray, pray, for today their tears are real.

There are saints, and when my brother died I prayed to be like them, to be a woman rescued from my life, risen into the sky on a slender shaft of light, my body left behind, a lovely husk of shell and stone and glass. Day after day I prayed, until my knees were raw, my fingers numb, and I grew weary of saints. One evening I left the church and went to the wise woman of our village. She was skilled in the future, she took me to her home and rubbed my palms with ash. I had no tears, or if I did they were solid within me by that time. The trouble I was in, you see, it was very serious. My mother was dead, having caught the fever she seemed to sense around us always. My brother had used our few savings to buy a motorbike. I swear it was not from vanity or greed. We had a plan. My brother would deliver eggs and vegetables to the villagers. I would learn to weave. We would save, and when I was ready we would buy a loom. We were so young, and we did not imagine anything that could keep us from our dreams.

I tell you it was not pride, not at first, but I think that day when my brother died he was overcome. By speed, by the force of the wind in his hair. This is what I imagine. He drove so fast that the tears gathered in his eyes. He turned, just for a moment, to brush them away, to see who might be watching, and when he looked back it was too late, he was already lifting in the air. The cow screamed, he heard it as he soared over the road and into the dry river, empty now, hard as concrete beneath that beating sun. The bike rode on, riderless, and crashed at last into a tree. The cow lay for three weeks where it died. I saw its body bloat, a balloon of skin taut against the stink of death, then later still, withered to the bone. My brother landed on his head. When they brought him to me there was blood coming from his ears. Within a day he died.

So I knew what must happen to me. The funeral costs, the cow to replace, the motorbike reduced to a twist of torn bright metal. I was young, but no one in the village would marry me now, a girl of ill luck, weighed down with debts and grief. The wise woman knew it too. She looked at my hands, gray with ash, shaking her head at what she saw. Pain and cold. I shuddered at this, thinking death, but she said no, not death, only cold. She told me there were places where it is so cold that for months there is no rain.

"No rain," I repeated.

"What comes from the sky there falls like dust," she said. "I have not seen it, but I know that it is so cold it burns you like fire. You must be strong. I see you in this place. You must prepare."

She would say no more. Her fingers, stained brown with herbs, placed the things I would need in a small cloth bag. Precautionary things, medicine to make me invincible, a barrier around me that would let nothing in. She asked me if I knew what to expect and warned me that the first time was painful, but prized by many. Then she gave me his name, and the address of that place.

"Go to him," she said. "he is not kind, but he guards his own."

SHE MUST HAVE known, when she sent me. She must have seen it.

They put me in a small white room, and for many hours I was alone. Once I tried to leave, and then they took my clothes away and sent me back. One door. One window. A single bed. No food, for hours, only a sink. I drank water until I imagined myself rinsed clean inside. Sitting by the open window, looking at the flat gray wall of another building, I drank and cried for my brother and my mother and myself. Then I closed my eyes and tried to imagine them, tried to reach them. I was gone then, too. I was floating, halfway to another world.

Then the men came. I was very still, somewhere outside myself, watching them from the blank space. And so it was not painful. I did not scream or bleed. More men came, and more, and I was so far away, so distant and so cold, that I did not even count or mark the ways they differed from each other. The next morning I was given a new room, the room I was to live in. Two other girls were there. One, a tall woman applying bright red lipstick, had strong bones, her hair cut to her shoulders and pulled back severely. Nangka. The other was called Dahlia; she was slight and pale, and her hair was longer than my own.

"So fast," Dahlia said when I came in. She was disappointed; the room was crowded with three of us. Nangka turned from her mirror and walked over to me. She held my chin with her long fingers, her hard lacquered nails. She examined my arms.

"No bruises," she declared, dropping my arm with disgust. "She didn't fight."

"What good would it do?" Dahlia asked, already bored. "What good would it do, to fight?"

I kept myself apart, and they did not like me. It's true that I joked with them, I placed my bets, but inside I kept myself separate in a pure place, an arrogance of silence, and they hated me for it. Pale Dahlia ignored me, the bold Nangka was my torment. She piled her jars and lotions on my table, and dug her fingers into my arms when I complained. Her nails were bright, razor-sharp, the color of the blood she drew. What good would it do, she said, mocking me, to fight?

We had three white walls, three beds in a row, a small table by each bed and a wardrobe for our clothes. Our working clothes. Bright, like bird plumes or the scales of parrot fish. Silky, so that worn they seemed a second flesh, warm against the skin, luxurious. We washed out lipstick, the smell of smoke. We ironed away the wrinkled evidence of sweaty palms, the spilled froth of drinks. This was by day, that we washed. We did each other's hair, compared the craziness of men. What they wanted us to say, what they asked us to do. But never what we said. Never, never what we did. I spoke and heard myself speaking from where I sat in the purest part of my brain. Nangka was rough and coarse, she spoke like the city she came from, a voice full of choking fumes and wild unexpected sounds. Dahlia was like me, quiet, from the country. We did not talk about the past, but I knew this about her. I recognized her hesitancy, understood her silence.

One day when I had been there three months, Nangka was doing my hair, piling it on my head and poking it with pins like daggers. Dahlia moved through the room, stepping in and out of the scope of the mirror. The sky was clear that morning, the sun moved in a square on the floor, and I, far away inside myself, was almost content. The night was a distant future. My skin was clean.

Then I heard Dahlia laughing. I turned and saw her with my package from the wise woman, which she had taken from my drawer. I had learned, of course, of other precautions. Girls talk among themselves. I had put those things away unused. But I was still so angry to see them resting in her slender hands. My voice rose high, and I descended from that pure place I had lived in.

"Give it to me," I demanded. "It's nothing of yours." But already she had pulled it open.

"Oh," she said, holding up a paper of herbs. "What have I found?" She tossed it to Nangka, who dropped my hair and caught it, spilling dry seeds from the brittle paper.

"My God," she said. "You are a dope, a country idiot, if you depend on this."

Next Dahlia lifted out my necklace with the cross and locket. These had been my mother's, and they were my only things from home. I did not understand it, why she hated me so much. We were alike. But then I understood: that was precisely why.

"A sweetheart?" she said, dancing around the room with the open locket. She leaped onto my bed and began to make small kissing sounds. "Someone you hope to marry?"

"My brother," I said. It was my voice, I was saying it, and the sound of my voice knocked me from the pure place forever. I was there, then. I was in that room. "My brother," I repeated. "He died."

"Oh, really," she began, but Nangka turned her voice on her at once, chased her from the room with words as strong as stones.

She turned back to me, and put her hand on my shoulder. We looked at each other in the mirror.

"I had a brother too," she said.

IF YOU HAVE had a brother and then lost him, you will know the kind of bond that connected us then. Hidden in the daylight corners of that place, our heads together over washing and lipstick, the demanding tresses of my hair, we talked. Nangka told me of a city life I had never imagined, of days without grass or flowing water, of a father who beat her brother until he ran away and joined the army. He was only seventeen when they sent him to the uprisings on another island, sent him to a village church and a bayonet through the liver. When she spoke of him it was in a flat soft voice that expected no answer. Her hands were in my hair and then she dropped them to my shoulders. The long nails of her thumbs rested against the chain that held my locket and my cross.

"The things that are done," she said, "have no good logic, no explanation. You should sell that thing," she added, nodding at the cross. "It's nothing for luck, but the gold is good." Her eyes had gone so dark that I could think of nothing but the night they brought me from the country.

"Nangka," I said. I reached up and took both her hands. Her fingers were thin and cool and dry. In a moment she pulled them away and dipped them into my hair again.

"Yes," she said. "Yes. But tell me about your brother now."

And so I did, everything I could remember. She said she could imagine him, that our brothers would have been friends. "Tell me," she said. "Tell me what they would have done together." I closed my eyes, and I talked about the river as if it were there before me. We used to go every morning to wash ourselves in the light of the new dawn. Since we could not swim we held on to the jetty with our hands, we pulled ourselves underwater and made a game of how long we could stay there. My brother was half fish, he could stay down for more than 150 counts. For me it was less, but no less wonderful. When my lungs began to spark I shot myself up. I threw my head back, water rushing from my hair, and drank the air. Each time, I opened my eyes to a new world, clearer and more vivid than the one I had left. The air was so clean, the colors so pure, the ordinary things vibrant with a life I had overlooked.

In this same way, with Nangka as my friend, my eyes opened. The new world was shabby, but I saw. I saw how worn our silk was in the daylight. I felt the roughness of our sheets, and heard the noise around us always: factory whistles, the rush of water in old pipes, jackhammers in the street below, the tinny music as they cleaned the bar. And the men. It might have been the first time, the way I took it when I finally woke up. When they made me undress, when I felt the soft damp press of flesh, I thought I would go mad. There were complaints against me. I was warned. Until Nangka, afraid because she saw that I was not, decided it was up to her to save me.

IT WAS MONTHS ago that we left, nearly a year now, and yet there are things I am not used to in this place. One of them is this: Whenever I hear trains at night, I think it is the wind. Rising and blowing, rattling the windows of this foreign house, they jar me out of sleep. I reach to close the windows, to pull the wooden shutters, to shake the man beside me and take him underneath the house until the storm subsides. Then I am truly awake, fierce and ready, and I realize that the shaking, the gathering noise, is only one of many trains. In the dark I listen to it rumble past and disappear, its noise thinning into the night. From the bed I can see the flash of light each window makes, and sometimes I can see faces, caught for an instant like a photo. I search these moments, seeing so many things. A coffee cup held to the lips, an expression of pain or laughter or surprise, once a couple kissing. Everyone is pale, like the snow that falls, every face is pale and pink. I cannot see my mother here, or my brother, and I cannot see the face I truly seek, Nangka with her bright lips and skin the color of smooth nuts, her hair hanging to her shoulders like a black wave before it breaks. Even when I hold a small piece of her hair, a piece I stole when no one was looking, I do not see her. She is somewhere in this pale country, somewhere in this snow, but after all these months I no longer expect to see her. Like me, her traveling is finished, I am sure. Like me, it is possible that she rarely leaves the house. I sit in the window until I shake with cold, I hold the soft piece of her hair.

It was her idea, this cutting.

"Yes," she said. "It's what we must do first."

I put my hand to the soft masses wound around my head. Never cut your hair, my mother said. Whatever you do. It is your oldest possession.

"My hair was longer," Nangka went on, seeing my face. "My hair went to my knees. It took me hours to comb it. Hours to dress it up each day." She laughed. "The wedding style. After all, it was not meant for every day. At first I could not let them cut it, though I knew I should. I went that first time, and let them cut only to my waist. I went back every month and lost another inch. Until now." She pointed to her black hair, which brushed against her shoulders. She pointed to her bangs. "Today I will get the last piece cut, and you will do all of yours. You must be brave," she said. "Men like long hair, but not too long. It marks you as a villager. Now tell me again. Practice what we will say."

"You are my sister," I told her. "You are my oldest sister. Our parents died last year. We have never been apart."

"Stop staring," she said, tugging at my arm. "Look straight ahead." I was walking without thinking, my eyes drawn back and forth by the lights and flowers. I had never walked in the city before.

"I can't hear you," I said, stopping to press my hands over my ears.

"Of course you can." This time her tug was harder. She stepped in front of me and took my face in her hands. "Do you want to stay in that place forever? Listen to me. Are you a virgin? Are you?"

I blushed. We kept walking. "Yes," I said. "I am."

Nangka smiled. "Good," she said. "You said that exactly right. Now, why do you want to marry a foreigner?"

"I want to make a good home. I want to have children. I want to see the world."

"But we are sisters."

"Yes," I said. "We are sisters. And we do not want to live apart from each other. We never have in our lives."

"All right," Nangka said. We had reached the beauty parlor. There were rough pictures of women drawn on the glass wall with paint. They were not smiling, any of them. Their hair grew up in waves and towers. They looked at the air with their lips puckered, their eyes half-lowered. Inside there was a woman whose skin was coarse, whose hair fell around her head like an upturned bowl.

"Just an inch," I begged, feeling her hands on my hair. "Please, no more than that."

"There is no time," Nangka said. "We have no time to go slowly. I'm sorry."

"This hair is thick," said the woman. She weighed it in her hand like a slab of meat. "If I cut it all at once I'll do it free; hair this long I can sell."

I closed my eyes. My mother combed my hair every morning, and once a week she rubbed my scalp with scented oil. She was proud of my hair. During festivals she wove flowers into it. *This*, she had said, stroking it. *This is your great beauty.* But what good was it to me now, a false bride? I nodded, very slowly.

Nangka took my hand.

"You'll be happier this way," she said. "Wait and see."

She was right, though I wept when I saw it. The sharp ends touched my shoulders and my hair, my great beauty, was a fat braid hanging from the wall.

"Stop crying," Nangka begged. "It was necessary. And it's not so bad. You are still pretty, look." She held up the mirror. My hair was gone, but she was right, my face was just the same.

"There," she said, seeing me recover. "And doesn't your head feel light?"

It was true, my head felt as if it were floating, disembodied. We walked to the agency and I kept glancing into windows, surprising myself, feeling giddy and off balance when I turned my head too swiftly and nothing weighed it down.

At the agency I stayed close to Nangka.

"You see," she told them, "she is my younger sister. Of course she is shy, she has just come from the village. We want to stay together. Sisters. We want to make good homes in a new country. We want to be good wives. Cook? Of course. And cleaning, we are very good at that."

In the mornings now, while we waited, our short hair gave us free time. We studied. Nangka had a map. She had a dictionary with polite words in English.

"Now we are here," she said, pointing to the islands, hundreds of them scattered like green ink against the sea. She pointed out the places we might go. One was huge, shaped like a fat bull with no horns and stubby legs. Another was like a wild boar, chasing a bright bird across the water. This last one was an island and much smaller, but it was the one I liked. There was so much water.

"I don't know," Nangka said. "It's very cold there. Colder than you can imagine." She paused, listening to footsteps in the hallway until they died away. The boldness of what we were doing made her brisk and worried.

"Stop dreaming," she said. "We must practice." She read from her small book.

"Good morning," she said. "How are you today?"

"Fine," I replied. "Thank you very much, I am fine."

I WAS RAW, I was green, I was a girl who had never seen snow. How could I know, when they showed me this man, how to judge? He was pale, that's what I saw, pale and rather fat. He wore glasses and behind them his eyes looked like small gray clouds. He said he was a water man. He had drawn a dam, and now he was here to build it. When he left he wanted to take home a wife. He had chosen me from a photograph the agency had given him. He said he would interview two others. I kept my head bowed in the polite way, though it was harder now. My hair swung against my shoulders and my head kept drifting up. He asked me questions about my life, he asked me to stand up and walk back and forth across the room.

"Your parents," he said. "Is it true that they have died?" I nodded, still silent. And then I knew a way to judge him. I looked up, directly at him.

"I had a brother too," I said. "He was killed by a cow." I watched him very closely, but he did not laugh. He listened. He listened to my story.

"I'm sorry," he said.

And he did not laugh at me, not once.

"That's lucky," said Nangka, when I told her. "He is kind." We sat in the bare morning light, our books hidden beneath the mattress, speaking in whispers, comparing our fortunes.

"And yours," I said. "Nangka, how was he?"

"Ugly," she said. "Like a rambutan fruit. He was hairy, and underneath the hair his skin was red. Even his nose was red, like a hibiscus. His hair is as dark as mine. It covered his whole face."

"But kind?" I asked. "Was he also kind?"

"I don't know," she said. She was looking at the wall then, remembering. "He asked strange questions. I kept my head down. He came over and unfastened all my buttons, one by one. He opened my blouse like a curtain. Yet he did not touch me. He stared, but he did not touch me."

"Not kind," I said.

"No," she agreed. "Not very kind. But he is from the same wild-boar island as your water man."

Now I LIVE on this wild-boar island, but it will not tell me what to feel. If there were palm trees, a brown river, lean wooden houses against the jungle and hibiscus, I would know. Even in that city, with all the noise, the scent of cooking food and open drains, of smoke and sewers, I woke up and I knew. But here the sky is a watery gray, the snow softens everything, pales all color. I am always cold, it seems, though the water man has a house with heat, and has bought me many sweaters. Jim, he says, smiling. Call me Jim. He is a kind man, but when I look at him, when I look around, there are only white things, cold things, and I feel nothing about them, nothing, I feel nothing at all.

That we escaped at all was a miracle of course, a kind of gift, and I must remember that. We were very lucky. No one followed us when we left that morning, no one saw us go. The only things I took were my locket and the clothes I wore, a crisp white skirt and blouse I bought with the money I got for my gold cross. It was so early that all the shops were closed. The streets were filled with a blue-gray light, and not even the fishwives were open yet. Our footsteps echoed against the metal shutters of the shops. Nangka wore a simple dress of dark blue silk, which she had stolen months ago. Her lips were a clear red, her hair was dark black, her skin the color of cut wood just after it has rained. She was beautiful, I thought. She said we both were.

We sat together in the center of the long airplane. Other girls were with us. They leaned into the windows, pointed out shoreline and cities, or the vast expanse of sea. Some of them slept. Nangka and I did none of these things. We barely even spoke, we were so nervous. At the landing my ears filled up with something and gave me so much pain I wanted to scream, and when I had to say good-bye to Nangka I could hardly hear what she said. But I saw her, I kept her face in my mind. I told myself there was no reason to worry, her new address was folded in my locket by a picture of my brother. I touched its metal, warmed by my skin, and I let her walk away with that man, out into the night.

I wrote her many letters:

Dearest Nangka,
After I left you we came to this place by train. It was early morning. The houses are so close together here, like at home, but each one has a small gate, a fence around the garden. The water man says there are flowers, but not now. The air smells wet and earthy. He says it is too early for the fire, though I am always cold. Yesterday I gathered sticks and branches from his

garden. I saved them in the kitchen and asked could we please have a fire. I did not understand his expression, and then he laughed. He showed me the switch. First there is a humming, then a light that moves like fire, but you can touch it. Later there is heat that bakes my skin dry. Nangka, I felt so foolish I wanted to die, but he is a kind man. The floors in this house are soft with rugs, and the walls have a paper that is fuzzy when you touch it. Nangka, please write to me, is this how it is for you?

Dearest Nangka,
My sweet friend, did you get my letters? Every day I wait for the mail but there is never anything from you. Today we went to the shops at the end of the block. It is so strange, Nangka, there was nothing there I could recognize, though he wants me to cook. Everything is wrapped in plastic, I cannot feel the oranges or the meat, and nothing has a smell. When I was home alone there was snow. I did not know what it was at first. Then I remembered the wise woman and went outside to feel it. It is white and burns like the smoke that used to come from the factories to our room. At first I was not cold and I stood there for a long time. Then I saw a face in the window next door. It was the old woman, looking at me, and when I waved she dropped the curtain. Then I went inside and I was suddenly very cold. I sat in a blanket and watched the lines of white growing on the fences. I thought about that old woman. The water man, Jim, is kind, but the other people here are not kind. I see them looking at me always, and they do not smile. Nangka, I think of you always, is it the same for you?

Dear Nangka,
I am so worried. Here are some stamps. I am sending you these stamps so that if he does not let you out you can get a letter to me. Wait for the mailman. Nangka, I miss you. I would rather be back at that place with you than to be so lonely here.

I sent these letters with diminishing hope. Still, I put them in the box every day. I did not hear and did not hear, and soon my own letters began to come back to me. I saved them, and one day, desperate, I showed them to Jim.

"She has moved," he said, pointing to the yellow sticker.

"Yes, but where? Where is she now?"

He shook his head, and handed me the letter back. His skin was very white then, and his fingernails were blue, like the envelope.

"It doesn't say, I'm afraid. She didn't leave an address."

"She wouldn't do that," I said. "We are like sisters."

It was too late when I realized my mistake. Jim studied me. He said, "I thought you *were* sisters." But when he saw me folding with loss, he put his arm around me. "There," he said, "it doesn't matter. Look, do you have her new name? Do you know what man she came with?"

I remembered him at the airport, face like a hairy fruit, when he put his arm around Nangka's shoulders and drew her away. I remembered how small she looked beside him, her last smile to me. I remembered that he was not kind.

"No," I whispered. "No."

"You're shivering," Jim said. He turned up the heat and put another blanket around my shoulders. When he frowned I could see the fine red lines surface on his forehead, a map of his thoughts. He listed things we could do. Write the agency. Contact the embassy. It was possible, he said, that we could find her. At least we could look.

"But you mustn't hope," he said. "It isn't likely, and you mustn't get your hopes up."

THREE MONTHS HAVE PASSED, and still I do not hope. Nor do I pray, though I have found a church, and I sometimes go there. One day I was shopping, holding a ham swathed in plastic, when I saw the nun. She wore short skirts, which surprised me, skirts that brushed her knees, and dark black tights. Her hair was covered by only a black cloth, and no wimple framed her face. She was pale, her hands were as white as soap. She was a nun, and I followed her. A block, half a block behind, I followed her, marking the way in my memory. She was young, I could tell from the way she walked, the long swing of her legs. It was spring by then. The sun was cool on my face and hands, and the trees looked like half-plucked chickens with their small pale leaves.

The church she went to is big, but though I come here often, I am nearly always alone. I sit in the front pew, near the statues that crowd around the altar. These are faces I recognize, smooth expressions of grief and rapture I find familiar. I do not have these feelings anymore, such extremes of pain or ecstasy. My life on this cold island has a pattern, but my feelings have paled like the skins of the people here, my smiles are smiles of habit only. It is true I do not suffer. I think if I went back, saw the hibiscus and brown river of my childhood, pain would flower in me to match the colors I could touch. Even here, in this place that is a shadow of my other life, the memories stir. My brother had dark eyes, and the skin beneath his fingernails was the rosy pink of coral. My mother smelled like jasmine, she wove bright waxy orchids in her hair. When she sang to me there was bougainvillea outside the window, fuchsia leaves like flames. There was green all around us, deep and rich, and when the rains fell they ran like juice from the sky. Even Nangka, with her city voice, knew the power of red on the lips, of deep blue silk that fell around her calves.

This is what I think of at that church. I see the statues, and I am reminded, faintly, of what to feel. I close my eyes and see first my brother, pulled from the river on that day he did not drown. He is pale beneath his skin, like these statues, but he is alive, and that night my mother wears a red dress to church, she tosses flowers into the baptismal fountain to celebrate his life. I go on like this, remembering, feeling a surge of life and color. But then there are the other things, which also come. My mother with a fever that sent water streaming from her skin, my brother turning his head to wipe the tears of wind from his eyes. Or Nangka, head tilted back, her hair wet and heavy, before that last inch was cut away. The worst memory is Nangka, turning past the strange arm to give me one last smile, while behind her the rain was falling, sealed from us by glass.

I open my eyes, then, filled with memory, and seek the faces of the statues, which at home would let me weep. But here they are so pale, and like me their tears are frozen in their eyes. They are as cold as mountain earth, but all the same I seem to hear them speak.

Listen, they whisper, their voices as urgent as wind before the rain. *Let me tell you. Let me tell you how it began.*

Gold

ON THE DAY THAT GOLD WAS DISCOVERED NEAR HIS VILLAGE, Mohammed Muda Nor had worked all morning tapping rubber. At one o'clock he walked out from the airy rows of trees, waved to Abdullah, the entry guard, who was already eating his lunch, and started down the dusty road home. The call to prayer wavered from the village mosque, and it seemed to Muda that he could see it, waves of sound shimmering concurrently with the midday heat. It was the end of the fruit season, one of the last hot weeks before the rains began, and the weather was a fiery hand against his back. Muda walked with his straw hat pulled down low over his forehead, so he didn't see the children running toward him until they were quite near. They circled around him and pulled in close, like the petals on a closing flower.

"Pachik Muda." It was his oldest nephew, a boy named Amin. He was wearing shorts and holding the hand of his youngest sister, Maimunah, who stood brown and naked beside him. "Uncle, our mother says for you to come quickly to the river."

Muda stopped to consider. He was hungry, and the river was in the opposite direction of his home. He had risen before dawn and had worked hard all morning. Each tree required a narrow cut in the bark and a cup, precisely set, to collect the rubbery white sap. There were hundreds of trees in his area. He had worked hard, and he was hungry.

"Tell your mother," he said, "that I will come later. Right now I am going for my lunch." He expected them to run off then. They were the children of his sister, Norliza, and they were rarely naughty. But instead Amin released his sister's hand. He reached out and tugged at Muda's sarong.

"My mother says to come," he repeated. "Please, Pachik Muda, she says it is important."

Muda sighed, then, but he turned and followed the children back along the road. Red rambutans and smooth green mangoes hung from the trees. He plucked some of these and ate them as he walked, wondering what he would find on the riverbank. Norliza had worked the rubber too, before she married, and she would not take him lightly from his rest and prayers.

When he reached the river he saw a cluster of women standing on the grassy bank. Norliza was in the center, her sarong wet to the knees, holding something out for the others to see.

"Norliza," he called. He was going to scold her for consuming his time with her bit of woman's nonsense, but before he could speak she ran to him and uncurled her fist. The lines in her palm were creased with dirt, so that the skin around them looked very pale. The words he had planned stopped in his mouth. For on her palm lay a piece of gold as large as a knuckle. It was wet with river water, and it caught the noon light like fire in her hand.

"The children found it," she said. "I was digging for roots." Norliza was a midwife, known in the village for her skill in herbs and massage. She came into the jungle every week to search for the healing roots and bark. "I was digging there, near the trees by the river. The children were playing next to me, sorting out the rocks for a game. This one they liked because of its shine. At first

I did not realize. It was only when Amin washed it in the river that I understood." Her dark eyes gleamed with an unfamiliar excitement. "To think," she said. "To think he might have dropped it, and I would never have known."

Muda reached out and took the knot of gold. It was smooth, almost soft, against his fingers. He ran his thumb against it again and again. Some of the women drew close to stare. Others, he noticed, were already moving away with the news.

"It's not real," he said loudly, and dropped the lump of gold back into his sister's hand.

"Muda!" she said. She looked up at him from dark eyes. Once she had been the most beautiful girl in the village. Now the dark eyes were connected by a finely etched skin, and the expression on her face was reproachful. He took a deep breath and spoke again.

"I've worked all day in the rubber, and you waste my lunch time with this foolishness. You are a silly woman," he added, though it gave him great pain to see how she flinched under the eyes of the other women. A ripple of murmuring voices moved through the crowd. They had lived in the village all their lives, and he had never spoken to his sister sharply. Even the women who had reached the road paused and turned back to watch. "You are a foolish woman," he repeated. "Foolish. And I am going home."

He turned and walked away with slow dignity. He didn't look back, but when he was certain he was out of sight he began to run with a speed he had not summoned since he was a boy.

Khamina was washing dishes when he burst inside. His lunch was set out on the floor—a plate of fish stuffed with coconut, a vegetable curry, several small bananas—but he paid no attention to it. Instead he ran to the wooden porch where his wife was squatting amid a pile of soapy dishes.

"Khamina," he said. "Give me your cooking pot."

She stood up in surprise and gestured to the soapy wok soaking in the water. Then her eyes narrowed, and she looked him up and down.

"Muda," she said. "Why are you running through my house with your shoes on? Where is your mind? Today I scrubbed these floors, and here you are dragging the rubber field across them."

"Khamina," he said. He had scrubbed the pot and was now pouring water over it, clearing away the soap. "Let me tell you something. It is no time to complain about a little mud. This is an important day. My sister Norliza may be here soon. If she comes I want you to tell her that I have gone back to the river. Tell her to come there at once. She is not to speak to anyone. Do you hear me? Not to anyone! Tell her to come alone."

Muda splashed water on his face. Then he picked up Khamina's cooking pot and left the house. She followed him, stepping over the food he had ignored, standing in the doorway to watch him running through the heat of the day, her black pot swinging from his hand.

The sun was so hot that day that it consumed the sky and filled the air with a harsh metallic glare that had driven all the animals—chickens, cats, and mangy dogs—underneath the houses for shade. Nonetheless Muda ran the entire way back to the river, not even pausing at the fork that led to the rubber plantation. When he reached the river he saw that Norliza and her children were still there, crouching by a shallow hole they had dug. The knuckle of gold was resting on a flat gray rock. When Norliza saw him she jumped up at once, wiping her damp hands against her sarong. She snatched the gold from the rock and ran to him.

"Muda, you fool," Norliza said, planting herself before him. He had run so hard that he could not answer and stood before her gasping for breath. "How could you speak to me so in front of the women from the village when I have made the greatest discovery in the memory of any person alive? Muda, you are my brother, but you are also a fool."

To her surprise Muda smiled at her, then broke out in laughter. No one had spoken to him this way since he had become a man.

"Norliza," he said, when he could speak. "Take care of what you say. I am not one of your children, and I am no fool. You might as well say so of a crocodile, sitting still and thoughtless as a log in the river."

"This is gold," she insisted, but in a softer voice. Strands of hair had fallen against her face and she brushed at them with the back of her hand.

Muda reached out and once again held the nugget in his hand. He could not get enough of the soft feel of it on his skin, and worked it between his fingers.

"Yes," he said. "It is gold. Now show me exactly where you found it before all the women in this village return, with their husbands and their neighbors, to dig."

Once Norliza understood, she worked as Muda had known she would—quietly, quickly, and with the fierce determination of a woman who had always been poor. Together they drove stakes into the ground, marking off a plot that stretched along the river and reached to the edge of the jungle. When the stakes were secure he tied ropes between them. Then he climbed inside the area they had claimed and began to dig. Norliza sent the two oldest boys into the shallows of the river where they washed the stones she and Muda took from the red earth. The younger children ferried dirt and rocks back and forth in the cooking pot. The older boys sorted the stones into two piles for their mother to examine: those that shone, and those that did not.

On the long run from his house Muda had lost his straw hat, and now his hair was like lit kindling against his neck and ears. From time to time he went to the river and splashed water over his head, but he did not stop to rest. In the rubber trees he had learned how to work efficiently in the midday heat. There he knew how much work had to be finished and how long it would take, and so he rested often in the hot afternoons, sometimes curling up in the old caretaker's huts, other times leaning against the slender trunk of a tree. Here the heat was greater, the work harder, but there was also no limit to what he might find. He moved surely and swiftly and without a single break in the movements of his hands.

Muda was a poor man. As a child this had never bothered him. Everyone in the village was poor, after all, and in the next village it was just the same. He had not thought of it as a lack. There was always fruit to eat, the river was full of fish, and water buffalos were killed for wedding feasts. As a child, running in the murky water of the rice fields, or shimmying up the young coconut trees to shake down the fruit, he had been happy.

At sixteen all of this changed. He was offered a job in the rubber plantation. That first day, he had walked the six miles from his house to arrive, scared and shy, before daybreak. In those early months he worked as he was working now in the earth, all his attention focused on the rows of graceful rubber trees, on the thin streams of white that flowed into the cups he placed. Due to his industry he won a bonus that he used to buy a motorbike, the first in his village. He was the envy of the men, and he knew he could have any of the young girls, swaying in their tight sarongs as he sped past them, for his wife.

It was then that he began to notice the new cars and expensive suits of the plantation owners. They came once a month to inspect their investments, and Muda watched them with awe, their shiny leather shoes, the odd flap of their ties, as they disappeared beneath the trees. When they were out of sight he crept up to one of the cars, a gold Mercedes, and ran his fingers across the smooth hot metal. Inside the seats were upholstered in a leather as soft as a monkey's palm. He thought of his own small motorbike, how it sent sparks through the girls and put envy in the eyes of his former schoolmates, and tried to imagine how it would feel to own this gleaming car. Then the men were coming back; he moved silently into the trees and watched them drive away, the golden car disappearing in a cloud of fine red dust. Later, deep in the forest, making the thin cuts in the bark, his fingertips still held the various textures of the car. He worked at the rubber harder than ever, determined that one day such a car would be his.

The next year he married. Khamina was not the prettiest girl in the village, but she was famous for her pandanus weaving, for deft fingers that could shape the fragrant leaves. She made a mat for his bike to rest on, and when they were married she covered the whole of their little house with woven mats. At night they lay on these. He was surrounded by the smell of cut grass, by the warm fleshy scent that rose like clear smoke from Khamina. In that year his plans for the rubber trees diminished. He thought: Next week I will get to the plantation early, I will tap another dozen trees, I will earn another bonus, and another, and some day I will be rich. But he did not do that, preferring to linger near the smooth tempting body of his new wife, and within a year the first baby came. He was working just as hard but suddenly there was less money, not more, and as his other children came he was working more and more hours just to earn enough to feed them. Now, as he dug, he did not think of the endless rows of rubber trees. He did not regret the white sap falling silently, spilling over in the cups and wasting on the earth. What he remembered was the buttery car of the plantation boss, trimmed with brilliant gold.

In the late afternoon the other villagers began to arrive. When they saw what Muda and Norliza had done, excitement spread among them like a swift river wind. Muda heard their sighs, their gasps and exclamations, he heard the stakes driven into land, the sound of digging and excited voices. But he did not look up, and he did not change his pace.

He did not look up until a shadow fell across his back like the brush of a cool hand. It was Khamina standing over him. She had been a delicate girl, lithe and nimble. Now her sarong found no indentation at the waist and the fabric of her blouse pulled tightly against her breasts and arms. Even the skin on her face was drawn tightly over her cheekbones. Her lips were thin and trembled with anger.

"Muda," she called out sternly. All the heads turned at once to look at her. They were familiar faces, each one known to her for as many years as she had lived on earth, but she ignored them and looked directly at her husband. "Muda," she said. "What has possessed you?"

"Khamina," he said, standing up. "This is a great day in the village, Khamina. We have discovered gold."

"Gold?" she repeated. Behind him Norliza came up with the nugget displayed in her palm.

"It is true, Khamina. Gold."

"One piece," she scoffed.

"There must be more," Muda said. "To find only one nugget would be like finding only a single leaf on a tree."

For a moment it seemed she would be pacified by these words

and by the bright irregular lump in Norliza's dirty palm. Then her eyes, following the trenches Muda had been digging, fell upon her cooking pot. With a cry she reached down and swept it up, shaking out the red dust and rocks he had carefully assembled.

"I have one cooking pot," she said. "It is not for carrying dirt. And I have one husband, whose job is in the rubber trees. What are you doing here, Muda? Abdullah has been to the house twice looking for you. Your trees have spread their sap all over the ground. Muda, I did not marry a ditchdigger."

She turned then toward home, holding the dirty pot out to her side. She walked quickly and Muda knew that she was hurrying because the dusk was coming. Khamina was religious, but she also believed in spirits, and she did not want to be alone on the road at the hour when they came out.

Khamina was not alone in her fears, and before the sun set many people went home. Muda watched them leave, wondering which among them would seek his job in the rubber trees. Still, despite Khamina's words he did not leave. Like others, he lit torches along the riverbank and kept digging long past the time he could see clearly. Finally Norliza put her hand on his shoulder and told him to stop. She handed him some rice she had brought from home. He rinsed his hands in the river and began to eat, sucking the sticky grains off his fingers. He had missed his lunch, and in the cool night air from the river he was suddenly very hungry.

"What will you do?" Norliza asked finally. Only a few people were left, quietly digging. "Will you come back tomorrow?" Muda shaped some pebbles into a small hill. Then he dug his hands into the center of it and let the smooth stones rain across the ground. As they fell an idea came to him.

"I will spend tonight at the mosque praying about this matter."

She nodded. It had been their father's habit to sleep in the mosque when faced with a severe problem, waiting for guidance. They sat quietly for several minutes. Muda continued sifting through the stones. He liked their smooth feel, the warmth they still retained from the heat of the day. It was Norliza who noticed that one stone caught the moonlight in a different way, and Muda who picked it up and rinsed it in the river. It was another nugget, much smaller than Norliza's piece. But it was gold, all the same.

"Your fate," she said, wonder in her voice.

"Yes," Muda said. He felt the wonder too.

Khamina could not answer him when he handed her the gold and the story of the sign he had received, but she was not happy. She closed her lips and refused to make him food to take to the riverside, and after a few days he realized that she had sent the children to her mother's house and had taken over his job in the rubber trees. This shamed him. However, his days were full of hard work and the excitement that had possessed him on the first day did not die. Even when a day passed, or sometimes two or three days, in which no gold was found, Muda maintained his hope. Some people gave up; others began to grumble and speak of quitting. The mood of the group would grow dark and futile, and the pace of the work would slow. Then, suddenly, there would come a shout. No find was as big as the first one Norliza had made, but each one was enough to revive the spirits of the gold diggers. For every person that quit, two others came to dig, and soon the area was a swamp of mud and deep holes that filled with water when they were left overnight.

Muda dug. Even at night he dreamed that he was digging, and in his dreams his shovel touched vast boulders of gold, or caches of gold nuggets that he lifted up and let spill from his fingers. Once, in his dream, he unearthed a big car made purely of gold, and another time it was hermit crabs who came running to him, discarding their stolen shells, their soft bodies and scuttling legs all, miraculously, made from gold. He often woke from these dreams with a start, into the deep night, the soft breathing of his wife and children all around him. At these times he looked at Khamina's face, soft with sleep. She would no longer speak to him, and put his evening rice down with a tired thump. Even the children avoided him now; when he came in, late and muddy, they retreated to the edges of the room, staring, as if he were a river spirit that had come to carry them off. Once awake, Muda often could not return to sleep. Instead, he went to the river where he worked the rest of the night in the dark, as if by blurring the state between waking and dreaming he could bring the plenty of his dreams into the vivid light of day.

Yet he found no more gold. Many others had success; even Norliza had a small bag around her waist, heavy with nuggets she had sifted from the mud and water. It seemed to be a gift in her hands, that they knew where to seek, felt the shine that Muda could only see. Muda worked hard, sometimes digging far into the night, until the hole he had made reached up above his shoulders. Because Khamina had taken over his job, he worked with a great and ongoing guilt. Some nights he was afraid that if he went home he would not have the courage to return to the gold fields the next day. On those nights he went instead to the mosque. There, lying on the cool stone floor, he held his single piece of gold in his palm and prayed. For if this was truly a message from his god, why now was he being ignored, while all around him others profited?

One day the rains began, first as a light mist and then harder, so that a small pool formed in the bottom of his newest hole, and mud ran down his arms with each shovel he lifted from the earth. Late that afternoon, as Muda squatted on his heels by the side of the river, soaking wet and empty-handed, he thought that Khamina was right. He should give it up, this foolishness. He could not continue to live on hope. The night before he had been forced to ask for a loan of rice from one of his friends. Walking home, the rice had been an enormous weight in his hands. He remembered the joy of his wedding, and how that joy had dwindled into something much smaller, smaller with each child and the responsibility until it no longer buoyed him up, but hung from him like a weight.

He knew he should quit the gold fields. The thought of this relieved the weight, but to such a degree that he felt riddled with an emptiness, as if his emotions reflected the spoiled, hacked landscape of the riverbank. For he saw now that working in the rubber trees was a hopeless life. Many went there with dreams, but no rubber tapper would ever own a car the color of the sun.

People tried hard, he himself had tried, but there was no evidence of their effort in the village, where the houses were still lit by kerosene and the only running water flowed in the river. With gold they might drive themselves to ruin, but at least the hope was always there.

The rain was warm. It swept across the river like prayer veils in the wind and fell so heavily that he could not see the opposite shore. He was wet, and the dirt between his fingers was a warm, gritty mud. He rubbed it mechanically, feeling it melt away into nothing. Then he came upon something hard and sharp. Curious, thinking it was a piece of glass or tin, he rinsed the object in the river. To his surprise it was a tiny gold kris, a wavering Malay sword about ten centimeters long, inscribed with a verse from the Koran. Its tiny point was still sharp, but Muda could tell that it was very old.

"Norliza," he called through the veil of rain to where his sister was kneeling in the mud. "Norliza, come look at what I have found."

Muda was not devout, and so he was astonished by the reaction of the village to his discovery. The news spread quickly, until Muda could not go anywhere without people asking to see the kris. Even Ainon, the vegetable seller, held a newspaper over her head against the rain in order to have a glimpse, turning the kris in her brown fingers. She handed it back to him and quickly pressed her palms together in a prayer.

"You are blessed," she said. Then she chose the largest melon from the pile and handed it to him. "Take this one, please. Take it as a gift, and remember this old woman in your prayers."

No longer did people joke about his bad luck with the gold. Even Khamina was somewhat appeased. She served his rice more gently in the evening, and took to covering her hair when she went outside to shop. In the gold fields he felt the reverence of people like a circle of quietness around him.

One morning Muda arrived at the gold fields to find a dozen men in khaki uniforms handing out sheets of damp paper, announcing their news through a megaphone that cut through the mist and echoed back from the river's opposite shore.

"What is this?" he asked the nearest official, who turned toward him and thrust a paper in his hand.

"There's been a complaint," he said. He was a very young man, as young as Muda had been when he first went to the rubber plantation. "About illegal digging. Didn't you know? You must have a paper before you dig this land."

"Who complained?" Muda asked. He was not surprised to learn that it was a group from another village, latecomers who had found no gold on their faraway plots. Now these strangers stood around the fringes of the gold field, smiling because they already held the required papers in their hands. They looked greedily at the careful stakes and cordoned areas that, with a single government decree, had become ownerless.

"This isn't right," Muda said. "It isn't fair. When we go to the capital for our papers, these others will take our claims." His hand went to the kris around his neck. He'd started to wear it on a piece of string, and took some inexplicable comfort from the feel of its inscription.

The young man noticed his action. "Uncle," he said. "What's that you've got there?" Muda pressed the kris once before he opened his hand to display it for the officer. Its sharp point pricked his skin with an illuminating pain.

"This is my divine guidance," he began, and he told the young man how he had found the kris. "So you see, this decree of yours goes beyond unfairness. It works against the directive of the heavens, as well."

The young man looked uncomfortable. He pushed the cap back on his dark hair and shook his head.

"But what can I do?" he said.

"You can give us one day. Let one person go from each family for a paper. Let the others stay and dig. If there is someone without a permit tomorrow, that person must give up the claim. But we deserve this day of grace."

The young man went to talk with his superior, and then the two of them went to see still another man. Muda watched them talking, shifting their feet uneasily in the muddy ground. Soon the chief officer came over to hear Muda's story. He also examined the kris and held it in his palm. Then he picked up the megaphone and announced that the villagers would be given one day to file their claims.

It was Norliza who went from their family, running home for money and to change her clothes, giving Muda the small sack of nuggets she carried on her waist. She kissed each of her children twice on the forehead and told Amin, her oldest, to watch after them carefully. Then she, along with the others, was gone.

All morning Muda felt the unspoken animosity of the people from the other villages. He tried to work, but sometimes had a sense of foreboding so strong that the back of his neck felt cold and damp, as if suddenly beneath the shadow that would precede a blow. Several times he jerked swiftly around, but there was nothing. People worked stodgily at their claims, and when he looked at them the sense of danger disappeared like mist. Still, he would remember the feeling later, the drifting unease that became manifest early in the afternoon.

Muda was up to his waist in a new hole when he heard the shouts. He jumped out of the earth and saw Amin screaming, pointing frantically at the head of his sister as she surfaced from where she had fallen in the river. Briefly, he saw her head and shoulders turn in the slow current near the riverbank. It had been a calm river when the gold was discovered, but the rains had fattened it. Water surged with force near the center, making frothy, churning patterns that had fascinated Maimunah and drawn her to the river's edge. Now she drifted from the shore and entered the chaos. Muda, who could not swim well himself, did not think twice. The faces of his own children were in his mind as he leaped after her into the swirling waters.

The current was a thousand hands pulling him in different directions. He fought it at first, but each time he thrust his head above water he was pulled down again, rushed against the riverbed, whose stones, he thought, feeling them rub against his face and stomach, might well have been made of gold. Gold. His lungs ached, and he was thrust out of the water long enough to gulp a deep breath, long enough to catch a glimpse of Maimunah's terrified face, inches away from him. He dove forward, grasping water, and wished he had the power of his sister's hands, hands that could sift out gold from stones, hands that coaxed life into the world. Hands that would know how to fend off these river spirits who were dragging him below again.

Somewhere at the bottom of the river, rushed along so that his pockets filled with stones and water, he gave up. By some miracle the kris was still around his neck; he closed his hand around it and stopped fighting. He was a log, heavy, a log burning inside but motionless, bounced along with the current, tossed this way, then that. He was smashed into an underwater boulder with such force that he thought his arm must have broken, but even then he did not resist. And suddenly, as if he were a mouse in the mouth of the river spirits, they tired of their game and tossed him up into a calm place, a buckle in the river where the water was still and quiet.

This calmer water was full of debris. Broken branches floated near him, and he pushed past the carcasses of dead cats and lizards as he made his way to the shore. Maimunah was there. Her shorts had been torn away but her shirt was still on and was tangled in some branches. He feared she was dead, because she did not answer when he called to her. She was alive—when he touched her she turned her head to look at him—but he was filled with a deep fear because her gaze was still and blank, like calm water, and he thought that one of the river spirits had entered her while they held her underneath the water. He hooked his broken arm around a branch, wedging his elbow tightly into the mud. He was so exhausted, suddenly, that he thought he might slip back into the calm water and sink like a stone. It was only Maimunah that caused him to hold on. He collected her in his good arm, where she clung to him like a sea creature. He put his mouth very close to her ear, and he began to sing. The old songs, first of all, songs about the land, the trees, the tall grass that waved around the river. When his voice began to fade he turned to prayers that he remembered, interspersed with the verses from his lucky kris. In the end, he was reduced to only a phrase, muttering it over and over, his arms gone numb from the weight of the child and the tree. That was how the villagers found them.

The people of the village had not discussed the river spirits in years, but after Muda became so sick, they began to remember the stories. There were spirits of the water who could drag you underneath to live on air and algae, there were spirits of the currents who could enter your mind and set it spinning for the rest of your life. This was the one they feared had entered Muda. For ten days he was overtaken by a fever so strong that he twisted and mumbled on the floor of his home, and flailed at Khamina when she tried to bring him water. The imam came first, and then the local healer, who lit candles in all four corners of the room and chanted verses from the Koran, and cried out in the voices of the river spirits, trying to lure them out, to lure them home. In the end even he left, shaking his head, saying that these spirits were strong—there was nothing to be done but to wait, and pray.

On the eleventh day the fever broke by itself. Khamina had fallen into an uneasy sleep, propped against the wall across from Muda. She woke to a silence, a certain strangeness in the air. For an instant she thought he had died, but when she opened her eyes she saw him staring at her from across the room. He blinked, and asked quite clearly for a glass of water. Yet even after the fever had broken, he remained weak. People who came to visit him noticed that he hardly spoke, that his eyes wandered into the dark corners of the house, and that he was constantly touching the kris hanging from his neck. Often he was heard murmuring the verses that were inscribed there by a hand long dead.

In this time, when the villagers feared for his mind but not for his life, Muda himself was afraid of dying. During the fever he had dreamed recurring dreams of light, as strong as midday sun but without the heat. When the fever broke these dreams did not vanish. It seemed to him that he was walking in between two worlds, the familiar world of his home and one that he had dreamed, warm and unfamiliar and full of a white, soothing light. He did not wish to see anyone, not because he felt weak but because their voices seemed to come to him from so far away, through a sound like water rushing, that it cost him a great effort to listen to them. For several weeks he sat on the porch of his home, looking out into the white light that surrounded him day and night, and waited for some signal. He had it one day when the call to prayer came to him clearly, a low, sweet, peaceful voice that was not marred by the rush and static of other sounds. He listened to it, moved by its clarity, by the familiar rhythm of the words. He touched the gold kris on his bony chest. It took several days, but from that moment the world began to come back to him, until everything around him shone with a vividness, a clarity, he did not remember from before.

When he was well enough, Muda went back to his job in the rubber trees. Khamina rejoiced at first, thinking he had returned to his senses. She reestablished her place on the porch with her stacks of fragrant leaves, and for a few days she watched Muda carefully, hardly daring to believe again in the normal pattern of her life. Yet even when the village leaders came to explain how they had saved his plot at the gold fields, Muda was not tempted. He waved them away, saying only that the claim was Norliza's now, she could do what she wanted with it.

It was only as the days passed into weeks that Khamina began to understand that the madness of the gold had not disappeared, but had only been transformed. In the evenings, after the last call to prayer, she set Muda's rice out carefully on the leaves and waited for him to come home. But as in the worst days of gold, he did not appear. She discovered that he was stopping at the mosque on his way home, and that sometimes he stayed there far into the night, his forehead pressed to the cool stone floor in prayer. At home he often retreated to the porch with a lamp and his new copy of the holy book, and she sometimes woke in the middle of the night to see him there, the light flickering across his face as he murmured in the language of the imams. He grew thin and the fever-light in his eyes did not fade. He moved through his days with a terrible, strange energy. She was afraid, but she could not complain, not about the Koran, or about his hard work, or anything.

He took his new devotion even into the rubber trees with him. No longer did he nap throughout the long afternoons; instead, he prayed, a murmur that mingled with the rustling sounds of the trees. That was how the boys found him when the plantation owners came one day to his house. They followed the sound of his voice at prayer. He was resting in the rubber trees, drinking tea and turning the pages of his holy book. Muda heard the boys coming, and put the cup down slowly on the ground. When they burst into the small clearing, he saw the excitement and fear on their faces, and his hand moved without thought to cover the kris on his chest. He said one last prayer, then followed the children back to his house where the men were waiting.

It was the kris they wanted. That much he understood even before they spoke. The village chief was there, drinking the expensive Coca-Cola that Khamina had poured for all the visitors. The plantation owner did all the talking. He explained to Muda that he had heard about the kris from a government official. Did Muda know that his kris had probably belonged to a sultan's wife, over one hundred years before? She was a devout woman, and wore it on a thin gold chain around her neck. According to the family story, she had lost it one day while crossing the river in a boat. It was a miracle, really, that it was found. Now, the kris belonged in a museum. It wasn't as though Muda was giving it away, really. He could go to see it anytime. But this way others could see it too. They were sure he would want to share this kris. And it was, after all, a decree of the sultan.

Muda listened carefully, the kris resting in the palm of his hand as the man spoke. This kris was his, only his; that was something he knew. He thought about the way he had found it, how it had saved the gold fields for his village, how it had saved his life. The thought that someone could come and take it made him burn inside, go breathless. He started to speak, but the words died in his mouth. It would do no good. A decree of the sultan was not something you could argue with. The kris would be taken regardless of what he said. And so, when they finally finished speaking, he did not say a word. He put the kris into the hand of the rich man, a hand that was soft and damp with sweat. Then he stood up grace-fully and walked out of his house, but Khamina noted that for all his dignity the wild light had gone completely out of his eyes.

They had come in the gold car and Muda followed them as it left, walking steadily after the glimmering gold as it receded on the horizon. Even after it was long out of sight, the dust it had stirred up settling on the fruit trees, he walked. Finally all trace of the car was gone, and he squatted down on the side of the road in the shade. He tried to tell himself it was the divine will, but all the holy verses, even the one on the kris, which he had known in his fingertips, had fled from his mind. He sat like that, quite silent, in a vast emptiness. Across from him the golden dome of the mosque glinted in the midday sun, brightly, like a jewel.

In the Garden

ANDREW BYAR BEGAN HIS EXPERIMENT IN THE GARDEN, GO-
ing out in the dusky evenings after the help had dis-
persed for the day, after the cook had served the last
meal and washed the china and departed to catch the final trol-
ley, after the gardener had arranged the tools in a gleaming, orderly progression against the shed walls, had carried the remnants
of the weeding to the mulch pile at the edge of the grounds, and
had tended to the orchids hung like lanterns from the trellis—
that was when Andrew Byar went outside, the house behind him
lit like a great ship, his wife and grown sons moving through
their evening rituals beyond the panes of glass.

It was June, the air fragrant with jasmine, honeysuckle, and
mimosa. Catalpa blossoms burst like stars in the trees; their delicate custard scent infused the violent air. Andrew walked to the
shed, stepping quickly, almost stealthily along the path, as if he
were a thief and not the owner of these three verdant acres in the
heart of Pittsburgh, high on a bluff overlooking the flatlands on

the opposite shore of the Monongahela River. There his steel plants roared all day and night, bright as beating hearts, glinting in the distance like piles of burnished coins.

At the shed door he turned on the flashlight and stepped into darkness rich with the scent of raw wood and linseed oil and fresh, damp earth. He made his way to the workbench. Beneath it, shoved in a corner, was a wooden crate once used to ship fresh persimmons from the sea coasts of Japan, now buried under blankets. Dust billowed in Byar's narrow beam of light, and the smells of mildew and oil flew up as he dragged the crate to the middle of the room. He slid the lid off and groped inside for the strongbox hidden beneath a pile of old magazines, limp and yellowed. The box, smooth steel, was wrapped carefully in layers of oily rags, which fell in a soft pile by the polished leather of his shoes. He opened the latch with a tiny, intricate key he took from the inner pocket of his coat.

A ten-ounce bottle, fashioned of brown glass, was cushioned in a cloud of cotton. Ubiquitous, it might have held iodine, or smelling salts. Andrew Byar balanced his flashlight on the bench. He took a test tube from his pocket and carefully poured a clear liquid from the bottle, filling the vial to a line marked near the top, then stoppering it with a cork. He put the brown glass bottle back into the box, nestled the box into the rags and beneath the wilting magazines, and slid the crate back to its position beneath the bench, the moldy blankets. Flashlight in one hand and the test tube in another, he went back outside, striding past the swimming pool and down the gravel path between the camellia bushes laden with rosy white flowers, until he came to the trellis where the orchids hung.

Here, he paused. From this clearing the house was visible only in pieces through the trees, magnificent elms and oaks and sycamores hundreds of years old, rare remnants of the virgin forests felled a century before to build the city. He stood watching for a moment, glimpsing the glassy light and shadowed brick amid the leaves, imagining his wife in her evening bath, plush towels on the floor of Italian marble and rose petals scattered on the water. Recently, her hair had begun to gray, and each week a stylist came to the house and left her gilded, as pale and ornately framed as a mirror. Still, in her expressions, her slowing movements, Andrew Byar faced his own age. His two sons were home from college for the summer, apprenticed to the steel factory, which he had built from nothing and through which he had made his fortune. They were indolent young men, handsome and spoiled, and he had no confidence in them. This summer they had brought friends, steady rivers of young men and women whose bright laughter flowed through the house, who studded the tennis courts with their flashing limbs and shouts, who draped themselves over benches, sofas, armchairs, who swam laps in the natural spring pool or splashed in the shallows or drank martinis at its edge. Andrew avoided them and slept poorly, waking from nightmares where his empire, built at such sacrifice and with such canny skill, constructed so painstakingly from the hours and sweat of his whole life, had been frittered into nothing as they played.

The test tube in his hand had warmed until it seemed to give off its own heat. Andrew held it up, trying to discern if a faint glow came from within, or if this was merely a trick of the scarce evening light. The single brown bottle hidden in his shed had cost more than his pool, more even than the private train carriage fitted out with velvet and gold in which he traveled to New York City once a month. Yet if this liquid was, as he believed, an elixir of life, then no expense was too much, no cost beyond consideration, even if it cost him the earth.

He took the cork from the test tube. Slowly, carefully, drop by drop, he poured the liquid evenly into the soil around the orchid.

He stood still before the trellis then, until the darkness was complete, until the crickets and frogs filled his head with a frenzied singing that seemed near madness. Then he slipped the empty tube into his pocket and went home.

In this way his evenings passed for one month, then another. By day he was, as usual, consumed by business. He drew up contracts in his office or strode along the catwalks over the burning furnaces, while below men worked, shadows shoveling and hefting and shaping long bars of steel. The heat from the red-hot metal pleased him, as did the intricate dance between machinery and men, and he looked forward, too, to the end of every week when the accountant brought the production figures to his office high above the plant, sliding them across the mahogany desk in a black leather folder edged with gold leaf. Andrew Byar, born poor in Scotland, was a self-made man, and proud of it. He believed in the power of his own personal will, and he believed in science. Pittsburgh in the 1920s was a pulsing city, powered by great machines and fabulous inventions, and if soot sometimes fell from the air like dark snow, if the rivers grew choked and black, then Andrew Byar believed that science would find solutions. Already electricity had displaced the dangerous hiss of gas, the awkward churning of steam; in decades to come the city would gleam, a bright metropolis, sunlight scattering and refracting from the mirrored surfaces of a million well-oiled moving parts.

All made, of course, from steel.

Byar had profited from his keen understanding of new technologies, as well as from his instincts for risk and innovation. He trusted people less completely, knowing as he did about human frailty and failure—how many men had died in his plant through a single careless action, after all? How many times had a widow appeared in his office, begging for money to feed her fatherless children? He gave it, always, taking care to explain each time how the accident might have been avoided. Thus wise in matters of human failure and culpability, he had given his gardener a camera, with instructions to photograph the orchid in the garden every morning at precisely eight o'clock. Memory, with its unexpected currents, its tendency to favor hope over facts, was not something he would trust. Each day the gardener came into his study and put a manila envelope on his desk, and each day Andrew Byar dated this envelope and filed it in the oak drawer of his desk without opening it up.

At the end of the second month, when his family was in Europe, he locked the door to his study and took the sixty-one sealed envelopes from the drawer. Clear morning light poured through the windows, which ran floor to ceiling along the wall behind him. He hung the photos one by one, in chronological order, against the opposite wall, securing each to the plaster with a bit of tape. By the time he reached the last, his hands were trembling. Still, he was methodical, careful, precise. Not until the final photo was hung did he step back to survey the whole.

What he saw astounded him. He had begun with an orchid whose flowers were sparse, a plant well past its prime. Yet, nourished by this experimental liquid, the plant had flourished so profusely that change was clearly visible from one photo to another. After only a single week the orchid had burst its pot; twice more in these two months it had done the same, and now it was as large as a bush. Blooms cascaded from stems grown so long that they draped themselves over one another, trailed against the ground. He went immediately to the garden, where the orchid hung from the center of the trellis, its blossoms living jewels. He touched their waxy white petals, their deep purple hearts, with awe. What had been ordinary had become something from another world, a place more fertile and profuse, a place of unending plenty.

All day he was in a state of euphoric agitation, distracted in his morning meetings, pacing the factory grounds and glancing at his watch, willing the slow hours to pass. At last, evening began to gather, and he went home. He dismissed all the help and sent his car for Beatrice. *Wear white,* he instructed in a note, folding the dense paper once, imagining her at her dressing table, the dark words discarded amid her bottles of perfume. She would be late, he knew. Spirited and capricious, she would take her time; perhaps she would not come at all. He had seen her first one morning at dawn, an errant, early rising guest floating like a petal on the invisible and mysterious currents of the pool, her pale skin almost iridescent.

Dusk was softening the edges of the world. Impatient, unused to idleness, he arranged the setting carefully to pass the time, carrying a white wrought-iron table and chairs to the expanse of soft lawn. It was a night garden, bordered by low clouds of white alyssum. Moonflowers opened as Andrew worked, releasing their faint scents of lemon into the darkness. He hung the spectacular orchid from a low branch of a sycamore tree, each blossom like a candle in a chandelier. In a crystal bowl filled with water he placed white lilacs and camellia blossoms, so that the table seemed a part of the garden and yet appeared to float above it, too, to be suspended, hovering as bright and fleeting as a wish.

At last he heard her footsteps, rustling the gravel. And then he glimpsed her on the path, as pale and slender as the stem of a plant. Her white dress had a diaphanous layer, making her both vibrant and undefined, amorphous. She wore a fitted hat, close as a caress against her skull.

"What is it?" she asked, laughing, her lips cool against his own. "I can't wait to know. What is your surprise?"

They sat at the table. Andrew Byar pulled an unlabeled bottle from the canvas bag on the grass, the old glass smooth and undulant in his hands.

"This wine," he said, "is two centuries years old. A case of it was discovered on the bottom of the sea, part of a shipwreck off the coast of France in 1718. For all those decades it lay beneath the waters, and when they brought it up it was still intact. Think of it, Beatrice—the grapes that made this wine grew in the world when the garden where we sit was nothing but wilderness."

Beatrice smiled, intrigued, he could tell, and curious. It was the same look she had given him when she climbed out of the pool at sunrise, her skin so pale against her lavender suit, water streaming from her limbs, and found him standing there, watching her and waiting.

The cork crumbled; he poured the wine and raised his glass to hers.

"To the lost past," he toasted. "And to our future."

The rare vintage tasted darkly of burnt oak; it was dry, not bitter, with a trace of cherry. *Marvelous,* Beatrice murmured. When their glasses were empty, Andrew reached into the canvas bag and pulled out another bottle, which he put on the table beside the first.

"This one has a label," Beatrice observed.

Andrew smiled. The night air was as warm as breath. "Yes," he said. "It's the most recent vintage from the same vineyard in France where the first wine was made." He turned the modern bottle, keeping his eyes on her face. "Of course, in another two hundred years, when this bottle is opened, almost everything that is living now will be dead."

"You puzzle me," she said, and looked away, and he remembered that despite her youth she was sensitive to death; she had lost her only brother to influenza.

"Yes," he said, "it is most depressing, I agree. But Beatrice, what if you could live to drink this wine?" He put the bottle down and took her hands. "What if, in two hundred years, we could sit in this garden again, just as we are now, and open this bottle together?"

She laughed, and her laughter struck his silence like waves and fell away.

"I don't understand you," she said.

He stood then, and pulled her up. He showed her the orchid that had been so withered, now profuse with life. The year was 1922, and the Curies had transformed plain earth into something rare and unimagined. A secret of the universe had been revealed, and a restless world dreamed of transformation. In drugstores everywhere were special toothpastes, hand creams, bath salts, liniments, chocolates, all laced with radium, promising miracles. In factories across the country, women painted luminous faces onto clocks, licking the tips of their brushes to keep a fine point, tasting a bitter metal from the heart of the dark universe. The era was affluent, and most people could afford to have a little radium, but only a man as rich as Andrew Byar could have all he wanted. *Radi Os*. He whispered the name of his elixir, running his fingertips over the vial in his pocket. When he told Beatrice what the bottle had cost, she gasped. And when he poured the drops into her second glass of wine and his, this wine from grapes vanished for two hundred summers, she drank.

Paradise lost, he thought leaning back in his chair. Pale flowers opened in the darkness, amid the rising sounds of insects, and the wine warmed his throat, hers.

Paradise lost, now found.

ANDREW HAD CALLED THE CAR, it was waiting when Beatrice finally left the house, sitting quietly as a shadow by the gate. She walked, listening to the night sounds of crickets and wind in the leaves and the harsh crunch of the stones beneath her pale satin shoes. Her eyes would not stay down, she looked up into the night sky with its endless wheeling, scattering stars. Her father had a telescope and had tried to teach her the constellations, taking her to the roof of their own great house and pointing out, with infinite patience, the belts and flames and streaming hair, the cups of stars brimming over with night-darkened sky. She had studied it to please him, but she could never see what he was so intent on showing her. Celestial navigation, he explained, a science of the air: whole fleets had traveled with only these stars for guides. Beatrice stared until her eyes ached and stars burned phosphorescent against her closed lids, but even then the patterns eluded her. Often, just as she felt on the verge of seeing the stars coalesce into a shape, they seemed to swell, spilling over into rivers, shattering like a handful of rice strewn across blacktop. Her father sighed and put the telescope away. He could not imagine that his only living child would not share his love and aptitude for science.

The driver had the window rolled down. His cigarette ember made a bright arc as he reached to start the engine. Beatrice paused to tell him she would walk—the night air was so lovely—then passed through the gate into the street. Her footsteps were solid and lonely on the city sidewalks. The vast grounds of the estate rose wild and tangled beside her; a soft breeze stirred the diaphanous wrap she wore across her shoulders. The night was so dark that the random stars seemed nearly within her reach. Beatrice flung her head back to gaze at them, joy cascading through her flesh. She felt like a star herself, pale and radiant, as if every one of her cells were burning bright, as if she gave off her own particular light into the universe.

This feeling was something new: perhaps, though not certainly, it was the consequence of Andrew's elixir. When he put the drops into her wine, she had stopped laughing out of respect, though privately she had remained amused. She had drunk out of curiosity and politeness, repeating the formal, nearly silent exchanges that held their passion like a vessel, but also being true to a vow she had made to herself. For Beatrice was involved in an experiment of her own, one that had only tangentially to do with Andrew Byar. The wine had tasted old, of worn oak with a trace of mold. She let it linger on her tongue, imagining those vanished grapes, but she had tasted nothing out of the ordinary, not even the tinge of salt from all those decades beneath the sea.

It was not until later, after they had finished the wine and were walking along the rock path through the white garden, that it began. Moths, luna and sphinx, skimmed through the shadows and lit on the moonflowers, lifting their slow wings. Near the house, a bed of white nasturtiums seemed to flicker and spark. Beatrice slipped off her shoes and waded into the pool, a natural spring shaped by stones. *You look like a water lily,* Andrew said, and she glanced down at her dress, its hem soaked now and darkening. She smiled and pressed her palm to his cheek. He caught her hand and kissed it, his lips against the shallow concave below her fingers, his breath in the palm of her hand. She felt it then for the first time, how her flesh, where it had been touched by his, seemed to pulse with light, transformed, but she blamed this sensation on the wine, the starry light, the strangeness of the moonstruck garden. They walked across the grass. She stumbled, and he caught her arm, and she felt it again: the splay of his fingers like rays of sun on her skin. Inside the house, it was so different. Light trailed from his fingertips and marked her flesh, light soared through her like a comet in his bed.

Now she turned onto the avenue of stately homes, the white wrap slipping from her shoulders, her hair falling loose down her back. It was an extraordinary night, the air soft and warm, a caress. She heard the car following her in the near distance, and as she passed through the familiar gates of her father's estate, less grand than Byar's but magnificent all the same, she turned and waved to the driver, who looked straight ahead at the empty road and pretended not to see her. Then, still smiling, she followed the tree-lined path to the back garden, where she sat on a bench by the pond. On the rooftop her father's telescopes stood in a line, and beyond them, the stars.

Beatrice was twenty years old and beautiful, and she had made herself this promise: she would never be used, she would always be free. She would follow her heart wherever it might take her, and in this way she would discover her own true understanding of the world. It was an experiment as daring as Andrew's, as full of uncertain hope, though to those who knew her she was merely wild, spoiled, a girl whose family had never recovered from the death of her older brother, that young man of great promise who had survived the war only to die of influenza eight months later in the room where he'd been born. Three years ago, this was. Beatrice had been seventeen, and when the doctor emerged from her brother's room to break the news, she had felt her world splinter, like glass cracked and held only tenuously in its former shape. Her mother had collapsed, weeping, and her father had bent his graying head, revealing a vulnerable place at the back of his neck, reddened by his collar. Beatrice, however, had not moved. She had not dared. What had been held together, logical and orderly, was suddenly unbound. Her brother, whom she had loved, who had taught her to ride a horse and sneak to the train tracks to flatten pennies when the engines roared past, this brother with his pale hair and paler blue eyes, was suddenly, mysteriously gone from the world. Why? she demanded, turning her fierce anger on the friends and relatives and clergy who came to visit in the days and weeks that followed, but they shook their heads and could offer no answer more complete than the natural order of the world, a pattern fixed in place, preordained, divine.

Beatrice had been a dutiful girl, receiving the world and the rules of her society as true and inevitable, just as one accepted the moon rising or the servant girl bringing clean clothes into her room at dawn. However, she could not accept this. Walking the paths of the estate at all hours of the day and night, remembering her brother's laughter and the touch of his hand and the way sunlight made his pale hair look white, she began to question everything.

She began to push the limits of her world, too, tentatively at first, then more urgently. She was steadfast against the hue and cry that resulted, utterly determined to step beyond the strictures she had known. But she was not cynical. More than ever, the world seemed full of mysteries she could hardly comprehend, and the visible fell like a veil between herself and something else, something glimpsed at unexpected moments—a white curtain rising from an open window, or leaf shadows playing on the tiled floor of her room—images that layered and gathered, inexplicable but powerful. Yet her intuitions could no longer be contained by the structures she had accepted all her life, and this discovery made her feel breathless, as if she stood on the edge of an abyss, even while the world around her went on much as it always had, knit back together by the ordinary day-to-day. *Don't you see,* she wanted to shout, at her father bent over endless figures of steel sales and her mother arranging flowers and the cook cutting a hundred biscuits out for tea. *Don't you see that everything has changed?*

Had they looked up, she would have explained that the rules were like a net: they could not hold the fleeting thing they sought to capture. But no one did look up, and Beatrice slowly understood that she must discover the truth of the world on her own. And so, she decided, she would. She would embrace every experience; she would discard all preconceptions; she would see every moment as an open door, and she would step through each one wide-eyed, without fear.

Thus, when she emerged from the pool, water glistening cool on her pale limbs, and saw Andrew Byar watching her, transfixed, she had smiled.

And thus on this night, when the leaves stirred behind the hydrangea bushes by her father's house and a figure emerged, tall, dressed in black, invisible except for his hands and face shining out to her like beacons, she smiled once more.

"I thought you were never coming," she said, tranquil.

"I waited here for hours," the young man complained, sitting down beside her, taking her hand. Light shot through her; she thought of Andrew Byar and his garden.

"Poor Roberto," she said.

He was a distant relative of her mother's, come from Italy for the summer. Ostensibly to study, but she knew her father was seeking someone suitable to take over the business when he died. He had never considered asking Beatrice to do so, something which had not troubled her until she perceived that the rules of the world were light and hollow, easily knocked aside. Idly, she wondered if her father's decision might change if he knew that she was going to live forever, and she laughed.

"It is not funny," Roberto said, speaking in a formal, lilting English that she loved. "All day I have been dreaming of this time with you, and then you do not come. It is insulting."

"I'm sorry," she said, and she was, though she was not regretful. "I was called away unexpectedly. There was no way to inform you."

"Called away to where?"

"It's not discussible," she said lightly. "It is my own affair entirely."

He did not answer. She felt his presence beside her, dark and churning. The old Beatrice would have hastened to soothe away his anger, but now she sat quietly, waiting with interest to see what would happen next.

"I am in love with you," he said, angry at having been forced into this admission, or perhaps at the feeling itself. "I don't want to lose even a moment of our time."

She put her hand to his cheek, as she had earlier with Andrew. Offended still, Roberto turned his face away. Beatrice let her hand fall to her lap, wondering for the first time if what Andrew had claimed might be true. She had not really considered it, what it might mean to be ageless, to live outside of time. To explore every facet of the world, to follow every passion to its depths, because she would not have to choose one over another.

"What do you think?" she asked Roberto. "Would you like to live forever?"

"I have done so already," he replied at once. "Each moment you are gone is an eternity to me."

Beatrice laughed then, delighted by the way all doors opened to new places. Impulsively she kissed Roberto, sliding her hand behind his neck and her tongue into his mouth, where it bloomed like a flower struck by light.

SUMMER GREW RICH and dense, and then, subtly, it began to wane. A few leaves drifted to the ground, and overnight the dogwoods turned flame red. In his garden the orchid still flowered profuse and opulent, and elsewhere, in his car, Andrew Byar splayed his long, hard fingers on the custom-built walnut desk. The city was a rush of lights beyond his open windows, and from a distance came the roar from the steel plants, humming night and day. Recently, he had ordered a new furnace, determined to best his competitors, richer and more famous than he. They were old men now, men whose time of building and creating would soon end.

His, he believed, would not.

For two months and five days he and Beatrice had been drinking the Radi Os. It had become a ritual, and as with any ritual there were rules, intricate ceremonies that had taken on their own life, and which must not be broken. Each week they met in the garden, even though his family had returned and sometimes moved, visible, beyond the panes of glass. The alyssum had grown brittle, and the moonflowers had wilted, and the magnificent orchid would soon be moved into the greenhouse in anticipation of an early frost. Capricious still, as beautiful and willful as ever, Beatrice nonetheless joined him at the table each week, watching seriously and silently as he placed the drops into her glass. Any wine would do by now, any sort of dress, but they each assumed the same position at the table as they had on that first night, and they knew without speaking that they must finish their drinks in a single swallow. Dusk, it must be, though dusk came earlier now.

Sometimes they went inside afterward, and sometimes Beatrice merely rose and disappeared into the shadows. The eager talk of their early days, the chattering comparisons of change—flesh that quickened, fingertips that trembled—had given way to a pensive silence. They touched less and less often as the new sensations grew; even the most casual union was almost more than they could bear. One kiss, and his lips hummed for hours. A brush of their fingertips, and his hands carried her warmth, her imprint, like a brand.

Like a brand. It was so. Before the experiment, Beatrice had been a flicker on the edge of his mind, a pleasure, a reward, laughter falling amid the flowers in his garden at the end of the day. It had pleased him that she was the daughter of a significant rival, that she was pliant and easy, slipping so carelessly into his bed, apparently removed from any of the strictures and concerns that governed other women. A wild child, a free spirit, and he had chosen her because of this. Strangely, however, now that they had been sealed together by this secret, now that he saw her regularly and might go on doing so for decades or even centuries to come, she never left his mind.

Indeed, he had become obsessed with her, with her indifference. Here, after all, was the rarest gift, and he had given it to her alone, to Beatrice. Not to his wife with her gilded hair, not to his indolent sons, not to anyone else but Beatrice. She had been surprised and pleased and curious; it was true that she came faithfully each week to meet him. Yet not once had she expressed joy or wonder at having been so chosen, and lately this had begun to trouble Andrew Byar. He had given her this gift: why, then, should she still withhold her heart? Yet Beatrice remained as she had always been, amused and curious, but strangely distant, as if her own life were a book she was reading, one she might put down at any moment in order to gaze out the window at the sky.

Andrew's expectations had been so fully disappointed that he found himself regretful of the future. What if, in the uncountable days that lay before them, he became completely disillusioned with her? What if his companion turned out to be a woman he despised? The orchid thrived, cascading gemlike blossoms; released from the prospect of death, however, Andrew Byar's feelings for Beatrice were withering into dust. He saw her now in the harshest light, and became critical of the tiniest habits of her being: the way a muscle flickered her cheeks when she stifled a yawn or a smile, the irritating motion of her throat as she drank, her persistence in murmuring the foolish slang of the day whenever she was moved or delighted by the world.

In a decade, he wondered, in a century, would her quirks move him to violence? A life sentence, he mused: the phrase had taken on new meaning.

Yet at the same time he could not get enough of her. More and more often he dispatched his driver to seek her out, and more and more often she was not to be found. Her aloofness made him brood, it made him angry. He would cut her off, he thought sometimes, awash in anger, sitting alone in his great office, trembling with this unfamiliar inability to accomplish what he wished. Science had been Andrew Byar's life, yet science had not prepared him for this. Not for the rage he felt upon learning she met others, in the garden of her father's estate or on the rooftop or in the cars of trains. Not for the longing and misery that welled up to replace the rage, a depthless yearning that was what had driven him, finally, out in his car to confront her on this night.

He pulled into the circular drive before her father's house. A maid, fluttering and startled when he asked for Beatrice, explained that she was in the roof garden. Andrew brushed away her attempts to have him sit and wait. He strode across the foyer, following his instincts up the wide, curved staircase to the second floor and the steeper one to the third, where he discovered the open door and the ladder that went to the roof. He climbed, emerging into the crisp night air. Urns of flowers and small trees had transformed the rooftop into a park. Benches and tables offered places to rest and view the glittering cityscape below. Beatrice stood with her head bent over a telescope, her hair cascading over her shoulders, as the silhouetted figure beside her pointed out the belt of Orion, the Big Dipper and the Little, the flowing tresses of the Coma Berenices. "Surely you can see them," he exclaimed. He was wearing a hat, and he gestured at the stars with a folded newspaper. "Why, they are as clear as if I had drawn them there myself."

"Let me look again," she soothed. Dark hair slipped across her cheek, and in that instant Andrew Byar's anger faded. He understood that he could never deny Beatrice, any more than he could deny himself. What had begun as science and desire had become something more, something as essential to him as life itself, so that seeing her in this intimacy with a stranger, involved in a world of which he knew nothing, made him catch his breath in pain.

At this the two looked up, startled, from their telescopes.

"Andrew!" Beatrice exclaimed. Her father—for it was her father, Jonathan Crane, with his shock of white hair falling over his eyes and an old man's spotted hands—took a single step and said, "Byar, what the devil are you doing here?"

"I came to talk to Beatrice."

"Uninvited," Beatrice said sharply.

Jonathan Crane looked swiftly from one to another, his spare white beard cutting the air.

"Well," he said. "Beatrice is right here, as you see. Whether she will speak to you, I cannot say. But in any case, you may be of some assistance to me, Byar. Come here, and have a look. Beatrice insists that there is no order in the sky. Tell her, if you would, that she is wrong."

"Perhaps not wrong, exactly," Byar demurred, crossing the roof. Beatrice was staring at him; he felt her gaze like the sting of a slap. "Perhaps she prefers the stars to remain unknown."

"Perhaps I see my own patterns," she replied. "Perhaps I seek new patterns altogether."

"The world is as it is," her father said. "Come, Byar, have a look."

Andrew leaned over the telescope, gazing up at a familiar sky. When he finally stood, the old man was studying him with a gaze both unremitting and intent, reminding him of the many meetings at which they had faced each other just so, opposed on issues of steel production or charitable trusts.

"Orion," Andrew said, for the order of the stars was clear to him, and he could not see the point in saying otherwise. "And the Big Dipper, hung from the North Star as if from a hook."

"There you see, Beatrice?" her father said. "Even your secret lover can find the constellations."

Into the shocked silence that followed, the old man spoke again. "Yes, I know," he said. "All except for your intentions, Byar. Beatrice visits you, in secret, or so she presumes, every week. At those meetings you give her a glass of wine. Sometimes she goes inside with you, and sometimes she does not. I am her father, and I am asking what your intentions are."

Andrew Byar stared at his old rival. How had he been discovered so completely? His next emotion, however, was pure fear. For he had understood, in that moment when he emerged onto the roof and saw Beatrice, that desire had its roots in the possibility of loss. He understood, too, that if Beatrice were not present to solidify his belief, to confirm his confidence like light confirms a shadow, then belief might disappear from him entirely.

"This is my own affair," Beatrice was protesting, her voice clear, but trembling with anger. "You do not own me, either one of you, and you have no right to be discussing me like this."

"But I want to answer," Andrew said. Carefully, he explained the experiment to her father.

Jonathan Crane whacked the folded paper against his palm. "Ridiculous. Your ideas are nonsense."

They began to argue then, worrying the properties of radium as they had once exhausted the properties of steel. They argued with such ferocity and passion that they forgot Beatrice entirely. It was her father who noticed first that the quality of silence had changed; the rooftop with its intricate tile and urns of flowers was empty.

"You see how it is," he said gruffly, interrupting Byar. "She has gone. She chooses to ignore us both."

Beatrice was near enough, standing just beyond the doorway, to hear her father say this. She did not wait for Andrew to reply. How little they understood, she thought, descending the ladder and the flight of stairs to her rooms. How much they took for granted, and chose not to see. She had never made Andrew any promises; he had mistaken her silence for complicity, that was all. The experiment was no more her passion than were the distant and abstract patterns of the sky. Why be limited to seeing the stars as bulls and goats and scuttling crabs, when from another vantage point—from, say, the moon or Jupiter or Saturn—they might resemble something else entirely? Or beyond even that, within another way of perceiving, within a new framework of thought, a person might discover patterns beyond what her father or Andrew Byar or anyone else imagined. They did not, after all, have the slightest insight about the mysteries of her own heart. Why, then, should she trust their vision of the world?

Well, she would not. It did not take her long to pack a suitcase.

The house was silent. Roberto had proposed to her, and in the wake of her refusal he had in turn refused her father, turning his back on the steel trade and returning to Padua to study botany. *I am free of you now,* he had written on one terse postcard, and she had considered this for a moment before she wrote on the bottom, *Your freedom brings me joy,* and sent it back.

One suitcase, but it was heavy. She lugged it down the stairs and through the marble-floored foyer, grateful for the murmuring of the fountain, which masked her footsteps. Outside, Andrew's car was waiting. The driver started the engine the instant he saw her in the doorway. Well, why not? Beatrice thought, though she had intended to call a cab. Tonight she would accept a ride—yes, why not? The driver tossed his cigarette into the gravel and got out to put her bag in the back. Beatrice slid across the cool leather seat, folding her hands on the walnut desk, inhaling Andrew's peculiar scent: cologne and cigars and an underlying whiff of steel. The liquid in his little bottles was odorless, but the car was filled with the aromas of money and autumn air, close counterparts, somehow. *To the station,* she instructed, and the driver pulled away. She glanced back at the house, wondering if Andrew and her father were still on the roof, discussing the stars or the stock market or her own stubborn nature. No matter, really. She would take the first train, wherever it might go. She picked up Andrew's pen. Across the production figures, which he would see as soon as the car returned to fetch him, she wrote in bold black letters, *My freedom brings me joy.*

BEATRICE TRAVELED for nearly a year, to Boston and Chicago, New York and Philadelphia and Washington, D.C. Stories of her wildness rippled in her wake, how she drank too much and danced barefoot in the snow and took lovers with careless abandon. Scandalous photos appeared in the society pages: Beatrice with her slender arms around one neck or another, the delicate rise of her breasts visible beneath her risqué dresses. Beatrice dressed up like a man, dressed up like a bear, wearing a corona like a star. She was always laughing, but people noted that her wildness had made her thin, had lent a feverish quality to her eyes. They watched Andrew Byar slyly, too, commenting on how

gaunt he'd grown, waning like a moon in her absence. Or perhaps it was the strikes, which had begun just after the new furnace arrived and three hundred workers were laid off in the
name of progress. In bloody protest, whole production lines had
shut down for weeks, rendering meaningless the neat projections
across which Beatrice had scrawled her liberation.

On the verge of summer, the stories of Beatrice's escapades
suddenly ceased. The photos stopped. Her father made discreet
inquiries, only to discover that no one had seen Beatrice since a
party at an estate in the far reaches of the Adirondacks a month
earlier, where she had danced frantically, people said, frenetically
and without ceasing. She was there, dancing, and then she was
gone. Just like that, disappeared, though no one had thought too
much about it at the time. Perhaps she had stepped out onto a
terrace for a breath of air, perhaps she had gone for a stroll.

No one had seen her pause on the side of the swirling room
and light a cigarette. Or they had seen her and had not noticed,
for the party was wild and everyone was drinking, and in the ki-
netic mosaic of the evening Beatrice was only one more fragment
of color. She drew the smoke in deeply, watching the flash of
arms and ankles, the beaded dresses glinting. Then she slipped
through the French doors onto the terrace, closing them behind
her, so that the visual intensity of the party was separated from its
noise, which came to her distantly now, muffled. She inhaled
again, folding her bare arms against the night air. She had begun
to smoke at some point, in Chicago, she thought it had been,
where a young man had left his cigarettes on a table and she had
slipped them into her purse. Chicago or Boston or New York:
this was one discovery, that it really didn't matter. Whatever
truth she'd been seeking, trying on the laughter and the costumes
and the men, she simply had not found. One by one she'd discarded them, and now she stood here, at a party that was real, but
also unreal, a place that was not her own. Her Pittsburgh life was
lost as well, no more now than a dream. She had heard rumors of
the strikes, of course, and through them rumors of Andrew. She
had seen his photograph twice, and noted how he'd aged.
Strangely, she found that she missed the meetings in the garden,

so secret and exhilarating. She missed even Andrew and her father, for without their orderly views of the world to work against, to define her, the freedom she had gained had fallen flat. The room beyond the glass doors swayed and pulsed. Beatrice threw her cigarette, still smoldering, into the wet grass, and walked alone to the lake.

It was dark. Waves lapped at the shore. She slid her shoes off and waded to her ankles in the frigid water, so recently ice. In recent weeks the sensations of light had slowly left her, replaced now and then with mysterious shooting pains that came and went and finally came and stayed. In motion, she did not feel them, which was one reason she lived as she had. She squatted down and cupped the icy water in her hands, listening to the distant call of loons. A flash of white on the opposite shore caught her attention. She looked up, then held herself as still as the water, searching the line of trees.

Maybe it was nothing, or maybe nothing stranger than nasturtiums glinting sparks in the dusk of Andrew's garden. But it seemed to Beatrice that she glimpsed her brother, standing as naturally amid the trees as a deer, one hand in his pocket and his head tilted at an angle, the forest at his back. For a long time, until her legs ached and began to tremble with the exertion of stillness, she did not move. When she stood, he was gone. But she was convinced that he had been there, that she had glimpsed something vital through these trees. Barefoot, still, she left the lake and followed him.

It was a near-wilderness, and night. In the house, people laughed and sang and fell asleep on sofas even as the music played, ices slipping from their hands. Days passed before her disappearance was discovered. Two weeks before search parties were dispatched, and yet another ten days before Beatrice was found, not by anyone looking, but by a group of boys attempting to become Eagle Scouts. Thin as a leaf, her clothes torn and dirty, she was sitting on a rock by a stream. She did not seem at all surprised to see them. "Oh, hello," she said, standing and brushing dirt from her hands. "I've been wondering when somebody would come."

The boys clustered around her, astounded. To them she seemed like an enchanted creature, a deer that spoke, a shaft of light assuming human form. They were afraid at first, hesitant to offer her their arms. The unplanned hike back took most of a day, for the boys, inexperienced, were forced to stop often and consult their compasses. Also, Beatrice was weak. She walked slowly, and at first she walked in silence. After a few hours, though, she began to tell them stories, fantastic stories, of her weeks alone in the woods. Later they would argue over them, agreeing on the details but never the whole. She had eaten the earth, she claimed, she had broken open maple trees no bigger than her finger and drunk the rising sap. She had stood in a shockingly hard rain, water dripping from her fingertips, from her hair, and watched a herd of elk move across a clearing. She had been following her brother at first, sighting the glint of his hair one moment and the flash of a limb another, but in the end he had disappeared, and she had been left alone. This she did not tell the boys, fearing it would frighten them, as it had frightened her, to hear of the dark nights she'd spent, sleeping on moss or pine boughs, the nights so pure black that she couldn't tell, finally, if the darkness was coming from within her or without. As it was, she frightened them anyway. Her arm was no more than a living bone beneath their hands as they helped her across streams and over fallen logs. They imagined a dark forest of the heart, the pulse of blood and weave of branches, and they let her go as soon as possible.

Beatrice saw the fear in their eyes; she heard them saying, later, that she had lost her mind. In the wake of this derision she grew silent, aware that she could never explain how solitude, so unfamiliar and so perilous, had altered her forever.

In his great house on the bluffs, Andrew read of her rescue. No longer well himself, he spent most days in his sunny office, going through his papers, or sitting in the solarium with his wife. He studied the brief story on the back page, which chronicled Beatrice's emergence from the forest, leaves woven in her hair, dirt ground into her dress.

When she returned to Pittsburgh, he went to meet her at the

station. She stepped from the train, dressed simply in a white silk skirt and a gray cashmere sweater. She was very thin. *She is dying,* he thought, which is what Beatrice thought, too, when she saw Andrew standing on the platform, as hunched and gray as a comma. Her heart swelled up with sadness, as well as with a sudden, inexplicable love. She knew as vividly as if she had seen it herself that the orchid was withered in the greenhouse, its flowers gone, its very leaves and stems marked with burns. She was twenty-one years old.

"I loved you," Andrew whispered as she passed him. "You must believe me, Beatrice, I chose you out of love."

"No," she said. She spoke evenly, for her fear and bitterness had faded during her weeks in the forest. "It was not love between us then, never enough love from either you or me. I was your experiment. And you were part of mine."

They did not speak again, though within months they were living in the same sanatorium. What they had observed in one another was terribly true: they were dying. Geiger counters clicked and chattered on their breath, voicing the disintegration of their cells. The slightest touch raised bruises, the color of pale lilacs against thunderclouds, on their arms. The families came, bearing flowers, wine, books, news, the small comforts of the day-to-day, and if they passed one another in the halls they averted their eyes: whatever connection had existed between Andrew and Beatrice was ignored, as if ignoring might erase it.

One afternoon, when everyone had left, Beatrice stood, filled with an insatiable restlessness. She must move. The staircase was grand, built of hickory and curving down to the main floor, where French doors opened onto the gardens. It took her half an hour to descend. Outside, the grass was warm, thick, springing up beneath her bare feet. She felt a wave of pure astonishment at its texture, as if each blade pressed separately and softly against her flesh.

No one was in sight; the sunlight was a warm hand, moving and returning. She thought of Andrew, how solemn he had been as he put the drops into their glasses, how deeply he had believed in— had depended on—the certainties of science. She had never shared his belief, but she had no regrets. It was not, as some argued, misguided love or self-sacrifice or the whimsical nature of a young girl's heart that had brought her to this moment. She had been no vessel for another's dreams, no casualty in Andrew's single-minded pursuit of scientific knowledge. It had been life she wanted, life she had embraced, no moment lost or left unexplored, no light or darkness left unseen.

Beatrice paused to rest on a ledge of stone. High up in the brick building, a curtain flickered in a window, lifting for an instant like a veil. *I create the universe,* she murmured, knowing it was in some strange sense true, for she understood now that the world was a shimmering place, shaped anew in every instant by the mystery of perception, each atom in constant if invisible motion. Except that suddenly for Beatrice the motion *was* visible. The earth beneath her feet felt as volatile as ocean waves, and the transitory beauty of the garden, the subtle shifts and alterations of even the boulders, left her breathless.

The wind lifted. Branches hummed, and then the stones began to groan, resonant and strange. All around her borders dissolved, spilling trees and flowers from their shapes; the air was stained with color. Within herself, beyond herself, there was this swirl and glitter: this was the wondrous and terrifying knowledge she had gained. Beauty, too, and even a coherence in the way her thoughts themselves were splintered, coming to her in layers and rushes: her brother's bright hair and the feel of a horse about to leap beneath her, her father's reddened neck and the scent of baking biscuits floating through the house on a rainy day. And Andrew's face in his luminous garden, so solemn and so full of hope. *The elixir of life,* he was saying, and now the stones were speaking, too, a chant reverberating through every cell of everything, living and inert, a sound so powerful that even her own body began to blur and lose its form, cascading into the unstill world like petals falling, like water shattering, like every minute particle of light.

Rat Stories

WHEN CLAIRE STEPPED OUT ONTO THE VERANDA, CARRYing a tray of drinks to her guests, the rat that had been crouched behind the fern ran up the wall and scurried across the iron railing. Claire noted it calmly from the corner of her eye, the humped gray body and trailing tail, and it was only the sudden scream from Inez, who leaped up and stood quivering on her rattan chair, that caused Claire to drop her tray. Steve hurried to console their frightened guest, placing a firm and steady hand on the small of her back. Raoul and Paul both lunged to catch the falling drinks, but missed. Glass shattered, gin and whiskey spread out in pools, ice cubes skidded to all four corners of the intricate tile floor.

"Shit," Claire said, first in English and then in French. She had been a diplomatic hostess, switching back and forth between languages all day. "Shit shit shit."

"Claire," Steve warned. He had helped Inez down from the chair and stood with a hand protectively on her arm. Steve directed agricultural projects in the Third World, and Inez had arrived from the main office last week in order to assess his work. She had come several times in the past year, visits that threw the office into an uproar. After so many nights of listening to Steve rant about Inez, her imperial demeanor, her outrageous demands, her lack of understanding of the practical constraints of this or that, it was very odd for Claire to see him standing next to her, solicitous and gracious, the perfect host. But this visit was important. Inez was here to renew Steve's funding, or not. The stress of these last weeks had left Steve paler than usual beneath his dark beard, his forehead creased with worry lines. Since the day Inez had arrived, stepping onto the shimmering tarmac in a peach-colored suit and wide-brimmed straw hat, Claire had hardly seen him. "That'll be enough, Claire," Steve said now.

They had been fighting all day—all week, for that matter— and if they had been alone she would have crossed the room, slapped his face, maybe, and asked him what did he think she was, the bloody maid? These were his guests, after all, not hers, and it was also not her fault about the rats in the house, or about foolish, powerful Inez leaping onto a chair, her knees locked together in fright. But they were not alone and would not be for hours, so instead Claire gazed down at the pool of spreading liquor, at Raoul leaning over to pluck sparkling shards of glass from the floor. Raoul was an educational consultant, the only person at the agency, aside from Steve, Claire could say she truly liked.

"No, no, that's fine, Raoul," she said, touching his arm. "Leave the glass. The maid will see to it. I'll fetch us a fresh round, in the meantime."

By the time she came back with the second tray, the mess was gone and everyone was seated again. Inez, her long legs curled beneath her, accepted the gin with a feeble smile. "Thank you," she murmured, taking a deep drink. "I feel so silly, but I have a deep terror of rats."

Raoul took a gin for himself and handed a whiskey to Paul, a young man who had been introduced as an assistant to Inez. Always before, Inez had traveled alone, and so tonight Claire was very curious about Paul, who, though at least twenty years younger than Inez, had hair that was already a striking, lustrous gray. Claire suspected an affair between them, and she was longing to ask Raoul, who was short, slender, witty, and who whispered sly jokes and gossip to her at agency parties. But she had not had a moment alone with him all evening, and he was flying out again tomorrow. She tossed her long braid back over her shoulder and sat down. Raoul took a long swallow of his drink and nodded at her, pleased.

"Just the thing," he said. "Nothing like gin in the tropics." He smiled at Claire. "Now," he went on, "you mustn't mind Inez, who is still suffering from jet lag. Ordinarily she's the perfect guest."

"Inez is a *wonderful* guest," Steve protested.

Raoul waved his hand dismissively.

"No, she's not herself tonight. But you mustn't feel embarrassed, Inez," he went on. "They're dreadful creatures, rats. When I was in Africa, the place I stayed was an old mission that was infested with them. When the first missionaries came, you see, the natives had given this particular hillside to them gladly, because it was supposed to be haunted. No one would live there. People had always used it as a kind of dump, and over the years the rats had taken hold. Well, they built the mission anyway, but they couldn't get rid of the rats. There was no eradicating them. Some of them were huge, too, as big as possums. I got used to it, but even so I used to carry a club with me whenever I went out at night. They were *that* big. My assistant was more courageous. He used to squash the smaller ones with his bare feet and think nothing of it. It was just like swatting flies, to him."

"Oh, Raoul, really, how disgusting," Inez said. She shook her head and sipped her gin and gazed moodily over the dusty street where a group of naked children was playing. Everything about her was long, Claire noted, her hair, her limbs, the bones in her face. "I couldn't bear to see that, I'm absolutely sure."

Raoul shrugged, winked surreptitiously at Claire. He smelled faintly of cloves. "You get used to it," he repeated. "Good grief, Inez, after the places you've lived, I would expect you to be completely immune."

"I know, I know," Inez lamented. "I certainly should be. But it gets no better. I find myself worse each time. I can't stand the thought of them running over my feet."

"Never mind, Inez," Steve said. His voice was deep, soft, comforting. He wore a batik shirt, darkly printed, and the dying sun cast his tanned arms in gold. Claire gazed at him, remembering nights all over the world—in Nepal and the Sudan, in Laos and once in Myanmar—when he had spoken that way to her. It had not happened for a long time now. The last sunlight slanted across the balcony, illuminating Steve's face, the play of light and shadows making his features seem both strong and even. He offered Inez a smile that Claire herself had not seen in weeks, then reached over to top up her glass with tonic. "I'm sure that particular rat was a complete aberration," he lied. "I'm sure we've seen the last rat of the evening."

"You are always so calm, Steve," Inez said. "It is a very reassuring quality, you know." She smiled up at him, but she still didn't put her feet on the floor.

Just as well, Claire thought, remembering the nest they had discovered just that morning, after days of mysterious tracks and rustlings, and whiffs of the telltale vile odor, like damp, rotting fur. *Now I understand,* Steve had said, stepping back from the tangled nest, stuffed with bits of cloth and vegetation, the dark, wiry rodent hair. *Now I know where that phrase comes from, "I smell a rat."*

Paul put his glass on the table and cleared his throat. He had been silent all evening, polite but mysterious, and now everyone glanced in his direction. He was attractive, Claire thought, his thick gray hair falling in waves against his tan face, like the sea against sand. He looked like a hero out of the Ramayana, sitting here on her veranda. She leaned forward to hear what he had to say, wanting not to like him, wanting to think Inez unhappy.

"They used to eat rats," Paul said evenly, "at the place I was staying in South America."

"Don't tell me about it," Inez insisted. She waved one long hand in the air and shook her head. "Please!"

Paul smiled. His teeth were white and perfectly even. "I will, though," he said. Claire studied him closely, wondering if it was courage or just ignorance that made him push on this way. People who worked for Inez generally did whatever necessary to keep her happy. "I think you need some shock therapy, Inez. Maybe what we really need to do is trap a rat and let you touch it."

"We could oblige," Claire put in, drawing a dark look from Steve, feeling as free and giddy as if she were standing at the edge of a precipice. Inez's face was now so taut that two small lines had deepened on either side of her mouth. "Our maid bought these traps, like little cages. Once the rats are caught, she smacks them on the head and tosses them out into the street. You've seen them everywhere, I'm sure, dead rats slowly becoming part of the road."

Paul chuckled, Raoul shook his head, amused, and Inez choked slightly on her gin.

"Claire," Steve said. The anger in his voice was like ground glass, glittering, so seductive and so fine that only she could feel its sharpness. "Darling. See how you are distressing Inez." He smiled and gestured to the cut-glass dish, nearly empty, on the table. "We're almost out of cashews here," he said. "Don't we have any more?"

He was so polite! Such a wonderful man, Inez must be thinking, and so handsome with that dark beard, those vivid blue eyes. Only Claire heard the thick weave of anger cushioning his every word. She gave him a dazzling smile. "I don't know," she said. "Why don't you go and see?"

The cashews were in the freezer, carefully sealed away from rodents. They both knew it. Steve hesitated, then put down his glass and maneuvered past Inez. When he brushed Claire's shoulder his animosity reached her like a cold breeze, and anger bloomed darkly in her own heart. Steve was worried, she could tell, that she would mess up his funding, though he should know better. After all these years, of course she would be a proper hostess. For the sake of the funding, she would keep the rest of her rat stories to herself. But she saw with satisfaction that Paul and Raoul had already become engrossed in the topic.

"I'm serious," Paul said. He put down his drink and leaned back in his chair, running his hands through his thick hair and clasping them behind his head. "If you want to conquer your fear,

Inez, you must first face up to it. It worked for me. I was in the Seychelles for a while, doing an engineering project. And I always noticed that the workers had lost a few layers of skin on their fingertips and their toes. I thought no more of it until this happened to me, once or twice, that I had this funny reaction with my skin. At first I thought it was some kind of disease. I even looked up the symptoms of leprosy. One day I became concerned enough to ask a doctor. He was an Indian doctor, a Sikh. He wore a pure white turban on his head. He took one look at my fingertips and laughed. 'Oh, Mr. Paul,' he said. 'I see you are being bothered by our cunning rats. They come in the night, don't you know, and numb the fingertips with their breath. Then they can nibble at the first few layers of skin undetected.'"

Claire smiled. Inez's long face had twisted into an expression of near pain. "Thank you very much, Paul," Inez said. "I shall never sleep again."

Paul shook his head with some impatience. He held up his fingers, which were long and square tipped. For a moment everyone was quiet, gazing at Paul's unblemished hands. "My point is not to disgust you, Inez. I'm trying to explain. Just think of how I felt, with those rat marks on my fingertips already. I went out and bought all the rolls of wire I could find, and I rigged up a veritable fortress in my room. My skin healed, but I still didn't sleep well. I kept thinking of the little rat teeth, white, like the points of knives. I woke up in cold sweats, dreaming of them. Finally, I decided if I could touch a rat, in a controlled situation, that is, then I might be able to move beyond the fear. And so I trapped one, at night, in a cage like Claire described. My God, it was a big one too, and black. But I made myself touch it, and it wasn't so different than, say, touching a cat. I poisoned it, soon after. It wasn't pleasant, but the dreams stopped, and since then I haven't worried at all about rats."

Inez, listening, had drained her drink. "Well, I admire you, Paul," she said, putting her sweaty glass down on the table. "But I couldn't possibly touch a rat. With me it is a genuine phobia. I'm not scared of any other animal. For instance—here's a real story for you—I was living out in the countryside in Indonesia in this lovely little villa. It was next to a river, perfectly marvelous, with the coconut trees swaying overhead and all sorts of wildlife. Monitor lizards as long as you are tall, Paul, and once I even saw an alligator slide off the banks into the water. I used to like it all well enough, watching it from the balcony on the second story.

"Well, one day I came home from work early. It was one of those steamy hot days you get in the interior, and I was drenched with sweat. Shrugged out of my clothes right away, grabbed my sarong, and padded off for a bath. The tub was on the left side of the room, the sink directly to the right, and I went for the sink first because I wanted to brush my teeth. So imagine this, now. I was standing there at the sink, my mouth all frothy with toothpaste, when in the glass of the mirror I saw something dark move in the tub. A lizard, I thought first, though I knew instinctively that it was not. I froze right there, with the toothbrush in my mouth, and watched in the mirror as a cobra rose up against the white porcelain of the bath."

Steve had stopped in the doorway with the crystal bowl full of cashews, and Inez paused in her story to smile and wave him to his chair. She was flushed, two bright spots of color on her pale cheeks, and her long fingers moved like narrow shafts of light. Raoul and Paul, who had both drawn forward in their chairs, took advantage of the pause to replenish their drinks. Claire studied Steve as he placed the nuts in the middle of the table. He was smiling, but a muscle twitched in his lean face. So much of life turned out to be a matter of luck, good or bad, Claire thought, reaching for a cashew. This party, for instance, was something they had planned quite carefully for weeks, and yet it had nearly been ruined. Everything had been ready, the marble floors polished, the windows sparkling, the roast in the oven, when the vilest smell in the world had begun to permeate the house. Wordless, she and Steve had met in the kitchen, setting aside their dust rags and their animosity. Steve turned off the gas and yanked the oven away from the wall, and together they had tilted it forward to look into the space behind.

The stench—baked urine, singed hair—had sharpened, and with the stove balanced between them they had heard frantic movement.

And then, as if in sudden consensus, the rats had begun to leap from their nest in the stove. One after another, thick black rats followed by their smaller babies. Like Inez, Claire had wanted to scream and run, but because she and Steve were balancing the heavy stove between them, there was nothing to do but wait for the rats to leave. One of them had slid right down her arm. Even now, hours later, Claire could feel the wiry rat claws on the skin. She shivered, shaking off the sensation, then spoke to Inez.

"How vulnerable you must have felt," she said.

"Oh, I was terrified." Inez had been gazing pensively into the foliage, but now she looked up and grew animated again. "I just froze. I don't know if you've ever seen a cobra, outside of pictures, I mean. Well, they are *evil* looking. Black and swaying, with that decorated cowl. I held perfectly still for an instant, and watched it sway and hiss at me in the mirror. There were several yards between us. I had to decide if it was close enough to strike. Finally, I bolted and ran like hell out of the bathroom, screaming bloody murder for the maid and the gardener."

"Thank the heavens," Raoul said as Inez paused, "for maids and gardeners."

Inez shook her head. "So you'd think. But they were more terrified than I was. The gardener gave me a forked stick about four meters long and explained how to use it, but he refused to even go upstairs. So I had a drink and then I went up by myself. The snake was gone, so I sat down on the toilet and waited. Sure enough, after an hour it came back, stuck its head up from the drain and slithered out. I pinned it with the stick and cut off its head with a machete the gardener had given me. The blood—oh, it was *awful*. But my point is, it didn't bother me a bit to touch that snake, not once it was dead. But I'm still quite sure that I could never bring myself to touch a rat, even one that was very, very dead."

"Inez," Steve said, raising his glass in a toast. "That's an amazing story. I'd like to make a toast to you. High points for bravery."

Claire raised her glass along with the others, and even smiled, though she thought that Steve had gone too far, was sliding over the edge into obsequious behavior.

"Yes," Raoul said, clinking his glass against Steve's. "Well. Perhaps you ought to acquire a python, Inez, to eat your rats. I saw one devour a cat once, and it was quite effective."

They all laughed and stood up. The darkness had descended with tropical suddenness. Frangipani blossoms glowed faintly all around them, their heavy scent drifting through the air. Steve, deferential as a footman, took Inez's elbow, and Claire turned away abruptly, leaving the nuts and dirty glasses to the rats that lurked behind them in the dark leaves.

The original dinner, which had begun to bake with the rats in the oven, had been thrown away, and Claire had rushed to the nearest restaurant for an order of biryani rice and curried chicken. Now the maid served it up in steaming bowls, as if it had been concocted in their own kitchen. The three guests ate heartily. Lovely curry, Raoul murmured, helping himself to more of the golden rice. Extraordinary biryani! Even Inez ate with gusto, as if she were filling up all the long narrow hollows of her limbs. Only Steve and Claire, the scent of baking rats still vividly with them, ate sparingly. Nevertheless, the dinner conversation was polite and lively. At the end of it, after a dessert of fresh mangoes and dark coffee, Inez sat back and answered the unspoken question that had shaped the evening.

"Steve," she said. "Claire. What a lovely dinner party. And I think we both agree," she added, nodding toward Raoul, "that you are doing good work here. I feel sure your funding will be extended. It is what I will recommend."

"That's splendid," Steve said, and Claire heard the relief rushing through his voice. "I'm just delighted."

"It *is* wonderful," Claire agreed. Already the worry was easing from Steve's face, and she thought yes, good, now we will get our lives back once again.

They stayed for a second cup of coffee, and Claire had her earlier suspicions confirmed when Paul excused himself, pleading an early morning, and Inez, her eyes lingering on him as he left, got up a moment later. She smiled languidly as she rose, stretching her long arms. "My wrap," she murmured. "I have an early morning, too. Did I leave it on the veranda?"

"I'll look," Steve said, standing up immediately, and Claire knew he was thinking of the rats. "You wait here."

"Nonsense," Inez said. "I'm coming with you. Otherwise, you won't know where to look. Besides, I want to finalize a detail or two with you."

Steve shot a look at Claire, who shrugged. Inez had already announced her decision; what harm could rats do now? She watched them walk through the living room, Inez trailing a sweet perfume, her white dress luminous in the darkness.

Raoul put his hand on her arm. "Delightful, Claire," he said. "And congratulations. The funding decisions were next to impossible this year. You really made an impression here tonight."

"Despite the rat?" she joked, and Raoul laughed.

"Because of the rats," he said. "I really think so. Inez loves to tell her cobra story, and she so rarely gets a chance."

"And who is Paul?" Claire asked, taking a step closer to Raoul and lowering her voice. "Is there something going on?"

"Going on?" Raoul repeated, and Claire saw, to her surprise, that he was flustered.

"Between Paul and Inez," she said. "I thought I sensed . . . something."

"Oh, maybe," Raoul said, and shrugged. "Who knows, with Inez. Anything could be happening. The woman *is* a cobra."

Claire laughed.

"Lovely evening," Raoul said again, kissing her cheek.

Claire saw him to the door, and on an impulse she went outside, into the garden. There were no streetlights, but the moon had risen high above the city and the frangipani tree glowed, the white blossoms cascading to the ground. Claire hugged her arms, inhaled deeply, feeling the sweet release of a job well done, of success. Later tonight she and Steve would go over the evening, relishing the happy outcome, laughing, finally, at the near catastrophe with the rats. It would be like the old times, days and nights they had spent working in the most remote villages, living in thatched huts and hauling water from communal wells. Hard experiences, in some ways, but they had lain together every night, whispering their dreams and plans, the stars so close in the well-

ing darkness that they might have reached out and plucked some
from the sky. Now Claire pulled a frangipani blossom from the
tree, fingering its waxen petals. Things had seemed so much sim-
pler when she and Steve were young. They had gone out in the
world to make a difference, and for many years had done so, without all these complications.

The rustling came from the veranda and at first she tensed,
thinking it was another rat. Then she saw the dull ember of Inez's
cigarette, the glow of her dress, and Steve's voice lifted through the
foliage. Inez laughed, a soft sound, and Claire took a step, meaning
to call out. But a movement stopped her. They were two shadows,
that was all, Steve dark in his printed shirt, Inez pale in her white
dress, and she watched them pull together, intertwine. The kiss
lasted for a very long time, it seemed. Claire stood in the garden
and watched them as she might watch two strangers, conscious not
of anger or jealousy, but rather a letting down, a disappointment
so vast that she felt herself paralyzed by its weight. It was only after they drew away from one another, Inez laughing lightly and
touching her long fingers to Steve's face, that Claire roused herself.
She hurried back and met them in the foyer. Everything was no
more or less than usual, Inez sliding into a white silk jacket, Steve
reaching out to shake her hand.

"Divine," Inez said, brushing her lips against Claire's cheek.
"Delightful, Claire. All my thanks."

"Well," Steve said when she was gone. He closed the door and
leaned against it. "Sweet success. No thanks to you and your rat
stories, I might add."

"Rats weren't the only thing I might have mentioned," Claire
said, noticing the slackness in his jaw, the odd asymmetry of his
nose, as if he were a person she had never met before.

Steve didn't answer. He looked at her steadily, then closed his
eyes. "I don't know what you're getting at," he said.

Claire ran her hands across her arms. Hours had passed, yet
she could still feel the tiny rat feet scraping down her skin. "I think
you know very well what I mean," she said.

Steve pulled himself away from the door and walked across the
room. Now that the long worrying was over, his face was youthful

and relaxed again, almost boyish. Claire found it hard to move, hard, almost, to breathe. She knew she ought to say something about the kiss she had witnessed, but she could not seem to summon the words. What would he say, anyway? That it did not matter? That it did? Either way, what would they do next? There was a time when Claire's opinion had influenced all Steve's actions, but now she feared her words would not touch him in the least.

Steve did not seem to notice her distress. "I got the funding," he said pensively, with a hint of venal joy. "I think that's what really matters."

"Is it?" Claire asked, turning back to survey the table, empty now except for a slender vase full of white and purple orchids. Already the maid had finished the dishes and gone home.

"Yes," Steve said. He was looking at her now, standing in the doorway to the bedroom, one hand on the door frame, the other hanging loosely at his side. In his face she saw such exhaustion and such sadness that she knew the kiss she had witnessed was not the first between them, or the last. "I don't mean to be cruel, Claire," he said, "but right now that's the main thing, yes."

That night Claire slept fitfully. She did not think directly of the long kiss she had seen, or what it might mean. Instead, she thought about the story she had not told, which remained vividly alive in her mind. She could not forget the feel of the rat feet, or the smell of the rats as they burst from the oven, one after another, abandoning their burning nest. There was the ruined roast, splattered on the floor, covered with rat tracks. There was the oven, turned on its side, the hairs and sticks of the rat nest spilling out the back. Neither she nor Steve had spoken as they scrubbed. The maid was on half salary, and half days. Inez was coming to dinner. Every time Steve swore, Claire had felt it run through her like a blow. Now the day had reached its uneasy conclusion, but the scent of rats, the feel of their wiry feet, lingered still.

Once during that night she started awake in the dark room, thinking she heard the thump of rats in the wall, and later she woke again with a twitching in her extremities, convinced that rats had nibbled at her fingertips and toes. But her flesh was intact, the skin smooth and firm and whole. She curled up, drawing her limbs close together beneath the sheet. Was it really possible, she wondered, to have your flesh eaten while you slept? Steve's hand was flung out across the pillow. She leaned close to it, breathing lightly on his fingertips at first, then making an experimental nip at his flesh. He didn't stir. Claire, disturbed by this evidence, tried again. Your guests, she thought. Your agency, the compromises that you made. This was the hand that had pulled Inez close on the veranda.

She bit harder than she meant to then, and the hand jerked suddenly away. Still sleeping, Steve opened his eyes and looked straight at her, confused, unseeing, caught within his dreams. "What is it?" he said, putting his hand on her heart, his warm fingers like a fan against her skin. "What's happening?" Then his panic eased; he rolled over and drew himself to the far side of the bed, leaving Claire with a smooth expanse of sheet on either side. Above, the ceiling fan whirred and clicked. Yes, Claire thought, listening to Steve breathe, and listening beyond to what might have been palm leaves rustling, or the faint scratching of rats in the walls. Tomorrow he would run his thumb across the dull ache in this finger. He would look at her, uncertain. Let him wonder, Claire thought. In the morning, let him wonder. This was another story she would not tell.

The Story
of My Life

Y OU'D KNOW ME IF YOU SAW ME. MAYBE NOT RIGHT AWAY. But you'd stop, lots of people do. I bet you'd look back twice at me, and wonder. I'd be an image lingering in your thoughts for days to come, nagging, like a forgotten name on the edge of your mind, like an unwelcome memory twisting up through dreams. Then you'd catch a glimpse of me on television, or gazing at you from a poster as you hurried down the sidewalk, and you'd remember. I'd come into your mind like a vision then, a bright and terrifying light.

Some people see it in an instant. They call out to me and stop me on the street. I have felt their hands, their vivid glances, the demanding pressure of their embraces. They have kissed my fingertips, have fallen to their knees and wept, have clustered around me, drawing the attention of a crowd. Once a girl even grabbed my arm in the parking lot at school. I still remember the darkness in her eyes, the panic clinging to her skin like mist, the way she begged me to give her a blessing, to relieve her of her great sin, as if I had a direct line right to God.

"Hey no," I told her, shrugging her away. "You've got that wrong. You're thinking of my mother."

You've seen my mother too, guaranteed. See her now, the star of the evening news, standing with several hundred other people in a parking lot in Buffalo. It is hot for May, the first fierce blast of summer, and heat waves rise around these people, making them shimmer on the screen. But that, of course, is pure illusion. The truth is, these people never waver, they never miss a step. Theirs is a holy path, a righteous vision, and if they must stand for twelve hours a day in the blinding heat, thirty days in a row, then they will do it like a penance, they will not think twice. This Buffalo clinic is at the edge of the university, and the protestors with their graphic signs draw increasing crowds. For days we have watched the news clips: ceaseless praying, bottles of red paint splattering brick walls, scared young women being escorted through the hostile crowd by clinic workers in bright vests. Mounting tension, yes, the sharp edges of impending violence, but still it has been a minor protest, something witnessed by motorists on their way to work, then forgotten until the evening news.

It is nothing compared to what will happen now that my mother has arrived.

See her. She is young still, long-boned and slender, with blond hair that swings at the level of her chin. She favors pastels, crisp cottons, skirts that brush against the calf, shirtwaist dresses and sweater sets. On the evening news the cameras pick her out, her pale yellow dress only a few shades darker than her hair, the white collar setting off her tan face, her sapphire eyes. Unlike the others with their signs, their chanting anger, my mother is serene. It is clear right away that while she is with this crowd, she is not of it. Her five assistants, surrounding her tightly like petals on a stamen, guide her slowly to the steps. The banners rustle in the hot wind, fluttering above the famous posters.

See me, then, my sweet smile, my innocence. It is a black-and-white shot, a close-up, taken three years ago when I was just fourteen. My mother strides before these posters, passing in front of one of me after another, and when she pauses alone at the center of the steps, when she turns her face to the cheering crowd and smiles, you can see it. The resemblance was striking even then, and now it is uncanny. In the past three years my cheekbones have become more pronounced, my eyes seem wider. We could, and sometimes do, pass for sisters. My mother waves her hand and starts to speak.

"Fellow sinners," she says, and the crowd roars.

"Turn it off, why don't you?" Sam says. We are sitting together on the sofa, drinking Coca-Cola and eating animal crackers. We've lined the elephants up, trunk to tail, across the coffee table. Sam's eyes are the same deep blue as my mother's, and the dark curls on his head are repeated, again and again, down his wide chest. When I don't answer he turns and presses his hand against my cheek, then kisses me, hard, until I have to pull away from him.

We look at each other for a long moment. When Sam finally speaks, his voice is deliberately grave and pompous, twisting the scriptures to his own advantage.

"Nichola," he says, drawing a finger slowly down my arm. "Your body is such a mystery to me." There is longing in his voice, yes, but his eyes are teasing, testing. He knows I know these verses, the ones my mother always uses to begin. *My body is no mystery to Thee, for Thou didst knit me together in my mother's womb.* He must also know that it seems near sacrilege to me, what he says, the way he says it. And truly I am flushed with his audacity, the breathless danger of his words. I am thrilled with it. Sam watches my face, smiles, runs his hand down my bare arm.

"You know what comes later," I remind him, hearing my mother's voice rising in the background. *"Deliver me from evil men.* Remember?"

He laughs and leans forward to kiss me again, his hand groping for the remote control. I get to it first and sit up straight, keeping a distance between us. I am saving myself, I am trying to, though Sam Rush insists there is no need because one day we will marry.

Not now," I tell him, inching up the volume. "She's just about to tell the story of my life. It's the best part."

Sam catches my wrist and pulls the remote control from my fingers. The TV snaps off and my mother disappears to where she really is, 257 miles away.

"You're wrong," he says, sliding his hands across my shoulders, pressing his lips against my collarbone.

"What do you mean?"

"That's not the story of your life," he whispers. I feel his breath on my skin, insistent, pressing the words. "This is."

MY MOTHER WORRIES, or ought to. After all, I have her looks, her blond beauty, her narrow hips. I have her inclinations. But my mother has a high and shining faith. This is what she tells me every time she leaves the house. She holds my face in her two hands and says, *You'll be good, Nichola, I know that. I have the strongest faith in you, I know you are not a wild girl like I was.*

Well, it is true in a way, I am not a wild girl like she was. Sam Rush is the only boyfriend I have ever had. And for a long time I was even good like she means. Those were the days when she used to take me with her, traveling around the country from one demonstration to another, standing in the rain or snow or blazing heat. There are snapshots of my mother and me from those days. In many of them I am just a toddler perched on her hip, while she squints into the camera, gripping half a banner in her free hand. She wore pantsuits, all creaseless polyester, with wide cuffs at the wrists and ankles. She had maxi-skirts and shiny boots and her hair was long then, falling down her back like the thin silk of corn. For years she was just a part-time protestor, like anybody else. But then she got religion, and got famous, all in a single afternoon.

I was five years old that day. I remember it, the heat and the crowd, my mother's pale blue dress, and the way she held me tightly when the preacher started speaking. "Amen," my mother said. "Amen, oh yes, AMEN." I remember the expression on her face, the way her eyes closed shut and her lips parted. I remember how we moved so suddenly toward the steps where the preacher stood with his microphone, leading everyone in prayer. Another moment and we were up there with him. My mother put me down and turned to the crowd. When she took the microphone from the startled preacher and began to speak, something happened. She called my name and touched my hair, and then she said, *I am a sinner, I have come here today to tell you about my sin.* People sighed, then, they drew in closer. Their faces filled with rapture.

I know my memory on these points is pure, not a story that was told to me, or one that I saw much later on a film. We have a copy of the newsreel now, down in the archives, and it is still a shock each time I watch it and see how many things I missed. I felt so safe, standing up there with my mother, but I was too young to really understand. I didn't see the anger on the preacher's face as my mother wooed his congregation. I don't remember how the crowd changed beneath her voice and followed her, forming a circle before the clinic doors and lying down. I did not even notice when the police arrived and began hauling them away. But on the film, it happens. My mother and the preacher pray while the circle around them is steadily eroded. I see myself, as the circle shrinks, lifted up and handed blindly into the crowd, to a woman with a patchwork skirt who smelled very clean, like lemons. And then, I see on film the most important thing I missed that day. I see the way my mother rose to power. She stands right by the preacher, praying hard, until just he and she are left. That handsome preacher glances at my mother, this interloper, this surprise. It's clear he's thinking that she will be taken first. He expects her to be humble, to concede the stage to him. My mother sees his look and her voice lifts. She closes her eyes and takes a step back. Just a small step, but it's enough. The police reach the preacher first. He stops praying, startled, when they touch his arm, and suddenly it is just my mother speaking, her eyes open now, sustaining the crowd with the power of her voice alone.

People rise up sometimes, start their lives anew. That day it happened to my mother. She burned pure and rose high above the others, like ash borne lightly on a flame. When they came for her she did not cease her prayers. When they touched her she went limp and heavy in their arms. Her dress swept the ground and her sweet voice lifted, and on the news that night she seemed almost angelic. They carried her away still praying, and the crowd parted like a sea to let her pass.

People rise up, but they fall down too. That preacher, for instance, fell so far that he disappeared completely. Others are famous one month, gone the next. They hesitate when boldness is required, they grow vain and self-important and go too far. Sometimes, they sin. In those days before she rose herself, my mother watched them, and she learned. She is smart, careful, and courageous, and her story gives her power when she steps before a crowd. Still, she says, it is a brutal business we are in. There are always those who would like to see her slip. She trusts no one, except for me.

Which is why, when I hear raised voices in her office one afternoon, I pause in the hallway to listen as they talk.

"No, it's too much," Gary Peterson, her chief assistant says. He is a young man with a thin mustache and a great ambition, a man who is a constant worry to my mother. "If we go that far we'll alienate half the country."

I glimpse my mother, standing behind the desk with her arms folded, frowning. "You saw what happened in Florida," she insists. "A clinic closed, and not a soul arrested."

A cleared throat then, a low and unfamiliar voice I can't quite hear. I know what they are talking about, however. I watched it with my mother on TV. In Florida they piped butyric acid through holes in the clinic walls. Soon everyone spilled out, doctors and nurses, secretaries and patients, vomiting and choking, the building ruined with that smell of sewer gas and rancid meat. My mother watched this happen, amazed and also envious. "That's bold," she said, turning off the TV and pacing across the office. "That's *innovative*. We're losing ground, I'm afraid, with the same old approach. We have to do something stunning before we fade away entirely."

And so I wonder, standing there, what idea she has asked them to consider now.

"It's too risky," another voice insists.

"Is it?" she asks. "When we consider the children who would be rescued?"

"Or lost," Gary Peterson interjects. "If we fail."

They go on. I lean against the wall, listening to their voices, and press my hand against my lips. It smells of Sam, a clean salty smell of skin, the old vinyl of his car. In another week or so my mother goes to Kansas City, and Sam has put it to me clearly: He wants to come and stay with me while she's away. He's going crazy, that's what he says, he can't wait any longer. He says it's now or never. I told him I would think about it, let him know.

"Anyway," I hear Gary Peterson say. "Your plan involves Nichola, who isn't exactly reliable these days."

The men laugh and I go still, feeling myself flush bright with anger. They are talking about a year ago in Albany, about the day Gary Peterson made children block the clinic driveway. "Go on," he said to me, though I was sixteen, older than the others. He put his arm around me. Gary Peterson, tall and strong and slender, with his green eyes and steady smile. I felt his hand on my shoulder. "Go on, Nichola, please, these little boys and girls need someone like you to be a leader." The pavement was hot and dusty, scattered with trash, and the cars barely slowed when they swept in from the street. I was scared. But Gary Peterson was so handsome, so good, and he leaned over and whispered in my ear. "Go on, Nichola," he said. "Be a leader." And he kissed me on the cheek.

I was drawn in then. I remember thinking that my mother was a leader, and I would be one too. Plus I could feel his lips on my skin long after he had stepped away. I looked to where my mother was speaking on the steps. The protest was going very badly, just a few stragglers with signs, and I knew she needed help. And so I did it. I spread myself out on the asphalt in a line with all the others. The sun beat down. Some of the little ones started crying, so I led them in a song. We sang "Onward Christian Soldiers." It was the only song I could remember all the words to. Everyone got excited, and someone called in the TV crews. I could see them arriving from the corner of my eyes, circling us with their black cameras. That film is in the archives now, thirty of us lying there, singing. All those sweet small voices.

The camera crew was well established by the time the first doctor got back from lunch. She cruised into the driveway, determined to speed past the growing group of protestors, and almost ran over the smallest child, who was lying at the end of the row. Her car squealed to a stop near that girl's left arm. She got out of her car, livid and trembling, and went right up to my mother, grabbed her arm. I stopped singing so I could listen. That doctor was so angry.

"What in the name of heaven," she said, "do you think you are doing? If you believe in life, as you claim, then you do not put innocent lives at risk. You do not!"

My mother was calm, in a white dress, angelic. "Close your doors," she said. "Repent. The Lord will forgive even you, a murderess."

"And if I had hit that child?" the doctor demanded. She was a small woman, delicate, with smooth gray hair to her shoulders, and yet she shook my mother's arm with a power born of fury. "If my brakes had failed? Who would have been a murderess then?"

Lying there on the hot asphalt, I saw her point. The others were too little to understand, but I was sixteen, and suddenly I saw the danger very clearly. Other cars were pulling up, and there we were, a pavement of soft flesh. Their tires could flatten us in a second. Gary Peterson was hovering near the cameras, talking to the reporters. More crews had come, and the crowd was growing, and I could see that he was very pleased. If one of us were hit, I thought, we would make the national, maybe the international news. I was suddenly very frightened. I waited for my mother to recognize this, to understand the danger, but she was intent on making her point in front of the doctor and a dozen TV cameras.

"Repent," my mother yelled. "Repent and save the children!"

As she spoke another car drove up, too fast and unsuspecting, and bumped the back of the first. The doctor's car jerked forward a foot, so that the last little girl was lying with her arm against the doctor's tire, the bumper hanging over her face. She was crying hard, but without making a sound, she was so scared. That was when I stood up. "Hey, Nichola." Gary Peterson was shouting, and then he was standing next to me, grabbing my arm. "Get back down," he hissed at me, still smiling. "No one's going to get hurt." But already I could feel him fixing bruises on my arm. "No," I said, "I won't." And when he tried to force me, I screamed. That's all it took—the cameras were on us. He let me go, he had to, and stood there while I helped those children up, one by one, brushed them off, and led them out of danger. We made the national news that night after all. My mother was upset for days, but Gary Peterson, who made the front page of several papers, was quite pleased.

It's because I am so angry that I step into the doorway.

"Nichola!" my mother says. She must see from my face that I have overheard the conversation. She nods at me seriously and asks me to come in. "There you are, honey. Come say hello to Mr. Amherst and Mr. Strand and of course to Gary. They are here to discuss the upcoming work in Kansas City." She glances at them then, and smiles, suddenly calm, almost flirtatious, all the tension gone from her face. "We're having a little disagreement," she adds.

They smile at this small joke, and look soberly at me. We get all kinds of people here, from the real religious freaks to the bored rich ladies from the suburbs, and I can tell which is which by the way they react whenever I show up. The religious people, they get all emotional. They say, *So that's your little girl, your baby that was saved, oh she is sweet.* Some of the ladies even weep to see me, the living embodiment of all their strivings and beliefs. These men, though, are not moved. In fact, they seem uncomfortable, as if I remind them of something they'd rather not know. My mother calls me her secret weapon when dealing with such people. Against these men, with their college degrees, their congregations, their ways of doing things, I am my mother's strength. Because there is no one who can argue when they see me, the walking, talking evidence of my mother's great sacrifice for life.

"Nichola," my mother says softly, glancing at the men. "I wonder if you could help us out."

"Sure," I say. "What do you need?"

"These gentlemen would like to know—just as a sort of general inquiry—exactly what you are prepared to do, Nichola? What I mean to say is that there's some concern, after the incident in Albany, about your level of commitment."

Our eyes meet. I know that I can help her. And even though I feel a little sick, as if a whiff of butyric acid were puffing through the air vents as we speak, I do.

"I'd do whatever I could to help," I say. This is not exactly a lie, I decide.

"Anything?" Gary Peterson repeats. He looks at me hard. "Think about it, Nichola. It's important. You'd do anything we asked?"

I open my mouth to speak, but the next words won't come. I keep remembering the hot asphalt against my back, the little voices singing. My mother's expression is serious now, a frown streaks her forehead. This is a test, and it will hurt her if I fail. I close my eyes, trying to think what to do.

Nichola. I remember Sam's touch, the way his words sometimes have double meanings. *Your body is a mystery to me.*

And then I open my eyes again and look straight at them, because suddenly I know a way to tell the truth, yet still convince them.

"Look," I say. "You know I am His instrument on earth."

Gary's eyes narrow, but my mother smiles and puts her arm around me, a swift triumphant hug, before anyone can speak.

"You see," she says. She is beaming. "I told you we could count on Nichola."

Something shifts in the room, then. Something changes. My mother has won some victory, I don't know what exactly.

"Perhaps you're right," Mr. Amherst says as I am leaving. I hurry, relieved to get away. Whatever they are planning doesn't matter, because I already told my mother I won't go to Kansas City. "Perhaps it would be best to escalate the action, to make an unforgettable impact, as you suggest."

I smile, heading up the stairs. I smile because my mother is winning her argument, thanks to me. And more, I smile because today Sam Rush kissed the inside of my elbows and said that he could not live without me, that the blood is always pounding, pounding in his brain these days. Thanks to me.

"You are asking for trouble with that outfit," my mother says the next day, when Sam drops me off after school.

I flush, wondering if my lips are red, like they feel. Parked in his car, we argued for an hour, and Sam was so angry that I started to get scared. He kissed me at the end of it, so hard I couldn't breathe, and told me to decide tonight, no later. *You love me,* he insisted, gripping my arm like Gary did. *You know you do.*

"Nichola," my mother insists, "that sweater is too tight, and your skirt is too short. It's provocative."

"Everyone dresses this way," I tell her, which is not entirely true.

My mother shakes her head and sighs. "Sit down, Nichola," she says. We are in the kitchen, and she gets up to make some coffee. She looks so ordinary, so much like any other mother might look. It is hard to connect her with the woman on TV who can hold a crowd of thousands enthralled. It is hard to picture her standing on a platform, offering up the story of my life, and hers, to the tired crusaders. For that is when she tells it, when people are growing weary, when the energy begins to lag, when "Amazing Grace" goes terribly off-key and the day is as hot or as cold as it will get. She stands up on the stage then with her hand on my shoulder and says, "This is my daughter, Nichola. I want to tell you the story of her life, of how the Lord spoke through her, and thus saved me."

She tells them how it started, how she was young and beautiful and wild, so arrogant that she believed herself immune to the consequences of her sins. From the stage she gives them details to gasp about, how beautiful she was, how drop-dead gorgeous. How many men pursued her and how far she let them go, how high she climbed on the ladder of her ignorance, until the world below seemed nothing but a mirage that never would concern her. They envy her a little, despite themselves, and after a while they begin to hate her just a little too—for her beauty, for the power that it gave her. My mother makes them feel this way on purpose, so that when she tells them of her fall they can shake their heads with secret pleasure, they can murmur to each other that she got what she deserved.

My mother knows her audience. In her weakness lies her strength. She tells them how she wound up a few months later, pregnant of course, abandoned by her family and her friends. They sigh then, they feel her pain, her panic. They understand the loneliness she felt. When my mother flees on a Greyhound bus the crowd is with her. They wander by her side through the darkest corners of an unfamiliar city. She grows fearful, yes, and desperate. They, too, grow numb and lose hope, and finally they climb with her to the top of the tallest building she can find. They stand at the edge, feeling the wind in their hair and the rock-bottom desperation in their hearts, and they swallow as she looks at the city below and prepares herself to jump.

It is such a long way down. She is so afraid. And she, poor sinner, is so beyond herself that she does on impulse what she would never plan: she prays. She whispers words into that wind. She takes another step, still praying. And that is when the miracle occurs.

An ordinary sort of miracle, my mother says, for she heard no voices, saw no visions, experienced no physical transformation. No, on that day the Lord simply spoke to her through me. She tells how she grew dizzy suddenly. From hunger, she thought then, or maybe from the height, but she has realized since that it was nothing less than the hand of grace, a divine and timely intervention. She stumbled and fell against the guard rail, sliding on the wire mesh, scraping her arm. Brightness swirled before her. She put one hand on the cold concrete and the other on her stomach, and she closed her eyes against that sudden, rising light. For a moment the world was still, and that was when it happened. A small thing, really. An ordinary thing. Just this: for the first time, she felt me move. A single kick, a small hand flailing. Once, and then again. It was that simple. She opened her eyes and put both hands against her flesh, waiting. Still, as if listening. Yes, again.

At this point she pauses for a moment on the speaker's platform, her head still bowed. Her voice has gone soft and shaky with this story, but now she lifts her slender arms up to the sky and shouts, *Hallelujah, on that day the Lord was with me, and intervened, everything was saved.*

"Nichola," my mother says now, sitting down across from me and pouring cream into her coffee. I watch it swirl, brown gold, in her cup. "Nichola, it's not that I don't trust you, baby. But I know about temptation. I know it is great, at your age. Next week I am going to do that mission work in Kansas City, and I want you to come with me. It will be like the old days, Nichola, you and me. We could stop in Chicago on the way home, and go shopping."

She offers this last one because she can read my face, like a mirror face to hers, but with opposite emotions.

"Oh, Nichola," she says wistfully. "Why not? We used to have such fun."

She is right, I guess. I used to think it was fun. I sat on the stage with my mother and watched her speak. I felt the pressure of all those eyes, moving from the posters and back to me, as my mother told our story. That was when I was still a kid, though, and it was before the protests got so strong, so ugly.

"Look, I already told you. I'm too busy to go to Kansas City."

"Nichola," she says, an edge of impatience in her voice. "I promised people that you would."

"Well, unpromise them," I say. "They won't care. It's you they come to see."

"Oh, Nichola," she protests. "People always ask for you. Specifically for you."

"I can't," I say. I'm thinking of the heat, the hours of standing in the group of prayer supporters, of the way there is no telling, anymore, what anyone will do. "I'm so busy. I've got a term paper due. The junior prom is in three weeks. I just don't think I can leave all that right now."

"Leave school, or leave Sam?" my mother asks.

I'm starting to blush, I can feel it moving up my cheeks, and my mother is looking at me with her gentle eyes that seem to know everything, everything about me. I fold my arms, my left hand covering the place where Sam held on to me so hard, and then I say the one thing that I know for sure will change the subject.

"You know, I've been wondering about my father again," I tell her.

My mother's face hardens. I watch it happen, imagining my own features growing still and thick like that.

"Nichola," she says. "As far as your father is concerned, you don't exist."

"But he knows about me, right? And don't you think I have a right to meet him?"

"Oh, he knows," she says. "He knows."

She pauses, looking at me with narrowed eyes, the same expression she wore in the office, negotiating about Kansas City with Gary and the others. Her face clears then, and she leans forward with a sigh.

"All right," she says. "What if I told you that you'd get to meet your father, if you come with me to Kansas City?"

"What are you saying?" I ask. Despite myself my heart is beating faster. This is the first time she has ever admitted that he is alive. "Is that where he lives?"

She shrugs. She knows she has my interest now. "Maybe," she says. "He may live there. Or maybe he lives right here, or in another city altogether." She sits back and looks at me. "I don't think that you should meet him, Nichola. I think once you do, you'll wish you hadn't. I'm keeping it from you for your own good, you know. I just don't want you to get hurt."

She waits for me to say what I have said every other time: that she is right, that I don't want to meet him after all.

"All right," she says at last, when I don't speak. "All right then. Here's the deal. Come with me to Kansas City, Nichola. Do exactly what I ask there. And then, I promise, I'll tell you all about him."

I sit still for a moment, tempted, but thinking also of the dense crowds, the stink of sweat in air already thick with hate, with tension. I try to imagine a face for the father I've never known. I think of Sam, of the answer he's expecting, and how afraid I am right now to tell him anything but yes. My mother waits, tapping her fingers against her empty cup. I wonder why she wants so much for me to go. I remember what I promised in her office.

"I don't want to do anything . . . anything terrible," I tell her. I say this so stupidly, but my mother understands. Her face softens.

"Oh, Nichola," she says. "Is that what this is about? I know how much you hated that business with Gary. It won't be anything like that, I promise you." She leans forward and puts her hand on my arm, speaking in a confidential voice. I can smell the coffee on her breath, her flowery perfume. "It's true I need you to do something, Nichola. Something special. But it's not a terrible thing, and anyway it's more that I just need your support, hon. It's going to be big, this protest. The very biggest yet. It would mean such a lot to me if you were there."

It is because she asks like this that I can't say no. I hesitate. That is my mistake. She gives me the smile she uses for the cameras, and pushes back the chair, stands up.

"Thank you," she says. "I prayed for this. You won't regret it, honey."

It's true that for a few minutes I feel good. It's only when she's gone that I realize how much I have given, how little I have gained. It's only then that the first slow burn of my anger begins.

My mother's bedroom is done in rose and cream. A few years ago, when she started getting paid a lot to do Christian TV talk shows, she hired a decorator to redesign the whole house with a professional look. The decorator was one of those angular women with severe tastes, and you can see her mark everywhere else— black-and-white motifs, tubular furniture, everything modern and businesslike. It's only my mother's room that is different, soft, with layers of pillows and white carpet so thick it feels as though you are walking on a cloud. Sometimes I close my eyes and imagine I could fall right through. I wonder if this is how my mother thinks of heaven, a room like white chocolate with a strawberry nougat center.

I know where she keeps things. I have sat on her bed, amid a dozen quilted and ruffled pillows, and watched her paste newspaper photos into her private scrapbook. She trusts me, the one person in her life she says she can trust, and I would not have imagined that I'd dig into her secrets.

Still, when my mother leaves the next day, when she phones me from downtown and I know for sure she is safely away, I go into her bedroom. I know just where to look. The box is in the closet, wedged into the corner, and I pull it out from beneath my mother's dresses. It smells of her perfume. I untie the string and lift the things out carefully, the scrapbooks and the yearbooks, the photos and the letters. I note their order. I arrange them precisely on the carpet.

At first I am so excited that I can barely concentrate. I pick up each letter, feeling lucky, as if the secrets inside are giving off a kind of heat. In fact, however, I find absolutely nothing, and soon enough my excitement begins to fade. Still, I keep on looking, pausing only once when the phone rings and Sam's voice floats into the room on the answering machine. "Nichola," he says. "I'm sorry. You know you are everything to me." I listen, holding still, feeling shaky. I told him not to call today. I listen, but I don't pick up the phone. Once he hangs up I go back to the papers on the floor.

I read. I sort. I skim. Much of it is boring. I sift through a pile of checkbooks, old receipts, a stack of unsorted pictures of people I have never met. I shuffle through the letters from her fans. It's just by chance that I see the one that matters. The handwriting is so like mine, so like my mother's, that I stop. I turn it over twice, feeling the cool linen paper in my hands, the neat slit across the top. I slide the letter out, and money, two hundred dollars in twenty-dollar bills, falls into my lap. I unfold the paper slowly, and then I begin to tremble as I read.

> *I don't know if you got my other letters. I can only hope that they have reached you. I don't understand why you would do this, run off without a word. Yes, we were upset at your news but we are your family. We will stand by you. I am sending money and I am begging you, Valerie, to come home. I cannot bear to think about you out there in the world with our little grandbaby, in need of anything.*

I put the letter down and finger the bills, old, still crisp. My mother told me that they kicked her out, that they severed ties with her forever. At least, that is what she always says, speaking to the crowd, how she begged them to forgive her and they would not. How she was cast out into the world for her sins, alone to wander. I came up here looking for my father, but I sit instead for a long time with that letter in my lap, wondering about my grandparents, who they are and where, and whether or not they have ever seen me on TV. Sam phones again. I hear the longing in his voice, the little flares of anger too, and I do not answer. Instead, I read that letter again, and yet again. The return address is smeared, difficult to decipher, but the postmark helps: it was sent from Seattle and dated six months after I was born. Seattle, a place that I have never been. I put the letter aside and go through everything again. I look hard, but there is nothing else from them.

I am still sitting there a long time later, studying that letter, when the fax comes through. There's a business line downstairs, but my mother keeps this one for sensitive communications that she does not want her secretary—or Gary Peterson—to see. It has never occurred to me that she might not want me to see them either, so when it falls from the machine I'm hardly even curious. I'm still thinking about the grandparents I always thought disowned us. I'm trying to figure out how I can find them. I scan the fax, which is from Kansas City. It starts out with the usual stuff, hotel reservations and demonstration times, and I'm about to toss it down when I see this line: *So glad that Nichola has seen the light at last.*

What light?

I read. The words seem to shift and change shape beneath my eyes. As with the letter, I have to read it several times before I can get the meaning straight and clear in my mind. I'm sure that in all my life I have never read so slowly, or been so scared. For in my hands I have their plans for Kansas City. The usual plans at first, and then references to their bold plan too, the one that will keep them in the news. I can see at last why my mother needs so much for me to join them. Like pieces of white ice, her lies melt clear in my hands, and suddenly I see her true intentions. What did she promise me? *It's a small thing, not terrible, not at all.* But it is terrible. Oh yes. It's the worst thing yet.

Suddenly the room seems so sweet to me, stifling, that I have to get out. I feel I am inhaling sugar, and it hurts. I leave the fax on the carpet with the other papers, and outside I lean against the narrow black banister, breathing deeply. I am so grateful for the clean lines, the clarity, the sudden black and white. Because it is obvious to me now that what I have taken to be the story of my life is not that at all. It is not my life, but my mother's life, her long anger and relentless ambition, that has brought us to this moment, to where we are.

Kansas City swelters in the heat, and every day my mother speaks of sin, her voice a flaming arrow. The crowd listens and ignites. The National Guard spills out of trucks and the nation waits, to see how this protest, the longest and ugliest in the history of the movement, will end. I wait too, watching from the fringes as she steps from her cluster of bodyguards, smiling shyly at the crowd, which cheers, enraptured, ready to believe. *I am just a sinner,* she begins, softly, and I look right at her as the crowd responds; I whisper, *That's right, you are a sinner and a manipulating liar, too.* She goes on speaking to the nation. I watch her, as if for the first time; I see and even admire her skill at this, her poise. For the very first time I see her clearly. I watch her, and I wait to see if she will make me do this evil thing.

It is on the third day that she leaves the stage and comes to me. It is late afternoon and her face is tanned dark. There is sweat on her forehead and above her upper lip. When she puts her arm around me her skin feels slick. She seems tired, but exhilarated too, for the protest is going very well. *Don't ask,* I think. Maybe she just wants to go for dinner. *Please, don't ask.*

"Come on, Nichola," she says. "It's time for you to do that favor."

We take two cars, the one with me and Gary and my mother, the second with tinted windows and three men I've never met. We drive for a long time, it seems, maybe half an hour, and as we reach the suburbs they tell me what they want me to do. It is, as my mother said, a simple task, and if I did not know better I would do it without flinching, I would not think twice.

"Okay, Nichola," Gary says, stopping on a suburban block where lawn sprinklers are hissing against the sidewalks and the trees are large and quiet. The other car parks in front of us. "It's about a block down, number 3489. She comes out every night at 8:30 to walk the dog. You know what to say?"

"Yes," I tell them, swallowing hard. "I know."

"Good luck," my mother says. "We'll be praying."

"Yes," I say, getting out of the car. "I know."

I walk slowly through the dying sunlight, feeling their eyes on me. Number 3489 is big but ordinary, with fake white pillars and a wide lawn, flower beds. There is no sign of a teenage girl. I keep walking, but slowly, because I am scared and because I do not know yet what I'm going to do. Behind me in the car my mother trusts that I will keep my word, and before me in the house the doctor and his family finish dinner, do the dishes, glad that today, at least, no protestors have gathered on the lawn. You can see where the flowers are all crushed from other times. There are bars on the lower windows, too. In a few minutes the daughter will come out of the house with her Scottish terrier on a leash and take him for a walk. My job is simple. I must walk with her, make her pause, and talk to her. About the dog, about videos, about anything that will distract her so she doesn't see them coming. That is all. Such a small thing they have asked of me, a five-minute conversation. They have not told me the rest, but I know.

At the end of the block I pause, turn around, start back. It is 8:35 and I can see the sun glinting off the chrome edges of the two parked cars. This time when I near the house two people are outside, on the lawn. I hesitate by the hedge. A man is squatting by his car, soaping up the sides. A bucket and a hose lie next to him on the ground. The car is old and kind of beat up, too, more like Sam's car than my mother's. On the thick grass a small white dog is running here and there, sniffing at bushes and spots in the lawn, while the young girl whistles and calls to him. The dog's name is Benjy. I do not know the girl's name, though her father is Dr. Sinclair. At the demonstration they emphasize his name. *Sin*clair, *Sin*clair. His daughter has short hair and is wearing a T-shirt, shorts, and sneakers. She is holding a leash in her hand.

Suddenly, her father, who has been washing the car with his hose, stands up and sprays a little water at her back. She shouts out in surprise, then turns around, laughing, letting the water rain down around her. The little dog runs over, jumping up, trying to get in on the fun, and suddenly I wonder what it would be like to be that girl, to have grown up in this ordinary house. I know I should walk away, but I can't. I can't get enough of looking at them. In fact, I stare so long and so hard that the father finally sees me. Our eyes meet and he turns his head, suddenly alert. I start walking across the lawn then, trying not to think.

"Hi," I say, when I get close enough.

"Hi," the girl says, looking at me curiously. Her father smiles, thinking I'm a friend of hers. I had this idea that they would know me right away, like I know them. I thought that they would look at me and see my mother, but they don't. They just stare. I'm so surprised by this that for a moment I can't think of what to say. So I just stand there, looking at this doctor. I have only seen him from afar, as he darted from his car into the clinic. Now I notice how small his ears are, how many wrinkles there are around his eyes. His smile fades as the silence grows between us. He takes a small but perceptible step closer to his daughter.

"Can we help you?" he asks. Despite his wariness, he is kind.

"Look," I say. I glance back at the road and then reach up and release my hair, shake it out to my shoulders. They ought to know me now, it should strike their faces like ice water. They should turn and flee without another word from me. But they do not. The doctor gives me an odd look, true, and glances past me then, to the quiet street, the row of bushes that hides his house. There is nothing there. Not yet. They are waiting. He looks back at me, and after a long moment more, he speaks.

"What is it?" he asks. His voice is very gentle.

His daughter picks up the little dog and smiles at me, to help me speak. She is younger than I am. I think about how they want to shove her into the back of the second car and drive away. A few hours in a dark place, and then they'll let her go. They don't want to hurt her, though I'm sure they are prepared for anything to happen. Scare her yes, they want to do that. They intend to show her the wrath of the heavens, and to this end the men in the car are waiting with their ski masks and their Bibles. Perhaps she will be saved, but that's not the point. What they really want is to terrify her father, to make him repent for the lives that he has taken. They want the world to know that there are no limits in this battle.

I look straight at the doctor then. I don't smile. "Dr. Sinclair,"

I say. "You should know better than to trust a stranger. It's very dangerous. Especially tonight. I wouldn't walk that dog."

I'm ready to say more, but he understands at last. He reaches for his daughter, and they hurry to the house, leaving the bucket of water, the hose still running. I see the front door close and hear it lock behind them, and I wonder if they watch from their barred windows as I walk through their backyard to the alley, then out of sight. I walk for miles like this, between the quiet yards of strangers, and when it's finally dark I get on the first city bus that I see.

It's hard to do this. I know I'm leaving everything behind. My mother and Sam, my whole life until this day. But it was not really my life, I know that now, it was always just the reflections of the lives of other people. I finger the letter my grandmother wrote, the money folded neatly. Seventeen years is a long time. They may not be there anymore. They may not want to see me if they are. But it is the only place I can imagine to begin.

Already, though, I miss my mother. I will always miss her, the force of her persuasion, her strong will. I wonder how long she will wait before she realizes that I've failed her, that I've gone. Outside the window Kansas City rushes past. The air is black and hot, and sprinklers hiss against the sidewalks. The bus travels fast, a lean gray shadow between the streetlights, and elsewhere in the dark Sam gives up on me and turns away. I imagine that my mother waits much longer. It seems to me I know the exact moment when she finally sees the truth. She sighs, and presses her hands against her face. Gary Peterson starts the car without another word. They drive off, and at that moment I suddenly feel the pressure ease. The other people on the bus don't notice, but all this time I have been growing lighter and emptier, until at last I feel myself emerge.

See me then, for the first time.

You do not know me.

I am just a young woman, passing through your life like the wind.

FOR THE BEST IN PAPERBACKS, LOOK FOR THE

In every corner of the world, on every subject under the sun, Penguin represents quality and variety—the very best in publishing today.

For complete information about books available from Penguin—including Penguin Classics and Puffins—and how to order them, write to us at the appropriate address below. Please note that for copyright reasons the selection of books varies from country to country.

In the United States: Please write to *Penguin Group (USA), P.O. Box 12289 Dept. B, Newark, New Jersey 07101-5289* or call 1-800-788-6262.

In the United Kingdom: Please write to *Dept. EP, Penguin Books Ltd, Bath Road, Harmondsworth, West Drayton, Middlesex UB7 0DA.*

In Canada: Please write to *Penguin Books Canada Ltd, 90 Eglinton Avenue East, Suite 700, Toronto, Ontario M4P 2Y3.*

In Australia: Please write to *Penguin Books Australia Ltd, P.O. Box 257, Ringwood, Victoria 3134.*

In New Zealand: Please write to *Penguin Books (NZ) Ltd, Private Bag 102902, North Shore Mail Centre, Auckland 10.*

In India: Please write to *Penguin Books India Pvt Ltd, 11 Panchsheel Shopping Centre, Panchsheel Park, New Delhi 110 017.*

In the Netherlands: Please write to *Penguin Books Netherlands bv, Postbus 3507, NL-1001 AH Amsterdam.*

In Germany: Please write to *Penguin Books Deutschland GmbH, Metzlerstrasse 26, 60594 Frankfurt am Main.*

In Spain: Please write to *Penguin Books S. A., Bravo Murillo 19, 1° B, 28015 Madrid.*

In Italy: Please write to *Penguin Italia s.r.l., Via Benedetto Croce 2, 20094 Corsico, Milano.*

In France: Please write to *Penguin France, Le Carré Wilson, 62 rue Benjamin Baillaud, 31500 Toulouse.*

In Japan: Please write to *Penguin Books Japan Ltd, Kaneko Building, 2-3-25 Koraku, Bunkyo-Ku, Tokyo 112.*

In South Africa: Please write to *Penguin Books South Africa (Pty) Ltd, Private Bag X14, Parkview, 2122 Johannesburg.*